PRAIS

THE TREE OF LIFE

"A captivating story—interwoven with history and thought provoking current issues, all told under the backdrop of a massive natural disaster that unfolds as an entertaining page-turner with a message of hope and redemption."

— Don Stephens, Founder of Mercy Ships

"... a riveting, courageous, inspiring, global, and fascinating medical thriller...an all-too-real scenario of world strife, mixed with God's faithfulness to those who seek Him with all their hearts."

— Diana Weinberger, author of *When Mountains Don't Move - A True Story of Faith Under Fire*

"Dr. Tim's skill as a writer to portray such a diversity of geography, ethnicities, activities...my oh my! My pulse didn't settle down for several hours after finishing the book. His descriptions of medical emergencies, injuries, procedures, surgeries, were spell binding [as well as] his handling of the ethnic diversity with kindness. In the midst of such drama and violence, the beauty of emerging faith and deepening relationships brought enrichment to the whole."

— Deyon Stephens, Co-Founder of Mercy Ships

"...a story of many truths. Author Timothy Browne transports the reader alongside Dr. Nicklaus Hart to ground zero of a major earthquake in Turkey and exposes the realities victims suffer and the impossibilities medical teams face. Truth about the region's history, modern culture, and complex conflicts are deftly woven within the intense plot, creating a relevant and important novel in today's world. But the most important truth revealed in this authentic and vivid story is even in the face of brutal hate, we are called to love."

— Karen Sargent, author of *Waiting for Butterflies*, 2017 IAN Book of the Year

Dr. Nicklaus Hart Series

Maya Hope
The Tree of Life
The Rusted Scalpel

Timothy Browne, MD

Please visit
TimothyBrowneAuthor.com
and sign up to receive updates
and information on upcoming books by Tim.

Follow Tim on Facebook
@authortimothybrowne

the TREE of LIFE

A MEDICAL THRILLER

A Dr. Nicklaus Hart Novel

TIMOTHY BROWNE, MD

The Tree of Life, *a medical thriller*
A Dr. Nicklaus Hart Novel, Book 2
by Timothy Browne, MD

Copyright © 2018 by Timothy Browne
All rights reserved.

First Edition © 2018

ISBN-13:   978-1-947545-05-2 (pb)   978-1-947545-06-9 (pb/BN)
           978-1-947545-03-8 (hb)   978-1-947545-07-6 (hb/BN)
           978-1-947545-04-5 (epub)

Cover design, Book layout & design by Suzanne Parrott
Tree on Cracked soil, ©Ammak / Shutterstock.com

Library of Congress Control Number: 2018935928

Printed and bound
in the United States of America.

To the people of Haiti
And to all people effected by natural
and man-made disasters—may you find comfort and peace.

To: Jules
We are made to love
and be loved—thank you
for showing me this.
… "I'll always remember the song they were playin'"…

ACKNOWLEDGEMENTS

My deepest hope is that one day my writing ability catches up to my life experiences. I am so blessed in the adventures and people that have impacted my life, but I'm equally blessed to be surrounded by people that care about what I have to say and make it readable. I definitely should have been paying closer attention to Ms. Gruba's high school creative writing class. I guess you can't just make up your own sentence structure.

To my Beta readers, thank you for diving into the story and helping flush out areas that were not clear but mostly for your encouragement to continue to write.

To my story editor, Burney Garelick who has the hardest job of all when she receives the raw manuscript. Thank you for not just sending it back, but caring for it like a grandmother would her grandchild. Loving unconditionally and gently offering advice and wisdom.

To my editor, Erin Healy who not only found spots that the story fell short, but is a master craftsman of words. Thank you for helping me become a better writer.

To Suzanne Fyhrie Parrott for the amazing artwork, design and your patient guidance in publishing. As a new author, I quickly realized that writing the books was the mere beginning of the journey. It reminds me of standing at the bottom of my beloved Mission Mountains in Montana and pondering how I could possibly get to the top. But Suz, you have been the perfect guide… thank you.

To my family…you mean everything to me. To my boys, Timothy, Joshua and Jacob, their beautiful wives, Jamie, Sarah and Devlin, and their growing families. You all make the work worth it. To my wife, Julie…you have lived the adventure. I love you all more than there are stars in the sky!

CONTENTS

Then the Lord God formed a man from the dust of the ground and breathed into his nostrils the breath of life, and the man became a living being. Now the Lord God had planted a garden in the east, in Eden; and there he put the man he had formed. The Lord God made all kinds of trees grow out of the ground—trees that were pleasing to the eye and good for food. In the middle of the garden were the tree of life and the tree of the knowledge of good and evil.

— Genesis 2:7–9

Adam named his wife Eve, because she would become the mother of all the living. The Lord God made garments of skin for Adam and his wife and clothed them. And the Lord God said, "The man has now become like one of us, knowing good and evil. He must not be allowed to reach out his hand and take also from the tree of life and eat, and live forever."

— Genesis 3:20–22

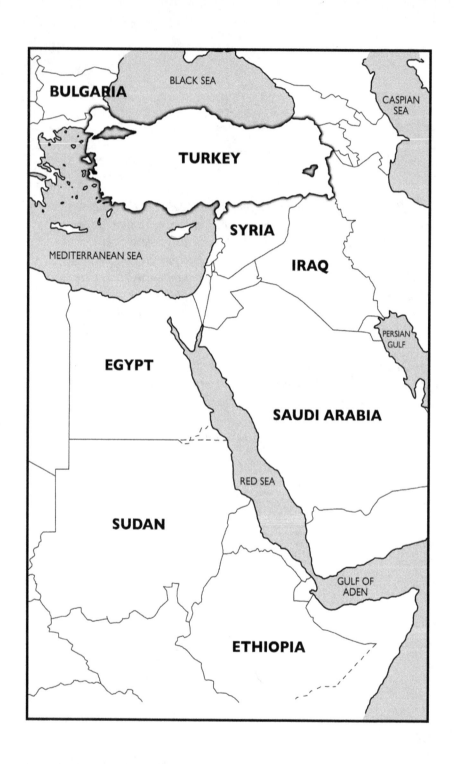

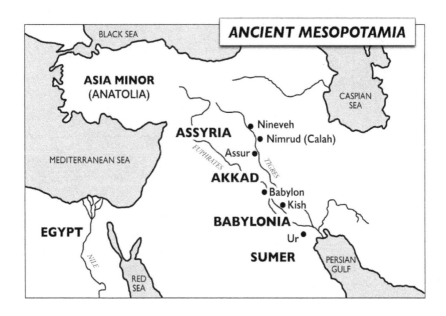

PROLOGUE

SHAKEN

Ibrahim stood at his bedroom window, wiggled into his jeans and pulled his T-shirt over his head. He scrunched his feet into his shoes, not bothering to tie the laces. His friends had started the game without him, and he flew down the staircase and through the living room to the front door.

"Ibrahim," his mother yelled.

His mother's plea stopped him at the open doorway of the family apartment, long enough to gulp down the fresh air and stretch for the sun like a prisoner released from his cell. After being confined inside for two tortuous days, he was free.

His mother had tried her best to entertain him during that time, but he was restless and refused to be comforted. She'd given him games, and cards, and books, but the games were stupid and he hated to read. His father, for the most part, was silent, parked in his corner chair reading old newspapers, and his bratty little sister irritated him like a buzzing mosquito he couldn't swat. Worst of all, there was no television to watch. Their set had broken a year ago, and his father wouldn't get it fixed. But now he was free and couldn't wait to be with his friends. He took the apartment steps down to the street two at a time as his mother appeared in the doorway.

"Ibrahim, Ibrahim," his mother called. "Tie your shoes, and please do not wander too far."

He crossed the street, paused on the sidewalk to fix his laces and closed his eyes. Sunshine hugged his shoulders. He was alive. His other senses woke up to his freedom, and his nostrils flared with the aroma of fresh bread wafting from the corner bakery. His ears tuned to the everyday sounds of his neighborhood springing back to life—steel gates rattled as shops opened for business, a taxi parked at the curb honked for its passenger, and men and women chatted and bustled on their way to work.

His friends called to him to play, and he heard his mother holler again, louder this time.

"Ibrahim, please answer your mother."

He ignored her. Like many seven-year-old boys, he craved his mother's attention, but not now. He had waited long enough and his friends were watching. It was time to enjoy his freedom. He meant no offense; he loved her very much, and knew both she and his father loved him. He was their only son, and they'd given him one of the most significant names in Turkish history. The great Ibrahim was the father of the world's great religions— not only Islam, but Judaism and Christianity as well, where he was called Abraham. Ibrahim's parents reminded him often that he, too, would grow to become a great man.

"Ibrahim!" His mother's voice grew tense.

He opened his eyes and waved to his mother as she stood in the doorway of their small apartment complex across the street. Her long black hair, uncharacteristically uncovered, fell around her shoulders. She looked pretty with her hair down.

"Ibrahim, please stay where I can see you."

His mother glanced nervously up and down the street. She had good reason to be concerned. Rumors that the militants were nearby had flooded the city. No one seemed to know for sure, but his father said the newspapers were filled with reports of ISIS taking over northern Iraq and Syria. He had listened intently to his parents discuss the group's goal of establishing an Islamic State in the ancient area of Mesopotamia, which included the region of eastern Turkey...their home. That morning at breakfast, his father murmured something about politics to his mother but nevertheless appeared happy to return to his job at the bank.

The entire population of Ibrahim's city of Van had taken shelter for the last two days with only a few people daring to venture outside their homes. Everyone waited for violence, but the only sign of war had been a battalion of their own army rolling through the city, headed to the border between Turkey and Iraq to provide security. All was quiet.

"I'll be back for lunch, Mama," he shouted over the sound of a large diesel truck rumbling down the street.

She blew him a kiss. He wanted to blow one back, but not in front of his friends, who rolled a soccer ball to him. He skillfully footed the ball, bounced it onto one knee, then the other, and sent it back to his friend.

He couldn't help glancing at his mother to make sure she had seen his performance. She shook her head and smiled. When he flashed her a grin and a thumbs-up, she waved at him to go on and play.

He had taken three steps toward his friends when it struck.

Everyone froze for a moment, turned to each other, then scattered. One man dropped his grocery bags, spilling vegetables all over the sidewalk. Men and women screamed, but their cries were silenced by a horrific, thunderous roar unlike anything Ibrahim had ever heard. *Was it a bomb?* Instinctively, his head snapped in the direction of the passing truck, expecting it to be obliterated, replaced by a huge crater in the middle of the street.

The truck was intact, but the terrible sound increased, louder and louder, deafening: roaring, grinding, exploding. Thick dust and heavy fear choked the air. Ibrahim could no longer focus.

Instinctively, his attention snapped back to his apartment and his mother. Maybe the rumors were true and the militants had just attacked with a rocket.

The cataclysmic roar intensified as the street heaved upward and split in two. His nostrils burned with the rancid smell of natural gas. His world was shaking so violently it could be only one thing—

Earthquake!

Disoriented, Ibrahim saw his mother fall down the steps, then he realized he too was flat on the asphalt. Life reeled in slow motion. He crawled toward his mother. He could see her shaking, trying to pick herself up. He heard her scream, but he couldn't hear the words.

He glanced back at his friends in time to see a huge concrete slab teeter from a building and slam to the ground. They disappeared in a cloud of dust.

Ibrahim pushed himself up only to be knocked down again by the earth's seismic waves. Screeching steel triggered him to cover his head. The sign advertising cigarettes crashed onto the car parked beside him, smashing its windshield and piercing his skin with shards of glass. Waves of thick, swirling dust saturated the sky.

"Mama!" Ibrahim yelled, but he couldn't hear his own voice.

His throat burned with the acidic powder forcing him to gag and cough hard.

The street shuddered so violently that standing became impossible. Dripping blood, he pushed himself to his hands and knees in time to watch the three-story apartment building next to his began to crumble.

His mother's eyes were ablaze with terror as she forced herself to her feet and screamed at him. He strained to hear but couldn't. She kept her center of gravity low and her arms stretched out for balance, only to be knocked back to the pavement. She would not give up. She pawed at the ground, pulled herself up, tumbled, and regained her balance, forcing herself off her knees.

A large power pole slammed to the concrete, landing just feet from her, and its transformer exploded into a shower of sparks. The severed natural gas line lit like an acetylene torch and roared to life, the heat scalding his face.

Paralyzed with fear, he cried to her, "Mama, Mama."

Determination filled his mother's eyes as she stood at the edge of the large fissure that ripped the road. She squared her frame to leap.

He screamed to tell her their apartment complex was collapsing—his sister was still inside. The front of the building split off and fell toward them.

His mother was in midair when the wall hit, slamming her to the ground and crushing her body. She landed only inches from him, but he couldn't move closer to her. Blood flowed from a split in her scalp. With a glimmer of hope, he saw her eyes were open.

"Mama!" He reached for her. "Mama, please." Her eyes emptied of life and went dark.

He tried to pull himself to her, but it was impossible, he couldn't budge.

"Mama," he called, clawing the ground and stretching his body. Searing pain gripped his legs and he screamed. His legs were trapped, clamped to the asphalt with unforgiving debris. Ignoring his pain, he lunged toward her. He forced his body forward, reaching for her, grasping, but he was only able to touch her long, beautiful hair.

"Mama."

He gasped for breath. The air was thick with dust and smoke and death.

His world dimmed. He knew no sound, no air, no pain... he knew nothing except his mother's hair clutched in his fingers.

"Mama."

CHAPTER 1

AN ACCIDENT
MIDNIGHT–THURSDAY

Blood dripped from the operating table onto the floor. Dr. Nicklaus Hart winced at the bloody mess in Trauma 2 at the Regional Medical Center of Memphis, the MED.

"He fell off the back of the speedboat," explained Dr. Ali Hassan, Nick's trauma fellow.

Nick cringed. The eighteen-year-old would never be the same. It was a miracle he had survived.

"The rest of the boys were badly shaken up, but from what I understand, the driver panicked as the boat was swept by the current and threw it into reverse. I guess the propeller hit him like this." Ali demonstrated with both arms and one leg pushed out in front of his body.

Nick adjusted his surgical cap as he stared at the mangled flesh that used to be arms, and at the ripped-open knee, exposing a shattered patella. He shook his head and sighed.

"We better cover him with every antibiotic known to man. God only knows what is growing in that water." He wrinkled his nose at the mixture of blood and skanky water.

The anesthesiologist painted the boy's skin around the clavicle with sticky brown betadine and expertly slipped a large-bore subclavian line into the vein running under the collarbone. This would allow him to pour in much needed fluid, blood, and medication. The team had done a masterful job in resuscitating the young man, who had arrived at the emergency department in full code with no pulse and minimal blood in his system.

"What in the world were they doing on the Mississippi at ten o'clock at night?" Nick asked and cursed the heavy mist that had fallen over Memphis, obscuring landmarks and making the air disagreeably damp and chilly. "How did they ever find him in the river?"

"They were waterskiing and just hanging out, I guess... drinking and smoking weed. Not a bad thing I suppose, because their lighters were handy for finding this guy in the dark. One of them knew enough to throw tourniquets on his arms when they got him back in the boat."

The team of three anesthesiology residents adjusted dials on the respirator, injected medications into the IV and changed out one bag of blood for another. It was a blessing at the MED, a teaching hospital; there were plenty of hands for situations like this when Trauma 2 hummed with activity.

Two separate scrub teams set up sterile tables of surgical instruments, and several nurses performed their duties with precision—slipping a catheter into the boy's bladder, making sure he was positioned carefully on the table, fetching last-minute instruments and medications, and helping the resident doctors get into their sterile gowns.

"You able to talk with his parents?" Nick asked, looking at the mangled hands and arms. The left hand was barely recognizable with only the thumb remaining on the palm. Dead-looking mounds of muscle replaced a healthy forearm. The right side was even more unnerving with a near perfect, uninjured, pulseless hand attached to the rest of the arm by shiny white tendons stripped of their muscles. Shredded skin covered what was left of the elbow.

"They're all from Mississippi. And yes, they know it's bad. I talked with his stepmom. His dad was too upset to speak. The family should be here by the time we're done."

"Show me the x-rays and tell me your plan."

They walked to the large bank of lighted panels. Ali had already placed the most relevant films on the view box for his attending.

"I was kind of surprised to see the spiral fracture of the right humerus." Ali pointed to the upper-arm bone film. "I guess the propeller twisted the arm all the way up. The skin flap was pulled up to here." He indicated on his arm above the elbow. "I could put a finger into the fracture. The elbow is trashed, but I think we should try to keep as much length in his arm as we can, so I thought we could put external fixation on the humerus after we debride all that we need to. I want to save as much skin as we can for coverage."

Ali didn't have to mention amputation; that was a given. Nick saw shards of bone in what was once the forearm. There was nothing to repair.

As he studied the x-rays, the nurse, Jasmine turned on the stereo, and music from AC/DC filled the room. He frowned. "You mind finding something a little more soothing?" he hollered above the organized chaos. She rolled her eyes and changed the music, and he heard James Taylor singing "Fire and Rain."

He turned back to Ali. "And your plan of attack?"

"When I explored the wound in the ER, the patella was split. We'll do the amputations, wash the heck out of the leg and the stumps of his arms, put the ex-fix on the upper right arm, and place wound-vacs on everything. Of course, we'll be coming back to the OR every day for a while until it's all clean, and then we can fix the patella and humerus," Ali said.

Nick squeezed his fellow's shoulder. "You did well, Ali." He couldn't help but notice the large scar that ran from the corner of Ali's mouth to his ear. Ali had told him it was from a tree branch, but when he wouldn't make eye contact, Nick figured there was more to the story. He shrugged it off. Probably none of his business anyway.

Jasmine thrust a clipboard of papers to be signed into Ali's hands. He smiled at her and accepted his assignment gracefully. Jasmine frowned at Nick, causing his eyes to move from her shapely figure back to his fellow.

Nick liked the man. With the stress and bedlam of the MED it was easy to be unkind, but he rarely saw Ali get rattled. Ali was only a few years younger than he, and Nick often felt conflicted as to whether he should consider his fellow an equal or a surgeon-in-training. He was becoming confident in Ali's ability to make good decisions and leaned toward the former, but it was his responsibility to remain the teacher.

Ali had completed his orthopedic residency in Seattle, at Harborview, Nick's alma mater. Ali interviewed at many medical centers for a trauma fellowship, but when he didn't secure a spot, one of his professors, who happened to be a close friend and colleague of Nick's, called and asked for a personal favor to pick him up as a fellow for the MED. The professor told Nick that Ali was a bit older than most candidates because he had done a five-year general-surgery residency before changing to orthopedics, and that was possibly why other programs had overlooked him. It was unusual to have someone trained in both specialties, but Nick had a growing sense of gratefulness to have Ali as his trauma fellow for the year. Ali had been at the MED for two months and was adjusting well. He was competent, but he understood his limitations; this was something Nick appreciated.

Ali handed the clipboard back to Jasmine and smiled at Nick.

"Sounds like you saved this young man," he complimented Ali.

"Thanks, Dr. Hart, but it was really the EMTs and the folks in the ER who did that. I just hate seeing what that propeller did to this kid. It's going to be difficult for him to wipe his own nose." Ali shook his head.

One of the residents washing the mangled arms with betadine called to Ali. "Hey, Turk, you mind helping out here?"

Ali looked at Nick, waiting to be excused. Nick thought the other residents called him Turk because he was originally from Turkey but wondered if the nickname bugged him. He looked into Ali's dark eyes for a clue. If it did, it didn't register in his face. Ali was consistently polite and friendly to the entire staff.

He speculated that one reason Ali might have been turned down for a fellowship at the other medical centers was because of his religion. But being a Muslim in a predominantly Christian area like Memphis did not seem difficult for Ali.

Nick nodded toward the OR table. "I need to go scrub," he said to Ali. "Good job, man."

As he exited Trauma 2, he glanced at the clock on the wall. Midnight.

James Taylor was still belting out about fire and rain and lonely times. It seemed so fitting.

It's gonna be a long night.

***

Beep, beep, beep.
That sound. What is it?
Beep, beep, beep.
Where am I?
Beep, beep, beep.

Nick took a swipe in the direction of the annoyance and sent the contents of the nightstand crashing to the floor. The breaking of glass was enough to arouse him from a fretful slumber.

He peered over the bed. The nightlight revealed a broken lamp. He rolled back on the small twin bed, rubbed his head, and wondered what time it was. *Beep, beep, beep,* his pager rang out again.

His head cleared enough to remember where he was. *Crap. Oh, yeah, the call room.*

The beeping wouldn't stop on its own, so he reached over the side of the bed and searched for the scourge of his life— the umbilical cord to the residents and the ER. He pushed the button by feel and the message lit up. It was the ER and it was four forty-five in the morning, only two hours after they had finished with the boy from the speedboat accident.

Two hours of restless sleep. The worst part was he had a day's worth of patients in the clinic ahead of him. He pushed on his chest and sighed, remembering his nightmare, one that he often had. He was in the operating room; the case was going horribly wrong and when he looked down, he discovered he had forgotten to put on his surgical gloves. The medical staff would crucify him.

Nick startled when the house phone buzzed, indicating it had been knocked off its receiver and onto the floor. He fished for the phone and dialed the ER.

"Emergency department," an unfamiliar voice on the other end declared.

"Hart," was all he could croak out. He thought it strange that Conner, the always chipper front-desk clerk, hadn't answered the call.

"Hold one," the voice said.

Nick waited until the phone clicked. "Dr. Hart. Sorry to wake you. This is Ali. I'm afraid there has been a most unfortunate incident in the emergency department. A meth-head came in and shot up the place. Connor, the front-desk worker, and Riley, one of the triage nurses, have been killed. Security was able to stop the man before he got any further."

"What? Seriously? Riley…and Connor?" He asked, trying to clear the fog in his head. He sat up on the side of the bed and rubbed his face. He hated the ER, but his co-workers made it more tolerable. Riley was one of his favorites. She always worked nights, always quick with a smile, and always kind, even to the worst of humanity that came through the doors after midnight. His friends in the emergency department were the closest thing to family that he had in Memphis.

"I'm sorry, Dr. Hart, to break the news to you."

"What a screwed-up world," he said, glancing at his bloodied scrubs on the floor. "I'll head down."

"You should wait. The ER is on lockdown and it's a real zoo down here. Besides, the shooter was shot multiple times by security but he's still alive. We are on our way to the OR with him."

Nick's heart sank. His tank was empty. It had been that way for a while now and he didn't have one more ounce to give, especially to someone like this. Joy was nowhere to be found in his life; no wonder a dark thought had crept in, making him consider whether life was worth living.

He could pull it together one more time but what a crappy way to spend the rest of the night. Treat a guy that is likely whacked-out on meth, HIV positive, and has absolutely no resources to pay his bills. The jerk would probably sue the hospital for some reason and walk away with a few million dollars in his pocket.

Nick thumped his chest trying to beat the depression and sarcasm from his heart. "What's he have?" he asked.

"Gunshot wounds to the left shoulder and left arm, and one through-and-through to the leg that just needs to be washed out. The bullet to the arm shattered his humerus. We'll irrigate and debride the wounds and put an ex-fix on the arm to stabilize it temporarily," Ali said. "We've got this, Dr. Hart. I only wanted to give you a heads-up."

Nick thought for a moment. He was critical of the attendings that didn't get their butts out of bed to help the residents, but he was exhausted and laid his head back on his pillow. "All right, but call me if you need me," he said. "Or let him die for all I care."

CHAPTER 2

ATTACK

FRIDAY

Nick walked into the clinic wearing his white coat over his scrubs, but when he caught his reflection in the window, he saw that nothing could camouflage the dark circles under his eyes and his pale, unshaven face. He headed straight for the coffee machine. The older he got, the more his body ached like the flu after a night on call.

He thought he'd fallen back to sleep after the early morning page and conversation with Ali, but his head didn't feel like it. He woke up wondering how the case had gone. He intended to walk through the ER, but after hitting the snooze on his phone alarm a few extra times, he didn't have time before his morning clinic started. He would check on the crew during his lunch hour. The ER personnel were well acquainted with tragedy, but this was different. It was unbelievable that Connor and Riley were dead. Guilt hit him that he knew little about their personal lives. He thought they were both unmarried but wasn't sure.

He stirred three packets of sugar into his coffee and took a sip.

"Dr. Hart."

He turned to see Antonio Scott standing behind him, wearing a crisply pressed white coat over an expensive looking blue shirt and gold tie. Antonio was a hand surgeon and, like many he knew, was fastidious and wound tight to the point of being prissy.

"Hey, Antonio," Nick said, trying to sound cheerful. Because Scott was a colleague, he had tried considering him a friend but ended up holding him at arm's length. Nick had witnessed the man almost getting into a fistfight with another surgeon who dared park in his parking spot. But Scott was the top moneymaker for the group and the newly elected chief of staff for the MED. Most likely, the money and the promotion went hand in hand.

"You get your rest?" Antonio said sharply.

"Uh…" Nick looked at the man, whose face was already turning crimson, highlighting his ginger hair. He was of Irish descent and stood a full foot shorter than Nick. His sharp attire couldn't hide his barrel stature. "Call…you know," Nick shrugged, sensing a brewing storm. He sipped more coffee.

"Well, I sure the hell didn't. You hear about your patient?"

Which patient? Nick searched his mental files. The kid from the boating accident last night or one of the twenty or so patients he currently had in the hospital? His brow furled trying to understand the man's anger.

"I've been up since six a.m. dealing with your crap. You know about the shooting early this morning in the emergency department?"

Nick was not surprised that they had called the chief of staff about the incident. "Yes, I heard. What a—"

"Then the OR called me and told me your patient was dead. I asked to speak to you, but they said you weren't there…that you were sleeping."

"The meth-head? I thought the guys—"

"That meth-head happens to be the mayor's son. I just got off the phone with their attorney. Crap, Hart, why weren't you in there?"

Nick's mind raced. He thought of all sorts of things to say to his accuser. Scott was one of the worst resident abusers and rarely left his multimillion-dollar home in the middle of the night to get in his three-hundred-thousand-dollar Bentley to come help the team. The residents told Nick that the first thing Scott would ask about a patient was their insurance status. Scott probably thought call was easy, but only because the residents stopped calling him if the injured was uninsured.

Nick's cell phone rang, and he pulled it out of his pocket. He saw it was Ali. He had already missed three calls from him. He must have knocked the phone to silent or missed them as he tried reviving himself in the shower.

"Ali?" He answered the phone.

"Dr. Hart, thank goodness. I have been trying to reach you. I'm afraid I have bad news about the shooter from this morning. We got him to surgery and when the anesthesiologist induced him, he went into full code. I guess he had so much meth on board that the anesthesia made his pressure drop out, and they couldn't get him back. I wanted you to know before anyone else told you the news," Ali said.

Nick looked at Scott, whose face was nearly turning purple. He wasn't sure why the man seemed to dislike him so much. He suspected it was jealousy, especially after the attention he had received after his service in Guatemala three years ago. Scott was one of those people that thrived in the spotlight and wanted it all for himself.

"I'll call you back Ali, thanks."

"The mayor's attorney is already accusing us of letting his kid die for shooting up the ER," Scott said.

"And?" he asked sarcastically.

"Hart, you know how these things work." Scott's anger flashed. "Someone is going to have to take the bullet, and it's not going to be me."

"That's an appropriate metaphor," he said. He was in no mood to take any grief from the man.

"These are the kinds of stupid antics with which you seem to be well acquainted." Scott raised his voice and stepped closer to Nick, who didn't budge. "They're also the sort of thing that can stain your reputation, and mine."

"I'm sure you are very concerned about that," he challenged.

"Look, Hart...I know who you are. I am the head elder of my church and we deal with your kind all the time."

"My kind?" Their voices were echoing down the hallway.

The man shot daggers from his eyes. "I've heard about your philandering…your…sin." His anger made him stumble over his words. "And you call yourself a Christian?" His spittle hit Nick's scrub top.

One of the clinic nurses stood in the doorway and cleared her throat. She put her hands on her hips, gave them both a disgusted look, and pulled the door to the breakroom shut.

"I'm suspending your hospital privileges for the day as we sort this out. You need to go home." Scott said.

"You can't do that."

"You bet your ass I can. You want to leave on your own, or shall I call security?"

"I have full day of clinic."

"We have that covered," Scott said. "You have today and tomorrow to get yourself together. You're back on the call rotation on Sunday." He turned on his heels and left the room.

***

Nick slept hard and woke with a stiff neck and raw attitude after being sent home by the chief of staff. He rarely had an opportunity to sleep during the day, so he woke up feeling drugged. After a long, hot shower, he donned his pressed white shirt, blue jeans, favorite pair of cowboy boots, and a layer of Axe cologne. He didn't bother to shave.

He was angry at Scott for judging him and acting like a pious buffoon. He knew many of that man's secrets as well. He was not going to stand by and let the guy throw him or Ali under the bus. He had done nothing wrong; the residents performed surgeries all the time under the watchful eye of the fellow or fifth-year resident, with or without the attending's supervision. It was part of the training to help grow their confidence to be out on their own. He did regret joking with Ali about letting the patient die. Unfortunate words. But he hoped that Ali understood he was joking and hadn't repeated it.

Nick pulled up to the Madison Hotel in downtown Memphis. If he was forced to have the night off, he was going to make the most of it.

"Be careful with her," he said when he handed the keys to the young valet, who licked his lips when he saw the shiny-new aqua-blue Porsche 911 Carrera.

"Yes, sir," the boy said and enthusiastically jumped behind the wheel.

"You do have your driver's license, right?"

The boy gave him a sideways glance and sped off.

He watched his car turn a corner. The car was extravagant, but it was the one perk he enjoyed. Even the short drives from his apartment to the hospital seemed more joyful. He could have walked from his apartment to the Madison, but with the gun-and-knife club in full swing after sunset, it was just another good reason to enjoy his expensive toy.

Nick strolled through the posh lobby and into the elevator. He was headed up to the Twilight Sky Bar on the roof.

He stepped off the elevator and into the festive night air. The music and social scene were already hopping as he made his way to the bar. "Tito's and tonic." He nodded to the bartender and leaned on one arm against the stainless-steel bar top, surveying the crowd. It was too early for people to be dancing, but the lubrication was well underway.

Nick pushed back a wave of his sandy-blond hair, tossed by a breeze off the Mississippi. Two women in tight-fitting miniskirts put some extra swing into their steps as they passed him and smiled. The beauties, balancing on high heels and showing off their assets, left a trace of sweet perfume.

The taller of the pair slowed, raised her hands, wiggled her hips and sang, "It's all about the bass, about the bass..."

Her friend joined in, flashing Nick a mischievous smile and finishing the song, "...no treble." The pair giggled and continued trolling the bar.

He looked back at the bartender, who was smiling at him.

***

Nick lost track of how many Tito's Sonics he drank—enough to numb his run-in with Scott and too many to drive himself home. The girls invited him to continue the party at their place and were annoying the Uber driver with their boisterous laughter after Nick told them a joke.

He was sitting sandwiched between the pair in the back seat when his phone rang.

He pulled it from his front pocket and looked at the caller ID...it was Maggie. The phone was already on its third ring. He wanted to talk with her, more than anything. But he would sound stupid drunk...and there were the girls.

Fourth ring.

God, how I miss her.

Fifth ring.

I just can't. Nick let her call go to voicemail and hated himself for it.

"Maggie?" one of the girls said, looking at his phone. She must have read the conflict in his body language.

He nodded and put the phone back in his pocket.

"If I find you sneaking around on me I'm gonna whoop your butt," she said with a wagging finger. She broke out in a boisterous laugh that jiggled her large breasts.

CHAPTER 3

REGRET

SATURDAY

Nick lay exhausted in his own bed, wishing his regret and the ripe, musky scents of perfume would disappear. Much to the disappointment of the girls, he had called it a night and headed home. The morning sun poked through the blinds. This was his first day off in weeks, and he looked forward to the luxury of sleep, but his night was restless and empty, like a commentary on his life. As a practicing physician, he understood full well he couldn't continue to function without sleep. His life was out of control and he couldn't fix it by himself.

His phone vibrated on his nightstand and then its loud ringer resounded. He answered it reflexively without looking at caller ID.

"Yes," he said sharply.

"Well, good morning to you too."

"Oh…hey, Buck."

Buck Hanson was his best friend. After all, Buck had saved his life in Guatemala when North Korean terrorists tried taking him out.

"Hey, Buck. Glad to hear from you," Buck mocked him.

"Hey, you knucklehead, how about some breakfast?"

"Well, I…I kind of have a full day," he lied.

"Really?" Buck cut him off. "I called the hospital, and your nurse told me it's your day off. I'm down here at the front door of your apartment building so buzz me in before I knock down this flimsy door."

Nick pushed his tired body off his bed and propped the door to his apartment open. He had mostly avoided Buck lately even though he held him in high regard. Buck had served three tours in Afghanistan with the Marines until he lost both of his legs from a roadside IED. As Buck's stateside surgeon, Nick knew how bad it had been. But with help from the Wounded Warrior Project, Buck had regained his life and was fully functional with two high-tech leg prostheses.

As Nick hit the button to release the front door to the building, a wave of guilt and shame washed over him. He'd opened up to Buck in a big way after they returned from Guatemala, confessing his many shortcomings. Buck had listened patiently and led him through prayers of repentance. Nick believed his life had changed and was on solid footing. *Now I don't know.*

He laid back on the bed and covered his head with a pillow. He was just so tired of trying to figure it out. Why did he fall back into his old ways? What was wrong with him? He tried doing everything right: going to Bible study, reading his Bible, and even sounding like the other Christians around him. Maybe he was too weak to be a good Christian. Buck always seemed to have it all together. *What is wrong with me?*

"Time to rise and shine, sleepyhead." The bedroom lights came on, and Nick braced himself for Buck body slamming him with his full weight.

Nick groaned and then jerked involuntarily as a cramp gripped his calf. He pushed Buck off, grabbed at his toes and foot and pulled them toward his head for relief.

"Ha, serves you right for your erroneous ways," Buck said. "I'll go make us some coffee while you shower. Breakfast is on me."

Realizing that sleep was no longer possible, he swung his legs over the bed and headed to the shower. He stripped off his boxers, turned on the hot water, and stepped in.

Warm water hit his aching head along with thoughts about the previous night. He could hear the voice in his heart warning him not to escort the girls from the Madison. Why hadn't he listened? Especially when he knew he was going to feel like crap afterward. He must just be broken.

He reached for the soap and heard another voice in his head. It was his old high school football coach. He felt a firm finger thumping his chest and the gruff man towering over him, red in the face with spittle spewing from his mouth.

"Quit the team?" the coach yelled. "You little wimp. We are two weeks away from State and you're going to quit the team? And you want to do this to be with a bunch of pansies to go feed some dumb spics in Mexico?"

It had been his story to get out of playing football. His church youth group really had planned a trip to Juarez to work in an orphanage. But he was neither interested in the youth group nor Mexico, and he was not planning to go on the trip, but he hated football.

"Go pack your things and get the hell out of my locker room," the coach boomed. "You're not worth the powder to blow yourself up with." The coach gave him one more thump on his chest for emphasis and stormed away.

Nick subconsciously rubbed his sternum.

"Hey, I'm putting your coffee by the sink," Buck yelled through the steam.

"Thanks," he mumbled.

Depression wrapped around him like a straitjacket. He struggled to throw it off, but it choked his chest and squeezed the air out of him. While his hookups gave him a sense of relief, they also intensified his despair. It was such an enigma—like consuming a bountiful Thanksgiving feast but dealing with horrendous heartburn afterward.

He couldn't put his finger on the exact moment when his freedom in Jesus began to dissolve. Like life, it just happened, and before he realized it, he hadn't cracked open his Bible for months or attended any of Buck's Bible study groups. He was too busy dealing with life.

He turned the water off and stood in the steam, trying to clear his head.

At the last Bible study he'd attended, they discussed the parable Jesus told, of demons being chased from a man only to have them return in greater measure. He wasn't sure he completely understood. Buck had explained to the group; we can't leave our spiritual houses empty and vulnerable. We must be filled the Holy Spirit.

The whole idea frightened Nick. He wasn't sure he understood any of it. Then something hit him that scared him even more. Maybe he didn't believe any of it. Maybe it was all just a really good story. If he truly believed in God and Jesus, why did he turn his back on Him? *Why would I do what He tells me not to do?*

"Hey, hurry up in there. I'm starving," Buck yelled.

***

As they sat facing each other in a corner booth of the diner, Nick was sure that Buck recognized his severe hangover but was not about to lower his voice or give him a break. The clatter of plates and glasses and the chatter of customers made his head pound, and the smell of greasy sausage made his stomach rumble with bile.

"Wow, you look like hell," Buck said.

"Yeah, thanks." Nick held a coffee cup to his face with both hands and noticed a bit of a tremor. He shifted uncomfortably on the booth's red vinyl seat, trying to avoid the tear in the cushion worn through by what he imagined had been large, bacon-filled backsides enjoying seventy years of breakfasts. A small television set tuned to FOX News, hanging in the corner above their table, added cacophony to his interior and exterior chaos.

It could be worse. He was thankful that Buck was out of uniform and wore jeans and an old, plain gray sweatshirt. A chest full of military medals would have added to his sense of moral failure.

"I've gotta tell you what happened yesterday at our son's Little League game," Buck said. "The coach made the mistake of belittling our son after an error. My wife jumped up from the bleachers, marched down to the coach, got right in his face and gave him a piece of her mind. You could have heard a pin drop at the ballpark as Katy marched off. The guy is actually a friend of mine." Buck laughed loudly. "I stood up in the stands thinking I was going to have to go down there and pull her off his bloodied body. The guy sheepishly looked up at me, and I just shrugged my shoulders." Buck raised his arms with his palms turned to the ceiling and made a funny face. "I was like, dude, I have to live with her." He broke out into a loud roar.

Nick pushed on his sternum, but had to crack a smile. Katy was a petite woman, but he could picture her standing the man down.

"Sometimes I think I'm tough, and then I see her. She's like, fearless, man. I'm tellin' you."

They sipped coffee and sat in silence. Nick glanced at the TV and wished the talking heads would turn down the political rhetoric.

He knew Buck was waiting for him to go to his heart.

The silence began to crack the walls of his defense and release the angst inundating his mind and body. A tear rolled down his cheek and into his coffee.

"I…" He couldn't complete his sentence or the thought.

Buck waited.

"Damn it!" It came out unintentionally from deep in his soul. "Sorry," he apologized quickly, mindful of the other diners and staff.

He didn't know how to start. His feelings were entombed by thick walls of defense and his ego fought to defend them. If he confessed where his life had landed, he didn't know if he could stand the scolding he deserved. Shame and guilt rose in the sails of his grief and he pictured himself running from the diner.

Buck's hand grabbed his arm. He closed his eyes rather than face the gruff drill sergeant, probably sneering in disgust. The darkness didn't bring comfort.

Buck's grip tightened around his wrist until it hurt, forcing him to brace for the consequences, open his eyes, and look at his friend. But what he saw was neither disgust nor disappointment. He saw the look of his rescuer pulling him from terror on a dusty road in Guatemala. It was a look of understanding and compassion. Tears of joy streamed over Buck's battle-scarred face, and a wide smile spread across his chin.

"I got you." Buck's expression turned dead serious. "I got you."

He felt his blood pressure rise and his heart beat heavy in his chest. He hated that the battle of anxiety raged within him, even on his day off. No surgery was scheduled and no lecture planned, but it was still there: a painful, scary dread deep in his soul. His head spun and he was hyperventilating. He tried to slow his breathing.

"My God, am I going crazy, Buck?" he asked. He understood from experience the stigma of mental illness.

"Why would you think that?" Buck asked.

He held his heavy head in his hands. He didn't want to vocalize the thoughts of suicide that had been creeping into his head. He pressed at his temples trying to make the thoughts go away. The thoughts were an invisible threat, like an ambush waiting around the corner.

"I've wondered if the world would be better off without me," he finally said.

Buck sat back in the booth and blew air out his lips. "Yeah, been there," he said empathically. "I'm glad we're talking, because that's a lie—the world is better with you here."

"Why am I even thinking like this?" he asked.

Buck patiently waited for him to answer his own question.

Nick knew the answer—he was lonely. He was overworked. He had a growing sense of dissatisfaction with his job and all the battles he fought day in and day out against insurance companies, hospital administrators, and occasionally, even the patients. Worst of all, he felt trapped.

"Maybe I should walk away from medicine?"

"Maybe so," Buck said.

"How am I supposed to walk away from medicine when I've spent all my life and hundreds of thousands of dollars getting here? I can just imagine telling my friends that I'm walking away from it all. They would probably be first in line to admit me to the psych ward."

"You might be surprised," Buck said.

"Sure, I make a good living, but is it worth it? I don't even know what else I would do. Where is God in this?"

"You're talking about what you do, not who you are. The jobs we do are like sandcastles. Our real identity is who we are in God's eyes," Buck said.

"Yeah, maybe that's the problem…I just don't think I'm good enough to be a Christian," he declared.

Buck snorted. "That's the whole point, my friend. That's the whole point."

Nick frowned and crossed his arms.

Buck took a drink of his now-cold coffee and looked thoughtfully at his cup. He then locked eyes with Nick. "Jesus did not come to make bad people good," he said, pausing to lean in toward him. "He came to make dead people alive."

Nick's mind raced to grasp understanding but was interrupted by the blaring TV.

"This is a FOX News alert."

They strained their necks toward the screen. Dramatic graphics scrolled across the monitor as anchorman James Jones, holding a rolled-up sheaf of papers, stood in front of a large map of the Middle East.

"We have breaking news from Turkey. One of the largest earthquakes in history has been recorded. A 9.1 magnitude earthquake has just struck the eastern part of Turkey." Jones pointed his roll of paper to the map.

"Little word has reached us from the region, but we will be sure to keep our viewers up to date as information filters out of the area."

Nick looked at Buck.

"Again, stay tuned for more information out of Turkey as we gather reports of the 9.1 magnitude earthquake that just hit eastern Turkey."

He averted his eyes from Buck's stare.

"Maybe you need to go help?"

"Yeah, just what I need." He slumped in the booth.

CHAPTER 4

DUST FROM DUST

Ibrahim's delirious brain, not yet fully aware of what had happened, struggled to make sense and move his body locked in fractured heaps of crushed concrete, splintered wood, dented metal, dirt, and dust.

Pain
Noise
Air
Fire
Dust
NOISE
SEARING PAIN

With his body trapped in agonizing pain, Ibrahim searched for meaning. Maybe this was a dream, a horrendous dream. It was too awful to be a dream and more awful to be real. He tried to focus his eyes, but one saw only a kaleidoscopic blur and the other wouldn't open.

Why can't I move?

His pain was unbearable. "MAMA!" he wailed.

The sound of his voice jarred his brain when he saw her… his mother…his mother's head split open and bleeding. He saw her dead eyes. His body surged with anger, grief and pain, and he coughed up crushed concrete, dirt, blood and mucus. Searing pain gripped his right leg, crushing his mind.

He strained to reach his leg, but his arms refused to budge.

He fought to shift his body, but movement only intensified the agonizing pain in his leg. His stumbling, functioning brain fought for self-preservation when he realized he could barely breathe and was unbearably hot, sizzling like meat in a pan. Heat from a ruptured gas line seared his face and sucked oxygen from his lungs. In a desperate move to survive, he forced his head to turn and screamed as loud as he could, every cry reflecting his pain.

Ibrahim forced his left arm free from the rubble. He could see his fingers and carefully brought his hand to his face to clear some of the debris and give him room to breathe.

He smelled the earthy scent of concrete dust and heat. He heard the roaring of the gas torch. His head echoed with screams; he wasn't sure if they were real or imagined.

He tried to stabilize his lower body to minimize the pain. But as his brain and body started to function, so did his fear. He began to shake uncontrollably. He wondered if he was in that place between life and death, where sleep would overtake the pain of existence. He yearned for sleep, but the pain kept him alive. It was a tug-of-war, and he was losing. He called for help.

His mind flickered with an image of his mother standing at the doorway and calling his name. How he loved her, how beautiful she looked: her long black hair fell on her shoulders and framed her face. He heard her hollering to him.

"Mama," he called back.

He saw her smile as she waved at him.

He was transported to her lap. He sat with her in the rocking chair in their apartment. She read to him. It was his favorite story about the old lady who swallowed a fly. He and his mother laughed at their favorite part. The comforting fragrance of her perfume filled the room. When she finished, he begged her to read it again before bedtime.

Dust
Noise
Air
Fire
Pain
Dark
Sleep
"MAMA!"

CHAPTER 5

THE RUSSIANS

Vladimir gripped the steering wheel, willing the vehicle to cling to the road. Trying to concentrate on steering the SUV down the mountain road, his prominent brow creased above his large nose as the muscles in his jaw tensed.

"Aaaaa! You stupid idiot. Do you have to hit every bump in the road?" Antasha shouted from the back seat of the Land Rover. "Slow down. I don't think I can take much more!" She pounded her fists on the back of his seat and cursed in Russian.

"Antasha, I am sorry, but we must find you help."

"*Da, da,* but you are killing me now. Please stop so I can drink water without spilling it all over myself. Please stop."

Vladimir estimated that they were only fifty miles out of Hakkâri. He was focused on his driving, but the spectacular scenery they were driving through was hard to ignore. They were at the farthest southeast corner of Turkey, driving through the high peaks of the Cilo-Sat mountain range, following the raging Zab River.

Vladimir cursed and slammed his fist against the steering wheel. He hated to stop but could no longer tolerate her incessant crying.

"Okay, okay, Antasha Katrina. Here is a place I can pull off the road."

With a jolt, the Land Rover left the pavement and bounced as he pulled off the road into the dirt.

Antasha shouted and swore again. "My leg is moving," she cried. "My God, the ends of the bones are grinding together." Her breathing turned to panting. "I am going to kill you for this."

Vladimir's thick neck muscles tightened. "This is the thanks I get for saving you," he said under his breath. No matter the costs, he would have saved her. He cared for her deeply, and it was painful to hear her in such agony. His affection for her probably crossed some boundary, as they were associates for the Russian Foreign Intelligence Service, but that's not what his heart told him.

He shifted the car into park and got out to inspect the vehicle. He had no idea what was inside or if it contained anything of value, as this was not their car. He figured that the owner was probably dead. He moved his neck side to side and it snapped twice as he watched the other vehicles escaping Hakkâri pass slowly. The traffic was nearing a crawl. The day before, it had taken only four hours to drive from Van. But with traffic backing up, he had no idea how long it would take now to get back. He wasn't sure what to do or which way to go but Antasha needed help.

Stealing a glance at the scenery and breathing in lungfuls of fresh air, he estimated they were only thirty miles west of Iran and a hundred miles north of Iraq. There were major cities closer than Van in both Iraq and Iran, but that didn't help. There were no roads that connected into those countries and only a helicopter could transport them over the rugged mountains.

He moved to the back of the Land Rover and saw the hatch was smashed in. They were alive by dumb luck. As far as he could tell, the Ümit Hotel where they'd been staying had been destroyed. They only survived the catastrophe because they were outside sitting on the veranda, enjoying a local brew. The earthquake had happened in seconds—one minute they were gazing over the serene Zab Valley and the snow-capped mountains of the Cilo-Sat, and the next, they were on the ground with the hotel collapsing around them. At first he'd thought it strange for a train to roar through town. Then, when the roaring turned deafening and they were thrown from their chairs like rag dolls, he understood—earthquake. He saw the concrete hotel walls split and crumble like a landslide, throwing pieces of cinderblock everywhere.

He shuddered at the memory of the sounds and pulled at the handle of the SUV, but the door wouldn't budge. In the Foreign Intelligence Service he was called "the Hammer" by his colleagues. He hadn't paid much attention to their jibes; nevertheless, it only took him one blow from his elbow to shatter the vehicle's rear window.

Swiping off the shards of glass, he looked inside and had to smile. Staring back at him was a brand-new set of Giorgio Armani luggage. He pulled out the Armani bags and opened them on the ground: clothes, shoes, toiletries, magazines, and at last something useful—a bottle of cognac.

He felt a drop of liquid roll down his forehead and he reached up and felt of the warm sticky fluid. Blood. He found a white T-shirt from the luggage and dabbed his head, only then realizing how sore it was. During the earthquake, he had barely noticed the concrete block that cracked his head, as all his attention was focused on a large wooden beam collapsing over his beloved Antasha. By the time he could get to his feet, he thought she was dead, crushed by the unforgiving weight of the beam. Miraculously, the table where they had been seated had taken most of the blow.

He looked at his right arm and gently flexed it. His knotted biceps spasmed and he remembered pushing past his own physical strength and tearing the muscle as he lifted the beam from Antasha. She was alive, but her leg was badly deformed. His only thought was to get her to a doctor. He was thankful the beam had knocked her unconscious, and she did not feel the pain when he swept her over his massive shoulder with her leg dangling at an awkward angle. Fighting his way over the rubble, he shoved a man covered in ash and debris blocking their path. Staggering past him and stepping over a woman's smoldering body, badly burned by an exposed power line, he grabbed the first vehicle that had not been destroyed, threw Antasha in the back, gunned the engine, and raced toward the main road.

He figured the city's hospital would have been destroyed as

well and followed the flow of traffic out of town. He hoped he'd done the right thing, it all happened so fast.

He shook his head to dislodge the images, and his shoulders slumped as he saw the sun had moved from east to west. He presumed all their belongings had been destroyed, including their satellite phone. He would have preferred to call their agency in Russia to request a rescue. But that was not possible and there was only one way out—the road to Van.

He heard Antasha cry and dreaded stabilizing her leg. Tucking the bottle under his arm, he took magazines from one of the bags and a pair of lacy underpants from another.

He opened the Land Rover's back door, and Antasha's long, copper-colored hair spilled out. She was ghostly pale and sweating profusely, her body flung across the back seat. His thick fingers swept her hair from her delicate facial features and gently lifted her head. He saw her foot contorted at forty-five degrees to her knee.

He uncorked the bottle of cognac with his teeth and held it to her mouth. Her bright red lips puckered around the bottle top, and she took a large gulp of the liquor.

Somehow, she formed a grin. "Oh, Vladimir, you know how to treat a lady." Then her leg spasmed and her grin twisted into a grimace. She coughed violently.

"I need to set your leg, Antasha Katrina."

He offered her another swig and then took a Montblanc titanium pen from his shirt pocket. She had given it to him as a birthday present. "You might want to bite on this."

He gave her what he hoped was a reassuring smile and went around to the other side of the car, where he opened the door and examined her leg. He had no idea what to do but realized her leg would be less painful if it was straightened and stabilized. He strained his brain to remember first-aid training from his military days.

He could see the sharp ends of the bone tenting the skin. He was thankful the fracture wasn't open and figured that since the leg was already broken, whatever he did couldn't make it worse. "I'm sorry, AK," he said as he pulled her foot and twisted it back upright. He felt the bones crunch under his huge hands.

Antasha screamed and bit down on the titanium pen. Sweat poured from her forehead, and she panted like a laboring mother.

He eased his pull and felt the ends of the bones fall into place. With a sigh of relief, he wrapped the magazines around the leg and tied them in place with the panties to fabricate a makeshift cast. Then he arranged her straightened leg on the seat.

He went back to the Armani luggage and found some expensive looking clothing, which he used to support and pad Antasha's leg to keep it stable for the rest of the journey.

He closed the door and returned to the other side of the car to offer her more cognac, but she had passed out from the pain. He removed the pen from her mouth, noting the imprints of her teeth, and put it back in his pocket.

He lightly touched her cheek with the back of his hand and took a swig from the bottle. "I'm sorry, AK."

CHAPTER 6

TURK
SUNDAY—POST-QUAKE DAY ONE

Nick was glad he had taken the previous day to rest after breakfast with Buck. His outlook on life was rosier after a solid night's sleep, but he had to make some changes. His relationship with medicine was such a love-hate affair, but for this moment, it was good to be back with his ortho team. Sunday was typically quiet in the operating rooms of the MED, but this hot August Sunday was hopping with frenzied activity. The weather usually kept the shootings and mayhem at bay; it was too darn hot to fight. But on this day, it was as if the earthquake in Turkey had sent aftershocks to Tennessee.

He walked out of OR 3 and into the staff breakroom. With Ali Hassan and a competent fifth-year chief resident in his operating room, Nick had just overseen his team masterfully remove the shattered head of a hip and replace it with a metal ball joint. He only had to offer a suggestion here and there; they knew what they were doing. After his chastising by the chief of staff, he had to think twice about leaving them alone to close the large incision and apply the necessary dressing. Knowing Scott, he was probably at church or brunch at the country club. He was certainly never around the hospital on the weekends, which was probably why Nick's suspension wasn't longer.

The breakroom was full of chatter from doctors and nurses in scrubs of various colors, eating, resting or watching TV. Both the general surgery and the orthopedic teams were exceptionally busy treating admissions three at a time. Cosmic alignment or coincidence, surfers and surgeons accepted the triads; waves came in sets of three and so did patients. As soon as his team finished fixing one broken hip, two more awaited. One step forward, two steps back. It was a long day.

His phone rang. When he saw her number on his caller ID, he answered his cell phone immediately. "Maggie!"

"Hi, Nicklaus."

"Hey, Maggie. Are you in Guatemala? How are things at the Hope Center?"

"Yes, of course I'm in Guatemala."

He heard sorrow in her voice. "Everything okay?"

There was a long pause, and he felt his pulse quicken.

"Maggie?"

"I was actually just calling to say hi. I didn't know my voice would betray me so fast. We lost one of our babies Friday. Her mother brought her in a few days ago with terrible pneumonia. We did everything we could…"

Her voice trailed off. She was crying. "I'm so sorry, Maggie," he said, trying to sound empathetic in his fatigue. He regretted his tone the minute it left his mouth. The guilt of not returning to Guatemala in the last year had started to fade, but surged with Maggie on the line.

"You okay?" she asked back.

He knew Maggie could read his voice as easily as he could read hers.

"I'm good. Just tired I guess. I just came off a pretty brutal stretch of call." He lied about his guilt, not the call. "How's everything else at the Hope Center?" he asked, changing the subject.

"We just got the tractor that the MED raised money for." Her voice became more chipper with the news. "Here, I'll text you a picture now."

There was a pause and his phone dinged. He laughed out loud.

"Farmer Russell." He grinned at the picture of Maggie wearing a huge smile and an equally large brimmed hat. She was surrounded by the kids from the orphanage, dwarfed by the huge green tractor.

Since the murder of Maggie's husband and Nick's best friend, John Russell, the Hope Center had more than doubled in both its physical size and its capacity to serve the children. The publicity the center had received after the North Korea incident put it in the spotlight, and it benefited from a generous outpouring of donations.

He chuckled at the photo on his cell phone. "You look just too darn cute on that tractor." She wore a yellow sundress and her long black hair blew in the wind under the brim of her hat. "I guess I'm going to have to buy you some overalls," he teased.

"Only if you bring them down in person."

"Are you ready to marry me then?" he asked playfully.

"Are you ready to become a dad to 163 kids?"

It was their standing joke, but the serious, unspoken answer lodged in their hearts.

There was an uncomfortable pause.

He never could nor would take John's place, and Maggie, though she longed for intimacy, felt strongly steadfast to her deceased husband.

Maggie finally broke the silence.

"When do I get to see you again?"

"I'd like to come down with the group of ortho residents next month," he lied.

"I saw you in my dream last night," Maggie told him. "You were on a plane. I kind of hoped you were coming to see me. Then," she added sadly, "when I saw the news about the earthquake, I knew."

"Knew?"

"That you might go."

"Yeah, you and Buck. He told me the same thing yesterday," he said with more irritation than he'd intended. "I have no plans to go to Timbuktu...Turkey. It's clear on the other side of the world and I have plenty to do here." He could feel heat rising in his neck.

"I just know how badly you would be needed." There was a long pause before she spoke again, this time seriously. "I want you to know, Nick, that I will be praying for you without ceasing. You know I love you, don't you?" Maggie read him too well. "Nick, are you sure you're okay?"

"Yeah, really, I'm good," he lied again. "I'm at the hospital is all."

"I understand. Call me when you get a chance…I miss you."

"I miss you too, Maggie."

As he hung up the phone, the breakroom chatter stopped. Someone had turned on the TV to a booming report of the earth-shattering news. News anchor James Jones was speaking.

"The death toll is at three thousand, but that is expected to be the tip of the iceberg. We are just getting a few pictures now of the devastation and hope to have them up for you momentarily." Jones looked offstage at his production staff, pleading for the pictures.

"The United States Geological Survey has put the epicenter of this monstrous earthquake just outside the city of Van, Turkey," Jones continued. A map of Turkey appeared with a flashing red target centered over an area in the eastern portion of the country.

"Van appears to be about fifty miles from the northern Iranian border and seventy-five miles from northern Iraq." The map zoomed in on the area. "Armenia is here," he said, pointing up and to the right of eastern Turkey. "An interesting part of the world, to be sure, being almost at the crossroads of Syria, Iraq and Iran." He appeared to be filling air time, waiting for the pictures and staring daggers at his staff. "While we're waiting for pictures, I have Rick Johnson from the US Geological Survey. Thank you, sir, for speaking to us. What can you tell us about this area? It seems earthquakes are common there."

"Thank you, James, for having me. This region of eastern Turkey is susceptible to earthquakes because of the convergence of four tectonic plates." He adjusted his glasses and ran his fingers over a large screen showing the fault lines.

The geologist pushed a button on his keyboard, and a map came up bearing hundreds of targets. "These are the quakes in this zone in the last one hundred years. You can see the susceptibility of the area to seismic activity."

"What do we know about this particular earthquake?"

The man pushed another button on the keyboard, and all but one target disappeared. His voice was bright with enthusiasm. "It appears that this was a 9.1 magnitude quake, one of the largest in recorded history. The epicenter is here, just outside of Van."

Nick looked away from the TV when his fellow and the chief resident entered the break room. He smiled at them, nodding and expecting reassuring nods in return to verify everything had gone smoothly.

But Ali ignored his greeting and immediately focused on the TV.

"Hey, Turk," a general surgery resident joked, "it looks like your country has been hit by the big one."

Ali kept his eyes on the TV and pulled off his surgical cap. Nick could see the color drain from his face and realized his fellow had been too busy caring for patients to see the news.

The bull's-eye on the geologist's screen rippled like a rock tossed into a lake. "This earthquake should have been felt in Iran, Iraq, Armenia and even Syria," he said. "The solid rock formations of this area are conducive—"

"Thank you, Mr. Johnson," Jones said. "We now have those pictures from Van that we have been promising."

Johnson vanished from the screen and was replaced with a grainy picture. Jones was quick to explain. "Sorry, folks, these are being transmitted via cell phone." The pixilation of the pictures increased in increments until an unfathomable scene of destruction appeared.

"Wow." Jones frowned. "Can anyone tell me what we're looking at here?"

He waited while someone whispered something to him off camera.

"*Yu zun cu il* university." Jones attempted to repeat what he'd heard and threw up his hands. "Can someone please spell that and put it on the screen?"

YUZUNCU YIL UNIVERSITY appeared on the screen over the scene of devastation.

Nick noticed Ali pale and look as if he was going to be sick.

"Okay, folks." Jones rushed to speak. "I apologize for the

lack of information here, but I'm sure you can understand how challenging it is to get anything out of a disaster zone in God-knows-where Turkey. But this pile of debris appears to be part of the *Yuz-un-cu Il* University."

"It looks bad for these poor folks," he added, trying to sound empathic. "We'll be right back with more breaking news. Don't go away."

"*Yuzuncu Yil*," Ali said with a strong Turkish accent, still staring at the TV.

Nick put his hand on Ali's forearm. "You know this place?"

"*Yuzuncu Yil?*" Ali repeated, almost in a whisper. His shoulders drooped and he put his hand to his forehead and turned to Nick. "*Yuzuncu Yil* University is outside of Van. Van is my hometown."

***

Why am I doing this? The last twenty-four hours had passed in a flash for Nick as he squirmed in the vinyl chair at the Memphis International Airport hugging his backpack and watching the TV at his gate. Not only had he granted Ali permission to go home to Turkey to help, but he had volunteered to go with him.

Nick talked with his chairman of the orthopedic service and received the blessing to take a two-week personal leave of absence. The word of his trip filtered up to the chief of staff who was not as understanding and left him a curt message on his cell phone.

"You can run off and perform your little do-good stint, but *your* problems with the mayor's son are not going away. Their attorney has requested all the medical records and we expect them to file suit. They and *I* will be here awaiting your return."

Scott was obviously not going to defend him.

Sweat dripped down Nick's back. He wasn't sure if it was the thought of facing the attorneys and Scott on his return, or the unknown of the earthquake affecting him, but he had no idea what lay ahead. All he knew was that he was about to wade into one of the worst natural disasters the world had ever seen.

The news kept hammering reports that the city of Van was virtually destroyed, and within a hundred-mile radius, other towns, too, had not fared well. The area accounted for a population of well over one million people. It was too early to know death tolls, only that they were going to be significant.

He looked at his watch. Their flight to Houston left at three, and then they'd go on to Berlin. With a direct flight to Ankara, Turkey, in the center of the country, they would arrive at almost three in the afternoon the following day. From there, they would catch a one-hour flight out of Ankara to Erzurum, the closest city to Van with an operational airport. Fortunately, Ali's cousin lived in Erzurum, and he would drive them to Van, a five-hour trip on a good day. If everything went smoothly, they could be at ground zero in two days.

His thoughts were interrupted as the TV screen scrolled a list of charities people could donate to that promised to send aid to Turkey: the Red Cross, the Red Crescent, Samaritan's Purse, Hope Force International, SIGN Fracture Care International and more. Then a banner flashed across the screen accompanied by a voiceover: "The United Nations is putting together an international task force to serve in Turkey."

The gate agent announced their plane was boarding.

What have I gotten myself into?

CHAPTER 7

ALIVE

Ibrahim gagged on the water, the rancid taste of concrete having soured his stomach. But his throat ached and he took another sip. Immediately, he retched, vomiting on a man lying next to him.

His brain was still confused. A girl who offered him water looked familiar, but she was obscured by layers of dust. She sat slumped next to him. How did she get there? She could have been a ghost, except for the blood on her cheek. *Where am I?* One thing he was sure of, this was not *Jannah*, the Islamic heaven his mother had talked about.

"Mama?" It hurt to talk. A sharp pain shot up his leg, and his body trembled. "Where is my mama?" He had no idea where he was or what was happening except that he was no longer on the hard ground and the weight of the debris was off him.

The girl said nothing but reached out and gently touched his face. It was a soft touch, but he pulled away in panic. His eyes darted to the left and then right. He sensed he was moving—his brain focused on the sensation and his eyes searched for answers. He was definitely moving. He was in the bed of a pickup truck. How did he get here?

A man lay to his other side—was he dead or alive? A dirt-covered bone stuck out of his upper arm, and blood oozed down the side of his head.

The man moved. His head fell against Ibrahim, who screamed and drew back in horror—the man's eyeball hung from its socket.

Ibrahim squirmed, putting distance between himself and the dead man. He pushed on the soft ground under him and gasped when he saw it wasn't dirt but flesh. He lay on a corpse. He tried to scream, but no sound emerged. He gulped for breath, but the air had been sucked from his lungs.

Frantically, he reached for the hand that had touched his face. "Mama!" he cried.

He found the hand, but it was limp and lifeless.

CHAPTER 8

THE ROAD THROUGH HELL

The city of Başkale, halfway between Hakkâri and Van, lay in ruins. Vladimir was discouraged that it had taken twelve hours to drive fifty-five miles and the night had descended so quickly into darkness. But they were farther along than the other drivers trying to escape the quaking earth. When a landslide had swept across the mountain road and brought traffic to a standstill, it was Antasha's navigational skills and Vladimir's driving expertise that allowed them to defy the odds and maneuver the four-wheel-drive Land Rover over an old mining road around the impasse. But it hadn't been easy.

To the point of annoyance, Antasha had loudly vocalized her fears of flipping and plummeting into the raging Zap River. After she'd downed half the bottle of cognac and he had further stabilized her leg with splints fashioned from tree branches, Antasha had moved to the front seat—better to comment on his driving. He heard her without replying, concentrating on the passage and, with steely determination, conquering the rocky terrain.

He reached up and clicked on the dome light. Despite her criticism and the perilous drive, he was incurably smitten with her and couldn't help stealing glances at her. She was so beautiful even with her makeup long gone. Her pale skin highlighted her copper-colored hair and dark eyebrows.

She caught his glances and glared at him through her aqua-blue eyes. "What?"

"Nothing. Just making sure you're okay."

"*Da*, keep your eyes on the road." She huffed and turned off the interior light. She was not one for affection or sympathy.

He swerved too close to the edge and Antasha grabbed his arm, digging her nails into his skin.

"Watch the road, you idiot!"

He easily brought the Land Rover back on course.

Sometimes he was put off by her sharp edges. He had never heard much gratitude come from her lips, and he certainly didn't expect to hear it now. But that was okay. This was business. Besides, he was a patient man.

He would wait forever because he loved everything about her—her brilliant mind, her indomitable spirit, and her beauty. She was turning him into a *Pushkin*. He smiled thinking of the great Russian writer, then he caught her grimace again. She knew he loved her; he'd never hidden his feelings. He believed she was fond of him, the way a woman is fond of her dog. But that was enough for him for now. In time, she would love him as he loved her. He was sure of it because on a handful of occasions she had granted him enough intimacy to sustain his hope.

"Vlad, we have to find supplies and gas."

He glanced at the near-empty gas gauge. But Başkale was in shambles—collapsed, burning buildings. There were no service stations or grocery stores, no signs of life other than human silhouettes illuminated by the flames, prowling the ruins, salvaging whatever they could find. He had no idea where to find supplies and gas.

Antasha shifted her fractured leg from the dash, where she had elevated it to keep the swelling at bay. "Turn here," she commanded, pointing to a dirt road on the right.

He frowned at her.

"The city is too dangerous. Turn here."

Vladimir didn't know much, but enough to obey her.

"I saw farmland out this way when we drove through before," she explained. "We can find supplies there."

Of course, she's right. She's always thinking, always scheming, my beautiful Antasha. After all, it had been her foresight that had saved them many times in their sixteen years as partners for the Foreign Intelligence Service.

She'd shared little about her past, but he did know that she'd grown up on a small farm outside of St. Petersburg, and she was the only daughter of immigrant Jews. But that was it. She refused to talk about her youth, saying only that her parents were long dead.

As they drove down the road, apartment complexes on either side were collapsed in ruins. Car lights focused on mounds of rubble and people desperately pulled at pieces of concrete, searching for loved ones or possessions. The moonless night and the flames of broken gas lines added to the desperation.

He dodged sharp debris to avoid puncturing a tire. They'd rolled up their windows to escape the smoke, but they could still hear the wailing. He slowed when they saw two women kneeling at the edge of the road, grieving over a child's lifeless body. Just beyond the women, a man carrying an injured woman in a wheelbarrow waved frantically at the Land Rover. As they approached him, the man stepped in front of the vehicle.

"Watch out!" Antasha screamed.

Vladimir swerved just in time to miss a head-on collision, but not enough to avoid clipping the man's shoulder with the side mirror, sending him and the wheelbarrow spinning to the ground.

He frowned at Antasha, but she was unfazed and motioned him forward.

"We cannot stop for anyone," she insisted.

In the rearview mirror, he saw the man and his passenger scrambling in the dust. Vladimir continued down the road.

It wasn't long before the collapsed and burning apartment buildings gave way to one-story flats in remarkably good condition, and within minutes they drove into farmland. When the road ended at a three-way intersection, Vladimir looked to Antasha for direction.

By now they had left the fires behind, and since the power was out, there were no lights to indicate houses or stores or cafés to guide her choice. They would have to guess.

"Go left," she said.

Driving another half mile, she instructed him to take the next left. He turned where she pointed, and almost immediately their headlights shone on a large, partially collapsed barn.

"Good guess," Vladimir said.

Antasha pointed to a grassy path worn down by tire tracks. "The farmhouse must be down there. Let's check around the barn for gasoline."

Vladimir drove to the back of the barn and smiled when he saw two large petroleum tanks mounted on stilts. "You're a genius."

She ignored his compliment. "One will be diesel and the other regular gasoline. Don't get the two mixed up or we'll be screwed."

Vladimir jumped out of the Land Rover and cleared access to the tanks by pushing away broken timbers that had fallen from the barn. Fortunately, the tanks were intact and gravity operated. He tapped the sides of each; both appeared to be at least half full. One nozzle had the staining and pungent odor of diesel, so he grabbed the second.

He aimed the nozzle toward the ground and pulled the handle. In the dark, it was difficult to tell, but it smelled like gasoline.

Antasha rolled her window down. "Light a match to check it."

"Yeah, very funny, AK."

He reached up to pull the hose off its holder when he heard something and froze in his tracks.

"*DUR!*" A loud voice came from around the corner of the barn.

It was a word Vladimir didn't understand, probably Turkish. But he did understand the sound of a shotgun shell pumped into its chamber, and he wasted no time dropping the nozzle and raising his hands above his head.

A man wearing an old red hat and holding a shotgun appeared in the taillights of the Land Rover. He continued to yell Turkish obscenities, shaking his head and waving his free hand frantically. His message was clear: they were not welcome.

Vladimir could tell that the farmer was not only angry at the intrusion but possibly afraid of him. Vladimir knew he must look like a monster in the middle of the night. His size could be intimidating, and the dried blood on his head didn't help his appearance. He had to say something to put the man at ease, to ask permission for the gas.

"DUR!" the man yelled again and waved the working end of the shotgun toward the road.

Vladimir stepped closer to the man, who retreated, his eyes full of fear. He raised his voice, yelling in broken English, "Away! Go!"

Vladimir caught the man's eyes looking beyond him. But before he could react, a loud blast shook the night, and a bullet whizzed past his head. *What the hell?*

The shot had come from Antasha. She had intended to hit the farmer, but due to the cognac, her aim was off. The shot missed its mark and ricocheted off the side of the barn.

The farmer recovered quickly and aimed his weapon at the Land Rover. Vladimir sprang into action. His long legs quickly closed the distance to the armed man. He delivered a spinning roundhouse kick to the shotgun, discharging the weapon. His momentum carried him forward, and he smashed his fist into the man's face, knocking him backward.

Vladimir picked up the man's shotgun by its warm barrel and threw it into the bushes. When he saw Antasha leaning out the open window holding her gun, he snapped angrily, "I had this under control." As much as he loved her, he hated it when she was reckless, especially when it was obvious that he had the situation well in hand.

"Whatever." She shrugged. "Just get the gas into the car."

He did as he was told.

As he filled the Land Rover, he saw the farmer stagger to his feet holding his bloodied face and stumble back to the farmhouse. *Tough old bird.*

Gas spilled from the full tank and he tossed the nozzle onto the ground, fastened the gas cap and jumped into the Land Rover. He gunned the engine, spun the tires, and took off down the road.

As soon as he caught his breath, he decided he wasn't done chiding Antasha. Without looking at her, he said, "I had this. You could have killed him."

They sat in silence, bouncing down the side road toward the main artery to Van.

Antasha reached for his shoulder, and he thought she was going to make the first move to reconcile. She pulled her hand away quickly and turned on the interior light. When the light came on, she gasped, "You have been shot, Vlad."

CHAPTER 9

THE FLIGHT
TUESDAY—POST-QUAKE DAY THREE

The plane hit a pocket of turbulence and Nick jerked to consciousness. Disoriented, he thought he was waking up in the call room but then remembered boarding in Berlin where many of the women masked themselves in burkas and the flight attendants covered their heads with scarfs. He'd been in such a deep sleep, he'd forgotten for a moment that he was airborne and in flight for more than fourteen hours. He scanned his surroundings, decided all was well, and stretched his legs. His hands were cold, and when he rubbed them together, they felt swollen. His vision and mind cleared and he looked at Ali, who sat next to him.

"You get any sleep?"

Ali shook his head absently, his eyes focused on his computer screen.

"Any news?" Nick tried to engage him.

Ali frowned. Dark bags hung under his eyes.

Nick shifted in the uncomfortably small seat and tried again. "Find out anything?"

Without a word, Ali turned his laptop toward him. Photographs from the scene of the earthquake filled the screen. Nick focused on a picture captioned DOWNTOWN VAN that showed indistinguishable piles of rubble. Two men bent over one pile, their hands frantically searching for something. Nick clicked to the next picture of what appeared to be a four-story building pancaked into a single level. Judging from scattered fruits and vegetables, the bottom floor was once a market. A woman knelt in front of the chaos, sobbing.

He looked at Ali. His head was pressed against his seat back, eyes closed, his color ashen. Closing the laptop, Nick sighed deeply and leaned back in his seat. He didn't know what to say, so he sat in silence.

Finally, Ali spoke. "I also got an email from home…from my wife, Astî. She has been trying to phone her parents as well, but there is just no way to get communications in or out of Turkey," Ali said. "She told me that rescue teams have arrived and sent back those pictures by satellite phone. They use words like *unbelievable, horrific, apocalyptic…*" His voice trailed off.

Claustrophobia flooded Nick. Between being crammed into the window seat with the man in front of him reclined back as far as possible, Ali's anxiety, and his own sense of fear, he wanted to get up and move, but the thought of pacing the aisle of an airplane in flight only inflamed his worry.

Without thinking he asked, "So there's no word from your mom and dad?" He immediately regretted his question.

Ali grimaced, closed his eyes and crossed his arms over his chest.

Nick did the same and concentrated on slowing his breathing.

Finally, Ali spoke. "I have not seen my parents in five years." Ali buried his head in his hands. "My wife's parents live in Van also. All our parents are in their seventies." He paused. "I don't see how they could survive something like this."

Nick pushed on his sternum and thought of his own parents. He reached for his backpack under the seat in front of him, found some Tums, and popped two in his mouth.

He had called his folks from Berlin. In the rush of preparation for the trip, he realized he had forgotten to let them know he was headed to Turkey. Their first reaction was fear, then they peppered him with questions—Where will you operate? Who is looking after you? Is it safe? What will you eat?—most of which he couldn't answer.

His dad was overly protective. "Son, watch out for those crazy, radical ragheads."

He had cringed at his father's racial slur. He tried his best to deflect their questions and lied about all the details being taken care of. He didn't want to worry them.

After a long and uncomfortable pause, his dad got to the heart of the matter. Nick could tell his reticent father was in tears. "Son, your mom and I are so very proud of you. I…I wish I was going with you."

After he had hung up, he thought about his dad's parting wish. It surprised him and filled him with a familiar anxiety, still trying to measure up to the old man. After all this time, he'd never thought about working with his father in the same OR. The elder Dr. Hart had retired years ago and rarely spoke of medicine. *Wouldn't that be something?* He shrugged.

He turned to Ali and grabbed his shoulder. "Let's just pray that they are alive. That by some miracle…" He couldn't finish his sentence.

"Yes, if Allah wills."

They looked at each other and nodded. They had much to learn about each other. He felt guilty for learning so little about Ali's personal life in the two months they'd worked together. At the MED, it had been all business.

"Yes, if God wills," Nick answered back. He shifted in his seat and stretched his back and tried to strike a more optimistic tone. "Hey, I talked with my friend Buck last night. He's a sergeant in the Marines, and he promised he would work to procure whatever surgical and orthopedic supplies he could find and figure out some way to get them to Turkey."

"That is kind of your friend."

"If anyone can get it done, it's Buck."

They sat in silence until both spoke simultaneously, but Ali deferred to his boss.

"So, the guys at work call you Turk," he said. "I've wondered if that bothers you."

Ali grinned.

"No, not really." He smiled as if withholding a secret.

Nick looked at him inquisitively. "There must be a story here?"

"When I first came to the US, people knew I was from Turkey, so they assumed I was Turkish."

Nick was puzzled.

"I am from Turkey, but I'm actually Kurdish. When I explained, they looked at me exactly like you are now." He smiled. "But when I kept insisting, some of my acquaintances started to call me Kurd. And then, somehow, that morphed into Kurd the Turd."

Nick nodded with understanding.

"Turk became the best option," Ali said, and they both chuckled.

Nick wanted to know more. "I've heard of the Kurdish people, but I'm sorry to admit that I have no idea about their history."

"How far back do you want to go?" Ali said, looking at his watch. "Our history goes back to ancient Mesopotamia, probably thousands of years before Christ."

Knowing Ali was Muslim, it surprised him that the name of Christ rolled so easily off Ali's tongue. He thought of saying something, but decided to leave it for another time.

"Mesopotamia? It's somewhere in my memory bank, but I honestly don't remember much about it," he said, drumming his finger against his forehead.

"The land of rivers, or the land between two rivers, to be exact. You know—where it all began." Ali patiently waited for him to acknowledge his meaning.

Nick wanted to laugh out loud, as he knew he carried the same bewildered expression that most residents get when their attending grills them about some aspect of orthopedics. The residents rattle off rote facts until they run out of information and the attending makes them all too aware of how little they know.

Ali was much more kind. "Where it all began," he said, "The Garden of Eden, Adam and Eve, the prophet Noah and his family." He opened his laptop and typed *Mesopotamia* into Google.

Nick nodded and frowned. "Those are Bible stories. I remember them, but I never thought…" He stumbled over his words. "I guess I never stopped to think about where all that took place. Mesopotamia—I must have been sleeping through that Sunday school lesson."

Ali's smile relaxed him. "I grew up in this area with its rich history. It is at the very heart of the beginning of time, at least for mankind." Ali searched through several maps and clicked one to open it. A map of the Middle East appeared, colored in green with a large area of red that was marked Mesopotamia. It covered the modern-day boundaries of eastern Turkey, northern Syria, Iraq and the western portion of Iran.

"Unbelievable." Nick was surprised about his unfamiliarity with the history.

Ali continued. "It is thought the Garden of Eden was located somewhere in this area." He pointed to the map on the screen. "Here is Turkey between the Black Sea to the north and the Mediterranean Sea to the south." He pointed to each body of water. "Istanbul is here at the far western side, where Turkey meets Europe. We are landing right in the middle of Turkey in Ankara. Right below Ankara is Syria and then, of course, Israel and Jordan. When we drive farther east to Van, we will be north of Iraq and just west of Iran."

Nick swallowed hard.

Ali paused for him to catch up. "This is the ancient city of Ur," he said pointing to an area of southern Iraq near the Persian Gulf. "This is where the Euphrates and the Tigris dump into the Persian Gulf."

Nick stared blankly.

"This is where it is believed that the prophet Abraham was born. Here is another spot you have heard about." He pointed to the far eastern portion of Turkey. "This is where the tallest mountain in Turkey lies." Ali probably enjoyed himself, mentoring his attending. "This is Mount Ararat."

A light bulb flashed on in Nick's mind. "Where Noah's ark was thought to come to rest." He was relieved he finally knew something. "I had no idea of the importance of this area."

"Yes, and we are just scratching the surface."

The man sitting in front of Ali fully reclined his seat, almost crushing Ali's computer between the seat and the tray. Ali took it in stride and pulled the computer from the tray, closed its lid, and caught his plastic cup with few remaining ice cubes before it slid off.

"So, back to the Kurds," Nick said. "Are they the ancient people of Mesopotamia?"

"Well, not like you are thinking. You must remember during this ancient time, the people gathered in tribes. So, the Kurds probably arose from one of those tribes long before Christ. There are many legends about the Kurdish people," Ali said. "It is legend that the first town built after the flood was a town called Judi. Melik Kürdim, who is rumored to have lived no fewer than six hundred years, ruled it. He invented his own language. It was different than Hebrew, and he called it Kürdim. This area that he controlled probably came to be known as Kurdistan." Ali shook the ice in the bottom of his cup and finished the last few drops of water. "There are other stories of Kurds," Ali continued, "how they were angelic servants of King Solomon. Others believe that there was an Assyrian king with two snakes growing out of his shoulders who was conquered by a man who would become the father of the Kurdish people. There are a lot of stories. It's hard to know which to believe," he smiled at Nick.

"Geez, I thought my family history was complicated. I think we traced our roots as far back to my great-grandfather emigrating from Ireland. Guess that's not very far in the scheme of things," he half smiled, and they both laughed.

A flight attendant interrupted to offer them some water. Ali accepted, Nick declined. It would only make him want to get up for the bathroom again, and the less he moved inside the airplane, the better.

"And you are Muslim?"

"Yes, Dr. Hart, Shia Muslim."

"Shia? You are going to have to start drawing me a flow chart." They laughed again.

"Think of it this way, Dr. Hart. You are an American, yes?"

Nick nodded.

"And I overheard that you are originally from Montana?"

He nodded again.

"And are you Christian?"

He kept nodding but felt bad that his faith was not more obvious.

"What denomination are you?"

"Episcopalian."

It was Ali's turn to look confused.

"Think of it as being Catholic, but without the guilt," he explained.

Ali laughed, but Nick wasn't sure he understood.

"What is your heritage?" Ali asked.

"Like many Americans, pretty mixed. Some Irish, some English, some Scottish."

Ali rubbed his head. "I don't know the ancient people of Ireland, but they probably migrated out of Mesopotamia, through Europe and beyond."

"I thought I recognized you," Nick said. "You're my long-lost cousin, Ali O'Hara." They laughed loudly, causing the burka-clad woman in the same row to shift in her seat.

"My cousin, two thousand times removed," Ali said and they laughed again.

The woman shot them a disapproving look, and Ali lowered his voice.

"It is like this, Dr. Hart. You are an Irishman from America who is an Episcopalian Christian. I am a Kurd from Turkey who is a Shia Muslim. We probably have lots more labels, but that sums it up for now."

Nick wasn't ready to drop the subject. "Who are the Sunni and Shia? I have heard the words before."

"Most Muslims are either Sunni or Shia. Think about it like your Christian denominations. Like the Catholics and the Protestants."

"Do Sunni and Shia believe different things?"

"Well, in some ways yes and some ways no. The main split happened after the death of Prophet Muhammad, 632 years after Christ. When the prophet died, there was a disagreement over who would take control of Islam. Some thought an elected leader should and others...well, others thought it should be a genetic succession—the two groups became the Sunni and the Shia." He held out his hands as though offering the two beliefs.

"And what about ISIS that we hear so much about?"

Ali pursed his lips and nodded. He thought for a while. Then he glanced around anxiously and lowered his voice.

"Dr. Hart, that is where it gets complicated. Most of the ISIS fighters are Muslim, and most of those are Sunni." He paused as if to consider how to say it correctly. "I think every belief can get hijacked by radical ideology. One of the main beliefs that these radicals have is that we are living in the end times, and their recreation of the ancient caliphate will usher in the apocalypse, the final great battle between good and evil to be fought in the town of Dabiq in Syria."

Nick was beginning to think he was in over his head. "What's the caliphate?"

"This would be the official Islamic state, led by the caliph, who would be the successor to the prophet Muhammad. The caliph would be the supposed leader of Muslims worldwide."

"You say this like you don't believe it."

"Like I said, I am Shia. I…and most Muslims, I might add, think differently."

Ali took a sip of water, glanced around again and lowered his voice even more. "Personally, I think it is a land grab. This ancient land of Mesopotamia has been battled over and won and lost more times than we can count. If we could hear the cries of the ones who died there, it would be deafening."

A loud ding startled Nick, and the pilot's voice announced they would begin their descent into Ankara. The seatbelt light flashed on.

Sweat beaded on Nick's upper lip.

"Dr. Hart, you are right to be nervous. We must be careful. There will be ISIS sympathizers around us. You would not want to fall into their hands."

CHAPTER 10

HELL

When someone grabbed him by his waist and pulled him off the idling truck, the bones in Ibrahim's leg gnashed together and he screamed.

He gasped for breath and heard a voice. "I'm sorry, little one. You do not belong with the others."

It was a man whose face was covered with a surgical mask. Ibrahim couldn't tell if he was good or bad. He was surprised the man took such care in putting him on the ground. But when the man attempted to straighten his crooked leg, he hollered. The man let go, jumped back and stood over him, blocking the sun.

He stared at the shadowy figure and wet his pants. His brain screamed, *ISIS!*

The man reached behind his back and Ibrahim shielded his face. He anticipated a blow and tightly closed his eyes.

There was a thud beside him and he flinched. He squinted and saw a half-full water bottle. Thirsty as he was, he didn't dare reach for it.

The man said nothing and turned away. Ibrahim watched him warily as the man pulled a girl from the truck and put her gently on the ground beside him. He recognized the girl; she had been in the truck sitting next to him on the pile of bodies. She was alive but barely conscious, moaning.

Without moving, Ibrahim watched the man probe the mangled bodies in the back of the truck, a shapeless mass of skin, bones, blood, and fecal matter. The man closed the tailgate and climbed into the passenger side. The truck pulled away, bouncing over a pothole in the road and jouncing the mass of humanity in the back.

Ibrahim's head spun and he vomited, but only bile came up, leaving him with dry heaves. He wiped his mouth on his debris-covered sleeve, gagged and coughed again. The fine white concrete dust seemed permanently caked on his clothes and skin and in his hair.

Despite fear and the pain in his leg, he forced himself to sit up. He grabbed at his upper leg to hold it still and calm the spasm in his muscles that made his bones grind together.

He glanced around and saw he was in some sort of compound. The cinderblock wall surrounding the area was mostly destroyed. A five-story building across the road was intact but leaning at an angle against a huge pile of wreckage. When he saw the mangled, wrought-iron balconies sculpted together by a crazed artist, he realized it had been an apartment building.

A field of broken bodies lay as far as he could see and appeared as ghosts and zombies, covered with white paste and blood. It was worse than any war movie he'd ever seen. A woman close to him stared blankly. Her large dark eyes contrasted with the whites of their orbits, blinking through her ethereal mask. He thought she was alive. A horrific chorus of moans and murmurings hovered above the ground like smoke.

Nothing was familiar. The pain in his leg told him he was alive, unless he was in *Jahannam*—hell. He remembered his father teaching him about the seven gates of hell, where there was always pain.

This must be the first gate, Jaheem, the blazing fire.

He hated when his father talked about hell; it was too scary. He wished he had asked more questions. He didn't think a person would be in pain when dead, but maybe he was wrong—maybe this really is Jahannam.

What have I done to be sent to Jahannam?

Ibrahim looked beyond the compound and saw columns of smoke and raging flames devouring the city.

Yes, it's Jaheem.

The girl behind him moaned and shifted in place, turning onto her side. The sun was setting quickly, turning blood red and disappearing through smoke and haze. Ibrahim was cold, and his body trembled. He pushed himself closer to her to feel her warmth. He hugged his arms around her to stop his shaking. He closed his eyes and fell asleep.

CHAPTER 11

MESOPOTAMIA

"Welcome to Mesopotamia, Dr. Hart," Ali yelled over the clamorous crowd at the airport in Ankara. They left their gate and walked down the concave terminal toward the immigration and customs desk. Even though the corridors for arriving and departing passengers were separated by a glass wall, the barrier failed to silence the vociferous travelers.

The airport was the size of any regional airport found in a midsized town in the States, but it was jammed with people of every nationality. Many congregated in large groups with nearby piles of luggage. Turkish troops in black SWAT uniforms carrying M15 rifles policed the crowd, trying to bring order to the chaos.

"I guess we're not the only people going to the earthquake zone," Nick hollered back.

The atmosphere was electric, and he felt the hair stand up on the back of his neck. He noticed some men in red reflective vests with hardhats hanging from their belts trying to calm several barking dogs straining at their leashes. The dogs were as anxious to get on with their task as he was.

"Must be a rescue team," Ali shouted.

Nick looked at Ali and nodded. He detected relief across Ali's face for the first time since they had left and wasn't sure if he was grateful to have made it safely or if he was glad to be back in his country. Whichever it was, he squeezed Ali's shoulder and saw his eyes well with tears.

"It is wonderful to see all these people coming to help my country," Ali said, fighting his emotions and quickening his pace. "We'd best be getting along. Our plane to Erzurum leaves in two hours, and with these crowds, it may take a while to get through customs, pick up our bags, and make it to our flight."

As Nick pushed forward through the crowd toward the CUSTOMS AND IMMIGRATION sign at the end of the long corridor, he glanced through the large windows at the serene scene outside the airport. It was a startling contrast to the inside frenzy and looked so refreshing—peaceful farmland bathed in the afternoon sun. He let his shoulders relax and took a deep breath.

Ali interrupted his thoughts as they approached long lines at customs. "I'm afraid, Dr. Hart, you will need to queue up over there." He pointed to another line.

He realized he hadn't been paying attention and had followed Ali into the Turkish citizen line. "Right," he apologized and started toward the longer line.

"Dr. Hart, I will meet you at the baggage claim. I will pull our bags for us."

Before they parted, he touched Ali's arm. "Hey, Ali, I'd really like for you to call me Nick. We're equal partners. No more teacher-student thing."

Ali broke into a broad smile. "Sure thing, Dr. Hart. That means more to me than you know. Thank you." He nodded and rejoined his line.

Nick queued up and reached in his pocket to turn on his cell phone. It chimed and he pulled it out to see who'd left a message. It was Antonio Scott again. Nick hesitated and thought about ignoring it. But he probably wouldn't have service for a while and put the phone to his ear.

"Hart, the mayor's attorney has filed suit and is making a real media circus out of *your* mess. I'm calling to advise you that you better call your mal-practice insurance and lawyer up. What a mess you've left."

Scott cursed as he hung up the call and Nick felt the sting of the tires of the bus he'd been thrown under.

Nick rested his chin on his phone. *Crap. One more thing.* He glanced over at Ali, waiting with his countrymen, unaware of the legal storm brewing for them. He hated the fact that Ali would be swept up as well. The attorneys would throw a wide net and sue everyone involved.

Ali saw him looking his direction and smiled back. Maybe he should wait and tell him later. There was too much going on to think about a stupid lawsuit. He smiled back at Ali.

Although he always saw Ali in hospital scrubs, he wasn't surprised at Ali's civilian clothes—black trousers held in place by a brown belt bunched at his skinny waist, a plain white short-sleeved button-down shirt showing a triangle of an undershirt at the neck, and scuffed brown loafers left over from college days. Not exactly a fashion statement, but he liked the unassuming man. No one would guess that under the mild-mannered nebbish lay an extraordinary human being and surgeon.

He noticed Ali step aside to allow an elderly woman to cut in line ahead of him. He hoped that his short list of friends had just increased by one.

CHAPTER 12

AFTERSHOCKS

Ibrahim watched the men in masks lift a woman's body and heave it into the back of the pickup. Her head bounced awkwardly against the truck bed and he turned away in sadness and respect. He seemed to be the only one that paid the scene any mind.

The shrieking and wailing from the day before had become a drone of moans and murmurs. Bodies lay everywhere, their injuries highlighted by the crimson blood against the white powder that coated everything. Three people walked among the injured giving aid.

An old man and a young woman supporting each other hobbled to claim the small space vacated by the dead woman tossed into the back of the truck. When the couple crumpled into the space, he saw the young woman's forearm was severely deformed, and the man's ankle bone was open and exposed.

Ibrahim tried shifting his leg, but even the slightest movement increased the pain. He was overcome by thirst and remembered the water bottle at his side. He picked it up and shook it. He was so thirsty he could drink the half-empty bottle in one swallow, but as he propped himself up on one elbow, the girl lying next to him moaned.

He turned to her. Her face, partially obscured by her hair, was a dusty mask, and her eyes were half open but vacant. He pushed her hair back and she blinked. He looked at the water and then back at the girl. His throat ached with thirst.

He grimaced as he lifted her head with one hand and poured some water between her lips. She coughed, gagged, and retched a mucus plug onto her tattered shirt.

Her coughing threw his leg into spasm, and he bit his lip to keep from crying. When she caught her breath, he tried again, putting the bottle to her lips. This time she took a sip and swallowed. Her eyes rolled back as they closed, then she curled into a fetal position.

He looked at the less-than-half-empty bottle and took a small sip. Then he screwed the top back on and put it down beside him. Nothing but misery surrounded him, and he looked to the sky. It was a brilliant blue. A buzzard floated in the thermals, and an elephant-shaped cloud lazed in tranquility. His eyes blinked trying to grasp the simultaneity of the horror that surrounded him and the bliss of the sky. It was more than he could comprehend, but at least now he was warm. It had been a cold night, huddling next to the girl and trying to share body heat.

With the sun on his face, his eyes blinked mindlessly. He tried to grasp understanding and remember better days. He closed his eyes and pictured himself with his mother on their small balcony, identifying animals they saw in the clouds. He was lying in her lap, looking up at her smiling face framed in a blue summer sky. Her white teeth sparkled when she laughed. She smiled at him and lifted a lock of hair that had fallen over his cheek. "Oh, my Ibrahim, my darling child. You are the most handsome boy. You are so smart. You will be a great man someday. You were born for greatness."

She tickled him, and he squirmed. "Mama, stop it."

He didn't want her to stop, but his eyes burst open at a terrible noise—a grinding, thunderous rumble, the fierce, frenetic shaking of the earth. Instinctively, he looked for something to hang on to, but there was nothing and no one except the limp hand of the girl next to him. The roaring, shaking earth played counterpoint to human screams. He wanted to run, but fear and pain kept him grounded. He watched the people that still had life cover their heads and dig their hands into the earth.

The shaking accelerated like tribal drums beating a war dance, and he was sure the ground beneath him would fracture, and he'd fall into the abyss of hell. He heard someone call for Allah.

"Mama!" he screamed.

Then, as fast as it began, the shaking stopped. People around him continued to wail, pleading with Allah.

CHAPTER 13

ALMOST THERE

"Which way, AK?" Vladimir waited for an answer, but Antasha didn't reply. She was deeply engrossed in a large fold-up map spread out in her lap. They were coming to an intersection and he needed to know which way to turn.

An official sign alongside the road read SCENIC VIEW TURNOUT. He decided to stop and turned out of the morass of traffic, then parked at the base of a large knoll. Through the front window of the Land Rover was a spectacular view—rugged, snow-capped mountains framed a green valley cradling a small hamlet.

Vladimir stretched his back and tried shaking the fatigue from his head after the endless trip from Başkale. After their detour around the landslide, they'd met bumper-to-bumper traffic on the road to Çavuştepe and had been stuck on the route for two days. Who would have ever imagined such a traffic jam?

Those forty-eight hours had been particularly exhausting for him. He'd had to keep one eye on the road and the other in his rearview mirror, anxiously checking for the police to catch them after the encounter at the farm. Of course, if the police had caught up to them, there would have been no escape with the road jam-packed with vehicles, inching along like turtles. If Antasha had her way, the confrontation would have ended with a horrendous bloodbath.

Vladimir winced. He was still sore, physically and at Antasha. She was so impulsive. The blast from the shotgun had taken off the top of his right deltoid muscle.

He scowled at her, knowing she wasn't looking. She ignored him, immersed in the map, which only added fuel to the fire. He could smell his injured shoulder—the odor was stronger than dried blood. He really needed a long, hot shower. They had barely enough water to stay hydrated, and he'd used some of it to wash his wound and a little more to scrape the dried blood from his head. He had dug through the expensive luggage in the back of the Land Rover and found a clean white T-shirt to dress his wound. He told Antasha how to wrap it.

Her legs stretched across his lap. Her right foot was swollen and her toes looked like sausages topped with bright red tips from her painted nails. Her swollen foot had turned blacker and bluer. Gravity had carried the blood from the fracture down to her foot. He shifted in his seat, and her legs twisted.

She squealed. "Watch it, you moron." She kicked his thigh with her good foot, causing her fractured leg to spasm. He looked out his side window to keep her from seeing his grin. *Serves you right.*

She swore at him in Russian and fumbled with the map folds. "Who uses these things anymore?"

He'd found an iPhone in the expensive luggage, but with no service, it sat useless in the cup holder.

"We're almost back to the big lake, the one we drove around—Lake Van," she said. "Right up there at the intersection." She pointed to the map and turned it toward him. "If we go to the left, we will go through southern Turkey, just skirting the border of Iraq and Syria. That is the fastest way back to Istanbul and the hell out of here. But in places the road passes only miles from ISIS territory. If we go north, we'll go through Van, around the lake, and then the long way west to Ankara and on to Istanbul. Maybe we can catch a flight out of Ankara. What do you think?"

He ignored her, staring out the side window, reading an official historical plaque.

She kicked his thigh with her healthy heel. "Where shall we go?"

Anywhere but here with you, he thought, though it wasn't true. He would always want to be where she was.

"Vladimir?"

"Did you know I'm Armenian?" he asked brightly.

"Really?" she rolled her eyes. "What's that got to do with anything?"

He pointed to a flag on top of the knoll next to them. "Those are the ruins of the Fortress of Haykaberd."

"Big deal."

He paraphrased from the plaque. "Armenian folklore says the fortress was founded in the first millennium BC by Hayk."

She exaggerated a shrug, tilted her head and raised her open hands.

"Hayk was a descendant of Noah. It says here that Hayk was a man of giant stature, a mighty archer and a fearless warrior. Also, he was very handsome and friendly and he had curly hair, sparkling eyes, and strong arms." He paused, grinning at Antasha. He lifted both his arms in a muscleman pose but grimaced when his injured arm cramped. Undeterred by the pain, he flexed his left arm, making his huge biceps bulge and roll. "This is the land of my people."

"Yeah, except for the curly hair." She smacked the scab on his bald head with the folded map.

He ignored her taunt. "Apparently, somewhere close to here, Hayk defeated Nimrod, the son of Cush and the great-grandson of Noah. He also defeated King Bel, the Babylonian invader."

"Bel?" she asked. "*Oui, oui*...a beautiful French belle, like me?" She struck a pose and tossed her tangled hair.

"Hardly. Bel was a wicked giant of Titan mythology. There was a gigantic battle along the shores of Lake Van, and Hayk slew Bel with a nearly impossible shot from a long bow." Vladimir was excited. "I remember in Armenian history class hearing about the Battle of the Giants. Can you imagine what the world was like around 2000 BC?"

"Who cares." She went back to the map, but paused in thought. "Wait a minute. If this guy...what's his name?"

"Hayk." Vladimir was enjoying himself.

"If Hayk fought a battle in 2000 BC and built a fortress in 1000 BC, he would have been over a thousand years old."

Vladimir sat with his hands raised and a huge smile across his broad face. Antasha looked like the lights in her mind had come on and she finally understood why he was telling her the story.

"That's old," she said with a reciprocating smile. "But take that stupid grin off your ugly face."

He watched Antasha crinkle the map into her lap and look out over the beautiful mountains of Turkey. He knew she was probably thinking about their assignment here as well.

When their chief at the Foreign Intelligence Service had called them into his office and told them they were being sent to Turkey under orders from Putin himself, they thought the chief had gone mad. He'd handed them a bulky folder marked TOP SECRET and told them it was filled with both ancient and modern documents. Vladimir had opened the folder. On its cover page were several hand-scribbled words: *The Tree of Life*. He and Antasha had glanced at each other in puzzlement.

The chief had told them, in all seriousness, "That is the president's own handwriting. There are reports of people living in Turkey who are centuries old. The president wants to know why." Their chief had lowered his voice. Vladimir couldn't read whether he was trying to hold back his own skepticism or being dead serious. "I don't know what your knowledge is of the Bible," their chief continued, "but the early patriarchs lived for hundreds of years. This is all in the file, but I need to tell you that in 2002, Putin met with a priest that had emigrated from Turkey. On the priest's death bed, he kept murmuring about the *Hayat Ağacı*… the tree of life." Their chief was dead serious. "The priest told Putin he was over two hundred years old."

They'd laughed as they left the FIS building. "What a pile of crap," Antasha had said. "But who cares? We've been given a vacation to Turkey, all on the government's dime. I could use a vacation, and I hear it's pretty nice this time of year."

What a vacation it's been so far. Vladimir winced. His shoulder was aching more and more.

Antasha shoved him yet again with her good foot. "Look, Vladimir. The line is moving."

He pulled himself together and started the Land Rover. It lurched forward, causing Antasha to shriek and curse at him again.

A patient driver paused to let them reenter traffic.

At the north-south intersection was a lone policeman directing traffic. Antasha reached between the seats for the grip of her pistol. Vladimir reached to restrain her arm.

"Which way, AK?" he asked.

"The fastest way home," she said and pointed to the left.

With his eyes on the policeman, he saw a barrier blocking the road. The policeman waved them to the right and north. Vladimir hesitated. The policeman blew his whistle and waved frantically, urging them to move and follow the traffic flow north.

He did as he was told. "I guess we're headed to Van."

CHAPTER 14

WHIRLYBIRD

"There is just no way to get you there," the gate agent repeated for the fourth time. "Your flight has been canceled."

Nick and Ali had sailed through customs and immigration. Their bags had arrived safely, and they were waved through without having to open their bags for inspection. Nick's worry about getting his surgical instruments and medications into the country had been unfounded.

Bags in hand, they had raced to the gate to catch the flight to Erzurum. Unfortunately, when they talked to the gate agent, the news was bad.

"But we must get to Erzurum," Ali had repeated. As trauma surgeons, Ali and Nick knew the first forty-eight hours after an earthquake were critical, and more time than that had already gone by; it had been three days since the quake.

"Please step aside," the agent said and signaled for the next person to step forward.

Ali refused to budge. He looked at Nick for help, but all he could do was shrug.

The one-hour flight to Erzurum had been scheduled to leave in forty-five minutes. Ali's cousin was supposed to meet them there to drive them to the earthquake zone in Van. But even that was not certain; they had tried calling him many times since landing in Ankara, but all the circuits were busy.

Ali continued to press the gate agent. "Madam, you do not seem to understand. We must get to Erzurum tonight." His face was flushed with anguish.

"Sir." She raised her voice, and the other passengers turned to listen. Then she sighed and said with resignation, "I would fly you myself if I could, but they have shut down the airport in Erzurum."

"Who in the world would make such a decision?" He slapped the top of the agent's desk.

"The United Nations has closed the airspace." A pilot in uniform standing off to the side of the desk crossed his arms defensively when they looked at him.

"And they can do that?" Ali challenged the man.

The pilot responded in Turkish, his voice loud and sharp. Nick could feel tensions rise when two Turkish soldiers watching the exchange took steps in their direction.

Nick grabbed Ali's shoulder. "Hey, bud, let's step out of line and talk this through. I'm certain that neither of us would do any good locked in a Turkish jail."

Ali resisted, but an elderly man with a large mustache standing in line behind them said something to him. Ali relented and Nick guided him through the crowd to the middle of the terminal.

"What did he say to you?" Nick asked.

Ali hesitated and studied the floor. "He called me a Kurdish *cacık*." He looked up without focusing. "*Cacık* is the white sauce you put on gyros."

Nick didn't understand.

"Dr. Hart, it is Turkish slang for *fool*," Ali explained in defeat.

"That SOB called you a fool?" He looked back at the line they'd been standing in and started toward the man with the mustache, seeking vengeance or at least an apology.

Ali held him back. "It is okay, Dr. Hart. This is no longer the United States."

They stared at each other.

"It is just the way things are here."

He sighed. Apparently, he had a lot to learn. "How did he know you are Kurdish?"

"Probably my accent or the way I look. I don't know. Just like people in the States know if you are from New York or New Orleans."

"Funny, you all sound and look alike to me," he joked, trying to relieve the tension.

"Very funny, Dr. Hart."

Before he finished his thought, Ali's eyes locked onto something and he quickly walked toward a large group of people.

Nick's stomach fell as Ali waded into the crowd centered around a large, bald man in uniform. Many of the people surrounding the man wore matching canary-yellow T-shirts with a large cross on the back and the words *Calvary Chapel Church of North Carolina*.

Nick hurried to catch up to Ali and bumped into one of the men.

"Excuse me." Nick apologized and excused himself several times as he pushed his way to Ali.

When he got close enough, he was surprised to see the bald man was a United Nations officer in a combat uniform. His blue beret was folded neatly under his shoulder epaulet, which was adorned with a colonel's eagle. The emblem of the American flag was attached to his shoulder. Ali had squared himself off with the colonel and was already deep in conversation and conflict.

"Son, I would advise you to take a step back." The colonel's voice boomed over the crowd.

Nick reached Ali and grabbed his shoulder. Ali refused to desist, standing toe-to-toe with the colonel.

The soldier's face was chiseled and angry. "Yes, I know you want to get to Van, you and these thousand other do-gooders. What don't you understand about no?"

"But, sir, if we can only get to Erzurum, I can get us to Van."

The colonel scoffed at him. "I'm telling you, even if you get to Erzurum, you are not getting into Van. Hell, son, it may be months before anyone actually drives there. Half a mountain is blocking the road."

The colonel surveyed the crowd. "That goes for the rest of you folks. Ya'll better get comfortable here in Ankara for a while until we figure this thing out," he said in a Texan drawl.

"You need doctors?" Nick blurted, immediately regretting opening his mouth when the colonel shot him a wary squint.

"What kind of doctors?"

A hush fell over the crowd. "I'm...we are surgeons." Nick swallowed hard. "Orthopedic surgeons."

The colonel checked the clipboard in his hand, looked up, and smiled. "It looks like you have yourselves a ride after all."

A voice at the back of the crowd spoke up. "I'm a scrub nurse."

"Come on up here, little lady," the colonel replied, waving her forward. He pushed a button on his walkie-talkie, held it to his mouth, and said, "I've got two bone-cutters and a nurse. Over."

"Roger that, sir. Ask if they need an an...esthes...iologist?" The man on the other end shouted and stumbled over the word.

"Anesthesiologist." Nick said, nodding enthusiastically.

"Roger that," the colonel replied. "Meet us down by the Huey."

"That's funny." Nick smiled. "I thought he said Huey."

The colonel cut him off. "Gentlemen, lady, follow me." With his large arm, he cut a swath through the crowd, clearing the way for himself, the nurse and the doctors. Ali and Nick glanced at each other with amazement and hurried to match the colonel's stride.

"You ever been to a hot zone?" the colonel said, glancing over his shoulder.

When the three shook their heads, he said, "In that case, you sure the hell better buckle up."

CHAPTER 15

GROUND ZERO

Nick examined the spartan interior of the UH-1 Huey Helicopter and its passengers. No one else seemed to suffer from the anxiety he was feeling. Why was he the only one who hated to fly? Ali was straining against his shoulder harness to peer through the open door, probably trying to get his bearings and searching for a clue to his family's situation.

Will, a seventy-five-year-old anesthesiologist from Texas, sat back with his eyes closed, apparently dozing. Nick wondered how a man that age was going to fare in the conditions he anticipated.

Shellie, the nurse and scrub tech, carelessly chatted with the United Nations soldier from Nigeria sitting next to her. Shellie had short, sandy-blond hair, bright eyes, and a pleasant smile. The soldier seemed to enjoy the attention, his toothy-white smile glowing against his black skin. Nick looked away to avoid getting hooked into conversation. She had already given him too much information in the few minutes they'd waited on the tarmac. Shellie was from Ohio, the mother of two young children, and married to a fireman. That was about all he could remember, because he'd stopped listening, nodding occasionally, which seemed to satisfy her.

He leaned back and squeezed his eyes shut. When the helicopter banked severely he jerked his eyes open and gripped the shoulder straps that held him in place. He glanced out the window to see the ground approaching. Fear gripped his gut. The helicopter made a wide circle around the city of Van and then swooped to the ground, touching the tarmac with the skill of a surgeon. He breathed a sigh of relief. *Thank you, God.*

Stepping off the helicopter, they got their first sight of the disaster—the collapsed two-story steel-and-glass building of Ferit Melen Havaalani Airport. Its yellow identifying letters scattered like Scrabble tiles in the rubble among twisted black airport seats. A huge, eerie statue overlooked the destruction—a white cat with one blue eye and one green eye.

"What in the world is that?" he asked Ali.

"It's the Van cat. Our folklore says it was aboard Noah's Ark and came from Mt. Ararat to Lake Van." He turned silent and surveyed the damage.

Nick realized how awful the sight must be for him. "I'm so sorry."

Ali shook his head in disbelief.

A Turkish military jeep came roaring up. A young officer jumped out and Ali addressed him in Turkish. Nick couldn't understand what they said, but he could tell it wasn't good when the smartly dressed officer blinked back tears.

Nick stepped forward and Ali made introductions.

"Thank you for coming, Dr. Hart," the officer said in adequate English.

"Any idea where we're going?" Nick asked.

"Sir, there are three government hospitals here." He paused, his voice breaking. "Two are completely destroyed, and the other is being cleared and staffed by some Turkish doctors that have been flown in. They started surgeries today."

"Is that where we are going?" Ali asked.

"No, sir, I have been asked to take you to King's, a private hospital just outside the city. Many of the injured have been taken there. King's is a small mission hospital and orphanage. Miraculously, it survived the quake. There are very few facilities."

Ali spoke to the officer in Turkish. The man shook his head solemnly. He then nodded and they seemed to agree on something.

Ali turned to Nick. "One of his men will take you and the

team to King's. He has agreed to take me to my parents' home…"
He stopped short. "I hope that is fine with you, Dr. Hart?"

"Is it safe?" Nick asked.

"Yes, the soldiers will watch over you."

"No, I mean for you." Nick observed the setting sun.

"Yes, of course. King's Hospital is but a few miles from the neighborhood where Asti's and my parents live. I will hopefully meet you at the hospital shortly."

Nick climbed into the army jeep with Shellie and Will. He pressed on his sternum as he considered this ragtag team: a retired and tired-looking anesthesiologist, a perky nurse, and himself. He also realized that none of them spoke Turkish and no one had any idea what they were getting into.

Nick waved to Ali, fearing he may never see him again.

***

Settling into the front passenger seat, Nick watched two Hueys fly low overhead. "Do you speak English?" he asked the driver.

"No." He wagged his finger. Then he reconsidered, putting his thumb and first finger almost together. "A little," he said with a strong accent.

"Can planes land here?"

The driver struggled to find the words. "No." He wagged his finger again. "Runway is…how you say…broke."

He turned right out of the airport. Nick saw a sign that indicated Van was the other way. He pointed in that direction. "Van?"

"Yes." The driver nodded enthusiastically and said, "Won," as though correcting Nick's Turkish.

"Van?"

"No, Won." He held up one finger. "ONE."

He understood and nodded and said. "One."

The driver smiled at Nick. "Won." Then he turned deadly serious. "Won…broke." He cut the air with his hand, indicating the city had been leveled.

"I am so sorry."

"Yes, sorry...broke." The driver repeated the gesture.

"How many are dead?"

The driver frowned. "Many, many, many. Too many." He shook his head.

There was nothing more to say. Nick sat in silence.

He watched the road descend into darkness and wondered if they were going in the right direction. The road followed the curve of a large lake that sucked a blood-red sun into its still waters, turning broken buildings into freaky silhouettes. A swelling plume of black smoke blanketed everything.

Nick wondered what caused the column and was about to ask, but the driver seemed to read his mind.

"Gasolina," he said. He made a sound of an explosion and raised both hands in the air, momentarily taking his hands off the wheel.

Nick nodded and his mind flashed on war movies about the atomic bomb. This is what it was like. Large high-rises were either tossed on their sides or destroyed completely, reduced to football-size debris. A devastated civilization shattered like toothpicks spilled from the box. Nick saw a lone figure scavenging the wreckage for signs of life, memories, food, or water.

"My Lord," Shellie said from the back seat.

They rode in silence, shivering with a chilling sensation of moving through a battlefield.

Their driver navigated passage around chunks of concrete and splintered wood that blocked the road.

Then the smell hit them.

"Oh, that's nasty." Will covered his face with his shirt to block the odor.

"That's an understatement." Nick stuffed his face in the crook of his elbow. The driver pulled the handkerchief around his neck over his mouth and nose. But there was no way to mask the putrid smell of decaying bodies. Shellie gagged and vomited, and it was all Nick could do to keep his stomach contents down.

The driver pushed through to the lakeside where the air was fresher.

Shellie apologized, as she searched in her bags for something to clean up her mess. "That was just awful. Those poor people."

Nick was beginning to understand the hell they had entered. It had taken them two hours to go a couple of miles. With logistics like that, Nick wondered how they could transport the injured in this abyss, let alone find them. As the jeep carried the team into pitch-black darkness, Nick was grateful for the light emanating from headlights.

Why have I come here?

CHAPTER 16

KING'S HOSPITAL
TUESDAY EVENING—POST-QUAKE DAY THREE

The jeep driver dropped Nick and his two new medical associates off a block from the entrance to King's Hospital, apparently as close as he could get. He pointed the way down the dirt road and told them in broken English that he had to go back to the airport to help quell a mob of angry people. As soon as they climbed out of the jeep, it sped off. Nick saw the taillights disappear around a corner and the street went quiet. His skin crawled, overwhelmed by the dark, eerie stillness.

The only other time in his life he'd experienced this kind of darkness was when he was young and adventurous and rode his bicycle into a long train tunnel. He got to the middle and could see no light at either end. It was pitch-black, he didn't have a light on his bike, and he panicked. He threw his bike down, fell to his hands and knees, and crawled until he saw the light. The absence of light was terrifying, then and now.

Will startled him. "This is a fine mess we've gotten ourselves into."

A body stumbled against Nick with an apology. It was Shellie tripping over his bag. He caught her before she fell and she apologized again.

"I think we need to get out of the street." He stepped back and lowered his backpack to the ground, blindly rummaging through it until he found what he was looking for—a headlamp. He switched it on and affixed it to his head. He found two more headlamps in his backpack and handed them to his team members.

Will put it on easily, but Shellie fiddled with hers, giggling nervously and switching on the light directly into their eyes. Nick quickly averted his eyes and turned her around by her waist, adjusting her headlamp so the light illuminated the ground.

"Sorry," she said. "Thank you."

"Let's go," Nick said, putting on his backpack, grabbing the handle of his suitcase, and starting down the dirt road the driver had indicated. Bouncing his suitcase along the rutted road, a large dog startled him as it streaked across their path, out of the darkness, then disappeared into the night. He caught his breath and continued picking his way toward the hospital.

"Oh, my Lord," Shellie gasped. Nick followed her gaze with his light and saw a woman crushed inside a car. He put his arm around Shellie to keep her moving toward the hospital.

Ahead, the faint light of a flickering fire and muttering voices grew louder. Following the light and sound, he turned a corner to see two barrels of burning wood. He aimed his light at a crumbling cinderblock wall behind the barrels. Letters had been scrawled in black paint on an intact part of the wall: KING'S HOSPITAL. Whoever scribbled the words had misjudged the available space and squeezed AND ORPHANAGE underneath.

His light searched the space where the voices came from and froze. Hundreds of eyeballs glowed in his lamp, staring back at him. He tried to judge the size of the crowd, but even in his high-intensity lamp, he couldn't see the end of it. Men, women and children of all ages were standing, sitting, or reclining—all injured. He recognized their injuries—fractures of every kind—some wounds covered, others wide open.

The crowd went silent for a moment and then swelled toward them. Instantly, he was surrounded with humanity, pleading, pulling at him, and crushing. His head began to spin. He couldn't breathe. Will shouted, "Doctor, Doctor," but it only incited the crowd more.

Nick tried to protect Shellie, but he couldn't reach her for the grasping hands. Someone yanked his suitcase from his hand, but he managed to hold tight to his backpack.

He tried to catch his breath when a deafening gun blast exploded. It was as though someone had clapped a cymbal over his ears. The gunshot separated the crowd, but he panicked when something gripped his body, hauled him off the ground and through a large, wrought-iron gate, and deposited him on his feet. His knees buckled as he tried to get his balance.

"Ho, you're okay. I've got you, Doctor." A large black man in uniform smiled at him and steadied his shoulders. The man holding a smoking shotgun seemed to stand a foot taller than Nick.

"My name is Christopher. Welcome to King's Hospital."

Nick was speechless and stared at the man's enormous chest. Christopher was wearing a UN uniform with a Liberian national flag patch. Nick spun around in search of his companions and was relieved to see them beside him. He saw the wrought-iron gate close between themselves and the raging crowd. He took a step toward the gate but the same strong hand that had rescued him pulled at his shirt.

"No worries, Doctor, we will get your bags," Christopher said, seeming to read his mind.

He glanced back through the gate to see the faces of the injured people waiting in line. He turned to ask Christopher why they were not let in, but when he looked past the soldier, he understood. As far as the light from his headlamp could reach, there was a sea of humanity already filling the hospital grounds—injured, frightened, and desperate for help. He couldn't begin to count them, but judging from oil lamps glowing in the distance, he thought there were probably enough people to fill a football field.

He was about to ask Christopher a question when a diminutive Chinese woman in scrubs held an oil-burning lamp up to his face. "You doctors?" With the back of her other hand, she pushed blood-spattered glasses up her nose. She didn't wait for his answer. "I'm Fenfang Lee," she said in a nasally Chinese accent. "You call me Lee." She extended her hand to shake.

Nick hesitated as it was covered in dirt and blood.

"So many fractures, not seen anything like it. Oh, so bad. Open fractures, closed fractures, head injuries. Morgue over there," she gestured, "is too full."

Nick looked the small woman up and down as she continued to talk. It was obvious she hadn't slept for days; her cropped gray hair was matted and stood straight up, a smear of dried blood ran across her forehead, and a stethoscope hung from her neck.

"We need doctors so bad," she went on. "You doctors?" she asked again. This time she waited for an answer.

"Yes, we are," Nick said. "That is, I'm a surgeon, and Will here is an anesthesiologist, and Shellie is an OR nurse."

The woman looked at Nick through her filthy lenses. "Your specialty?"

"I'm an orthopedic surgeon."

"Thank lucky stars." She grinned a grimy grin. "I could kiss you right now."

He tried not to cringe. *Please don't.*

She clapped her hands. "Okay. An OR team. Let's put you to work."

Nick hesitated and looked at Christopher. "There's one more of us," he said. "Another bone surgeon, originally from Turkey. He's checking on his family and should be here soon." He hoped it was true.

"Thanks for letting us know, Doc. We'll watch for him." Christopher spoke to his men, making sure they understood.

"You have another surgeon?" Lee gasped.

Nick turned to her to explain, but before he knew it, she was hugging his waist. She let him go, grabbed his hand, and pulled him toward the hospital.

Talking all the way, Lee led the trio up the ramp of the empty hospital building to the third floor. Her voice and their lights bounced off mostly intact walls. Swollen, dark circles under the woman's eyes betrayed her nonchalant demeanor. A door to the surgical area fell from its hinges as they approached and slammed to the floor. "That need fixing," Lee said and stepped over it.

They walked carefully over supplies and equipment strewn on the floor around the scrub sinks and into an operating room.

"This is larger of the two operating theaters," Lee said.

They stood in silence, frozen like people at the bottom of an approaching avalanche not knowing what to do. The OR was dead and dark.

Nick judged the room with his headlamp—the empty table and the unlit surgical lights hanging over it. It was a perfectly modern OR. Shellie reached down to right two suction canisters on their stand. A cautery machine, pneumatic tourniquet devices, and what appeared to be a very new blood saver stood ajar from their normal positions, but otherwise unscathed.

Everything was ready, and everything was useless.

"That's the problem with technology," Will said, observing the dormant anesthesia machine. "It's not going to do us any good now." He tapped his fingers against the oxygen tank hanging from the side of the apparatus.

Nick traced their power cords to the wall, power cords with no power. His heart sank. The truth hit him for the first time, and the advice of the UN officer back at the airport echoed in his ears: "You ever been to a hot zone? You better sure the hell buckle up."

A loud rumble filled the room and the building wobbled under their feet. He bent his knees and threw out his hands to keep from being knocked to the ground.

"Aftershock," Lee said. The terrific tremor cracked the supporting outer wall of the OR, and tile fell from the ceiling. Nick and the others ducked and held their heads, hoping to save themselves from collapsing concrete that never came. It lasted only a split second. He stood warily and examined the crack. Fortunately, the wall was still intact.

"Now you know why hospital is empty," Lee said with a cackling laugh. "At one time, hospital full. The first one hit and"—she clapped her hands together—"BAM. No more patients." She cackled again.

Nick wasn't laughing. He was imagining the people's terror when their world collapsed and their friends and family vanished in an instant. He wanted to run away, grab the next helicopter out of there—flying be damned. Yet, he had come to assist. Was he going to stay and help? It could kill him. He had to make up his mind, right then and there. Was he ready to give up his own life to help them?

"What do you think?" Shellie interrupted his thoughts.

He leaned against the OR table and crossed his arms. He put his fist under his chin, regarded his team in the glow of their headlamps, and nodded, "I think we need to get to work."

CHAPTER 17

ALL THROUGH THE NIGHT

Antasha eyed the plummeting gas gauge, winced and knew it was imperative to find a hospital or get more fuel. She thought of the angry farmer and the shooting.

Not that she was sorry about it, but she had no idea that they would be trapped in the area and she was feeling a bit like a caged animal.

She tried to quell her pain and frustration and concentrate on the map, illuminated by the dome light. It wasn't easy. The map was not helpful, especially in the dark. She looked at her companion. Vladimir stared ahead with two fingers at the bottom of the steering wheel and his foot on the gas, easing the vehicle through the traffic. She studied his features, oddly highlighted by the dashboard lights.

We are so different. His huge neck muscles bulged, angling down to his massive shoulders. His sloped forehead gave way to a boxer's nose and a permanently scowling brow. The Hulk personified. She wanted to smile.

How can such a huge man be such a big baby? She sighed. She knew how hard he tried, how much he wanted to please her, how grateful he was for any kindness, how hard he cried after any intimacy. She had, on occasion, rewarded his persistence with a few moments of tenderness. After all, all work and no play was not healthy, even for government work, and Vlad could be fun. A pleasant sensation grew inside her, and she felt her cheeks blush. She squelched the urge and refocused on the stupid map.

He glanced at her for instructions.

"I just don't know, Vlad. I have no idea where we are. Everything looks the same. I think we are going in circles." She stared into the darkness and saw only destruction—occasional natural gas fires still burning out of control illuminating shadowy figures moving through the rubble.

They rounded a curve and came to a barricade. They'd taken a wrong turn somewhere. Before Vladimir could turn the Land Rover around, they found themselves surrounded by UN soldiers armed with M-15 rifles.

Antasha reached for the gun, but Vladimir's hand pushed the weapon deeper between the seats away from her grip and he scowled at her. With his other hand, he rolled down his window to face a soldier in a blue beret and a loaded rifle aimed at his head.

"Sir, put your hands on the steering wheel," the soldier demanded.

Vladimir obeyed. "Officer, I'm sorry. We are looking for the hospital." He spoke in perfect English. The man looked him up and down and then inspected the car with the light mounted on his M-15. Satisfied, he lowered his rifle.

"Sir, you should not be out here. It is not safe. A curfew is in effect."

"I'm sorry, but we have just come from…" Antasha gripped his leg. He understood her cue. "We have come from Çavuştepe."

"Tourists?" the soldier asked.

"Yes. We are visiting old Armenian sites. My wife was injured in the earthquake, and I'm trying to get her to the hospital."

The soldier shone his light at Antasha's splinted leg and nodded. "The government hospital is just up ahead, but I'm afraid I cannot let you pass. They are only taking critically injured patients, and there are thousands there already. King's Hospital is the only other functional facility in the area, and it is about thirty klicks from here. I hear it is also very crowded, but there are no other choices."

"How do we get there?"

"Take this road, approximately five klicks, then take a left to a traffic circle. Take the second right. Stay on the main road and follow it around the lake. But, sir," he warned, "it is not safe. There are many looters."

Antasha looked at the gas gauge. They would be driving on fumes.

***

Between the late-night gunshot and the aftershocks, Ibrahim couldn't sleep. His leg and back were sore from lying in the dirt, and he was nauseated by the ever-present smell of decay and feces. But the pain and the odors didn't concern him as much as his companion, the girl lying next to him. She was still warm, but she no longer moved or moaned. Maybe she was dead.

The night air was cool, but it brought relief from the flies that were beginning to swarm. A young boy had brought him a small sheet, and Ibrahim pulled it around his neck. The fabric smelled strongly of mothballs, but it was better than the alternative and cut the edge of the crisp night air.

Above him the Milky Way arched across the sky. With no artificial lights, the stars were bigger and brighter than ever. He felt small, like what an ant must feel in the middle of a grand city, or how a grain of sand feels on the shore of a great ocean.

Allah, are you out there? Are you real? What have we done to deserve this?

He closed his eyes and imagined his mother's face, her smile, and the scent of her perfume. He heard her singing and drifted into sleep.

***

The air was stagnant in the dark, claustrophobic OR. Nick couldn't shake images of the collapsed buildings or the stench of death or what it must be like to be trapped and suffocating under the stinking debris. It didn't help when the hospital walls groaned and creaked like a haunted house.

He fought back his fear and worked as fast as he could.

Time was wasting away for the hundreds of patients waiting in misery outside, but the task at hand seemed like an unscalable mountain. Only the collective will of the team was able to muster the momentum to prepare the OR. With no electricity or water, all they could do with the fine, white powdery dust coating everything was to brush it to the floor and sweep it out the door.

He kicked himself for sloughing off a disaster-relief symposium a few months back. He had believed he knew everything about trauma that he needed to know. Now he realized that was a stupid attitude. He had to make do without everything he had taken for granted. It was going to be tough without electricity, even though it was possible to operate using their headlamps. But what would they do without water?

Shellie brought up another challenge. "How are we going to sterilize the instruments?"

Will broke the hopelessness when he pushed the modern anesthesia machine to the corner and pulled out a case of medications from his suitcase. "So…spinals, locals, and maybe regional blocks," he said with confidence.

"How are you going to monitor them?" Shellie asked.

Will held up a blood pressure cuff and a stethoscope. "Like I did when I was in training forty years ago." He smiled. "Oh, here's one piece I'm glad I brought." He held up a small battery-operated finger-pulse-oximeter. "I tossed it into my bag at the last minute on a whim. I can monitor their pulse and oxygenation with this baby."

Nick realized he'd misjudged the older man and was glad to have his experience. He wondered how many more recently trained anesthesiologists would know where to begin without their fancy machinery.

"You miracle workers." Lee startled him from the dark hallway. "Just like America now." She stepped inside the OR with two wide-eyed women. "These nurses from King's," she announced. "Just arrived. They work in ward, but maybe help you." She turned to the frightened women and spoke to them in Turkish. She turned back to Nick. "My English not so good, my Turkish perfect." She laughed her cackling laugh.

"Is there any way we can get an interpreter up here?" he

asked Lee, knowing they would need to communicate with the new nurses and with the patients.

"I put on thinking cap. I see what I can do." Lee put a finger to her head. "Meantime, I ask them"—she pointed to the nurses—"show." She pointed to Shellie. "I forget name."

"Shellie."

"Shellie. I ask them show Shellie supplies. Dr. Hart, come with me. I show you most critical patients."

Before Nick could follow her, Will spoke. "Let's move the other OR table in here. We'll run it like a MASH unit. I can do both tables from the anesthesia standpoint, and when your friend gets here, you guys can double your efforts."

"Good thinking, Will."

Nick looked at his watch. He was worried about Ali. It was already midnight. Just like at the MED, the action starts at midnight. *One thing's for sure: I'll never ever complain about the equipment at the MED.*

"The UN is trying to get us generator and diesel," Lee said. "I tell them make top priority."

CHAPTER 18

ONE AND TWO

WEDNESDAY—POST-QUAKE DAY FOUR

Father, help me.

It was all Nick could think as he shook his head and looked helplessly over the compound's courtyard at the mass of throbbing humanity.

"Four hundred," Lee said. "Four hundred when we close gate. No idea how many outside. Do best we can." She sighed loudly and hung her hands in defeat, signaling a crack in her hardened persona.

"First days we make hard decisions," she explained, her voice trailing off. "People dying." Lee's emotional dam broke, releasing a flood of emotion. She covered her face with her hands and began to sob.

He wrapped his arm around the woman and pulled her close, and her whole body heaved in agony. He had only just arrived and was already overwhelmed. He couldn't imagine the horror of the first thirty-six hours.

"My God, Lee…" He searched for words, but finding none, he held her with both arms and let her grieve.

"I on vacation from China practice to care for orphans," she said between sobs. "Some vacation," she tried to joke. "Had no idea I go to hell."

A commotion at the gate caused Nick to pull away from

Lee. A group of UN soldiers escorted a scrawny Turk wearing a headlamp. He recognized him immediately. "Ali!" he shouted. "Thank you, God." Ali's dirty and partially untucked shirt hung from his slumped shoulders. Nick's heart sank when he saw how discouraged his friend looked. The soldiers marched Ali through the gate to the courtyard.

Nick grabbed Ali and hugged him. "I'm so glad to see you safe." Then he pushed him back and looked into his face. He knew the news was bad.

"I could not find them," Ali said. "Both houses are badly damaged, and no one was there. Nothing. No sign of them. At least…" He couldn't finish the sentence.

"I'm sorry, Ali. Maybe they're safe somewhere." Nick tried sounding optimistic.

"Maybe you're right, Dr. Hart. I'm going to hold on to that for now."

Nick introduced Lee.

"*Selamünaleyküm*, may God's peace be upon you," Ali greeted her.

"*Aleykümselam*, peace be upon you," she answered back, Ali's eyebrows raised with her knowledge of his language. They spoke briefly in Turkish before returning to English for Nick's benefit.

"Lee was showing us the lay of the land," Nick said.

"I number patients from most critical to less."

"Four hundred plus," Nick added.

"All this side, open fractures and severe injuries," Lee said, waving her arm over one side of the courtyard. "All other injuries, closed fractures," she said, waving over the other side of the courtyard. "In God's mercy, critical die quickly. All we give is comfort."

Nick and Ali nodded.

"We have to start with washing out the open fractures," Nick said. "The closed fractures will have to wait. When help arrives, we can splint as many as we can." He turned to Ali. "Unfortunately, the operating room is on the third floor, but there's a ramp all the way up. It's on the far side of the hospital. There are two ORs, but we have turned the big one into a MASH unit, so Will can run two tables at once."

"I just hope we get some help soon." Ali surveyed the sea of injured.

Nick squeezed Lee's shoulder. "You have done an amazing job. Now you better show us patients one and two."

"I know you guys bone docs, but is not skull, bone?" She swallowed down her grief and spoke with her characteristic cackle. "I have young girl I did not think survive this long. I sure she has head bleed. Come." She waved and led them into the sea of misery.

***

Ali knelt beside the girl who was partially obstructed by a boy that leaned against her, fast asleep. She appeared to be about fifteen, but she was covered in dirt and concrete dust, so it was hard to tell. Ali brushed back the girl's hair and opened one eye at a time, shining his headlamp into her eyes. One side contracted in the glow of the light, and the other stayed dilated and unresponsive. Even from his angle, Nick could tell that one pupil was blown.

Ali felt for a pulse at the girl's neck, and she moaned slightly.

The boy awoke and screamed, causing Ali, Nick, and Lee to jump. Ali pulled off his headlamp, aimed it at his own face and smiled. He put his hand on the boy's chest.

"There, there. We're not going to hurt you," he said in English and then Turkish.

The boy's cries turned to whimpers, and he winced and grabbed his leg. The muscles spasmed as the ends of the fractured bones ground together. Ali held the leg down, and the boy relaxed.

"*Selamünaleyküm, Selamünaleyküm,*" Ali said.

The boy blinked large dark eyes, "*Aleykümselam,*" he replied softly.

Ali stroked his cheek. "You are a brave young man. What is your name?"

"Ibrahim."

"Ibrahim, I'm Dr. Hassan, and we are going to help you. But first we must help your friend. Is this your sister?"

Ibrahim shook his head.

"Do you know her name?"

He shook his head again.

"It's okay. We're going to take her into the hospital and help her." Ali held onto the boy's leg and signaled for Nick to pick up the girl. The boy whimpered. "We will take good care of her," Ali told him.

Lee said something to an injured woman lying beside Ibrahim, and the woman placed her uninjured hand on Ibrahim's forehead.

Nick supported the girl's head as best as he could, knowing that picking up and moving a head-injury patient would never pass muster with emergency medical response standards. But there was nothing else he could do. If the girl was going to be saved, the pressure on her brain had to be relieved.

"Time's a-wastin'," Nick declared, and he, Lee, and Ali headed to the operating room.

CHAPTER 19

MAGGOTS

Nick, gowned and masked in the OR, glanced up from his patient to see Ali at the other table preparing for surgery on the girl's head. Light from everyone's headlamps bounced around the dark room, illuminating Shellie, Will, the two local nurses, and a young interpreter Lee had produced. Nick would operate on a middle-aged woman's open and terribly infected leg while Ali operated on the girl—an unheard-of scenario in any other circumstance.

Sterilization in this setting was a problem. They found a few sets of instruments that were already sterile and could get them by for the first three cases. After that, they would have to soak the instruments in rubbing alcohol and let them air dry until a generator arrived to fire up the autoclaves.

Nick's hands trembled and panic surged within him. To make matters worse, the earth shook again, a staggering tremor that rattled the building. Nick hung onto the table to steady himself and caught sight of Shellie gagging and vomiting in the corner.

The shaking earth slung Nick closer to the injured leg. It was severely infected and smelled of rotting flesh. Maggots crawled in heaping mounds, causing the dead muscle to look like it was moving on its own.

"I don't know," Shellie cried, "I don't know if I can take this." She retched again. "Oh, God."

Nick didn't know if he could take it either, even when the tremor had stopped. How could he be any more powerless in his life? He willed himself to stay in control, but a childhood memory fueled his angst. He saw himself as a kid, very angry at his aunt—he couldn't remember what for—but he was so angry that he grabbed her cherished china vase and threw it across the room, smashing it into a thousand pieces.

"What's wrong with you, Nicklaus?" He could still hear her voice and forced his mind to turn it off and return to the OR. *What is wrong with me? I'm losing it.*

Sweat dripped down his back, and he thought of Maggie and then Anna, his favorite interpreter and assistant in Guatemala. What would they do? They would cry out to Jesus, the only safe harbor in a storm.

"Jesus!" he shouted.

The OR team startled and the room went dead silent.

"Jesus," Nick repeated, softly this time, seeing their faces illuminated by their headlamps. He felt naked and exposed.

He raised a hand and stood up straight. "Okay. It's okay." His courage began to come back. "Okay."

He thought of what Buck had told him after a category-five hurricane hit the Mississippi coast and people were saying it was the wrath of God, that God had whipped it up to punish them. Buck had said that was nonsense. "Jesus doesn't bless storms. He rebukes them. Remember Jesus and the disciples in the boat when the storm hit? He rebuked the storm, and it quieted, and He encouraged the disciples to do the same."

"Jesus," Nick repeated while the team waited his direction. *Rebuke this storm.*

He looked at Ali at the other table holding a syringe of local anesthesia. The injured girl's head had been shaved, painted in betadine, and covered with an OR drape.

Shellie stopped gagging and picked herself up off the floor. He turned to Will, who was smiling at him. The old man was a perennial optimist. Nick looked at the two local nurses, who stared wild-eyed at this crazy American doctor.

He looked at the young interpreter. The earnest young man was gowned in an extra-large pink scrub top meant for nurses. It hung over his shoulders and was tucked into oversized pants and bunched at his waist by an old leather belt. Nick couldn't help but suppress a smile.

"We're quite a team," he said.

The young man translated.

"I don't know how we're going to manage this," Nick said, trying to find the right words, "but we're just going to have to. I know we come from different worlds with different beliefs and different faiths. But God…Allah, has brought us here to help. I don't know about you, but I'm scared shitless."

"Shitless?" the puzzled young interpreter inquired.

Nick grinned. "Very scared."

Everyone nodded.

He looked at Ali. "Bud, would you be willing to pray for us?"

"Yes, certainly, Dr. Hart."

Ali's prayer was brief and in Turkish.

When he finished, Nick said, "Thank you, Father. Thank you, Jesus."

Everyone added, "Amen."

***

With terrestrial and human tremors quieted and order restored, Ali injected the girl's scalp with a syringe of Lidocaine. Will stood by with a syringe of narcotics to inject in her arm if more anesthetic was needed. The girl moaned softly but did not struggle. Will signaled Ali to continue.

To tell the truth, Ali was a little surprised to be in charge. His brain flashed back eleven years ago when he was an intern and low man on the totem pole. He was doing a three-month neurosurgical rotation in London. The cases he assisted on were long and arduous, and he could still hear the carping of the prickly neurosurgeon. Ali was barely allowed to hold a scalpel, and the sarcastic surgeon loved to belittle him. "Don't suck on the brain. You're sucking on the brain," he'd bellow when Ali held the suction cannula. "You just sucked out the memory of his favorite dog," he ridiculed and laughed like a hysterical hyena. Ali had to develop thick skin.

Now he was in an OR with no electricity, and no one mocked him. The fate of this girl was up to him and her chance of survival was slim. Her brain could swell and herniate at any moment through the foramen magnum, and death would be instantaneous. Without a CT scan, Ali had no way of knowing if he was wading into disaster. The bleed could be so massive that there would be no way to stop it, and without cautery, even a small bleed could be difficult. The only suction he had was the bulb syringe.

It was a good thing Shellie and the local nurses had found some surgical clips in the supply room. These small metal clips could be squeezed together with a special instrument to close the vessels and save her life. That is, if she didn't die from a raging infection. He glanced at Nick working on the mangled, infected leg, then back at his patient's head.

He made the incision through the scalp wound. Blood oozed from the crack in the white bone. He hoped the piece of the skull that had fractured was large enough to lift off the dura. He looked at the antique skull saw, a small hatchet with serrated edges, which they had found in the instrument room and disinfected in alcohol. He shuddered to think of how many places in the world still used such archaic tools.

"Hold the girl's head steady so I can saw the bone," he instructed the nurse.

He was sweating and almost called for the air conditioning to be turned to high. Then he remembered they had no power.

The pressure behind the bone began to push it off the dura, and blood gushed all over his surgical gown as he removed the plate of skull. The brain had not herniated. The only good news was that the loss of blood would lower her blood pressure and possibly slow the bleeding. All bleeding stops eventually—it was a morbid joke beloved by that damn neurosurgeon who had tormented Ali.

He gently but firmly pressed a lap sponge onto the area. With no suction, finding the torn vessel was going to be difficult. He wiped his sweaty face on his shoulder. The last thing she needed was his sweat dripping into her cranium. He removed the lap sponge but replaced it immediately as blood swelled into the cavity.

Where is it coming from?

He tried to suction the blood with the pitiful bulb syringe, but more blood flowed almost simultaneously.

He heard Will's warning. "I know you wanted her BP down, but we're at seventy over nothing."

Ali held the lap sponge in place while carefully searching the edges to try to narrow down the bleeding in the quadrant.

"There it is." The artery slithered like an untethered water hose and he held out his hand for the surgical clip.

He swore under this breath and then yelled at the artery to cooperate. "Come on!" With one swift movement, he removed the lap sponge and thrust the surgical clip into place. It missed its mark. He thrust out his hand to the nurse for another one. He was close to panic. He could do more damage to the artery or tear another, and it would all be over.

The second clip caught only half the vessel, but it was enough to cut down the bleeding. The nurse was ready with a third clip. Ali grabbed it and the bleeding eased.

"Way to go, Ali," Will cheered.

"Okay," he nodded. "Let's do another clip for safekeeping and get the heck out of here."

***

At the other table, Nick faced the reality that amputations may be the most common surgery they would have to do—and he hated them. The woman's leg would have to come off. It was so badly damaged and infected that it would eventually kill her with sepsis and total organ failure. It would be a painful and agonizing death.

In a fully functioning OR, a plug-in pneumatic tourniquet would be placed around the top of the thigh to stop the bleeding from the amputation. But in this OR, the pneumatic unit sat useless in the corner, and he had no choice but to use a thick rubber exsanguinating bandage to wrap the patient just below the hip. The malpractice lawyers back home would have a field day with this. As he wrapped the leg in the rubber bandage, maggots fell from the wound to the floor.

Her leg would need to come off midthigh. He pushed away images of the woman trying to maneuver a wheelchair over dirt roads or sitting helpless along the sidewalks begging, unable to get an expensive prosthesis. But this woman's life was at stake, and an amputation was the only option.

CHAPTER 20

TWELVE HOURS

Fourteen amputations—eleven legs and three arms—in twelve hours, and Nick was exhausted. Two patients died from overwhelming sepsis, one on the OR table and the other after surgery. The word spread like wildfire from the hospital to the makeshift morgue. Everyone—medical staff, waiting injured, UN soldiers—tallied the amputations and the deaths.

Not only had the devastating quake crushed the infrastructure, its swirling dust and debris had awakened pathogens normally dormant in the antiquated sewers. The supercharged bacteria found their way to the open fractures of the injured and infected them, their wounds oozing with pus.

Nick could not have imagined the profusion of injury and disease. Throughout his career, he had seen many contaminated fractures, but never to this extent. It was as if a plague of biblical proportions had descended on the people of eastern Turkey.

So far, the medical team had only scratched the surface, and the prognosis looked grim.

Between surgeries, Nick stood with Ali and Lee on a hospital portico observing the waiting injured in the courtyard. "We have to go down and talk to them," he said. It was clear that all the amputations had increased their fear. "People are refusing to come in and be treated. I guess I don't blame them."

"We have to get you all something to eat." Lee gestured to Shellie, who lay stretched on a gurney with an IV dripping into her arm. "No operate without food." She waved her finger at the doctors like a mother hen.

Nick was beyond hunger. He looked at his watch tied to his scrub pants. "Is it really noon here?" He looked up into the clear blue sky, unable to comprehend the beauty of the day to the horror on the ground. He shook his head, incredulous.

Two large UN helicopters buzzed low over the hospital. "Any word on a generator?" he shouted as the noisy copters passed.

"Working on it," Lee replied. "Beautiful today but rain come soon. Tomorrow, next day. Need to make shelter for people."

They stood in silence, observing the restless crowd.

"I'm afraid I don't have much of an appetite," Ali said. "I do have protein bars. Happy to share. Everyone needs to take some water so we don't hit the floor like poor Shellie."

"We have water," Lee said. "UN brought truckload. Orphans passing bottles."

The children made their way through the crowd, giving water to thirsty takers. Nick remembered a pre-op rule. "We need to keep the patients NPO, nothing to eat or drink..." he began and then cursed. "These poor people probably haven't had much to drink for the last three days." He put his hands on the top of his head, realizing he was trying to practice standard US medicine. He sighed. "Anyone have some Advil?"

Lee produced a large bottle from her white jacket. "Just happen to."

He wasn't surprised by her efficiency. He took a couple of tablets and nodded thanks.

"I'll try to explain what we are doing," Ali said looking over the crowd. "Why we are performing amputations and that we will do them only if there is no other way to save their lives. We should probably operate on some people that just need their fractures washed out and let them leave with limbs intact. It will give the people confidence."

***

Vladimir cradled Antasha in his arms. It was the only thing that kept him from lunging at the man's throat. The beefy, black

UN soldier blocking the entrance to King's Hospital had been officious, and Vladimir was not happy.

"But we are Russian citizens," he had told the soldier.

"I don't care if you're from Mars. You are not going through this gate."

Vladimir ignored the cries from the people in the queue. He could subdue the large soldier, but the two soldiers standing nearby with M-15s were another matter.

People wearing white coats, standing on the hospital portico inside the gate, looked like medical personnel. He whistled loudly through his teeth and held up his injured Antasha. But they didn't see him and became distracted by the helicopters overhead.

The soldier crossed his arms and indicated with his chin and head that Vladimir was to move to the end of the line.

Vladimir realized he was defeated. He readjusted his hold on Antasha.

"You were sweet to try, Vlad," she said, patting him on the cheek. "Now take me to the back of the bus."

There was nothing more to say, and as much as he liked holding her, his arms were getting tired. The Land Rover's gas had run out three miles back and they'd had to abandon it and walk. He had to walk; she rode in his arms. He was glad to be rid of the vehicle, in case it became involved with the police after the incident with the farmer.

With Antasha in his arms, the walk had been horrendous. At first light, he had become more aware of the earthquake's devastation and thought it even worse than in Hakkâri. Hundreds and hundreds of people camped on the streets and in open spaces, apparently afraid to return to their homes. Haphazard shelters had been erected from sheets of plastic and cardboard supported by chunks of concrete or hanging from ropes attached to fallen trees and buildings. Men and women sat in shock, paying little attention to children running and playing as though it were a holiday. Campfires burned from splintered lumber and the smell of death was everywhere.

**

"Excuse me, sir."

Ali walked among the injured explaining the amputations and almost missed the small voice. He stepped back and saw two girls struggling with a basket of plastic water bottles. Then he looked down and saw the small boy lying in the dirt. Ali waved the girls over. He took two bottles and thanked them.

He sat on the ground next to the boy, twisted the bottle cap off, and lifted the boy's head. He put the bottle to his dry, cracked lips and the boy took three large gulps.

"Thank you, sir. Can you please tell me what happened to my friend?"

He looked at the boy with matted dark hair and sad eyes and realized it was the child who'd been leaning against the girl he had operated on.

"I'm sorry. What was your name again?"

"Ibrahim, sir."

"That's right. Thank you, Ibrahim. Your friend is very sick, but she is alive. I'm sure she's going to be just fine." His confidence wasn't real, but he chose not to upset the boy.

Ibrahim smiled. His two front teeth were badly in need of cleaning.

With a quick scan of the hungry people nearby, Ali snuck a protein bar from his front pocket and slipped it into Ibrahim's hand. He knew supplying one person with food was unfair to everyone else, but he could only help one at a time, and he was inexplicably drawn to the boy.

"Allah be with you, my dear child," Ali whispered. He left the other bottle of water with Ibrahim, got up, and went on with his information mission.

CHAPTER 21

ISIS

"Yes, my brother, if Allah wills," Abdul Awwal Fadhil said to his oldest brother. "But are you sure this is the right thing to do?" Abdul regretted the words as they left his lips. It sounded like he was questioning his brother's wisdom and authority, and that's not what he meant.

Abbas, his brother, was recently named first in command under Abu Bakr al-Baghdadi, the leader and self-appointed caliph of the newly declared worldwide caliphate. With the new position, Abdul had seen an immediate change in his brother's personality. Abbas had always been the most serious and focused of his brothers, but now he was distracted, withdrawn, and violent. He had become legendary at provoking the West with vivid and horrific images, and this ability accounted for his rapid rise in authority.

Abdul looked at his phone, waiting for a response that didn't come. He thought Abbas had hung up. When he was a kid, Abdul's friends had teased him, telling him his parents should have been more careful when they'd named his brother because the meaning of *Abbas* foretold his character: "the gloomy one." Of course, Abdul's own name was no better for his ego. It meant "servant of the first one."

"Abbas, are you there?"

"Yes, my brother, it is the right thing to do, and it is time."

Abdul hung up the phone and rested it under his chin. He would follow his three older brothers to the end of the world. He was proud of his fight for jihad. But the latest news made him hesitate. Like the rest of the world, he had seen the pictures of the earthquake in Turkey and the dead bodies stacked one on top of the other. Dying from a bullet or an explosion in the fight against the infidels would take him to paradise. That was one thing, but suffocating under a ton of bricks was another. If he died that way, would Allah still find his sacrifice worthy?

He stuffed the phone into his front pants pocket and took a long swig of his Coke. Two weeks ago, Abbas told him that ISIS would move further into Turkey in twelve months. The earthquake accelerated that timeframe. "Now was the perfect time to go," Abbas had told him and Abdul knew he was right. The earthquake created a void and they would fill it, just as they had done in Syria and Iraq. Now was time to enter deep within Turkey and reclaim a large piece of the caliphate.

He set his soda can down, wishing he had conjured the plan. ISIS fighters would disguise themselves as aid workers with the Red Crescent. Their convoy of relief supplies would camouflage AK-47s and rocket-propelled grenades that would supply the covert army they had been building for decades.

Abdul smiled. At least he had outlined the route. From Aleppo, the jihadists would drive east in northern Syria and then north to cross the border into Turkey and into Şanlıurfa, eighty kilometers from the Euphrates River. Abdul's brother loved the fact that they would pass through the ancient city of Ur Kasdim, Abraham's hometown in 2000 BC.

Abdul loved history and knew Islamic conquerors took the region in AD 638, when most of the Christians were slaughtered. His heart was filled with joy at the opportunity to do Allah's will. But his brain was filled with sadness. He had planned to begin his last year at the university to earn his degree in engineering and was looking forward to it, but now it would have to wait until next year. It was imperative that he answer his brother's call to action.

Allah be praised.

CHAPTER 22

THIRTY-SIX HOURS

"Augh!" Pain gripped Nick's right hand. With his left he tried to uncurl his fingers from the hemostat cramped in his palm so he could continue working on his patient on the table in the OR.

"Does anybody really know what time it is?" he crooned. "Does anybody really care?" he sang a line from an old song by Chicago, trying to hold onto some semblance of sanity.

He looked at Ali, slumped against the nearby wall, grabbing some shut-eye before his next patient was brought up to surgery. Ali's head hung awkwardly to one side. "How can you sleep?"

Nick flexed his fingers and watched a silent woman mopping the floor with bottled water, trying to keep the dust, blood, and body fluids at bay. She was one of two additional hospital employees who had survived the quake and returned to help. He had no idea what time it was or if it was night or day. All he knew was that his back was killing him.

When did we get here? Someone said they had operated for thirty-six hours straight. He was sleep deprived and found it difficult to keep track of time or the number of people they had operated on. There was so much to do. The hospital was still without running water and electricity, and everyone's nerves were frazzled from the battlefield conditions. Even Ali had lost his cool and yelled at a UN soldier for tracking dirt into the OR. Worst of all, Nick could feel anxiety fighting for space in his mind.

He shifted on the wooden stool someone had found for him and looked at the patient with a fractured forearm. He wondered if he could save her arm. At least he thought it was a female.

He looked over the surgical drape. *Yes, a woman.* She was conscious and wiping her eyes with her good hand. Will's arm-numbing block had worked well. Nick looked back at her injured arm and her chipped red fingernail polish. Something heavy had fallen on her arm and broken the bones and crushed the muscle. Maybe he should just whack it off. Easier for him. Not so easy for her.

Peace and fear warred inside Nick's head.

He closed his eyes and saw a vision of the woman's future. She was trying unsuccessfully to arrange her hair with the stump of her arm. Then, with vengeance, she was shaking her bloody, tendon-dangling, infected arm at him, her angry face ravaged with caked-on concrete cut with streams of tears.

"Help me," she begged him.

Nick's mind pulled at him. Coaxing him to escape to a safer place. A place without pain and suffering. The sound of a babbling stream rose within his soul.

A warm place.

A peaceful place.

Nick's head jerked up hard and he realized he had fallen asleep. It threw his neck into spasm. Without thinking, he grabbed his neck, breaking the sterile field and smearing blood on his skin. He sprang to his feet and knocked over the stool. The Mayo stand containing surgical instruments crashed to the floor. Bile rose from his stomach, and he fought to swallow it down. Sweltering air with the smells of betadine and blood sucked his breath from his lungs, and he grabbed his chest in panic. *I can't breathe.*

He ripped off his mask and gasped for air.

"I can't breathe," he said to his barely conscious patient and sleeping Ali.

The room collapsed around him. Anxiety flooded his mind and tangled his nerves. Darkness filled his vision.

My God, help me. He felt a falling sensation as if his mind might collapse into insanity. *Father, forgive me.* The weight of his past sins crushed at the self-built pillars of ego and independence from God.

Nick's subconscious mind raced halfway around the world. He was on his knees at the foot of his dying friend in Guatemala, pleading for her life and promising his own to God. If he truly believed, why did he turn his back on Him? Things done and left undone.

Screams ripped him from Guatemala with violent shaking.

Nick was ripped from his confused state. He realized he was on his hands and knees and was wide awake, but the floor moved under him, like riding in the bed of a pickup truck jostling down a bumpy road.

Another aftershock, more powerful than the previous.

Someone tugged at his waist, but his body resisted, stiffened and froze. He thought he was dying but sensed a presence pulling him from the grave. Every patient he cared for in the last forty hours seemed to scream into his ears. The cries of those being crushed by concrete and falling timbers rang in his head. The terror of a collapsing world gripped his soul.

Darkness.

He felt the panic of being buried alive and trapped, only able to move a hand or leg, barely able to breathe.

Suffocating.

Help me.

Voices called to him. *Air, I need air.*

The earth and the building around him groaned. He was unable to move.

There was one last lurch of the room and a loud, grinding sound and a crash.

Pain.

CHAPTER 23

THE WHITE SNAKE
THURSDAY—POST-QUAKE DAY FIVE

Abdul eyed the woman driving the truck with disbelief and annoyance. It was unusual for a woman to drive at all, but it was more unusual for a woman to lead a convoy of trucks. Aside from the impropriety, he was surprised at her expertise, shifting gears of the monster truck with such precision. A female driver had been his brother's idea, and he had to admit his brother was usually right.

"The fact that she is British and has blue eyes will disorient anyone standing in your way, including the guards at the border," Abbas had told him.

It was working so far, even though he resented that Abbas had put him in this position. He would have preferred to be at the university finishing his degree in chemical engineering. But Abbas knew best, and Abdul had prepared himself.

For the past year, he had abstained from alcohol and dating and was proud of his success. Such abstinence was prescribed in Salafist beliefs, the strictest Sunni Islamic teachings and the doctrine preached by ISIS. Because he had been morally upright, Abdul believed he was prepared to deal with the British woman driving the truck, but now he was not so sure.

He averted his gaze to follow a semi approaching them from the opposite direction, and when it passed, he couldn't help returning his gaze to the woman. He wasn't sure if it was her fair skin and blue eyes or her reputation as a well-known jihadist that intrigued him. Known as "the White Snake," she was still an enigma to him.

He forced himself to turn away and check the large side-view mirror. He watched the other three trucks in the convoy rumbling behind them and bounced his legs nervously. The worn truck tires hummed like white noise between radio stations. The vehicles, four US M939 6X6 military cargo trucks, had recently been captured in Iraq, taken to Syria, and painted with the Red Crescent symbol. ISIS loved to celebrate its capture of US vehicles to be recycled in the fight with the infidels.

Abdul adjusted his vest with a Red Crescent patch over its breast pocket. He squinted into the sky and hoped the large red crescent painted on the top of their truck's cargo would fool the US drones. If they weren't tricked, he figured he would never see the drone or missile that would vaporize them, and he wondered if, in that moment, he would even know what was happening. But he had promised Abbas to do his duty.

"Are you nervous?" the woman looked at him and asked.

"No," he said, glowering.

"Are you angry?"

He ignored her and surveyed the barren landscape that had not changed since they left Aleppo two hours ago. He turned to the open roadmap in his lap, fidgeting with its edge. He was glad they would soon cross the Euphrates River. He would welcome a reprieve from the monotony of the desert.

He caught sight of a road sign. The turn to Koboni was ten miles ahead. "One of my brothers is there," he said.

The woman glanced at him and raised an eyebrow under her blue and black scarf.

"In Koboni," he said.

She nodded. "I hear they have taken the city."

"Yes, from the Kurdish scum."

Abdul wished he were there, fighting for real, instead of stuck here with this woman, unarmed and exposed to everyone—US drones, Kurds fighting to the north, Shia pigs whose territory they were driving into, and even their own comrades, who might think their convoy was a humanitarian mission with valuable hostages to be captured. That would ruin everything.

"I know your oldest brother," the woman said, "but you obviously have another?"

"I have three brothers," he said, not looking at her. "Well, two. The second oldest was killed last year in Jobar, just outside Damascus. He's a doctor…was a doctor. He died from sarin."

Out of the corner of his eye, he saw her grimace and figured she had seen the pictures or at least heard the stories of horrifying death from the chemical weapon.

"I'm sorry."

"Allah's will," Abdul said and stared straight ahead.

CHAPTER 24

CALVARY AND THE CAVALRY

"Dr. Hart," a voice called, waited, and called again, urgently. "Dr. Hart, can you hear me?"

Nick's consciousness began to awaken deep within his primal brain. Waves of reality began to flood the higher thinking portions of his mind and return him to awareness.

Air.

Light.

He floated wide-eyed in a gelatin awareness, not yet sure where he was.

"Dr. Hart, are you okay?"

He blinked and discovered he was sprawled face down with his head inches from a large concrete block embedded in the floor.

"Dr. Hart?"

Dazed, he turned and saw Ali, who was clutching him around the waist. Ali's headlamp blinded him. He looked away and raised himself up on his arms. As his eyes became accustomed to the light, he saw he was still wearing his surgical gown and bloodied gloves. He worked to pull off the gloves, and Ali helped him roll over and sit up.

Ali looked like an angelic figure backlit with bright sunshine. Nick smiled. "I truly did die and go to heaven."

"Dr. Hart?" Ali asked.

"Holy God, are you two okay?" Will yelled. "That was the biggest one yet." He knelt beside Nick and looked at his forehead. "That block took a layer of skin off."

His mind still reeling into focus, Nick felt the sting of the freshly scraped hide and heard Shellie sobbing somewhere nearby.

"She's okay," Will said and shook his head incredulously. "My God, that block missed your head by…" He paused. "Well, it almost missed your head."

Nick's mind began to focus, and his heart raced. He searched the room, wondering about the patients, if they'd been killed. Both OR tables were empty. Then he saw his patient standing in the doorway with the rest of the OR crew. Her injured arm hung limp, still covered by the surgical drape.

"Did everyone else—"

"Yes, everyone else made it out." Will finished Nick's question.

Nick noticed a ray of sunlight on the floor and followed it to where the ceiling had fallen. He saw a cloud float across a blue sky.

"Ali pulled you back just in time," Will said.

He looked at Ali's face, covered in dust, and then at the concrete slab. It had landed on the wooden stool, the very spot where he had been sitting, turning the stool into a pile of splinters. He looked back at Ali and grabbed his hands. "Thank you, my friend."

Ali wrapped his arms around his mentor's neck and the men wept. A small chunk of concrete fell and shattered nearby, startling them but causing no damage.

"Maybe we should get you guys out of here until the dust settles," Will said.

Nick looked at Ali and then up at the gaping hole in the ceiling.

Ali glanced around their OR and then up at the hole. "Didn't you just say you'd give anything for a window?" He grinned and helped Nick off the floor.

"Yeah, I guess you better be careful what you pray for."

***

Lee handed Nick a peanut butter and jelly sandwich. "Glad you okay." She leaned over and tamped down a corner of the large bandage covering the wound on his forehead. The ragtag team sat on the large patio of the orphanage in a corner of the compound. With the OR inoperable, there was nothing to do but take a break.

Nick looked at his team members. They looked exhausted and absorbed in their own thoughts. No one had said anything to him about the moments before the aftershock. Maybe they hadn't noticed his panic attack. Maybe they had and were being kind. Maybe he needed to give up medicine altogether. The stress was obviously getting to him. But what else would he do with his life?

He chomped a big bite of the sandwich.

"Not sure I've tasted anything this good." Ali smiled, interrupting his angst. Ali extended his sandwich to Nick as a toast and they bumped their PBJs in a celebration of life.

"Thanks again, my friend," Nick said. "I'm afraid…I'm afraid I'm not handling this very well." His eyes teared, and Ali put a hand on his shoulder.

"I think none of us are."

Nick began to speak when a young orphan girl in an oversized Seattle Seahawks T-shirt offered him a bottle of water. Her sad eyes and kindness melted his self-pity. He smiled, accepted the bottle, and noticed her elbow was swollen and bruised. He put the bottle down and held her arm to examine the large bruise. He bent her elbow back and forth.

"Does that hurt?" he asked.

She looked blankly at him.

"*Ağrı?*" Ali translated, asking her if she had pain.

Nick had his answer when tears formed in her eyes.

Nick patted her head, matted with concrete dust, and gently touched her elbow for signs of fracture.

Lee turned the girl's head toward her. "I think she one of dislocations we reduce." She inspected the girl. "Yeah, elbow dislocated."

"You do orthopedics in China?" Nick was surprised.

Lee laughed as if it was the funniest thing she had ever heard. "Oh no. I family doctor, do acupuncture. I no bone doctor."

Nick smiled at Ali and they nodded in greater appreciation of this woman. He looked over the compound full of injured people. "Well, you should be proud of what you have done here."

"You do what you have to." Lee shrugged, pretended she was holding an imaginary arm in her hands and pulled. "POP. You bone doctors not so special." She cackled again, and everyone laughed with her, except the girl who silently watched them in fear.

Nick saw the girl's apprehension and attempted to put her at ease. He took her arm and opened and closed his fist, suggesting she do the same. "All the nerves are working," he said. "Maybe we should get an x-ray."

"You want CT scan also?" Lee asked.

"Touché," he said, forgetting for a moment the hospital's limitations. "Well, you did a good job. Is she one of the orphans from here?"

"She is now," Lee said seriously. "Whole family gone. Before quake, we have fifty children. Now, three hundred. More coming."

The girl continued her task, distributing water to the people on the patio. Nick and the others watched her. He needed to stop feeling sorry for himself.

He turned his eyes to the other children walking among the tables offering sandwiches and thought about Maggie, the Hope Center, their lunches under the mango tree, the talks, the surgeries, and the patients.

God, how I miss her.

"You okay?" Ali interrupted.

He smiled. "I'm just thinking of a good friend in Guatemala that runs an orphanage there, but I have never seen anything like this. It's just unbelievable. And you—I don't know how you're holding it together. You must be worried sick for your family."

"We operated on a man from their neighborhood," Ali said. "He thinks he might remember seeing both my parents and Asti's, but he's just not sure." Ali paused and looked over the field of wounded. "You do what you have to do," he said, repeating Lee's words.

"I don't know if we're winning or losing," Nick said.

Lee looked down at her clipboard. "I think you getting through many of open fractures."

"Yeah, for the first round," he said.

Lee looked at him confused.

"The treatment for any open fracture is to wash it out until it's clean and then fix it," Nick explained. "We should be bringing every patient back every day to wash out their wounds, and that's just not possible." He looked to Ali, who nodded.

Will spoke up. "When does the cavalry get here?" His surgical hat sat crooked on his head and his seventy-five-year-old body looked haggard.

"We haven't even thought about the closed fractures," Nick said. "I know we have at least twenty or more people with femur fractures just lying out there in the dirt, probably twice as many with tibia fractures, and there are a bunch of kids out there with all sorts of fractures and only one OR. Who knows if the other is even usable?" He stopped, feeling his anxiety level rising.

"We will need to start splinting some people and put some of the kids in traction," Ali said. "I'm just not sure where we're going to put them." He looked at the hospital, empty after the last tremor.

"Well, I say we best pray," Will suggested. "One of my favorite stories is from the Old Testament. It's about Jehoshaphat, who was the king of Judah. His kingdom was about to be trounced by the vast army of the Moabites, Ammonites, and Meunites." He stopped and looked at Ali. "I'm sorry, son. I realize that I may be stepping on some toes here. I just realized that I learned the story a long time ago and don't even know who all the 'ites' are."

"No worries, Dr. Will. It's all our heritage. The Moabites and the rest were tribal kingdoms from the descendants of Lot, nephew of the prophet Abraham. It's all part of the history of Mesopotamia."

Will smiled at Ali. "You have a lot you can teach us, but right now, let's pray like Jehoshaphat. 'We do not know what to do, but our eyes are on you.'"

They sat in silence, each with their own prayer.

The loud thumping of a helicopter overhead broke their meditation. Everyone rushed to gather scattering cups and napkins. The large Huey circled the compound, blocking the sun, and finally settled on the far side of the orphanage.

Nick and the others went to meet them as passengers began to emerge.

A short elderly man in a straw boater hat, sunglasses, and yellow T-shirt was the first to exit, followed by several men and women wearing matching T-shirts. The short man's tanned face cracked a smile through a graying goatee, and he balanced himself on an ornate cane. He and Nick shook hands.

"Jack Bilton." He had a firm handshake and wore a large gold-nugget ring on his pinky finger.

Nick recognized the yellow shirt from the Ankara airport. "You guys are from—"

"Calvary Chapel Church of North Carolina." Jack pivoted to show the church name printed there.

Nick, Will and Ali burst into laughter.

Jack turned, looking perplexed. "I wasn't expecting that response."

Will stepped forward. "Pardon us. We were just praying for the cavalry. I guess you're it."

Jack appreciated the joke but then turned serious, taking off his hat and holding it over his chest. He looked at the hospital. "It survived, thank you, Jesus."

"It's a little worse for wear," Nick added.

Jack looked at him, waiting for more information.

"We just lost part of the OR ceiling in that last aftershock," he explained, touching the bandage on his head.

"What do you need?" Jack looked over the top of his glasses at him.

"Right now, I could use some rest."

The man frowned, twisted his lips and repeated, "Son, what is it you need?"

He wasn't sure how to respond.

Jack sighed. "Son, I helped build this hospital with my own hands, and I can see you are in an awful mess. Now, tell me, exactly what it is you need."

***

"It's like a war zone," Nick warned Buck.

"Yeah, been in one or two," Buck reminded him.

Nick looked at the satellite phone that Jack Bilton had lent him. There was terrible static, and it was hard to hear Buck.

"What's the news saying about this mess?"

"Pictures are flooding the networks and so is the support. They say the death toll for the earthquake was already over fifty thousand, with the number of injured estimated at more than twice that, and the homeless, twenty to thirty times more..." Static interrupted Buck's voice. "...numbers were expected to keep rising, but Turkey has finally accepted the States' offer for help. It's making my job a whole heck of a lot easier. Donations from the orthopedic companies have poured in and good ol' Uncle Sam is getting them to you as we speak."

"You leave tomorrow then?" Nick asked.

"The ortho supplies should get to Ankara in four days... Monday. I will be there to try to get them through customs and then to you."

"Call on this number. Jack seems to be able to get things done. Maybe he can help us. How he talked the UN into flying his team here is beyond me, but I'm glad they're here."

"I look forward to meeting him. I can't believe he's really the 'Stack 'em Deep, Sell 'em Cheap' RV guy we always see on TV. He must be worth a pile of dough."

"Seems to have a heart of gold," Nick said. "He's built missionary hospitals all around the world. King's is one of them."

"You doing okay? You sound awful and tired."

"I'm okay. Just hurry up and get here, you jughead."

Nick hung up the sat phone and lay back on the cot. The UN had set up living quarters for him and the other adults in the orphanage cafeteria, with men and women separated by a curtain. The OR crew was sent to rest while Jack's team examined the hospital. When Nick learned that Jack had brought two civil engineers, three men who worked in construction, and an electrician, he was impressed by the man's forward thinking. Jack had told the team they would assess the hospital's safety and see what they could do about the new skylight in the OR.

Jack also promised that whatever was keeping the generator

from arriving at the hospital would be solved by nightfall. Nick didn't doubt him.

He worried about falling asleep. There was so much work to be done. His brain was still slightly scattered, more from exhaustion than the earthquake, but he couldn't help thinking he should be doing something. He tried to get up, but his body refused to move.

I gotta get a life.

He looked back at the satellite phone and thought about calling Maggie. He really needed her strength. But he was afraid his emotions would get the best of him, and while she would understand, he didn't want his team to hear him break down. His meltdown in the OR made him feel vulnerable enough, but he needed to talk to someone. He decided to call Johnny Mack, an old friend and mentor he had not spoken with in two years. "Mac," as he was called by his colleagues, residents, and staff, was set to retire soon.

Nick dialed the number, and Mac picked up after the first ring.

"Mac? Mac, this is Nick Hart."

"Nick! You sound like you're talking from a submarine at the bottom of the ocean."

Nick laughed. "Mac, I might as well be. I'm calling from Turkey, from the earthquake zone."

"My God, Nick, I can't believe you're there. It must be terrible."

Nick choked back tears at the sound of his mentor's voice. He was one of the kindest men he knew and one of the smartest. "It's unbelievably bad. We got here three and a half days after the quake and have worked two days straight. We have no power, no water…Mac, you've never seen so many injured. I'm afraid it's pretty overwhelming." Nick paused to take a deep breath and could feel pressure pound in his chest.

"Well, I can't think of anyone more equipped to be there than you. Do you have help?"

"My fellow is here with me. He's from here, and he's great. But we could use some more hands. That's for sure."

"Consider it done. I'll put out a broadcast to the Ortho Society for volunteers as soon as we hang up."

Mac was the past president of the society, and his recommendation carried clout. "Thanks, Mac. That means a lot. I'm just not sure what I should do with all these open fractures. We're just inundated."

"Hmm." Mac collected his thoughts. "I have an idea. Now I don't want you to think it was from personal experience, but during the Civil War they used to treat open wounds with sugar or honey."

Nick chuckled. Mac wasn't that old, probably not even as old as Will. "Sugar or honey?" he repeated.

"Absolutely. They used the stuff to smear the wounds. It's pretty darn antibacterial. You know what a history buff I am. I found some of the archived medical reports in Virginia last year. One of the surgeons kept good records. He wrote that the wounds would be clean within a week. Apparently, even the ancient Egyptians used honey." He paused. "You guys have betadine?" Mac asked. "You think you can either get sugar or honey?"

"We have a bunch of betadine, but I'll have to check on the other stuff."

"You know, if I were you, and you can get your hands on it, I would mix up a concoction of honey and betadine. After you wash out the wounds again, I would pack them with that."

"Thanks, Mac, I figured you'd have a good suggestion or two."

Nick was about to disconnect the call when he heard Mac continue.

"Nick, I was in Vietnam. I understand what you're going through. I can hear it in your voice. A little shot of brandy and some rest will do you good."

Nick thanked him for the advice and disconnected the call. A slice of peace came from hearing Mac's voice. Nick's body melted into the cot.

Where's that shot of brandy?

CHAPTER 25

APPROACHING EVIL
FRIDAY—POST-QUAKE DAY SIX

Antasha flipped her red hair back with one hand as the handsome doctor walked past, but he barely glanced at her injured leg. She looked at Vladimir and shrugged—nothing was working for them. His usually effective show of brute strength had gotten them nowhere, and neither had her beauty and seductive charm.

Vladimir laughed at her.

"What?" She glared at him.

"You," he grinned. "You're not used to being ignored."

"I don't know what you're talking about."

"Yeah, right. Not to worry." He shrugged. "You've still got it. A shower and makeup will fix everything."

"Moron." She scowled.

It made her angry that he was right. Even the UN soldiers were immune to her beauty. One look into her small, compact mirror and she saw a goth freak. Her fair complexion had turned ghostly white and her naturally flowing auburn hair hung lifeless around her face. She'd found some red lipstick in the stolen SUV, but it made her look like a painted zombie.

But it wasn't her fault. It was hard to look sexy with a freakin' broken leg. The past days were a blur of dusty roads, hunger, pain, and fear. She counted on her fingers, trying to remember what day it was. When she couldn't come up with an answer, she asked Vladimir.

"What day is it?"

Vladimir looked at his watch. "Friday."

"Oh, my God, six days without a shower." She sniffed her armpits. "I can hardly stand myself." At least they were inside the compound walls now and there was nothing that they could have done to make it happen sooner. Gaining entrance was not based on anything she was used to, not power, not influence, nor even money.

That morning, a small Chinese woman in a medical coat had walked down the line of supplicants waiting outside the gate. She had randomly selected some of them and herded them through security. She had hesitated when she looked up at Vladimir. Antasha wasn't sure what made her pause—his gargantuan size or the fact that he obviously was not Turkish. When the Chinese woman finally spoke, she told him that he could carry Antasha into the compound, but he would have to leave once she was situated. By the time Antasha was settled, the Chinese woman had either forgotten about Vladimir or was too busy to care, so he stayed.

"We need to get the hell out of here," she said, looking around at the raging sea of injured bodies.

"Working on it," Vladimir said. "One of the soldiers told me the roads out of the region are still impassable. When I asked him if I could use a satellite phone, he just laughed."

She rubbed her swollen toes. She could see her leg was slightly crooked in Vladimir's homemade splint, but she was getting accustomed to the pain.

"You and I know this search for the tree of life is ghost chase," she said. "And now this. Putin may want to live forever, but he can have this world. I just want to get home to my bed."

A small girl in filthy clothes came up behind Vladimir interrupting their discussion. Her presence caught him by surprise and he jumped to his feet. The child stepped back, staring at him with wide eyes and dropped jaw, as though he were a giant. The girl nervously handed him two bottles of water and ran away, too quickly to hear Vladimir's thanks.

Antasha saw disappointment in his eyes. She knew he longed to have children of his own. But what he saw in the little urchins, she would never understand.

***

Ibrahim watched the huge man open a bottle of water and hand it to the woman with the long, scraggly red hair. She chugged it down, and he handed her the other bottle.

The man reminded him of the Beast, his favorite professional wrestler, and he stared to be certain it wasn't him.

His mother would never let him watch any programs from the US, but sometimes, he and his friends had watched WWE wrestling at the home of his friend's older brother. They loved watching the gigantic musclemen in ridiculously tight shorts throwing each other around like rag dolls. When he and his friends tried to imitate some of the moves, one of them would inevitably get hurt, and they would all be in trouble.

He sighed, letting the memory linger until he shuddered with loneliness and exhaustion. His eyelids drooped, only to pop back open when his mind's eye flashed on the recurring image of his friends getting crushed under the concrete slab.

***

Abdul studied the young soldier sorting through their paperwork for the third time, picking up the desk phone for the fifth time, dialing a number, only to replace the receiver without speaking. Abdul figured the phone on the other end was busy. He knew to be patient.

The soldier was not much older than he was. His uniform looked as though it had just come out of its packaging and displayed no military decorations. Abdul wondered if the soldier was a reservist recently called up to serve. Abdul's brother had told him that Turkey's military would have their hands full responding to the massive earthquake, managing the international attention flooding the area, and keeping the border safe from ISIS. He now saw his brother's wisdom in taking advantage of the distraction.

He waited behind the White Snake, who had taken charge of the truck convoy. The other drivers waited behind him. He tried not to shift from one foot to the other, while his ego screamed to be in charge. How disgraceful it must look to his comrades to submit to a woman.

He looked out the window of the small office as two soldiers inspecting the trucks climbed out of one of them. He was surprised the border crossing that separated the Syrian town of Tell Abyad from Turkey's Akçakale was deserted. Their contraband was well-buried under the medical supplies, but if the soldiers searched deep enough, the situation would not end well.

The young soldier spoke to the White Snake in Turkish. As she had done before, she replied in a very polite British accent that she did not understand. The soldier smiled at her and said something under his breath. Abdul thought the young man was blushing, having to speak to a British woman with the sultry voice.

The soldier looked beyond the woman at the five men. They all carried forged passports from different countries, even Israel. The soldier picked up the phone again, dialed, and banged the receiver in its cradle. He then stood, searched for his comrades out the window, and settled on the corner of the desk, facing the White Snake.

He smiled and rubbed his thumb and fingers together, the universal sign for money. "Money?" he said in Turkish.

"I'm sorry, I don't understand Turkish," she said.

"Pay money," he tried again and repeated the universal sign.

"I am so sorry," she said sweetly and shrugged. Abdul was surprised at how calm she was.

"Corruption?" the soldier said in desperation, pleading with her to understand.

Abdul resisted the urge to laugh. The young soldier was trying to shake them down, but the White Snake was unwavering.

"We are here from the Red Crescent, and we are here to help your people," she said, putting the emphasis on *your*. "If you don't want to let us in, I will be happy to talk with your supervisor."

They stared at each other. The soldier did not understand English but seemed to understand her tone. He was about to say something more when the two soldiers inspecting the trucks came into the office and spoke to him.

Abdul felt the muscles in his back tighten.

The young soldier sighed deeply and spread his hands in defeat. Then he gathered the passports and paperwork and thrust the lot at the White Snake.

CHAPTER 26

LET THERE BE LIGHT

Nick sat with the entire staff of King's in the orphanage cafeteria, which had become their combined sleeping, eating, and meeting area. The entire team's energy seemed to be renewed by a good night's sleep. It was time to set the day's agenda, and Jack Bilton and the UN colonel faced the group.

Jack wiped his head with a hanky. "The generator should be up and running very soon."

As if on cue, the overhead lights came on in a blaze of glory. Everyone cheered and high-fived, basking in the voltage that flooded the compound. Despite the roar of the diesel generator, the team heard a matching cheer of joy from the patients waiting outside.

Jack looked exhausted but was nevertheless beaming like a proud father. In his mideighties, he still had the energy of a teenager. "Well, that's the good news," Jack said. "Thank you, Jesus. There's something else," he added with excitement, "my men have declared the hospital sound and structurally safe. When we built her, we had earthquakes in mind, and she survived the shaking intact, with one exception." He grinned at Nick. "We've learned a stronger ceiling is necessary in the OR."

Nick clowned for the group, acting like he was dodging falling concrete, and everyone laughed. He glanced around the room and saw the group was relaxed, well rested, energized and filled with joy. Jack's generator not only flooded the room with light, it shoved aside the horrific darkness the team had experienced in the last few days.

"My guys worked overnight on the OR and have it temporarily supported and protected from the elements," Jack continued. "Ya'll now have water and power to the OR, which means you can scrub the rooms, fire up the autoclaves, and sterilize the equipment."

Jack held up a whiteboard from the orphanage classroom. "Here is the list of who's in charge of what. I understand we have a wave of volunteers coming, so we need to prepare."

He turned to Nick. "You men need anything for now?"

"My friend Buck Hansen should be arriving in Ankara in the next couple of days with all our orthopedic equipment. We'll need to get it here."

Jack nodded.

Will whispered to Nick, who nodded. "And we could use a couple of new anesthesia machines."

"Just give me a list," Jack said.

"Oh, and honey," Nick said.

A perplexed hush fell over the room and Jack raised an eyebrow. "I beg your pardon?"

"For my tea." Nick joked. Everyone stared at him as though he was crazy, but he quickly added, "I'm serious."

Jack furrowed his brows. "You really did take a blow to the head."

"Sorry," Nick apologized. "I know it sounds strange, but we really do need honey and lots of it. We're reverting to the time of the ancient Egyptians. They used honey in their wounds as an antibiotic covering. It was also a standard medical procedure in the American Civil War. We have seen so many open fractures, there is no way we're going to get to all of them right away. If we can pack the wounds with honey and betadine, it will buy us some time." He saw skepticism on the faces in the room.

"Honey?" Jack questioned the team.

A soldier standing in the back of the room holding an AK-47 raised his hand. Jack acknowledged him with a wave.

The soldier spoke with a strong Turkish accent. "Turkey is the leading producer of honey for the world. It is the best in the world," he added with pride. "My family is from Gürpınar, about twelve miles from here. They have been beekeepers since before anyone can remember. I know they would be honored to help."

Jack and the colonel looked at each other and nodded. The colonel spoke to the soldier in Turkish, and the soldier took off to arrange for the honey to be delivered.

Jack asked the team if there was anything else to discuss. When no one answered, he bowed to the colonel and gave him the floor.

The colonel spoke English with a French accent. "The tents and latrines have finally arrived. Setting them up will be a top priority today. Thank God the rains have missed us, but I don't think we will be as lucky in the next few days."

Then he looked at Jack and hesitated. Jack nodded to him to continue.

"I'm afraid I have bad news. The government hospital in Van did not fare so well during the last tremor. A good half of the hospital collapsed and..." He paused to clear his throat and choke back tears. "A number of our men and women have been killed, along with some of the doctors and nurses and the patients in their care."

This news sucked the joy out of the room.

Jack was first to speak. "We can't know what this means for us, but I suspect it means we're going to get more patients. The Americans and Israelis are setting up field hospitals at the soccer fields in Van but we have no idea when they will be operational."

Nick glanced at Ali. *When does the nightmare end?*

***

Nick was in a vacant patient room on the third floor, grateful for the electricity. He hoped the patients might soon feel secure enough to return to the building. Having order restored from the chaos and making patient rounds would make his job a thousand times easier.

He went into the bathroom, pulled off his scrub top, and stepped out of his pants. He glanced at his watch and saw it was Friday. He realized that only a week ago he was hooking up with the girls from the Madison, which made him flinch with guilt and remember his discussion with Buck.

"It's your drug of choice," Buck had told him. "We all turn to something to cover the pain we carry." Nick tried to block out Buck's words and was filled with remorse.

He looked at his watch again. He and Ali had left Memphis on Monday and started operating on Tuesday. He sniffed the odor emanating from his body. He didn't think he'd ever anticipated a shower so much.

As he stretched his arms over his head, he caught his reflection in the mirror over the sink. It was as if he were looking at a stranger. His blond hair was flattened, matted, and greasy from too many days under a surgical cap. His normal, suntanned face was gaunt and thin and covered with a scraggly beard. He looked down at his waist and could almost see his ribs. He'd lost weight.

He leaned closer to the mirror to inspect his beard. It had been years since he had grown a beard, and then it was lush, dark, and handsome. He was disappointed to see how gray it had become, but his eyes were the most unsettling part of his reflection. The eyes that stared back at him were those of a man he wasn't sure he knew, and it filled him with sadness. *Who the hell am I?*

The virtual, sickening smell of the gangrenous limbs he had been amputating swamped his memory. The thought of the amputations brought on a wave of failure and self-doubt. *Where are you, God, in all of this? Have you forgotten these people? Have you forgotten me?*

There was no answer. He felt more alone than at any time in his life. He imagined the two women with whom he had partied before leaving for Turkey and the pending litigation against him concerning the mayor's son. "Why can't I do anything right?" *No wonder you're mad at me.* Then he saw the disappointed face of a teacher when he'd been caught cheating on a math test. Condemnation and shame battered his brain, and he sank to his knees, his eyes filled with tears. "Why can't I be a better person? What is wrong with me?"

His unanswered questions made him weep. The agony of a life of striving was crushing his soul. *If only I worked harder, became more successful, then people would love me.* "You would love me," he cried out to God. "I want to know you, Father." He slumped his head and his arms dropped to his side in surrender. He wanted out of this prison of self-condemnation. *I thought life was going to be easier somehow.*

Nick's hamstring spasmed and he grabbed the sink to pull himself up. He gaped at the bloodshot eyes staring back at him in the mirror. All the striving, all the success, all the search for acceptance had gotten him nowhere. They had not rescued him from the sense that his life was insignificant.

"God, where were you? God, where are you?"

***

Ibrahim knew he was dreaming, but he didn't care. It all seemed so real and so beautiful. He sniffed the sweetness of freshly cut grass and relished the warmth of sun on his face. He was floating more than walking, but as he looked down, his legs moved normally, propelling him across the great expanse of green—a shade of green so vivid that it existed in three dimensions. The field was sliced by a winding river bubbling with sparking blue water—no, it was green—no, maybe more gold like honey.

A mammoth tree spread its beckoning branches over the river and sang like a choir of angels basking in the sun. Its leaves were kissed with gold and glistened in tempo. Not only did Ibrahim hear the music, he felt its rhythm suffuse his being. He checked to make sure his parts could survive the surge of energy that was flowing through every cell. But there was no cause for alarm; his body vibrated in harmony at the same frequency and he smiled as the sun kissed his face.

"*Oğlan, Oğlan*…Boy, Boy."

A hand on his chest shook him. Ibrahim's eyes sprung open to the pressure. He woke up quickly and lifted his arms in self-defense. As soon as he returned to consciousness, his leg ached and he winced. The dream was over.

The annoying voice persisted. "Boy, you want a sandwich?"

Ibrahim squinted into the light to see a boy staring down at him. The boy looked a little younger than Ibrahim and carried a large basket filled with wrapped food. Without waiting for a response, the boy pulled a sandwich from the basket, put it on Ibrahim's chest, and walked away.

CHAPTER 27

ABRAHAM

SATURDAY—POST-QUAKE DAY SEVEN

Abdul paused at the Pool of Abraham with the White Snake. But it was an unwelcome respite. One of the trucks had blown a tire outside Şanlıurfa, and the other men in the convoy were searching the town for someone to fix it or for a replacement. The White Snake suggested that she and Abdul separate themselves from the others. He was not happy that they'd gotten only thirty miles into Turkey.

"Isn't it amazing to think that Prophet Abraham lived here?" the White Snake asked. "Peace be with him."

Her British pronunciation—Abraham instead of Ibrahim—irritated him. Abdul had no comment; instead, he listened to the prayers spilling from a nearby mosque as he watched carp bubble and ripple on the surface of Balıklı Göl, known as the Pool of Ibrahim. As if to protest, Abdul tossed in a handful of fish food he'd bought from a vendor and created a splashing frenzy. *At least somebody can be happy.*

They sat on the wall overlooking the water, biding their time in the heat of the day. Abdul squirmed with beads of sweat rolling down his back and glanced at the White Snake. If she was sweaty and uncomfortable, buried head-to-toe in her burka, she didn't let on. She had to be steaming in the black robe and veil that soaked up the sun. When he felt her eyes on him through the veil's netting, he turned away, his nerves on edge.

He jerked to attention at the approach of two men speaking loudly in Turkish. His muscles tensed for confrontation, but when the men turned and continued down the courtyard of the Halil-ur-Rahman mosque, he relaxed. He was glad the White Snake had volunteered to cover her pale skin and blue eyes with the robe and burka so there would be no reason to attract attention. In spite of himself, he continued to think about her. He didn't even know how to address her. Under Sharia law, it was a sin to talk to her at all.

He wiped the sweat on his forehead and remembered the dream he'd had the night before. He hated that dream, and he hated himself for dreaming it. In the dream, he had almost succumbed to desire; her white skin had felt so soft.

"Here," she said. "I bought you this." She held out a small paper plate covered with a napkin.

He glanced at the offering and then back at the water.

"Please," she said. "It is raw *kibbé*." She pulled off the napkin and held the plate toward him so he could smell the spices covering the raw lamb meat. He couldn't help salivating.

According to legend, it was the prophet Ibrahim who was the first to serve this dish. Abdul wondered if she knew. His stomach rumbled loud enough for her to hear.

"See," she said. "Your stomach tells me that you want this."

He looked at the dish and then at the White Snake. Even though her face was covered, he saw by her eyes through the veil that she was smiling at him.

"Please," she repeated and practically put the plate in his lap.

Abdul shifted to avoid her touch as he grabbed the plate from her hand. He stared at the red meat, lifted the plate to his nose, and inhaled deeply. He savored the aroma of Tabasco sauce and mint leaves. The lamb looked fresh; it had probably been butchered only hours ago.

The White Snake dug into her burka sleeve, pulled out a fork and held it to his face. If he hadn't been so hungry, he would have jumped for cover. Considering the stories he had heard about her, the fork could have been a knife and she could have already slit his throat.

He took the fork without touching her and stabbed a bite of raw *kibbé*. The lamb melted in his mouth. He took another bite and sighed with contentment.

While he ate, they watched the fish dance in and out of the water. When he finished his meal, he put the plate and fork on the wall between them. The White Snake folded the plate and held it dutifully, as a typical Muslim wife would do when she and her husband were enjoying an outing.

"Do you know why they call this the Pool of Ibrahim?" he asked.

"Wasn't Abraham born here?"

"Yes, Ibrahim, he was born here," he said, trying to correct her pronunciation. Abdul tossed another handful of fish food into the water, and the carp leaped to the surface. "My father told me the story."

He paused, thinking about his father. *I wish he could be here.*

He sensed the White Snake shift, waiting for the story.

"Nimrod was the ruler of this area," he said, finally.

"Nimrod?"

"Noah had three sons—Shem, Ham, and Japheth. Ham's oldest son was Cush, and Cush is the father of Nimrod."

"Noah was Nimrod's great-grandfather."

"Yes, that's right. Ibrahim was Shem's son, cousin to Cush."

"So, Nimrod would have been Abraham's cousin once removed?" she asked.

"Yeah, I guess. Something like that."

He did not like that she always questioned him and that she acted so familiar, when they had only met a few days ago. He couldn't even remember her real name. He always felt inadequate talking to women, but this one was different. He realized his ease with her should make him happy, and he didn't understand why it made him angry.

"For some reason, Nimrod turned his back on Allah, and Ibrahim challenged Nimrod. Ibrahim told him that Allah was the one who gave life or death. Nimrod ordered two prisoners to be brought to him. He released one and took his sword to the other, cutting his head off, to make the point that he, too, could bring life and death. Ibrahim then told him that Allah brought the sun up from the east and challenged Nimrod to bring the sun up from the west."

He looked at the White Snake. He was relieved she was wrapped in a full burka because it was like talking to a statue, and it was easier to talk to a statue than a woman.

"This challenge enraged Nimrod so much that he ordered Ibrahim to be thrown into a great fire. As the story goes, the people gathered wood for four years to make the biggest fire the world had ever seen. But even in that great blaze, Ibrahim walked out unscathed."

"What does all that have to do with this pool?" the White Snake asked.

"When Ibrahim was thrown in the fire, Allah turned the flames to water and the burning logs to fish." Abdul waved his hands over the pool, and she nodded.

"What happened to Nimrod?" she asked.

"My father wasn't certain. He thought that Nimrod might have gone on to build the Tower of Babel. But Ibrahim left Mesopotamia and headed to the land of Canaan. My father said the true battle between good and evil is between the ones who believe and the ones that don't. The same battle that we are in today."

"It sounds like you and your father are very close."

"My father is dead." The reply came quicker than he intended, and it threw them both into silence.

"I'm so sorry," she said finally.

"Allah's will."

"Can I ask you how he died?"

Abdul held his hand like a gun to his temple and pulled an imaginary trigger. "He put a bullet through his head." Suddenly he was furious at the White Snake. He had never told any of his friends at the university how his father died. Why was he telling her?

He tossed what was left of the fish food into the pool, sack and all, and stood up. The chaotic cacophony of the fish reflected his emotions.

"We should go see if the others have fixed the tire."

***

Ibrahim was surprised when an Asian woman in the doctor's coat spoke to him in Turkish. He had never seen a person from Asia.

"We need to put your leg in splint so we get you inside," she told him.

Ibrahim moaned and tried to wiggle away when she touched his foot. Nevertheless, she took hold of his leg. He gasped, feeling his muscles spasm and his bones grind together. "Please stop, madam, please stop," he shouted and squirmed.

"Hold still!" she commanded. "You are only making this worse."

"Mama. Papa," Ibrahim cried. "Please, wait for my mommy and daddy to get here. Please."

She ignored his plea and he screamed. "You're hurting me." He dug his fingers into the dirt. "Stop pulling my leg!"

His hands went slack as heavy pressure crushed his chest. It was like the quaking, flaking concrete burying him. His need to breathe forced his eyes open, and he flailed his arms to free himself. But it wasn't concrete; it was a giant hand pressing his chest, keeping him still.

Just when he thought he was going to die, the hand eased up and he gulped for air. He was surprised that the pain in his leg had subsided. He watched the Asian woman finish wrapping a bandage around his leg and gently set it back on the ground. He didn't know what had happened, but one thing was for sure, his leg hurt a lot less than it had for days.

The giant knelt beside him, lifted his head with tenderness, and put a bottle of water to his lips. Ibrahim allowed the cool water to fill his mouth and flow down his throat. Between Ibrahim's gulps, the man pulled the bottle back, giving him time to swallow without choking. The giant spoke to him again, but he didn't understand.

After several more swallows, Ibrahim remembered. The giant was the man he'd seen earlier, the man who reminded him of the Beast. This close up he had never seen anyone with such a big nose or huge neck. And he'd never seen anyone with such kind eyes except for his mother's.

The big man held the bottle to Ibrahim's lips again so he

could take another drink. Now that he recognized the man, he thought the water tasted even better.

"*Da*," the man said, putting the bottle beside him and laying his head back on the ground. The boy watched his every move. The huge man turned and called to a passing UN soldier carrying an armful of blankets. The soldier shook his head, but when the giant stood and pointed to Ibrahim, the soldier nodded and allowed him to remove a blanket from the stack.

The giant rolled the blanket into a pillow and tucked it under Ibrahim's head.

"*Da*," he repeated and nodded. Then he put his hand to his own chest. "Vladimir," he said slowly. "Vladimir."

Understanding the giant was introducing himself, he touched his own chest and said "Ibrahim."

The man smiled and repeated the boy's name, but with a strange accent that sounded funny to Ibrahim. *Abraham.*

"Abraham," the giant repeated and smiled. Then he flexed his massive bicep and said it again. "Abraham."

***

Vladimir sensed the Chinese doctor staring at him. *She's going to make me leave.* "It looked like you could use some assistance with the boy."

"Thank you for your help," she said.

Vladimir smiled and started to walk away, hoping she would get distracted and he could return to get better acquainted with Ibrahim.

"You look like penny out of place." She grinned.

He turned back to her but said nothing.

"You lost or something?"

He wasn't sure what to say.

"We need to look at your shoulder. It doesn't look so good and doesn't smell so good either." She cackled.

He glanced at his shoulder and realized it was bleeding again. Bright red blood oozed around the large stain already on his T-shirt.

"You come to my clinic in hospital later. We wash it and take care of it."

She gave him some four-by-four bandages and started to walk away.

"Do you know anything about his parents?" he asked, pointing to Ibrahim.

The doctor looked at the boy and then at the man. "No idea. Many more patients to splint," she said and walked off.

Vladimir stood stunned at her indifference. He looked at Ibrahim as a wave of sadness washed over him. He forced a smile and a nod to the boy and walked back to Antasha.

"You feel better now, Boy Scout?"

He sat down next to her and sighed. "I'm just trying not to get us kicked out."

"Did you ask her about getting us into the hospital?"

"It wasn't exactly the time." He frowned and ignored her, wishing she wasn't so narcissistic. They sat in silence.

Touching his arm, she asked, "How is the boy?"

Vladimir continued to ignore her and blinked a tear from his eye.

CHAPTER 28

LIFELINE
SUNDAY—POST-QUAKE DAY EIGHT

Nick took a break between surgeries, sitting on the retaining wall between the hospital and the orphanage, watching the flurry of activity in the courtyard. With the OR back up and running and voltage pumping through the hospital, he and the crew were finding some rhythm. He was amazed at the transformation by the generator's power. The team's mood was slowly lifting—light pushed out darkness. Instead of ghostly figures moving in the shadows cast by headlamps, everyone was completely visible, and those dark corners lurking with foreboding had vanished. Never again would he take electricity for granted.

The open field around the hospital was being covered in large white tents, and a strong breeze of an approaching storm flapped the tent's canvas against the metal poles. UN soldiers in week-old pit-stained T-shirts tried to bring order to the chaos—setting up portable outhouses, rebuilding the compound retaining wall, and taking orders from Dr. Lee as she organized and recorded basic demographics for the patients and assigned them rooms. Many patients still refused to go into the building. He marveled at Lee's stamina and wondered how she was handling all of this. She was a rock. He didn't think he'd even seen her sit down.

Three black soldiers shared a cigarette on the other end of the retaining wall. For Nick, the aroma of the burning tobacco was soothing; maybe it was because, as a boy, he would often sit with his father on the back deck watching the sun set as his dad smoked his pipe. It meant that all was right with the world.

After his meltdown on Thursday night, he'd confided to Ali that his back was killing him. It wasn't exactly a lie, and it got him the relief he needed—muscle relaxants. With Ali's help, he had secured them from the anesthesiologist, and the drugs allowed him to get two nights of deep sleep. The repose and a few hot meals from the UN had given him a second wind.

They were back to irrigating and debriding open wounds between dreaded amputations. His hands continued to cramp and he tucked them under his legs and stretched them against the concrete. In his last surgery, he was using Mayo scissors to cut away dead tissue when his hand cramped so badly he had to have the nurse help him pry the instrument from his fingers.

"Hey, Doc," the UN colonel shouted, surprising him out of his thoughts. He turned to see the soldier approaching him briskly, carrying an open laptop. "Want some good news?"

"I'm waking up from this nightmare?"

"Yeah, roger that. My boys linked into a satellite, and we have Wi-Fi for a few hours. You want to Skype someone back home?" He handed Nick the laptop. "Just type the number you're calling here." He pointed to the screen. "I'm giving everyone about five minutes. I'll be back shortly."

"My one call from prison, huh?"

"Guess you better call your lawyer," the colonel joked and walked away.

Nick stared at the screen and the blinking cursor waiting for his command. For all the primitive conditions of the last week, he felt like he was holding a Tricorder device from *Star Trek*. He wasn't in the mood to talk with anyone. He thought about calling to the colonel and handing it back, but the colonel was chewing out soldiers for taking too long of a break.

Maybe he should call Buck and see how it was going getting the supplies to the country. Nick looked at his watch and realized it was Sunday, and Buck would already be making his way around the globe.

My parents. I should call my parents.

He entered a few numbers but stopped after the area code. He was just too tired. He deleted the numbers and tapped on the edge of the computer, considering other options.

He was just about to pull the top closed when he felt two small hands on his shoulders, followed by a small body pressing against his back and a chin resting on his shoulder. He turned his head slowly. A small boy stared wide-eyed at the computer screen and chattered in Turkish. The child's companionship brought comfort.

"What do you see?" Nick asked, not expecting to be understood. The boy stroked the dusty waves of Nick's blond hair and fingered his scraggly beard before pointing to the screen and asking a question.

Nick guessed at what he'd asked and said, "You want to see how it works, huh?"

He put his hands on the keyboard and typed in one of the few phone numbers he knew by heart—Maggie Russell's.

The boy watched his every move. A color wheel spun, and when a "z–wooosh" sound came from the computer, the boy giggled. The computer phone began to ring. The boy called to a friend passing by delivering water bottles. Equally excited, the water boy dropped his basket and took his position at Nick's other shoulder.

"Nick Hart!" a voice exclaimed.

Nick heard her voice before the video came into focus. Then, there she was. The screen filled with Maggie's smiling face, while a small screen-within-a-screen showed Nick and the two boys.

"Nicklaus?" Maggie asked again.

"Hi, Maggie." *God, it's good to see her.*

Maggie started to laugh and cry at the same time. "Oh, thank God. I have been so worried about you. My Lord, the reports coming out of Turkey are horrific. You look like you have just come out of the wilderness. Are you okay?" Her laughter and tears continued to build, and her words came all at once. "I called your folks to see if they had heard anything. Have you talked with them? You look exhausted. Look at that beard. I'm so happy to see you." She wiped tears from her cheeks.

Nick looked at his puzzled young companions, who were

trying to make sense of what they heard. "Women," he laughed. "You always have to let them get their fifty-thousand words in first." The boys grinned from ear to ear, even though Nick knew they had no idea what he'd said.

He used the computer cursor to enlarge the picture of the boys, and they erupted in delight seeing themselves on the screen. By now, a third boy had joined them, and the three of them made faces at themselves and giggled.

"Looks like you've made some friends in Turkey." Maggie smiled.

"Hi, Maggie." It was all Nick could say. His throat was swollen with emotions. He was thankful the boys had provided comic relief.

But Maggie turned serious. "Nick, how are you? It must be awful," she said. "Is it awful?"

He steadied the computer, which was shaking under the hands of the excited boys. "That's not an earthquake," he joked, masking his anxiety with humor. "Would you mind calling my folks and letting them know I'm okay?"

"Of course, Nick. But only if you tell me you're okay."

"Okay…I'm okay."

"Nicklaus Hart, I swear."

After a moment, he said, "You're right. It's awful."

A helicopter swooped behind him, and the boys loosened their grip on the computer to watch the chopper land.

"I'm sorry, Maggie, I've got to go. It's a bit chaotic here."

"Nick, please." He could see her pull her smartphone closer to her face. "Who are those children?"

"We're at King's Hospital. It has its own orphanage." He raised his voice over the racket of the chopper. "They told me before the quake there were about fifty kids. Now, who knows? Maybe hundreds," he said above the wake of the blades. "The worst part is the director was also killed in the quake. It's a real mess here, Maggie."

The helicopter landed and started to wind down.

"I am so sorry, Nick. Is there anything I can do for you?"

He patted one of the boys on the head. "Just call my folks. They'll be worried."

Tears welled in his eyes, but he didn't want to cry…not here, not now. Much to his surprise, he said, "Pray, Maggie. Pray for these poor people."

He could see the colonel heading his way.

"Maggie, I've got to go. They're only giving us a few minutes on the computer, and my time is up."

Maggie started to cry. "Oh, Nick. I love you so much. Please take care of yourself."

"I will, Maggie. I love you too."

Nick hit the red disconnect button, and Maggie disappeared.

"Entertaining the troops, I see," the colonel said, glancing at the boys and extending his hand to retrieve the computer.

Nick smiled halfheartedly and handed over the laptop. "Thank you, Colonel."

The colonel headed toward the hospital with two of the boys in tow. Nick watched him nod to Ali as they passed one another. Ali was headed for Nick, smiling like the bearer of good news.

"Who's your friend?" Ali asked when he saw the boy hanging over Nick's shoulder.

Nick tousled the boy's hair and swung him around, setting him on his lap. The boy giggled and he shrugged at Ali.

"Navê te çi *ye?"* Ali asked the boy his name.

"Alaz," the boy said.

"Alaz," Ali repeated for Nick. "Meet Alaz."

Nick tickled Alaz and made him squeal with laughter. Then he set him on the ground, expecting him to run off with his friends. But the boy clung to Nick's leg. Nick looked at Ali, pleading with his eyes. Ali spoke to the boy and directed him toward his friends.

"That didn't sound like Turkish."

"I was speaking to him in Kurdish."

"How did you know he was Kurdish?"

"I guessed. We tend to have skin that's a little darker," Ali said.

"Kinda hard to tell through all the grime." Nick couldn't help chuckling. "Thanks, Ali, I think he would have followed me into surgery. By the way, how many languages do you speak?"

"Kurdish, Turkish, Farsi, English, a bit of Arabic, and a few Turkish dialects."

"I'm kind of jealous," Nick remarked. "I only speak English, and sometimes I have problems with that. How do you say *thank you* in Kurdish?"

"*Sipas,*" Ali said.

Nick repeated the word. "How do you say it in Turkish?"

"*Teşekkür ederim.*"

Nick stumbled over the words. "Maybe I'll stick with Kurdish."

Ali stared somberly at the ground. His buoyant mood had changed.

"You okay?"

"Dr. Hart," Ali said with remorse. "I lied to you." He pawed the ground. "When you first asked me, I told you I got this scar on my face from a tree branch." The scar across Ali's left cheek looked angrier and redder beside his dark beard. "When I was five," Ali continued, "Kurdish was banned by the Turkish government. In fact, the words *Kurds, Kurdistan,* and *Kurdish* were officially banned, and we were to call ourselves 'Mountain Turks.'" Ali made air quotes with his fingers.

"What?"

"One day when I was in the market with my mother, I got separated in the crowd. I was afraid and cried out for her in Kurdish. That's when a man took out his pocket knife and sliced my cheek." Ali drew a line from the one side of his mouth up his cheek.

Nick was flabbergasted. "Are you kidding me? What happened to the man?"

"Nothing. It was I who broke the law."

Nick had rarely seen Ali angry, but he could see that retelling the incident made Ali furious. He felt his own anger rise. "That is messed up."

"That is Mesopotamia," Ali said.

"Why is there no Kurdistan?"

Ali frowned. "Well, frankly, you are in Kurdistan. The Kurds lived here, our history is here: Eastern Turkey, Northern Iran and Iraq, and Northern Syria. Sometimes modern maps are so deceiving. It's probably hard for most Americans to understand, especially the young people."

"Yeah, they hardly know anything about our own Civil War, never mind the history of this area. Is that why the Kurds fought Saddam Hussein in Iraq?"

"Yes, and in 1988 Hussein dropped mustard gas and sarin gas on our people in the Kurdish town of Halabja. I know some of my friends in Memphis think the fighting here is always over religion, and sometimes it is, but much of the fighting is over control of the land. That is why the Kurds are fighting ISIS…it's the land, Muslim killing Muslim."

"Like our Civil War. I guess I hadn't thought about that reality. Christian killing Christian," Nick mused.

"Those divides run deep. That's why I came to get you."

"What?" Nick responded with alarm.

"I have a man that is refusing to let me take him back to surgery," Ali explained. "He learned I am Kurdish, and he refuses to let me touch him. I told him all I was going to do was wash his wound and pack it with the honey and betadine, the Turkish delight, as you have named it. But the man started screaming that I was going to amputate his leg."

Nick felt the hair on the back of his neck stand up, and his face flushed. Having worked in Memphis, Nick was used to prejudice, but not to this extent. He was fond of Ali and knew what an excellent surgeon he was with the highest level of integrity. He would trust him with his own life, if it came to that. "That's a load of crap," Nick said, standing up and glancing around. "Where is this jerk so I can tell him we're going to amputate all right…at the neck."

Ali stepped in front of Nick. "Really, it's okay, Dr. Hart. I do not hold any malice against the man. It's hard to know what shoes he wears."

"Huh?" Nick shook his head, then nodded. "Oh, I get it. Don't judge a man until you walk a mile in his shoes."

Ali blushed. "Yes, that is right. I still have trouble with English idioms."

"It's okay. You do fine. You're a good man, Ali. You need to teach me how to be a good man, and I could use a lesson or two in Kurdish. But I'm still going to go tell the patient he needs blood or he'll die, and the only blood we have available is Kurdish blood."

Ali chuckled. "He's going to love having all those little Kurds running around in his bloodstream."

"We'll tell him it will probably make his skin darker," Nick joked.

They were both laughing so hard that patients in the courtyard turned to stare at them.

"Okay," Nick said, clearing his throat after the beneficial dose of laughter, "we'll just swap cases then. How do you think the Turkish delight is working?"

"I was pretty skeptical at first, but I'm rather shocked by its success. I'm certainly glad that we are doing fewer and fewer amputations."

"That's for sure. How many limbs did we have to take off?"

Ali looked at the ground and shook his head. "I don't even want to think about it."

"Buck should be here tomorrow with our ortho supplies, then we can start doing some reconstructive cases," Nick said.

Nick and Ali pushed away from the wall and went back to the hospital, picking their way through tents and patients.

"Oh, I almost forgot. I have some possible good news," Ali said. "I have seen a man who knows both my parents and Asti's parents. He thinks they may have survived and headed into the mountains with others to stay with relatives."

Nick put his hand on Ali's shoulder. "Man, what a relief. Maybe we could talk with the colonel to see if there is any way to find out more information."

"That would be kind of you, Dr. Hart...Nick."

Nick noticed and smiled but said nothing, not wanting to embarrass his friend. "Hey, speaking of good news," he changed the subject, "I saw the little girl with the head injury was off the ventilator this morning."

"It is pretty remarkable. I am surprised she lived."

"Well, she had a remarkable surgeon." Nick patted him on the back.

"I have to hope that she won't have much residual damage to her brain. There are few resources for a brain-damaged child here in Van. I think I would feel worse for that—"

The approach of a large, muscular man interrupted Ali. "Excuse me, Doctors. May I ask you a question?"

Since he was blocking their path like a Mack truck, they didn't have a choice. The man stood a half foot taller than Nick and a full foot taller than Ali and was as wide as both of them put together. He was odd-looking and definitely not Turkish. If he had had a handlebar mustache, he would have made a perfect strongman in a circus.

"I know how busy you are, but I was hoping to ask you about my friend," the big man said in a Russian accent.

"Who's your friend?"

The Russian pointed across the crowd to a woman with copper hair. The woman smiled and waved. "She has a badly broken leg, and I was wondering if you would examine her."

Nick looked at Ali, and they both looked over the courtyard. Hundreds of people lay in some stage of brokenness. He looked back at the man and was about to say something sarcastic, until he saw the concern on his hardened face.

"Uh, we are headed back to surgery right now, but Dr. Lee is getting things organized, and we hope to have everyone examined very soon."

He squeezed past the man. Looking back for Ali, the Russian held up his hands to the woman in defeat.

CHAPTER 29

ANGER

Abdul sipped hot black tea from the tulip-shaped glass. The gold rim of the glass was chipped, but he figured the china was their host's best. As he sipped, he glanced around the sparse one-room apartment. A Microsoft computer sat idle on a small portable desk with a dirty plastic chair tucked underneath. A twin-size mattress covered in a floral sheet lay on the floor at the other side of the room. It wasn't exactly what he had expected of the ISIS command center in Turkey; nevertheless, the cell had shown remarkable resilience and capability, with millions of dollars' worth of illegal arms passing through Cizre to Mosul, Iraq, only two hours to the south. The cell was credited with bombings in the capital of Ankara, as well as Diyarbakır and Istanbul.

"It is an honor to have the brother of Abbas Fadhil, first in command under Abu Bakr al-Baghdadi," their host and cell leader said. "*Subhanallah*, glory to Allah."

"*Subhanallah,*" the other cell members repeated to Abdul and the White Snake. Abdul and the woman sat in a circle on the carpet with the five men.

He returned the greeting. "*Baraka Allahu fika*, may Allah bestow his blessings on you."

"I am sorry to hear about your second brother," the leader said. "To Allah we belong, and to him we will return."

"Yes, thank you. Allah's will," he replied.

The carpet was old and threadbare, and he shifted his weight to get comfortable. He was not used to sitting on the floor; he preferred the desk chairs at the university. His discomfort was increased by the smell of body odor and bare feet that permeated the room.

"How did you know we were coming?" he asked.

The leader pointed to the desk and a black box that Abdul had not noticed. "Our PS 4," the man grinned, and the other men laughed.

Abdul had heard that ISIS was using the PlayStation 4 to communicate securely, but to see it in use was absurd. He had to join the others in laughter.

"And it is an honor as well to have Akleema Mohammad, the White Snake, in our presence," the leader said. "I have been told you were instrumental in the London bombings and helped four brothers escape, at the risk to your own life. May Allah bless you."

"May Allah bless you in return," she said and nodded to them.

"Welcome to Cizre, surrounded by the beautiful Tigris River," the leader said expansively, like the director of a chamber of commerce. "There is a saying in our city." He furrowed his brow. "If there's peace, it will start from Cizre, and if there's war, it will start from here as well. As you know, we are at the crossroads of Turkey, Iraq, Iran and Syria. As we speak, our brothers and sisters are fighting for their lives just two short hours from here in Mosul. If the caliphate is to be successful, then its heart, Cizre, must pump its life blood in all directions. But that will not be easy because it is very dangerous here for all of us. Cizre is populated by Kurds mainly and run by the Kurdistan Workers' Party...the PKK."

"Isn't that the group we are fighting in Syria?" the White Snake asked.

"Yes, but even our enemies are not safe here. The Kurds have revolted many times against the Turkish government and that's why the Turkish military has attacked the city. No one can be trusted here."

Abdul noticed the only light in this upstairs apartment flicker and go out, immediately followed by the rotating fan overhead. The clicking of its chain quit, and the room grew hot and steamy with the gamy smell of body odor. He wiped his sweaty face with his sleeve.

"We have been losing power daily since the earthquake." The leader apologized. "Would you like more tea before it grows cold?" He lifted the tin teapot off the now powerless portable heating unit in the center of the group. Both Abdul and the White Snake declined.

"I wish we could keep you here," the leader said wistfully. "I would have liked to show you the Tomb of Prophet Noah, peace be upon him, but it would be too suspicious to have you posing as the Red Crescent because, aside from the annoying blackouts, we have had very little damage from the earthquake. That is why we must send you away." He paused. "We are sending you farther east to Hakkâri. Hakkâri is south of the epicenter in Van, but it has also had considerable damage, and a man sympathetic to our cause runs the hospital there. We will store the armaments with him in Hakkâri for now, and you will help to set up another cell there. It is only four and a half hours from here, maybe five with your big trucks. You will be going into the mountains." He sighed. "You will find it is very beautiful."

***

The diesel truck strained as it lugged its cargo across the long miles from the Tigris River Basin up the Toros mountain chain, which formed the western section of the Himalayan mountain belt. Abdul and the White Snake rode in silence. He still hated that she was driving, but he had promised to submit to his brother's will. To tell the truth, he had been surprised how much respect the men in Cizre had afforded her and even more surprised how well she conducted herself among the pious Islamists.

Resigned, he settled into his seat and looked out the window. At least having her drive allowed him to conserve his energy and observe the scenery. It was August, but many of the highest mountain peaks were covered with snow. He decided to attempt harmless conversation and broke the silence. "Mt. Judi must be over in that mountain range somewhere."

"Mt. Judi?" she asked.

"Do you not know your Qur'an?" He started to scold her and stopped abruptly. Maybe he was being too hard on her.

"Please enlighten me," she said without sarcasm.

Abdul cleared his throat and began to recite. "It is written in Surah 11, 'And the word was spoken: "O earth, swallow up thy waters. And, O sky, cease thy rain." And the water sank into the earth, and the will of God was done, and the ark came to rest on Mount Judi.'"

"I thought the Ark of Prophet Noah, peace be on him, came to rest on Mt. Ararat," she said. "At least that is what I learned in Catholic school."

"Catholic school? You did not grow up Muslim?" Abdul's blood boiled but he suppressed his anger.

"Yes, Catholic. I have been grafted into Islam. I dated a boy in college who was Muslim, and the more he talked about it, the more I found peace."

Abdul smiled. "Your parents must have gone crazy."

"Funny. Not really. They don't even believe in God, so they don't really care what I believe. They thought I would grow out of it."

He looked at her. *Those eyes, they make me crazy.* He caught himself and continued to tell her about Noah's Ark. "Mt. Ararat is farther north, but still in the same mountain range. It is the tallest of all the mountains in Turkey, but I believe what the Qur'an says about Mt. Judi."

He watched her shift the monster truck from second to third gear as they reached the top of the hill. "What did you study at university?" he asked.

"I wanted to become a teacher…" Her voice trailed off and saddened.

Abdul waited for her to finish. He thought she blinked a tear away.

"But my boyfriend was killed in an automobile accident."

They rumbled a few miles in silence.

She spoke first and changed the subject. "I am sorry to ask, but I have not been able to get this off my mind. What happened with your father?"

He shot her a cold glare and looked away, gazing absently over the mountains. How he missed his father.

"You don't have to talk about it if it's too painful."

They passed the sign to Şırnak. Abdul realized that once they'd passed Şırnak, it would be another four hours to Hakkâri. He couldn't ignore her for that long. He swallowed. "My mother and father are both doctors. Were doctors...well, my mother still is. She is an obstetrician, but she has not practiced since my father..."

He wasn't sure he could continue. He felt his face flush and his head spin. He cranked the window down enough to let the cool mountain air fill the cab.

"My father was a cardiologist, one of the most famous in Saudi Arabia. He developed a new heart stent with his best friend." At those words, anger and bile rose in his belly, and he wondered if he was going to have to ask her to pull over. He found a plastic water bottle under the seat and took a swig. The nausea passed.

"My father trusted that terrible person who was our friend, like an uncle to us. My father invested millions into the project and trusted his friend to do all the business stuff. It was a deal done with a handshake...that is how my father was. After six years, a big company came to buy them out. That's when his friend betrayed him. His partner had been entrusted with the business dealings and put everything in his own name. When the company paid millions for the new stent, this so-called friend walked away with all the money. All he said to my father was 'things change.'"

Abdul swore in Arabic and thrust his foot against the dash of the truck. "If I ever see that man again, I am going to strangle the life out of him with my bare hands. My brothers and I have made that pledge." He took another swig from the bottle.

"The day my father found out he'd been robbed, he drank liquor for the first time in his life. It was the liquor and the shame that made him do it..." Abdul's head spun with the purging of emotion. "Many years ago, when they were still friends and they loved to watch American westerns, that thieving bastard gave my father a birthday gift, a vintage pearl-handled six-shooter. It was that gun my father used to blow out his brains in our kitchen. It was my oldest brother who found him."

Bile rose from Abdul's stomach and he leaned toward the open window. He almost couldn't get his head out fast enough. Vomit spewed down the side of the moving truck.

The White Snake slowed the truck and began to pull off to the side of the road, but he waved her on. He cleared the rest of the vomit from his throat and spit out the window. He swished water from the water bottle and spit that out as well. "I'm okay."

He sank back in the seat, put his head in his hands, and wept. He had not yet wept for his father, not even at the funeral. He had been consumed with anger. In the throes of his tears, he wondered why he had now spoken about it in front of this woman.

The White Snake pulled a handkerchief from the sleeve of her burka and gave it to him. "I am so sorry," she said.

He wiped his face with it. "That so-called friend moved to America. He and our millions live somewhere in California," he said, sniffing back tears.

The White Snake shook her head and tightened her jaw.

The rumble of the tires filled the silence until Abdul spoke again. "The worst part is my father could not have cared less about the money for himself. All he cared about was helping his sons have a better life than he had. He was very proud to set up an inheritance for his sons. When he lost the company and the money, he believed he let us down. The betrayal of his best friend was too much for him to bear. He had worked so hard. He worked all day at his practice and all night on the business… we hardly saw him for six years. I don't think he ever took a vacation." He paused. "I remember the day we sat in a restaurant, just the two of us. I was sixteen. My father drew his idea for me on a napkin. His idea!"

He swore and kicked the dashboard of the truck again, this time with such force a large crack ripped the plastic.

"I am so sorry," the White Snake repeated.

"Someday I will have my revenge."

CHAPTER 30

DEATH

MONDAY—POST-QUAKE DAY NINE

Nick stood with Ali and Lee at the bedside of a dying woman on the second floor of the hospital. Her husband, sitting beside her, gazed from one person to the next, pleading with his eyes, searching for hope. Nick looked at Ali, then Lee, and saw the exhaustion on their faces. It was Monday and supposed to be a fresh start. Buck would arrive sometime in the afternoon, and the second operating room would soon be up and running. New volunteers had arrived last evening, full of energy and raring to go.

The woman gasped with agonal breathing. Her breath stopped long enough that Nick thought it might be her last, until her chest heaved with terrible gurgling.

There hadn't been any deaths over the weekend, and nine days after the earthquake, the team hoped there would be no more. The UN had told them that the death estimate for the whole region was nearing 150 thousand, but it was expected to climb much higher. Maybe God's mercy had taken the victims at the start and spared them the agony this woman was enduring.

Nick wanted desperately to leave the room. *No wonder we are all afraid of death. A Stephen King story could not be more horrifying.* Her breathing reflex was likely coming from her brain stem. He hoped she wasn't feeling any pain and wondered if her spirit had left her body. *Lord, have mercy.*

He watched the woman's husband gently stroke her forehead and brush her hair to one side. He could see how much the man loved his wife. At the same time, he realized he had never known love like that. The intimacy of love meant being prepared for the deepest pain, for being separated by death. He thought of Maggie and everything she had endured with John's death. That kind of intimacy had eluded him—or maybe it was the other way around. Maybe he had avoided becoming entangled in deepest intimacy because he was afraid to love.

The sorrowful husband appeared to be in his late thirties. Lee had shared with them that the couple lost their two children the day of the quake. And now this. *How does anyone survive something like this?*

Ali had amputated one of the woman's legs days ago, and Nick amputated the other yesterday. Neither doctor was sure she would survive the second surgery, but it was a last-ditch effort to save her life. It was the only thing they could do. The antibiotics flown in by Jack Bilton's team were no match for the bacteria eating the woman from the inside.

The woman gasped loudly, and her breathing stopped. Nick could feel a collective hope from everyone in the room. It was almost a disappointment when she inhaled again. Her sobbing husband looked to Nick for help, but Nick couldn't bear the man's gaze and turned to Lee.

Lee tried to give them a way out. "You doctors go finish your rounds. I will stay with the woman," she told Nick and Ali. They looked at each other but neither made a move. Even though they had a long day ahead of them, it didn't seem right to leave their patient. Nick stood firm, crossed his arms, and closed his eyes. He inhaled deeply through his nose.

Why are you afraid of death? He heard the words come from deep in his heart. He pinched his temples with one hand, but he couldn't help answering his heart. He was afraid he didn't know how to live. What if he died before he figured it out? What if he died alone?

The woman's arms postured in spasm. Then she panted a few breaths and gave her last. Nick watched her mouth open in silent surrender as her body let go and relaxed into death. Her husband whispered a few words and gently kissed her forehead. Nick didn't understand the words, but he shared the man's grief.

Ali looked at Nick. They nodded at each other and quietly retreated from the room.

***

"No, no, no…" Ibrahim tossed his head. "Please stop," he cried. His leg didn't hurt very much, and that surprised him, but the men were doing something to it, and he didn't know what. All he knew was that every time they touched him, there was pain.

Two black soldiers had laid a stretcher on the ground next to him. They had poked him as if they were looking for signs of life and then argued. Ibrahim's eyes flashed between them, not understanding. Finally, the taller soldier seemingly won the argument. He knelt beside Ibrahim, sweeping his arms around the boy's body, supporting his leg, and lifting him.

It was the first time he had been off the ground in nine days. Even though the picking up hurt his leg, the warmth of the man's body was a comfort and reminded him of his father's scent after he had worked all day on their car in the hot sun.

The only time Ibrahim had ever seen a black man was on TV. The soldier had very white teeth and nearly coal-black skin. His hair was dark like Ibrahim's, but wiry.

"*Sakin ol, sakin ol,*" the soldier kept saying to him in an accent Ibrahim didn't know. He thought he was trying to tell him to calm down, but it didn't sound like Turkish.

The soldier carried him, navigating through the crowded courtyard, heading toward the large building.

"No, no, I don't want to go in that building," Ibrahim cried.

"*Sakin ol, sakin ol,*" the soldier repeated.

He tried to push away from the man's strong arms, but his exertion only made his leg hurt. The man went into the brightly lit building with white tile floors and blue walls and the strong smell of a cleaner his mother used. He saw people lined up on benches with bandages, slings, and splints covering different parts of their bodies. There was more activity inside the building than outside, with people shouting at each other and moving swiftly. "I do not want to be in this building," he repeated. The soldier just smiled at him.

"Abraham." It was the muscleman from outside. The giant got up from the bench, flexed his biceps, and signaled the boy with a high-five. As soon as the soldier was close enough, Ibrahim slapped his hand in solidarity.

As the soldier carried him down the hallway filled with wounded, Ibrahim turned back and watched the muscleman flex his arm again.

Ibrahim still didn't know what to expect, but when they left the building through the back door, he was surprised and relieved. The soldier carried him to a patio with a few steel tables separated by flapping bed sheets and set him gently down on one of the tables. He squirmed because it was cold and hard.

Two older Turkish women wearing plastic aprons, gloves, and surgical masks came at him from either side.

"Hi, little one. We need to get you cleaned up," one of them said and began peeling his shirt off.

He was glad she spoke his language. "Where are my mother and father?"

"We do not know anything about your parents, but we will get you cleaned up. Maybe someone inside will know."

It was the first time anyone had even come close to answering the question he had been asking all week. He thought it best to stop fighting, relax, and get clean.

***

Nick and Ali stood at the scrub sinks between the two operating rooms. Even though it seemed more chaotic with the new volunteers searching for supplies and adjusting to the environment, they were very happy to have the second OR running. Two anesthesiologists from England had arrived last night, giving Will the day off. If anyone deserved it, it was Will. Running two tables all by himself in the makeshift trauma room for the entire week was enough to exhaust the best of men. Nick was surprised to see Will at breakfast, sitting with the orphans and laughing as though it were a holiday. Will and Jack—Nick was impressed with the indomitable spirit of the older men.

"Who's going in which room?" asked Shellie, the nurse from Ohio.

"Hey, Shellie," Nick said and gagged, pretending to throw up. It had become a standing joke in the OR. No one was immune to the horrific sights and smells, but Shellie's stomach was more sensitive than the others.

"Oh, stop it," Shellie said and slapped his arm. "You better watch out, or I'll puke on your shoes again." She leaned toward him and pretended to puke. One of the new nurses passing by began to gag for real and they all laughed.

"There you go, Dr. Hart"—Shellie shrugged toward the nurse—"someone else to pick on."

Nick gave Shellie the once-over. She wore a bright red bandana instead of her surgical cap, and she'd shed a few pounds during the long week, likely due to stress and her sick stomach. But her transformation was remarkable. She was no longer the scared, country mouse trembling in the corner; she was now the confident city mouse and a trustworthy colleague. Nick realized that in a different world, he would be tempted to seduce her.

"Oh, Shellie, you know I love you," he teased back and attempted to make amends. "It seems like yesterday when I watched you help a patient onto the OR table and struggle with both the patient's IV and your own. I think you passed out at least three times. But look at you now—you're my hero."

"Oh, stop it," she said again.

"You really have done a remarkable job, Ms. Shellie," Ali said.

Nick saw Shellie's eyes well with tears.

"I didn't think I'd survive those first few days," she confessed. "Now I'm thinking this is what I was born to do." She straightened her back. "Well, if you gentlemen are done, I still need to know who is going in which room."

Ali and Nick smiled at each other.

"I don't care, Ali. You choose," Nick said.

"Then I will take the dirty room, and you take on the kids today," Ali said.

Ali was being polite, if a little subservient, but Nick was glad to accept Ali's choice. He didn't know if he could stand another day of smelly, open wounds. "Okay, but the deal is, we switch tomorrow. I know we need to start getting to the kids or else their fractures are going to start healing crooked, and then we'll have another mess on our hands. I talked with Jack last night. His guys are going to create a third OR in that storage room there," he said, pointing to a room off the central area. "What do you think of using that as the dirty room as soon as they get it done? We can keep washing out wounds in there, then we can use the two regular ORs for fracture work. Buck should be here pretty soon."

"That will work out well," Ali said. "What will you do with the kids today without equipment?"

"Shellie and I went through one of the storage rooms last night, and I found some old pins and an even older hand drill. I'm going to do whatever closed reductions and castings I can. We have a few kids that need some skeletal traction pins so we can put them in traction. I'm reverting back to my grandfather's era of practicing medicine."

"Or to modern-day Turkey," Ali put in. "Some of these rural areas still use that stuff."

"I'm just going to be happy to have our real tools and implants," Nick said. "I'm kind of sick of the smell of Turkish delight."

"I don't know, maybe we should patent it. It seems to be effective."

"Yeah, and we'll be rich, just in time for the next disaster." They both laughed.

"It might take us a while to sort through the orthopedic equipment that Buck is bringing," Nick said. "I hope we'll also be getting a few more ortho guys in the next day or so."

Ali looked down shyly. "Maybe when we get more staff, I could see about taking a couple of days to get to Hakkâri to see if our parents really did make it there."

"Oh, my gosh, yes. You can go today if you want to."

"You are very kind, Dr. Hart, but it will happen soon enough. At this point, they are either alive or dead, and there is nothing I can do."

"Well, let's pray for the alive option."

"Yes indeed."

***

Vladimir stood in the small exam room. The Chinese woman with the stethoscope around her neck had been in and out, grabbing supplies from the cabinets, murmuring to herself but saying nothing to him. He was getting tired of waiting.

Now she returned, swung open the door, and bumped into him. She looked up at him without apologizing. "You better sit down or I need ladder to see your shoulder."

He eased himself into the plastic chair, hoping it wouldn't give way under his weight, and watched the woman pull on exam gloves, snapping them at the wrist as she let go of each one. He was glad she wasn't checking his prostate.

"You think I have x-ray vision?" She looked at him through dirty glasses.

He got the hint and pulled off his shirt.

"Ewww, that not so good." She sniffed and pushed up her glasses with the back of her wrist.

He could smell the infection in his arm as well but was thankful she did not ask how it had happened.

"I'm going to wash it out now and start you on antibiotics, but if it's no better by tomorrow, I will have the bone docs look at it. They may have to take you to surgery to wash it out."

The woman reached for a bottle of sterile saline and a kidney-shaped emesis basin. The saline both burned and soothed as she poured it over his open deltoid muscle. "Something fall on you?"

"Uh, yeah, something like that," he said.

She squeezed hard on each side of the jagged wound. Pus and blood oozed, and a large clot of old blood plopped into the basin. Vladimir's head began to spin.

"You don't look so good. Put your head between your knees," she ordered, pushing his head between his legs with her elbow. "No way to catch you if you fall. I would hate for you to bump your head." She laughed.

Staring at the floor between his feet, Vladimir decided he didn't like this woman. But at least his head had stopped spinning.

"Weird," he heard her say.

He lifted his head slightly to look at her. She was poking something in the emesis basin. "I thought you growing little beetles in there." She plucked something from the basin and held it to his face. "Look like BBs. You fall on shotgun?"

He glared at the woman staring back at him. "Uh…"

"Never mind, I don't care," she said, not waiting for an answer. "More patients to see. Nurse will be in to put dressing on." She snapped off her gloves. "Take these antibiotics." She rattled the pill bottle in front of his face. "And see me tomorrow." She threw her gloves in the overflowing trash can and left.

CHAPTER 31

HAKKÂRI

Abdul stretched his back and grimaced. The truck's cab had been a horrible bed, and he had endured a terrible night's sleep. Worst of all was his battle with temptation. Throughout the night, Abdul awoke to the stirring of the British woman, who murmured in her sleep and sent his mind and hormones to places best untouched.

It had been the worst luck to have one of the trucks burst a radiator line on the way up the Cilo-Sat Mountains, on the eastern extension of the Toros range. They had made it only halfway from Cizre to Hakkâri. The trucks had chugged up the steep incline through hairpin turns with ease to the mountain ridge where the road dropped off hundreds of feet on either side. He had been about to say something about their good fortune when he saw steam billow from the truck behind them.

That meant all the trucks had to stop, and there was barely enough room to pull them all to the side of the road. The engine of the afflicted truck was too hot to work on. They waited for it to cool and as the sun set, they discovered that no one had brought a flashlight. No help was in sight as they had not seen another vehicle for miles. Abdul and his team were forced to spend the night in the trucks, and it hadn't been a restful night.

Abdul yawned as his phone dinged, waking the woman.

"I hope you're not getting text messages up here," she rebuked him.

He was irritated, tired, and hungry and almost swore at her. "Of course not. I know the danger. My phone just reminded me of *Fajr*, first morning prayer."

"It did?"

He smirked. "Yes. I have an app for that." He showed her the screen. "It also tells me the direction of the Kaaba in Mecca." He looked toward the growing light in the east. "We must hurry if we are going to perform *Fajr* before the sun rises."

Their doors creaked loudly in the thin mountain air as the pair exited the truck. The other men were already gathered by the side of the road, kneeling on prayer rugs with their heads on the ground.

The man in Cizre was right; the view was beautiful. The stars faded as daylight grew. He had never been to the mountains before and he inhaled deeply. The air was clean and crisp. *Thank you, Allah, for Your creation.*

He took a bottle of water, carefully washed his hands, and splashed what was left on his face. He must be clean to approach Allah. He pushed away the unclean thoughts he had about the woman. It made him angry that these thoughts came involuntarily; the more he tried not to have them, the more he did. *Allah have mercy.*

He spread his prayer rug out before him and began to pray.

***

Finally, the truck's radiator line was fixed, and they were on their way. Abdul had not said one word to the White Snake for the last two hours, as the diesel tires rumbled over the asphalt. If not for the beauty of the mountains, the silence would have been unbearable. They should arrive in Hakkâri within the hour. He smoldered with disgust. Why hadn't he thought of the solution? After all, he was the engineer. And it had turned out to be perfect.

When the broken radiator hose had been discovered, the men argued about what to do. Finding a new radiator hose was impossible. With no other traffic on the road, help was not available. They had made the decision to ditch the truck and load what they could into the other packed diesels. This created the problem of uncovering the carefully packed and camouflaged weapons. Where would they put those? They certainly couldn't pile them on top and risk being stopped when they entered Hakkâri. Leaving the truck full of armaments and medical supplies was no better a solution.

The only recourse was to leave the ailing diesel. As the men had begun the task of unloading the truck, the White Snake approached them, holding a box.

"You think this will help?" she asked.

"What? I suppose you found a radiator hose." Abdul smirked. "Stupid woman," he murmured loud enough that everyone heard, including the White Snake. It made the men laugh.

He couldn't have guessed she had the solution. Now he looked like an idiot.

The White Snake had ignored his comment and opened the box. It contained orange-sized foil packages. "Fiberglass tape," she said. "I found it in the medical supplies. After college, I worked in a medical clinic for a couple of years, and I used to watch the doctors wrap this stuff around broken arms. I thought maybe it would work around the hose."

She offered the box to one of the men, who recoiled as though it contained a snake. The man looked at Abdul, who nodded with resignation. "Take it."

The fiberglass tape not only worked well—it worked perfectly. The men wrapped it tightly around the split in the hose, and after they filled the radiator with water and started the engine, it did not leak a single drop.

The men cheered, and when they high-fived the White Snake, he was angry and clenched his jaw. They should not be touching that woman.

But it was more than that.

He was still angry and clenched his teeth. He had been bested by a woman.

***

Abdul had never seen the Alps, but the view was exactly how he pictured them—wild and majestic. The trucks came over a small pass and down into Hakkâri, sitting like an emerald mounted in prongs of rugged peaks. The city of sixty thousand appeared to be suspended in the bowl formed by the surrounding mountains. Fields of lush green spread from the city to rocky fields that shot straight up to the expansive chain. Occasional patches of snow filled crevices near the peaks. From his reading, he understood the city was over a mile high in elevation, and the mountains stood more than twice that. It made him short of breath and he gulped for air.

"Wow!" the White Snake exclaimed.

With the sight of the city, he forgot his anger, and his heart pounded with anticipation. Now maybe he would feel like a real jihadist. He pictured his oldest brother wrapping him in his arms in triumph. He wished he could call Abbas.

He was in the heart of the new caliphate, at the intersection of Turkey, Iran and Iraq. It was only six and a half hours to Mosel and eleven hours to Tehran. He had heard the Judeo-Christian version of the Garden of Eden story and knew some thought the original garden was within this area. The ninth-century painting of Adam and Eve always showed them wearing fig leaves in a lush jungle, but he'd never considered the garden might look like this.

Forgive me, Allah, but if I were the one to pick a spot, this would be it. But Islam taught that the Garden of Eden was in heaven, and Adam and Eve were banished from heaven and sent to earth as punishment for their sin. This did not feel like punishment.

"I see a mosque down there," the White Snake said, interrupting his thoughts.

Abdul strained but could not see it. From this distance, the city looked remarkably modern with many brightly colored high-rises surrounded by multilevel apartment buildings.

"Look to the right of the large red building," she said, "and then right again from that huge yellow apartment complex. See it next to the soccer stadium?"

"Ah, yes, I see it." He could see the gray dome of the mosque, but the single minaret next to the dome was nearly blocked by the apartment building. "Excellent. That is where the men from Cizre said to meet our contact."

***

From a distance, it did not appear that Hakkâri had sustained any damage from the earthquake, but as they drove through the city, they encountered a different story. The damage was significant. Tent cities made from plastic or tin or whatever could be scrounged filled every vacant spot among the debris.

One large apartment complex was flattened, and three men stood on the rubble, searching for anything of value. One of the men turned when he saw the trucks rumble down the street. He whistled loudly and shouted, and the other men did the same.

As the diesels entered the main boulevard of the city, more and more locals stopped and stared. Many people whistled and shouted. Abdul glanced at the White Snake with concern. She wasn't alarmed.

"We are the Red Crescent, after all," she said.

He nodded. *They think the Red Crescent is here to help.* He smiled to himself.

They passed the large soccer stadium filled with a tent city. As they rounded the bend, they saw the large mosque on the right. It appeared to have sustained little damage.

"We were supposed to meet the man in front of the mosque yesterday," the White Snake said. "I'm not sure what we'll do now."

She shifted the truck into a lower gear and slowed.

As the trucks stopped in front of the mosque, about twenty people gathered around them. One man climbed onto the running board on Abdul's side and tapped at the window, smiling broadly. Two young men climbed on the White Snake's side, saying something neither she nor Abdul understood.

"Well, so much for a stealthy entrance," Abdul said. "What now?"

The White Snake seemed uncharacteristically indecisive and nervous as the crowd increased three rows deep around the truck. She pushed the gear shift into first and edged forward, which only incited the crowd.

"Wait, wait, wait," Abdul said. He pointed to a man wearing a green shirt running toward them, shouting and frantically waving his hands. The truck lurched when the White Snake hit the brakes, almost throwing the man off the running board.

The man in the green shirt pushed his way through the swelling crowd and elbowed himself between the two men on the White Snake's side. She rolled her window down enough to hear what he had to say.

"Please, keep moving," the man ordered. He started yelling at the people in front of the truck and waving his arm, instructing them to get out of the way. He looked at the White Snake. "Please, drive."

She did as she was told, inching forward until the revved diesel threatened the people and they moved out of the way.

"You were supposed to be here yesterday," the man in the green shirt said and then shouted at the crowd. A man grabbed his sleeve, practically pulling him from the running board. He jerked his arm away and scolded the man severely in what Abdul assumed was Kurdish. Abdul noticed that most of the people in the gathering were darker skinned. *Kurds,* he thought in disgust.

"I am taking you to the hospital," the man in the green shirt said. "We cannot stop here. These people have not seen any relief supplies since the earthquake."

CHAPTER 32

JOY

MONDAY AFTERNOON— POST-QUAKE DAY NINE

Ketamine was the word of the day for Nick and his team in the pediatric operating room.

"What a great drug, especially if you're a kid or a dog," the British volunteer anesthesiologist said. He was about the same age as Will, and he told Nick that he had used ketamine all the time in the sixties and seventies. "It puts them in a trancelike state, gives pain relief, and best of all, they usually don't remember anything that happened. It works great for kids but sends adults on one heck of a trip."

Nick laughed. "I remember in residency, the guys gave an old man some ketamine, and he was picking butterflies off the walls for days."

He smiled at the small boy on the OR table. After a long day of reducing forearm fractures and elbow fractures, reducing tibia fractures and putting them in long leg casts, and putting femur fractures in traction, Nick thought this kid looked like all the other children. This boy had a femur fracture, and Nick planned to insert a skeletal traction pin above the knee to hang his leg in traction.

But the boy was terrified. He'd probably never been in such an alien environment filled with strangers. Nick tried to get him to relax by patting his head and stroking his forehead with his thumb. A large tear welled in the corner of the boy's eye and slid down his cheek. The boy appeared to be around six or seven years old with short dark hair, darker eyes and ears, and front teeth that he needed to grow into.

Nick hated the fact that he would need to put the boy in skeletal traction. He'd be in bed for the next four to six weeks and then in a spica cast for another four to six weeks. It would be difficult to care for the child in these conditions, but Nick didn't have the luxury of putting flexible titanium rods down the bone in one definitive treatment. He would have to be satisfied with archaic patient care. It was the best they could do, and the boy had nowhere else to go.

He wasn't having much luck pacifying the boy and looked for a nurse to come to his rescue. They were all busy, scurrying around setting up the instruments and fetching medications for the anesthesiologist. He looked back at the boy, who shivered and stared at him with large, inquisitive eyes. Nick pulled down his surgical mask and made a funny face. The boy's sullen expression did not change. Nick tried again by pulling his cheeks out in clownish distortion. Still nothing.

One of the interpreters entered the room and he called her over. "Can you help me talk to this young man?" He turned to the boy. "What is your name?" he asked, hoping that she would take it from there.

The boy's lower lip quivered and another tear ran down his cheek. The interpreter smiled at him, lowered her face to his cheek, and whispered in his ear. Whatever she said turned on a faucet of tears. She gently stroked the boy's head and rested her hand on his chest, all the while reassuring him in Turkish. Her whispers gave way to what sounded like a loving lullaby.

The anesthesiologist was ready to start an IV and looked at Nick. He tilted his head and shrugged. Maybe they could wait a moment. Sometimes, when the kids were inconsolable and time was of the essence, they had to be held down so surgery could start. But at other times it was clear that a minute or two wouldn't make a difference in the long day. The tender loving care worked, and the boy's chest slowed its heaving and his crying stopped.

The interpreter lifted her face and spoke sweetly to the boy. Finally, in a barely audible voice, the child spoke. She listened intently, then turned to Nick. "He is looking for his mommy and daddy. He says his name is Ibrahim."

Nick sighed. So many of the children he worked on were newly orphaned. "Hi, Ibrahim," he said. "We're going to fix your leg good as new. You're going to take a nap now, and I'll see you when you wake up." He nodded to the British anesthesiologist, and the interpreter translated for the boy, resting her chest over his to keep him still so the IV could be started.

Ibrahim caught sight of the needle and whimpered, but the anesthesiologist had the ketamine ready and quickly injected the correct dose. He nodded to the team, and they jumped into action.

Nick wheeled the new x-ray fluoroscopy machine over to the bed and scanned the broken leg. The femur was fractured midshaft, but because of the pull of the thigh muscles, the ends of the bones overlapped each other by a good three inches— making the leg six inches short. Left untreated, the femur would heal short, crooked, or malrotated, giving the child a significant limp the rest of his life.

Thank God for Jack Bilton and his resources. The C-arm x-ray unit had arrived the day before via helicopter. How in the world Jack pulled that one off was a miracle. The man had a heart of gold and a checkbook to match. Nick had no idea what a new fluoroscopy unit cost, but he guessed it was over a hundred thousand dollars.

The helicopter delivery had been a stroke of genius. The ceiling of the OR room that had been fixed was reopened so the copter could drop the crate right through the roof. It had seemed like a perfect solution, but they neglected to tell the patients about the plan. The large military transport helicopter hovering overhead shook the hospital like a huge aftershock and emptied the building. Dr. Lee was not happy. "You men like bulls in china shop. Now I have to get everyone organized again," she'd said and stormed off with her clipboard.

Nick smiled to himself as he felt Ibrahim's leg. *That woman can really get angry.*

When he squeezed the leg, the ends of the bones moved, and he was relieved that no healing had begun. He bent the knee and pulled up hard on the leg. He could feel the muscle stretch and the tissue tear as he started to lift the boy off the table. It seemed barbaric, but it was best to loosen up the fracture from adhesions that would have already formed between the bone and the surrounding tissue.

He wondered what happened to Ibrahim's parents and feared the worst.

He lay the boy's leg back down on the table, scrubbed the area with betadine, and with an old stainless-steel hand drill twisted a pin through the skin and the bone and out the other side. He removed the drill and picked the leg up by the pin. The pin flexed slightly as he pulled. Satisfied, he placed a metal bow on each side of the pin that would be attached to rope and pulleys that would suspend the leg overhead.

"Okay, that's the easy part. Now the kid needs to hang around for six weeks while this thing heals. Bring his bed over, and let's put it in traction before he wakes up."

As the words left his mouth, the OR door flew open and a red-faced nurse came running in yelling something in Turkish to the other nurses. It didn't sound good. Nick noticed the interpreter was paying close attention, and he waited to hear what it was all about.

"They want to know if you are done and if you can come with them," she told him.

"As soon as we get this little guy hung up in traction," Nick said.

"I'm afraid it cannot wait. It's something about a baby. Dr. Lee needs you now."

Nick looked at the anesthesiologist and the nurses.

The Brit was the first to speak. "We'll be fine. Go see what they need, and we'll take care of him."

Nick snapped off his gloves, and the nurse took him by the arm and led him out of the room. She pulled him to the central area, where a group of nurses and Dr. Lee gathered around a stretcher. A woman lay on the stretcher, naked and screaming. The nurse pulled him directly into the chaos.

"You remember your obstetrical rotation?" Lee asked.

He furrowed his brow and stared at her. *What are you talking about?*

The nurses stepped back and pushed him toward the stretcher. He looked at the screaming woman, checking for blood and signs of trauma. Nick gasped when he saw what the nurses directed him to—two tiny legs sticking out of the woman's vagina.

"Where is Ali?" It was all he could think to say.

"Scrubbed in," Lee told him. "You're it."

He was paralyzed. "My God, it's a breech baby." He watched the little legs kick like the baby was trying to wiggle its way out. The mother screamed like only a delivering mom can, so loud he couldn't think. He saw her staring at him, throwing her screams at him. He didn't need an interpreter to know she was asking for help. *Do something, you stupid idiot.*

A nurse handed him a pair of gloves, and he reflexively put them on. His hands began to shake, and sweat dripped from his forehead. He wiped his perspiration with the back of his arm and tried frantically to remember his very short rotation as a medical student in OB. He had helped in a few simple deliveries—catching the baby for experienced mothers—but he had never done a breech. He was not sure he had ever seen one delivered vaginally, only by C-section.

C-Section, that's it. He paused. No, that won't work with the baby partway out.

The birthing mother screamed and pushed. The baby's legs were purple. Nick realized that if he didn't do something, the baby would die and possibly the mother as well.

He grabbed hold of the tiny legs and pulled gently. The baby came sliding out to its chest. *Well, that was easy. Now what?* The baby was stuck in the birth canal at its shoulders. The panic in the room was palpable. Not only was the mother screaming, the nurses had joined her. They all yelled at him to do something. Nick's knees turned to jelly.

A stream of urine shot from the baby's penis onto Nick's scrub top. "A boy, it's a boy."

He grabbed the baby by the buttocks and twisted one way and then the other. Neither helped. The baby's legs turned from purple to blue, and they were out of time. He had to get at least one shoulder out. He stuck his fingers up the woman's birthing canal and felt for the baby's arm. *Anything.*

The woman panted from the added pressure of Nick's fingers. Instinctively, he pushed the baby back up the birthing canal enough to relieve some of the pressure.

An arm. I think it's an arm. He hooked a finger over it and pulled. There was a sickening snap, but as the arm broke, a shoulder appeared, followed by a head.

A thunderous cheer erupted. He cradled the baby in one arm and pressed his mouth over the meconium-covered face and gave the baby a puff of air. Then another. With the third, the baby sputtered and screamed with affirmation. He had never heard such a joyous sound. Another cheer filled the room, and the baby's mother wept with exhaustion and relief.

After a week of horror and devastation, here was a new life. Breathing and crying. Nick's tears flowed, and all the faces in the room were wet with tears of joy. It had been a miracle. He didn't bother wiping his tears; he let them fall like a spring shower welcoming a new season.

"What the dickens?" Ali said, entering the room. "You guys sure know how to make a ruckus, I thought you were torturing someone." He looked at the mother and then at Nick. "I guess you were," he laughed.

Nick lifted the baby toward Ali.

"Good job, baby doctor," Ali said. "When you told me you were going to do the kids today, I bet you didn't have this in mind."

"Yeah, but look." Nick moved the baby's left arm. It bent midway down the arm. "It looks like I broke the humerus."

Ali squeezed Nick's shoulder. "Man, that will heal in about a week in a kid this age. I gotta hand it to you. You not only got him out, you turned an OB case into an ortho case."

A nurse handed Nick a pair of hemostats to clamp the umbilical cord and a pair of scissors to cut it. Then Nick gently handed the baby to his mother. She smiled and held him to her chest.

"Tell her the baby's arm is broken," Nick instructed the interpreter. "Tell her we will put it in a sling and it will heal very quickly. Tell her I'm sorry."

Nick stood up and looked back at Ali. "You mind helping deliver the afterbirth? I think I need to go change my shorts." He laughed, his knees and hands still shaking.

CHAPTER 33

MERCY HOSPITAL

The man in the green shirt had stayed on the running board, holding fast to the truck and pointing the way. The other trucks followed. When the White Snake had stepped on the gas, the crowd outside the mosque had parted to let them pass. Their guide led them west to the outskirts of Hakkâri. As they'd motored through the city, Abdul understood why the people were so frantic—much of the city's infrastructure had collapsed.

Their guide told them the city was still without power and water, and only now, nine days after the quake, people were venturing into the remaining structures. He said it was only in Allah's great mercy that the earthquake had struck during the summer. All the people would have died if it had happened in January or February when temperatures were well below freezing.

Abdul was relieved when their trucks finally entered the large gates of the hospital compound. When they drove through, one of the four guards holding AK-47s slapped the truck's fender. The compound was impressive and he glanced at the White Snake to see her reaction. She smiled broadly back at him and shrugged.

After the stark condition of the ISIS office in Cizre, he had expected another dismal working space. But this compound was beautiful and newly constructed. There was no landscaping, and the asphalt surrounding the building was clean and black from a lack of traffic.

Several four-story cream-colored buildings with red trim and roofs appeared like the modern medical complexes of Abdul's home country of Saudi Arabia. The buildings sat in the middle of twenty acres of freshly scraped land. A fifteen-foot high cinderblock fence lined with razor wire encircled the compound.

"Where should I park?" the White Snake asked the man in the green shirt.

"Just pull up to the hospital entrance," he said, pointing to a large, glass-enclosed atrium. Abdul noticed that one panel of the atrium had been covered with a sheet of plywood; it had been damaged by the quake as well. He was amazed that the rest of the glass had survived the shaking.

The White Snake glanced at Abdul and snickered. "You're right, so much for a stealthy entrance."

The men in Cizre had told them they would be delivering the supplies to a hospital, but he had pictured something completely different. He had imagined smuggling the arms through the dark of night into some mountain cave or underground bunker. This was so open and exposed that he expected Turkish troops to pour out of the building at any moment.

He understood that part of the reason the Islamic State was surviving so well was their ability to compartmentalize all information. Only a handful of people were privy to the strategic plan and what was happening in different regions. He wondered if his brother was smiling for his little brother, encountering the luxury of this covert base.

The White Snake pulled the diesel to the front of the hospital, and the other trucks followed suit. A large sign with red letters over the entrance read MERHAMET HASTANESI. One of the truck engines backfired as it was shutting down, causing Abdul to jump. The White Snake laughed at him, and hot embarrassment surged at the back of his neck. He almost lectured her that Sharia law allowed him to beat her for insubordination, but he was interrupted by the man in the green shirt.

"Please, follow me," he said, jumping off the running board and heading to the entrance.

The men exited their trucks and filed toward the building. Abdul sensed their mixture of fear and awe. The automatic doors swung open as they approached. They entered a magnificent atrium of green marble, lined with flower gardens on each side against the backdrop of a large waterfall tumbling from the second floor.

Abdul, the White Snake, and the others stood in silent wonder.

"It is of my own design," came a voice from above, startling them from their trance. They looked up to the loft on the second floor and saw a large man in a navy-blue suit standing at the railing.

"Welcome to *Merhamet Hastanesi*—Mercy Hospital," he said, spreading his arms wide, his voice echoing off the marble. "Please come join me in my office." He waved the group up the stairs to their right.

Everyone hesitated and looked at Abdul.

"Please, you are my guests," the man on the second floor insisted. "Your trucks and supplies will be well protected. You are among friends here."

Abdul looked furtively at the White Snake and then quickly back at the man.

He needed to stop looking for guidance from the woman. He had already noticed his men were starting to follow her lead, and that had to change.

"Let's go," he ordered and headed for the stairs. He steadied his courage by clutching the gold railing that lined the curved staircase. At the top of the stairs, he and the team were welcomed by the large man in the suit. He was well dressed but fat, with a double chin that hung over the collar of his white shirt and rested on the knot of a baby-blue silk tie that matched the pocket square in his suit coat.

The obese man gave him a long, warm embrace. Abdul stiffened and sniffed. The man smelled like a mixture of cologne, tobacco, and fried chicken.

"*Subhanallah*, glory to Allah," the fat man proclaimed and gave him another embrace. "It is an honor to have the brother of Abbas Fadhil, first in command under Abu Bakr al-Baghdadi, our caliph of the new caliphate, peace and honor be upon him," he said, echoing the greeting of the men in Cizre. Abdul recognized his brother was high-up the chain of command in the Islamic State, but until now, he had no idea Abbas was so revered. He found it a little hard to believe. He loved his brother, but like most brothers, he knew him first as an annoying sibling.

"*Baraka Allahu fika*, may Allah bestow his blessings on you." He tried to pull away from the cloying embrace.

The man straightened his arms to hold Abdul by the shoulders. Then he kissed him on each cheek. "This is a great day," he said. "I could not be happier if Abu Bakr al-Baghdadi himself was visiting us."

Abdul blushed and stepped back. "Yes, thank you for your warm welcome," he said and looked at the floor.

When he sensed the man was waiting for him to say something more, he looked up. He was met with round, blue-tinted glasses and a beaming smile under a black handlebar mustache. The man had no beard, and that made Abdul suspicious. How could the man be a Salafi jihadist? Salifi jihadists belonged to the ultraconservative reform movement, and they all had beards. On top of that, Abdul saw grease on the man's naked chin, and he was embarrassed for the poser.

Abdul reached for his own chin and stroked his bare skin. He had tried to grow a beard last year. It was a barren scruff that looked ridiculous so he quickly shaved it off.

The White Snake stepped in and rescued him from his awkwardness. "Thank you for your warm welcome," she said to the man. Like most Muslim men, he seemed surprised that a woman would dare address him and stared at her with disapproval.

The light in his brain must have clicked on, and he blushed with embarrassment. "You must be Akleema Mohammad...the eh—"

"Yes, the White Snake," she said and smiled at him.

Akleema! It had been driving Abdul crazy that he could not remember her name.

"Akleema, the beautiful one, a daughter of Adam," the man said. "You certainly resemble your name." He blushed again. "*Subhanallah*, glory to Allah," he said and bowed slightly. "This, indeed, is a great day for the Islamic State. Please come into my office—all of you," he said, including the others in his invitation. "Oh, and please forgive me for my rudeness. My name is Omar Hussein. I am the CEO of this beautiful facility."

He waved them toward his office. They followed him but bumped into each other when he stopped suddenly, stepping back to the railing to gaze at the atrium and spread his arms over his magnificent creation.

"Do you like this?" he smiled broadly.

"It is quite beautiful," Akleema answered for the men.

"I hoped you would like it," he said like a proud father. "I had the generators turned on just for you."

***

Omar Hussein sat behind a large, ornately carved desk in an office lined with cherrywood paneling. The huge desk flattered the obese man, reducing his size considerably, making him look like a small child at the grown-ups' table. Abdul thought the man hadn't quite figured out how to raise his office chair to the correct height. He sucked back a grin as he looked around the room. The walls smelled of fresh paint, and an elegant crystal chandelier hung from the white ceiling. There were only four leather chairs placed in a semicircle around the desk, not enough to accommodate everyone. Taking charge, Abdul ordered his men to go back to the trucks so he and the White Snake could strategize with the administrator. It wasn't just the lack of seating; he was uneasy about abandoning the trucks and their cargo.

After his men had gone, Abdul watched a woman in a red dress and headscarf wheel in a tea cart and bow to Omar.

"Please serve our guests first," he chastised the woman.

She offered Abdul and then Akleema tulip-shaped cups of hot tea from a golden tray. Abdul lifted the blue-tinted cup toward his host. "Thank you for your hospitality." He noticed this cup was not chipped.

Omar accepted his tea and returned Abdul's toast. "It is you that I must thank. I am simply the CEO of this hospital. But you…"

Abdul thought the man was going to tear up.

"You are helping to fulfill the prophecy. It is your destiny. Those of us who believe in the Islamic State, the new caliphate, have longed for the day when an army would march into Turkey and establish the Islamic State here in our country." He wiped tears from his chubby cheeks.

"You are very kind, sir, but we are just a small group delivering supplies," Abdul said.

The man was taken aback. "Young man, I think you underestimate what you are doing. How old are you?"

"Twenty-two."

Omar sighed and smiled at him. "I am almost sixty, almost three times your age. I have been waiting for this day for decades. Like you, I left our home of Saudi Arabia in my twenties to come to Turkey. I began as an orderly in a hospital in Istanbul and worked day and night to struggle my way up the corporate ladder. By Allah's hand, I advanced until I became the CEO of a large hospital in Ankara. Two years ago, a representative from ISIS approached me about building a hospital here." He put *hospital* in air quotes. "As you can see, they funded us quite well. When the money comes through a Turkish foundation, no one ever questions someone's motives for building a new hospital to help their own people."

"Is the hospital operational?" Akleema asked.

"Almost. We were set to open two months from now, in October. But now, after the earthquake, we will have to wait and see, and that's a pity. So many people could use our help."

Abdul saw in his eyes that he was sincere about providing aid to the earthquake victims.

"As you know," Omar continued, "Sharia law requires us to live a certain way, but it also calls for us to care for the less fortunate of our people."

"Do you consider the people of Hakkâri your people?" Abdul asked.

The man sat back in his chair, which creaked loudly. With a tissue from a box on his desk, he dabbed at the grease on his chin. He folded the tissue and set it aside.

"You are a smart young man, Abdul. What did you study?"

"I am in my last year of engineering at the university."

Omar fingered his mustache, smoothing each side. "If you were building a tall building, what is one of the most important things that you would need?"

He thought it was a strange question but answered anyway. "A strong foundation, of course."

"Yes!" Omar exclaimed, as though Abdul had given him the million-dollar answer. "That is what we are doing here, building the foundation. We could not build a military base here, so we did the next best thing…we built a hospital." He smiled at Akleema and Abdul.

"Are the people of the area sympathetic to the Islamic State?" Akleema asked.

"No. That is why we must be as cunning as wolves. I know I do not look like a Salafi jihadist. I could see the suspicion on your face when we first met." Omar paused and raised his eyebrows to Abdul, who looked down. Omar grinned. "It's okay. This is my costume. This is how a Turkish hospital administrator should look, not like a jihadist. You yourself do not look like a jihadist, baby face and all."

Abdul blushed, and the fat man let out a belly laugh that made Akleema laugh.

"All around the world, we are taking ground with our people appearing as everyday workers, as doctors and nurses, as lawyers and engineers," Omar said and laughed again. "Even beautiful white women have come to know the truth." He waved his hand at Akleema, making her pale face flush.

"So, what are we to do here?" Abdul looked at the man and asked, turning the subject to business.

Omar looked surprised by the question. "To work here and live here, of course," he said. "You are the Red Crescent, here to help the people…and that is what you will do. We will distribute the food and water that you have brought and fill the hospital with medical supplies to get it ready to open. You will be our guests." He paused, filling the chair with his ample frame, and sighed. "And we will wait. We will wait for our time to strike. We will wait for more fighters. We will wait for Allah's will."

Abdul and Akleema nodded.

"Tell us about Hakkâri," Akleema asked, sipping her tea.

Omar's face did not hide his emotions, and her request animated him even more.

"How far back do you want to go?" he began, then continued without waiting for a reply. "This area and its people may date back to the beginning of time, back to the time of Noah and possibly even back to the time of Adam and Eve. This area's history is of the Assyrians, the Babylonians, the Persians, the Greeks and the Armenians, the Romans, the Arabs, the Mongols, and the Ottomans," he said, counting them off on his fingers, "along with many others who conquered this area and were conquered themselves."

The woman who had served the tea opened the office door and asked if anyone wanted more. Omar shooed her away.

"Less than twenty years ago, thirteen carved stones, *stelae*, were found buried at the center of the city. They date back to the fifteenth century BC—back to the time of the prophet Moses."

"Who do the archeologists think put them there?" Abdul asked.

"No one seems to know." Omar answered. He got up from his chair and began to pace the floor. "There is too much history between then and now to go through, but, early in the twentieth century, prior to the Assyrian genocide of 1915, the region was populated with a mixture of Assyrians and Kurds."

"The Assyrian genocide?" Akleema asked.

Omar looked pleased and continued. "During the First World War, the Ottoman Empire—"

"The Ottoman Empire was an Islamic nation and the last caliphate," Abdul said to Akleema.

"Yes, indeed. The Ottoman Empire systematically removed"—the air quotes came out again—"the Assyrians, who were mostly Christians."

"How many people were killed?" Akleema asked.

"It's hard to tell. Of course, there are some who completely deny it happened, but most historians believe around three-quarters of a million people were removed." Omar watched her reaction, then shrugged and added, "But they were all nonbelievers."

Akleema nodded.

"So that leaves us with mostly Kurds in this area, around sixty thousand of them."

"Kurds?" Abdul said louder than he'd intended. "We are fighting against the Kurds. The Kurds killed my brother." He stood up, and his chair creaked against the floor as he pushed against it. He was furious. "Are you saying I am here to help the Kurds?"

Omar tried to calm him down. "You must remember, compared to the infidels, the Kurds are Muslim." He laughed nervously.

"They are pigs!" Abdul shouted and spat at the floor.

"Yes," Omar agreed. He stood up and approached Abdul with a friendly hand. "And what do we do with pigs?" He waited for Abdul's answer, but none came. "We feed them, and then we kill them."

Omar let the words sink in before continuing. "Do you know why the Ottomans killed the Assyrians?" He paused for effect. "The Ottomans killed the Assyrians to take their land. We are here to do the same. Without land, there is no caliphate."

"He is right," Akleema said to Abdul.

"Yes, young man, do not underestimate this day. Remember our prophet Muhammad, peace be upon him. Like you, he was a young man when he left Mecca to join his uncle on a caravan to Syria. Do not discount small beginnings. Your group is now the spearhead of our efforts here. On this day, you have become the leader of the Islamic State in Turkey, the heart of the caliphate. Now, my friends, let us go feed some pigs."

CHAPTER 34

REMEMBERING

MONDAY NIGHT—POST-QUAKE DAY NINE

Vladimir was relieved when Antasha waved from the far corner of the room. He had left her for only a moment to assist the UN soldiers from Africa, who were moving equipment from a couple of trucks to a storage room. Even with one arm, he was stronger than most men and had become an instant sensation with the soldiers when he carried a two-hundred-pound load with his good arm alone. The soldiers had pulled out their smart phones to take selfies with the big man. Even though Vladimir didn't smoke, he'd shared a cigarette with the men as a sign of friendship and the expectation of gaining information.

When he'd returned to their spot in the courtyard and found someone else lying on AK's mat, he panicked. Because he hadn't been there to protect her, he feared they'd taken her back outside the gate. He'd looked around frantically. Then he heard a voice, but he didn't understand the language. Someone tugged at his trousers and he looked down. It was the stranger lying on AK's mat, pointing him toward the hospital.

Now he stood at the threshold of the second-floor ward, which was full of women in hospital beds and cots. The room that appeared to accommodate twenty patients now had twice as many, and sometimes, two women shared one bed. All the women were in some state of brokenness.

He stood at the entrance, but the room was so crowded he didn't know if he could get to AK. He sucked in his breath and tried to make himself shrink, a trick not even he could accomplish. He waved to her and shrugged. He turned to look for another way when he was confronted by a nurse trying to squeeze into the room. She pushed by, forcing him through the entry.

Flattening himself against the door, he spotted a path to Antasha's bed and slowly shuffled his bulk sideways down the narrow aisle. If he could tip-toe, he imagined he'd look like one of the old Russian cartoons of a huge burglar tip-toeing across the room to some twinkling music. He knew all eyes were on him.

"Quit clowning around, you big goofus, and get over here," Antasha scolded. "Where have you been?"

When he reached her bedside, he attempted to squat in the space between her bed and the wall, but his massive frame was too big. He pushed her bed out with his knees, bumping it into the adjacent bed. He apologized to the two women crammed into it. "I'm sorry, I'm sorry," he said, even though they probably didn't understand. One of them moaned.

"This is embarrassing," he whispered to Antasha.

She shot him a dirty look. "You have no idea what embarrassing is. While you were doing whatever you were doing," she said, waving her hands, "I was being molested by two Turkish women."

Vladimir grimaced. "Really?" He started to get up. The room was getting hotter and claustrophobic and he gasped for breath.

"Oh, sit down, before you fall down," she said, patting her bed.

"What happened, AK? I am so sorry. I'm just trying to fit in and…"

"Oh, stop groveling."

"Really, AK, are you all right?"

She pushed herself up in the bed and smoothed the sheet on top of her body. "I'll be fine."

He took her hand, begging for more information.

She smiled smugly at him. "While you were gone, two soldiers carried me on a stretcher into the hospital and out to the back. Two women in plastic aprons stripped my clothes off, sprayed me down with a garden hose, washed me from head to toe, then sprayed me down again."

Vladimir cracked a smile.

"Yeah, you think it's funny? I'll take you down to the two dominatrixes and let them work you over. See if you think it's so funny."

Vladimir could not hold back any longer and let out a loud guffaw. He instantly regretted it when the women around them stared at him. "AK, really, I am sorry. I won't leave you again."

"Yeah, right. Besides, you missed the show." She smiled at him and twisted a strand of her hair. "Look at this wonderful thing I'm wearing." She lifted the sheet. She wore only a thin hospital gown. She turned sideways and flashed her bare bottom at him.

"AK." He flushed with embarrassment and pulled the sheet back over her, glancing around to see if the other women were watching them. Fortunately, most had turned away.

He looked back at her. "What am I going to do with you?"

"Well, I can think of a couple of things," she teased.

He looked at her with amused disgust. "I'm sorry I missed your Turkish bath. But you do look better, and you definitely smell better." He planted a kiss on her forehead.

"I wish I could say the same for you," she said and pushed him away. "What are we going to do now?"

"How does your leg feel?" he asked.

"Like crap, you moron. Especially with all this moving around."

Vladimir felt through the sheet and found the splint still in place.

"Ouch!" she squealed.

He looked at her and wasn't sure if she was faking the pain or not. Her blue eyes, accentuated by mascara, had regained their sparkle, and her copper hair, damp from her bath, still framed her petite features. Her lips were freshly painted. He marveled at her resourcefulness, to find lipstick and mascara in a place like this. He smiled at her. "I am getting to know some of the UN soldiers in hopes that they can help us." He lowered his voice to a whisper. "We may have a problem though. That Chinese doctor knows I've been shot. If she starts asking questions…" He glanced around to see if the women were listening, even though he was sure they wouldn't understand. "I say, screw Putin and his stupid dreams of the tree of life. We need to get the next helicopter out of here."

***

Ibrahim tried to force his eyelids open, but they stuck tight, as if they'd been slathered with glue. He tried to lift his right arm and then his left without success. His whole body felt immobile like a block of cement. But he could tell the surface he was on was soft, like a bed.

A bed. I'm in a bed. It was a novelty after lying in the dusty courtyard for so long.

Eyelids, arms, body, bed—they were strange concepts to be dealt with separately, each requiring a deep breath.

Breathe. Breathe.

Ever since the earthquake, every time he woke up, he woke to terror. But this was different. His breathing told his body to give in to the softness of the mattress. He was comfortable enough to think of something, a memory or a vision. *The man. Where is the man?*

But the thought was subsumed by a cool, refreshing sensation on his face. The coolness felt good. His leg ached, but there was something new. His leg was out of place and stretched above him.

Then he felt his toes move. *Who did that? Did I do that?* He swallowed air. *Breathe, breathe.*

The dampness on his face was pleasantly cool, and the rest of his body was comfortably warm. Something light and soft covered him and made him want to snuggle deep into it, as he did once upon a time in the noonday sun beside his mother.

Mama? Is that you?

A faint voice was nearby, coaxing him. His brain revved like an engine, dissolving a wall of wax in his ears. He could hear again. His body jerked and twitched, snapping on the other neurons like the lights in a dark room. He gasped with wonder and opened his eyes.

"It's okay, Ibrahim," the voice said in his language. "You are just waking up. Everything is fine."

He tried to identify the speaker. *Mama?* He squinted and saw the outline of a woman in a green scarf. He blinked and the outline became a form and a face. It was a woman with kind eyes and a big smile, but she wasn't his mother. *Where is my mama?* He closed his eyes. Fear, his constant companion, rolled over his awakened mind and drifted past when he remembered something. *What did the man tell me?*

"Can you open your eyes again, Ibrahim?" the woman asked. "Take a deep breath for me."

How does she know my name? He reopened his eyes and took a deep breath. He willed his brain to tell his right arm to touch his face.

"Be careful that you don't scratch yourself," the woman told him. With one hand, she took his hand, and with the other, she rearranged the cool compress on his forehead. "You are just waking up from surgery," she told him. "Do you hurt anywhere?"

Pain. That man took my pain. Don't you know that? He wasn't ready to speak.

He tried to lift his head, but it was too heavy to budge. Now he could clearly see the woman on his bed. He let his head sink into the pillow and turned his eyes to the ceiling. What he saw was his thigh stuck straight up above him and a pin stuck out of his bandaged knee. The pin and his thigh hung on ropes attached to some sort of apparatus. To make sure it was real, his brain directed his toes to move, and they obeyed. When they moved, his leg ached, but, to his great surprise, the pain was gone.

His mind was ready to speak, but was prevented by a dry throat and lips that stuck together. The kind woman dabbed his mouth with a cool cloth, and he tentatively licked his lips.

"Do you think you could drink some water?" She held the straw to his lips, and Ibrahim took a large drink. He let the cold water soothe his throat and swallowed.

"Okay, that's enough for now," the woman said and took the cup away. "How do you feel?"

Ibrahim looked around the room and saw other beds, full of children. "Where did he go?"

"Where did who go, Ibrahim?"

"The man. Where did he go?"

He watched the woman look around the room and back to him and smile. "There is no man here, Ibrahim. Just me and the other nurses. We have been with you the whole time."

"No," he said defiantly. "The man that was here. Where did he go?"

"Ibrahim, it's okay. You are just waking up from surgery, and sometimes the medicine can make you feel funny in the head."

"No!" he almost screamed. "The man came here and was walking around all of us. He knew my name. He told me he was here with me and that everything was going to be okay. He touched me, and my pain went away."

"I just don't know, Ibrahim, but everything really is going to be okay."

***

Nick was ecstatic to see his best friend and felt a loud pop in his back when Buck swept him off the ground in a giant bear hug. Even with his leg prostheses, Buck was nimble and strong.

"I think you've lost some weight," Buck said, setting Nick down for only a moment before swooping him into another hug. "Yep, for sure you've lost some weight." Buck nodded and set him down again.

Nick had been standing inside the compound gates with Ali and Dr. Lee, anxiously awaiting Buck's arrival.

"Man, I was starting to get worried about you," Nick said, glancing at his watch. "It's almost ten, and the sun set hours ago. The two trucks of supplies arrived this afternoon. I thought you'd fallen off the back of the truck and been left behind."

"The soldiers I rode with needed to drop some supplies off at the hospital in Van," Buck explained. "I told them I wanted to go with them and sent our trucks on ahead."

"How was the trip?"

"Long…and uneventful." Buck laughed. "I was rewarded with a comfy little Huey ride and then slammed with a not so comfortable jeep ride."

"Let me introduce you to the crew," Nick said. "Buck, this is Ali Hassan, my trauma fellow…no…my very able partner from the MED."

Ali smiled at Buck and shook his hand. "Sir, we are so glad to see you. Thank you for bringing all our tools. We have been working in conditions much like a century ago."

"My pleasure, Ali. It's the least I could do."

"Ali and the rest of the team have already been sorting through the supplies, organizing them, and putting instrument trays through the sterilizer for the morning," Nick said.

"As a matter of fact, we will start using them first thing tomorrow," Ali added. "We'll stabilize the open fractures with external fixators. Once we've fixed all the open fractures, then it's on to the huge backlog of closed breaks."

"Glad I can help." Buck shook his hand again.

"Buck, this is Dr. Lee," Nick said. "She is the most amazing person I know and has kept us all in line."

"Nick told me about you over the phone and what an incredible job you have done…"

"Okay, I have things to do." She shook his hand, added a brisk, "Nice to meet you," and walked off into the courtyard.

Buck looked at Nick and grinned. "She really is the Energizer Bunny."

"You'll meet the rest of the team at breakfast. Right now, most everyone has hit the hay. But before I get you settled, I want you to meet the man that has made this whole operation possible—Jack Bilton." He waved to the short man with the white mustache and goatee who had been talking with the UN soldiers guarding the gate. Jack heard his name and, leaning on a cane, limped toward Nick, Buck and Ali.

As soon as he was close enough, Jack grabbed Buck's hand with a strong grip.

"Sir," Buck said, "it's very nice to meet you. Nick has told me all about you and what you have done. Thank you for getting me here."

Jack looked Buck up and down. "You look like a fellow leatherneck." He held tight to Buck's hand. "Thank you, son."

Nick understood what Jack meant as he watched the old man stare down his friend, as he had already told Jack of Buck's sacrifices.

"You're a marine?" Buck asked. "Nick didn't tell me that."

"Well, he didn't know," Jack answered. "Some things we don't necessarily like to talk about. I was Seventh Regiment, First Division. Landed at Inchon during the Korean War."

"The Magnificent Seventh." Buck stepped back and snapped a salute to the man. "Ooh rah!"

Jack smiled broadly. "You give me too much credit," he said and tapped Buck on the chest with his cane. "That was then, this is now."

"Then my salute still stands, sir. Well done," Buck said, extending his arm to include the hospital Jack had built.

***

The candle flickered between Buck and Nick as they sat at a table in the eating area.

"Man, you've got a good group of people working with you," Buck said.

"Yes, and more coming in every day. At this point, I'm having a hard time remembering names," Nick said.

"As tired as you look, I'm surprised you can remember your own." Buck smiled.

"Yeah, thanks."

"Really, Nick...or should I say, Saint Nicholas. Have you looked in a mirror lately?" Buck burst into laughter and quickly covered his mouth when he remembered how close they were to the sleeping quarters.

"Yeah. HA. Like I didn't hear that one all the time in third grade, with a name like Nicklaus."

"But seriously, man, have you looked in the mirror? If your beard gets any whiter, we're really going to have to call you Santa. If you'd told me, I'd have brought some Just For Men so you could color it...look sharp for the ladies." His face turned red as he tried to choke back his laughter.

"You're a real pal, and you're making me feel so much better." Nick rolled his eyes. "When do you go home? I think there's a helicopter leaving first thing in the morning."

Buck raised his hand. "Truce."

They smiled at each other. A little banter couldn't scratch the depth of their friendship, after all they had been through together.

"Man, it's really good to see you, my friend," Buck said, grabbing his arm. "Christmas aside, you're my Saint Nick. How's it really going?"

"Well, not exactly saintly," Nick began and turned away when a surge of anxiety rushed through him like acid reflux. Just seeing Buck reminded him of his failures.

They sat in silence.

Nick puffed up his cheeks with air and blew it out. "What has it been? Nine days since we were eating breakfast and learned of this mess? Oh, yeah, my life has improved by leaps and bounds since you last saw me. As you are so quick to point out." Nick instantly regretted his tone. This was his best friend.

Buck ignored the barb. "I see a whole hospital and courtyard full of patients and hundreds more people outside this gate and they're all thankful you're here. You're a good man, Nick."

"Then why do I feel like such a piece of crap all the time?" he shot back. He looked away, but Buck stared at him. "This anxiety inside me seems to grow day by the day," he said. "I feel older than dirt." He sighed, uncomfortable with Buck's stare.

"Who are you?" Buck asked.

Nick looked into Buck's radiant green eyes and at the large, jagged scar that ran down the left side of his face. Nick would never tolerate any other man asking the tough questions. "Don't you think I've been asking myself that? I hardly recognize myself when I look in the mirror…maybe it's the white beard." He tried to break the tension with a laugh but failed.

"Really, Nick. Who are you?"

"Buck, I'm exhausted." Nick sighed loudly. But his friend would not let up. Neither would his steely stare. "Who am I? I don't know…I guess I'm an orthopedic surgeon…I'm a Christian? I'm a sinner? I don't know, Buck, what are you looking for?"

"Well, those are some good labels you're putting on yourself."

"Yeah, I've got even better ones than those," Nick said, looking at the floor as depression clouded his thoughts.

"Come on, Nick, people look at you and think you have it all. You have the looks, a great career, a super nice car. Women practically throw themselves at you. It's not enough, is it?"

Nick shook his head.

"Nor will it ever be," Buck said with compassion. "Look, you're an incredible doctor. After all, you put me back together, and I've seen what you've done for other patients. I tell people all the time about the kids you fixed in Guatemala, how you restored their lives. That was unbelievable. I think about how you saved Anna when her life hung in the balance back there." Buck sighed. "I just haven't been able to understand why the rest of your life is such a struggle."

Nick blinked back a tear. Buck was right.

"I've been thinking about you all this week and praying for you," Buck said, "and I think I have made a diagnosis, Dr. Hart." He smiled at Nick, who raised an eyebrow, giving him encouragement to finish. "I think you have forgotten who you truly are," Buck continued. "What your true identity is."

He furrowed his brow and shook his head. "I don't know…"

"Nick, it was you that told me how God touched you that night after you saved Anna. You saw the miracles. You tasted God's goodness. I saw how you came up out of the water when I baptized you after Guatemala. Remember that? Remember how you said you felt like a new man? What happened?"

Nick pressed his fingers into his temples. "It's like I know all that. I know it in my head, I'm just not sure it seems so real to me anymore. Like I just don't understand how to love God, how to be intimate with Him."

Buck nodded his head.

"Every time I think I'm gaining, I find myself swamped by life—too busy, too angry, too tired. Or I find myself in someone's sheets or passed out from booze. All I see is the disappointed look of a coach when I pray. I'm not sure I'm even saved anymore. I'm sure if I walked into a church they would throw me out on my ear."

Buck sighed and shook his head. "Well, maybe you would be tossed out by some churches, but not from our Father's house. He doesn't see my sin or yours."

Nick wanted to believe that was true. "Maybe I'm just thick headed or something," he said.

"Or maybe you're just human. You know what, Doctor? I think my diagnosis is correct. You've forgotten who you are. You're living in the wrong story. All that you said and more is why Jesus sacrificed His life. But when He said, 'It is finished,' He meant it—it's finished. That's the story you need to live in—your story starts from a place of victory."

"I'm just not sure I understand."

"Look, Nick, the fight is not out here," Buck said, waving his arms in circles. "It's in here." He thumped two fingers on his forehead. "That's the battle every one of us fights. When you were baptized, you died with Christ and rose with Christ to sit in heavenly places with Him. Christ in you, you in Christ, and together with the Father."

Nick ran his fingers through his hair.

"Unless you know your true identity with God, it's a hard battle to win. I love you, my brother, and I know the Father loves you. Now, let's get you some sleep…you look like crap."

CHAPTER 35

SHARIA LAW

TUESDAY—POST-QUAKE DAY TEN

Abdul knew the plan was brilliant—hiding in plain sight. They had unloaded the trucks that morning, although there was no rush to complete that task. This was their compound and they were in charge. When the hospital was functional, it would become more complicated, but for now, surrounded by a high fence, they might as well have been in an ISIS compound in Syria. Even the guards raised no suspicion in the community, as every hospital in the world used armed guards, always wary of terrorists. It made him smile.

The weaponry was stored in a secure basement room, and only he and Omar Hussein had keys. Abdul sipped a Coke and felt the cool breeze of the air conditioning hit his face. He was in the kitchen of the common area that would someday soon host visiting doctors who would staff the new hospital. Everything smelled of fresh paint, and several electrical outlets still lacked faceplates.

"You will be most comfortable in the new apartments next to the hospital," Omar had told them. He'd even had baskets of fresh fruit placed in each of their rooms and had apologized profusely for being able to run the generator for only an hour each day. He hoped it would be enough time to shower and enjoy the air-conditioning in the heat of the day.

Abdul took another sip of Coke. His thoughts were interrupted when CNN began to report an attack at the Istanbul International Airport. Abdul reached for the remote and turned up the volume.

"It is now confirmed that at least forty-one people are dead and another forty seriously wounded after this horrendous attack," the reporter said. She wore a red dress showing her cleavage and tossed her blond hair back from the wind. Emergency vehicle lights flashed behind her.

Abdul recoiled. Had they no sense of decency? She should cover herself up.

"Three men stepped out of a taxi here at the passenger terminal," the reporter continued, "firing at random, killing many as they were saying good-byes to loved ones. One of the assailants entered the terminal and threw three hand grenades into the security area. He was shot by police, but before he died, he detonated a large bomb strapped to his chest, resulting in a massive explosion that killed and injured many more people. The police kept two more assailants from entering the airport, but they detonated their suicide bomb vests directly outside the terminal."

Abdul sighed deeply and turned the volume down, as he fought the urge to chastise himself for not being part of the attack. The attack had to have come from the Cizre office. Only a few days ago, he had shared tea with three of the men who just gave their lives for Allah. They were heroes. His stomach churned with fear and regret.

He frowned at his comfortable surroundings and shook his head. Would his brother be pleased? Would his father? For that matter, would Allah be pleased? This did not feel like jihad. He should have been there.

CNN showed a video of a suicide vest exploding. Why didn't the men in Cizre say anything? None of them had acted like their days were numbered. *Allah, bless them for their courage.*

"Did you see the news?" asked the White Snake behind him.

He turned and smiled with pride for his brothers in arms, but his smile quickly faded when he saw her. He looked her up and down. She had shed her burka and was wearing a blue scarf that accentuated her blue eyes, but it was her sheer, white blouse through which he could see an undergarment that appalled him. Her tight jeans made him scowl.

Akleema caught his fierce appraisal. "I'm sorry you disapprove, but Omar told me this is how I should dress when we distribute food this afternoon," she said. "This is how the locals dress."

"Yes, but they are Kurds," Abdul complained, crossing his arms. "They do not follow Sharia law."

"I'm sorry, Abdul. You need to remember that we must try to fit in. Remember that my passport is British, and this is how I would dress back home."

"You would?"

"Well, for the most part."

"I don't think it is appropriate or pleasing to Allah," he scolded.

"I suppose I could change, if you like."

He looked at his watch and was surprised to see how late it was. They would have to leave in thirty minutes. "Suit yourself," he said, unable to resist a glance of her breasts.

Akleema took a shawl from the back of the couch and wrapped it around her shoulders. "I'll wrap up in this until we go. Is that all right?"

He gave her a slight nod.

"Do you mind if I have a Coke?" she asked and waited to open the refrigerator.

Again, he gave her a slight nod. He liked the fact that the infamous White Snake was asking for his permission. *Just how it should be.*

"Do you follow Sharia law?" he asked, as she sat down in a chair across from him.

The Coke fizzed as she pulled back the tab. "I try to. Like every good Muslim, I suppose. I mean I know the five pillars of Islam: to declare my faith by reciting Shahada, to pray five times a day, to fast during Ramadan, to give to the poor, and, of course, to make the pilgrimage to Mecca."

"Have you been to Mecca?" he asked.

"I'm afraid I have not. But I know many other parts of Sharia law, like my hand can be cut off if I steal, and if I denounce my faith I can be put to death. What do you think?"

"I think the only way we can be acceptable to Allah is to follow Sharia law completely. Isn't that what we are fighting for—to create the Islamic State where we can live in peace under the law?"

"Is that why you disapprove of how I'm dressed?"

"Of course. I don't think Allah will bless us unless we follow Sharia carefully."

"So, you don't think a woman should drive, or that a woman should have only one husband while her husband can have four wives?"

He watched her face flush.

"Or a man can marry a young woman and consummate the marriage when she is nine years old?" Her voice grew louder. "Are you one that believes a woman should be circumcised… mutilated and cut?"

She was angry, and he let her stew—enjoying watching her discomfort.

She tried staring him down but finally looked away.

Even though the White Snake was four years older, Abdul wanted to make sure she understood he was in charge. She may be known for slicing the throats of two infidel apostate journalists who criticized Islam, but this was his time.

***

The mob near the mosque was just as wild and rowdy as when Abdul and the White Snake had entered the city, but after hospital security and the local police had established order, the food and water distribution was going smoothly. Akleema was positioned at one of the trucks and Abdul at another. Omar stood beside the third. Omar had choreographed their positions to show the city how the international community had come to its aid. He wanted to showcase Abdul and Akleema as friends to the region. Other men from the hospital and from Abdul's team stood alongside the trucks or inside them, pushing the supplies forward.

The White Snake glanced at Omar. She could tell he was in his element. He looked like a grand politician stumping for mayor. It was clear he understood his role and was playing it to the hilt. She was surprised to hear that he spoke Kurdish well and even knew the names of many people in the city. A Kurdish man dressed in an old green military uniform embraced Omar and patted him on the back.

Abdul had been uneasy at the start of the task, not looking at the people, acting as if they carried leprosy. But she was thankful he had relaxed when the people shook his hand with gratitude and women handed him flowers.

She was surprised at how courteous and grateful most of the people were, even in their desperation. A woman with her head covered by a beautiful fuchsia floral scarf and wearing a matching dress approached Akleema. When she handed the woman a large bag of rice, the woman looked at her with dark eyes and a white smile. "Thank you," she said in English. "God bless you."

Akleema smiled back. "You speak English?"

The woman blushed. "Just little. Thank you," she said again but was jostled out of line by the man behind her. A soldier at Akleema's side took the man to task for his impatience. As the line readjusted, Akleema watched Abdul hand over a case of water. *What a baby face. He probably can't even grow a beard. Probably compensating by forcing his authority because he doesn't have the temperament to be a jihadist.*

She knew she shouldn't let him get to her. Still, she worried that his inexperience and impulsivity would get them all in trouble. She preferred to work with women, although it was easier to manipulate men, and she was very good at that. Even at six years old, when her uncle began molesting her, she knew she would use her wiles to her advantage. And she did. She had balanced the scales when she convinced her uncle to pay for five years at the university. It was, in part, because of that man that she had turned to Islam, away from the pious BS that he had espoused.

Abdul glanced at her, nodded, and turned to accept a case of water from a worker in the back of the truck.

Akleema nodded back and reflected on her first encounter with Abdul in Syria. With his short-cropped hair, full dark eyebrows, and eastern complexion, she'd thought him very handsome with tight, casual jeans and white T-shirt clinging to his tall, slender frame. Even though he was a few years younger, she could imagine being with him and smiled to herself.

A man standing in front of her and demanding something interrupted her thoughts. The man had elbowed his way to the front of the line, and she tried not to scowl at his rudeness. She turned to the inside of the truck and grabbed three plastic bags of food. She had intended to give all three to the man, but when he grabbed for them, she put two of them back, and with a satisfied smirk gave him only one.

When he protested vociferously, Akleema turned to the policeman next to her, who understood and instantaneously shoved the man out of line.

"Oink, Oink," Akleema said under her breath.

CHAPTER 36

DECISION TO STAY

Nick sat with Ali and Buck on the hospital retaining wall that had become their haven of respite. For the most part, the patients in the courtyard respected their space. Nick figured Dr. Lee had something to do with that. Both he and Ali were in their scrubs and between cases. Buck was in his army fatigue pants and a tight white T-shirt that accentuated his muscular chest.

Buck jumped from the wall and his expression turned to alarm. "Did you guys feel that?"

Nick and Ali shrugged and smiled at each other.

"Feel what?" Nick teased.

Buck shook his head. "I don't know how you guys survive this. Every time I feel the ground move, my mind flashes with the images of the devastation."

"That was a minor shake," Ali said. "They seem to be getting smaller and way less frequent. I hardly notice them anymore."

Nick nodded and took another bite of his sandwich as Buck settled back on the wall. Lunch was greatly improved today. Nick was chowing down on a peanut butter and banana sandwich to celebrate Jack's acquisition of bananas, flown in by one of the many helicopters making trips back and forth from Ankara. He hoped the potassium in the bananas would help his muscle cramps. "I haven't seen the main part of the city yet. What's it like?" he asked Buck between bites.

"Honestly, it's hard to even describe," Buck shook his head. "Jack let me Skype Katy last night after we got in, and I couldn't even begin to tell her. I mean, there is one point where the view looks like the kind of destruction an atomic bomb would cause. As far as you can see, only one or two buildings are still intact. Some buildings pancaked flat on themselves. The craziest thing is most of the structures were shaken so violently that even ten-story buildings were reduced to piles of rubble. Like pieces the size of a basketball. And, my God, the smell!" Buck pinched his nose. "It's everywhere, you can't escape it."

"We understand many people fled to surrounding villages, but even there, they found lots of damage," Nick said. "The UN commander told me that the roads out of this whole region are still closed and may not open for weeks. We're praying that Ali's and his wife's families have survived and fled to safety," Nick added. "We're trying to get caught up on all our patients enough so Ali can get out of here and search for them."

"Man, Ali, Nick told me about your families. I am so sorry. I asked my church to pray for them."

"That is very kind of you, Sergeant."

"Nick told me about that, too, how polite you are. My friends call me Buck. You can call me Buck. Please."

A squadron of three Huey helicopters flew low overhead.

"You may not realize it, but you guys are awful lucky to have this place," Buck said, pointing his thumb to the hospital. "The hospital we visited in Van is a mess. The OR is one large room separated into cubicles by plastic sheets. I can't imagine that's the most sterile environment."

Nick exchanged glances with Ali.

"The commander told me that both the Americans and Israelis are close to getting their mobile hospitals set up," Buck said. "It took 'em a while to get clearance from the Turkish government, and because there's no landing strip, they had to chopper in the facilities one piece at a time."

"So much for the Mobile in MASH," Nick said, taking a bite of a banana.

"But once they're up, they're something else," Ali said with enthusiasm. "I saw one set up in Washington, DC, when I was visiting there. It was just a demonstration, but it had everything."

"Yeah, been there, done that," Buck said and rapped his knuckles against his leg prosthesis. "They saved my life in Iraq. I was so grateful, until they shipped me back home to Memphis, where I barely survived the care." He punched Nick and laughed.

Nick's arm stung. He mouthed the word *ouch* and grabbed his arm. "Guess I shouldn't have tried so hard," he said with a grin.

"Dr. Hart…" Ali began and started again. "Nick. What would you think if we start compiling a list of patients to send to each of those MASH units once they are operational?"

"Man, that's a great idea. At least we could see a glimmer of light at the end of the tunnel."

"Jack thinks we might have the third operating room ready by the end of the week," Ali said.

Nick thought for a moment. "The two orthopods that came in with Buck, one from California and the other…"

"Florida," Ali reminded him.

"Yeah, Florida. Nice guys, by the way. We'll let them earn their stripes for a few days. Tomorrow, I think we should have them wash out the open fractures and put on external fixators. You and I could start the long bone fractures in the main OR in the morning. We could alternate between nailing a femur and a tibia. That way, we could sterilize the particular instruments between cases and move along a little faster."

"That would be great," Ali said.

"I guess our main rate-limiting factor at this point would be the x-ray machine. We'll just have to wheel it back and forth between rooms. I hope those guys are used to sharing."

"Unless Mr. Bilton can get us another unit," Ali said.

"Yeah, just so long as this time we tell the patients what's coming."

Ali and Nick laughed, but Buck looked confused.

Nick swallowed the last of the banana, looked at his watch, and jumped off the wall. "A great story for another time," he told Buck. "Let's have the newbies finish out the day," he said to Ali, "and you and I should start going through the wards and prioritizing the patients. You want men or women?"

"Dr. Hart, you decide."

"No, Ali, you pick."

Buck stood up, exasperated. "Come on, you guys, let's settle this like real men."

He pulled a coin from his pocket, flipped it in the air, caught it, and flipped it onto the back of his other hand. "Heads, Ali, you take men. Tails, Nick, you take women." He uncovered the coin. "Heads. There you go."

"Wait a minute," Nick said and they all laughed. "Okay, I'm going to pop upstairs and get the guys started on the next case, and then I'm off to the women's ward. Buck, what are you doing this afternoon?"

"I'm going to help the UN guys put up another dorm for the kiddos. I can't hammer a steel rod down the middle of a bone, but I can surely pound a nail into wood. They're gonna have to figure out what to do with all these new orphans," he frowned. "It's chaos over there," he said, pointing in the direction of the orphanage. "I might Skype Maggie tonight. We sure could use some advice from her."

"Please send my love when you talk with her," Nick called over his shoulder as he headed to the OR.

***

He should have chosen the men's ward, Nick decided, standing at the threshold of the women's ward, where the buzz of conversation stopped as soon as the women saw him. He never imagined he'd feel so uneasy in a room full of women. His interpreter appeared beside him ready for duty. Even though he was a skinny kid not yet in high school, Nick was glad to have him because he spoke remarkably good English, Turkish, and Kurdish.

"You ready for this?" he asked the boy, who looked as uneasy as Nick felt. "You have a girlfriend?" he asked, trying to make him relax.

The boy averted his eyes and looked at his shoes, one of which was untied. Nick sighed. This might be a long afternoon. He tried again. "Is your family okay?"

The boy looked up and smiled. "That is my mother," he said, "in the back of the room with a bandage on her head."

"Really," Nick said. "This makes it pretty personal. How about the rest of your family?"

"My father and my sister were in the park with me. They are fine, as am I. We are lucky."

"Good, yes," Nick said, surveying the room filled to overflowing with broken women. "You ever get squeamish?"

"I'm sorry, Dr. Hart, I don't know that word."

"Do you pass out when you see blood?"

He eyes grew wide. "I don't know, Dr. Hart. I guess we'll see."

Nick put a hand on the boy's shoulder. "Well, it's okay if you do. I'm not feeling so well myself right now." The boy turned pale with apprehension.

"Okay." Nick smiled. "Let's do this. Why don't you introduce me to your mother?"

Nick followed the boy through the room, smiling and nodding at the women as he passed. They called to him, and the crescendo of questions grew desperate. Nick turned to the boy. "Tell the ladies that everyone will have a turn. Please. Tell them I promise we will get to everyone."

When Nick arrived at the back of the room, he saw a large man squatting in the corner next to the bed of a red-haired woman. He remembered seeing them in the courtyard and thought they were Russian. He smiled at them, and the big man stood.

Nick's interpreter stopped and hugged his mother in the bed next to the Russian couple.

Nick raised the clipboard he carried with patient names, identification numbers, and diagnoses. He looked at the number on a tag attached to the bed. *Sixty-three.* And he ran his finger down the list on the clipboard and matched the number with the woman's name and diagnosis: closed right femur fracture and scalp laceration.

"Hi. My name is Dr. Hart," he said to the boy's mother, and the boy translated. "Can I look at your leg?"

Nick attempted to pull the sheet off her leg, but the woman reflexively pushed the sheet back. He tried again, but she held it tight over her leg. Nick glanced around the room to see that most of the women were covered from head to toe with sheets and head coverings. *Oh right.* "Okay, you guys look away please," he said to the boy and the Russian standing nearby. "Please tell your mother that I can't fix her leg if I can't look at it."

The boy told his mother, then he and the Russian turned their backs. The woman was satisfied, pulled the sheet off her leg, and tucked it between her thighs. "Thank you," she told Nick.

Nick gently squeezed her thigh. It was swollen with the femur obviously shortened and deformed. But there were no breaks in the skin. "Can you wiggle your toes?" he asked, touching her warm, pink toes. He looked at her head and under the bandage. A large scalp wound in her hair was approximated with a couple of crudely placed sutures but appeared to be healing.

Nick sighed. What should he tell her? At the MED, he spent mountains of time explaining the diagnosis and the type of procedure they would do. How they would place a titanium rod down the center of the bone from the hip to fix the fracture. Because of the legal climate, he would go into considerable detail, describing all the risks associated with the surgery. But here, there was no the time for such explanations, so he simply said, "I am going to fix your leg tomorrow. Is that okay?"

The boy turned back and translated.

His mother nodded enthusiastically and kissed Nick's hand. He smiled and covered her legs with the sheet. The boy sprang to his mother's side with a big smile.

"You have a good boy," Nick said to the woman, expecting his interpreter to translate.

When the boy didn't say anything, Nick looked at him. "You know how this works."

The boy blushed and wagged his head from side to side and then translated Nick's message. His mother smiled broadly, said something endearing, and hugged her son.

"Tell her not to eat or drink anything after midnight tonight," Nick added, turning to his next patient, the red-haired woman whose uncovered copper hair and crimson lipstick were a startling contrast to the other women in the room.

"You've been very patient," Nick said to her and her gigantic escort.

"*Da*, as a child at Christmas," she said.

Nick laughed. "You speak English?"

"*Da*, like a good Russian."

"Ah, so you are from Russia. The other doctor and I guessed that. What in the world are you doing here?"

"We are having a wonderful time, seeing all the sights, meeting new people." She waved her arm across the room. "Staying in the fanciest hotels, eating gourmet meals, dancing—"

Nick found her sarcasm refreshing and laughed. "Okay, okay, I get it. Welcome to the Hotel California," he said.

"*Da*, what a lovely place," she finished the line from the Eagles' song.

Nick looked surprised. "And you know American music."

"Of course, Doctor. We have karaoke, you know. I am quite a star."

Was she flirting with him? He cleared his throat. "I am Dr. Hart." He reached out to shake her soft and supple hand.

"I am Antasha Katrina Volkova, but you can call me AK."

"A…K?" Nick didn't understand.

"AK. Like the AK-47. I was named after my uncle, who invented it."

"Really?" Nick asked.

"*Da*."

The way she smiled, Nick wasn't sure if she was serious or not. He turned to the big man and shook hands. Nick's hands were large, but they were dwarfed by the Russian's. "And you are?"

"I am Vladimir Molotov. You can call me Vladimir Molotov. I have no famous ancestor."

The man looked so serious, Nick couldn't read him. The man's prominent jaw, large nose, and oversized brows did not offer a clue.

"Are you husband and wife?"

"No," AK said definitively. "Vlad is my travel friend."

Nick thought he saw the man's massive neck tense. "Well, I'm sorry you have to be here." He looked at the number on her bed, then at the clipboard. "You have a tibia fracture, I see."

Nick started to reach for her sheet to pull it back, but

Antasha threw it off before he could touch it. Her hospital gown rode high at her waist. Now it was Nick's turn to be modest. He blushed and quickly pulled the gown down.

"No worries, Doctor. I'm not shy."

"But I am," Nick lied. He ran his hands over her upper leg and then down the splint and nodded. "You make this splint?" he asked Vladimir.

"Of course."

"I like the choice of underwear," he said, observing the panties Vladimir had used to hold the splint on her leg.

"So that's where they went," AK teased.

Nick asked her to wiggle her toes to check if she felt his touch and assess that status of the nerves in her leg.

"Oh, *da*, your touch is very gentle," she said. Her aqua-blue eyes shone like sapphires against her fair porcelain skin, and she twisted a strand of red hair. "What will you do for me?" she asked.

"Look," he said, swallowing hard and getting down to business. "You have a fracture of the tibia, your shin bone. We need to get x-rays, but I'm pretty sure it would be best to fix your leg."

Antasha looked at Vladimir. "We were kind of hoping to get out of here. Not that we don't appreciate your hospitality in this quaint little resort, but…"

"I understand. But I'm not sure the UN has the resources to transport people out yet. They are so busy getting supplies in."

"We may have the resources," Vladimir put in.

Nick nodded and wondered who these people truly were. "I understand, but one of the things to think about is that it may not be super healthy for you to travel right now with your broken leg. You have been sitting around for the last ten days, and your chances of forming a blood clot are rising by the day. Flying just increases that risk."

Antasha looked at Vladimir again, then at Nick. "When would you do the surgery?"

Nick shrugged and looked at the schedule on the clipboard. "Well, you could be number two on tomorrow's list if you want." He riffled through the many pages on the clipboard.

"Is this something you know how to do?" AK asked Nick.

He smiled at her. "Well, you will be my second at least. That's why they call it the practice of medicine."

"Oh, and my doctor is funny as well as handsome."

He smiled. "I am a trauma surgeon at a trauma hospital in Memphis, Tennessee. It's something I do day in and day out."

She looked impressed. "You work on Elvis?"

"No, I'm not that old," Nick said. "But speaking of old, I operated on a woman today who kept telling us she was 169. We figured she was just confused, but the crazy thing is, she was as sharp as a tack and very healthy. I told her once we got her fixed up, she might live to be two hundred." He chuckled.

The Russians looked at each other without cracking a smile. Maybe they didn't understand.

"Did she say where she was from?" Vladimir asked.

Nick thought for a moment. "I don't know. It sounded like Hakery or something."

"Hakkâri?" Vladimir asked.

Nick looked surprised. "Yes. She said it was a small village near there."

When the Russians said nothing more, Nick decided it was time to move on to the next patient. "Well, you guys think about it for a minute and let me know what you want to do. I have a few more patients to see," he said, waving the clipboard. He put his hand on the shoulder of his interpreter, who'd been standing by quietly. "Come on, my friend, places to go, people to see."

"Sign me up," Antasha called as he turned away. This time she was not looking at Vladimir. "Please fix me up, Doctor."

"I didn't mean to be such a good salesman." He turned back and smiled.

She flipped her copper hair back with one hand. "I trust you, Dr. Hart."

CHAPTER 37

THANKSGIVING
WEDNESDAY—POST-QUAKE DAY ELEVEN

It was a sweltering day and Abdul appreciated the luxury of air conditioning. It was easier to concentrate on the mission, but he knew the hour of power Omar had allotted them would be ending soon. He unplugged his phone from the charging outlet to send his message before the diesel generator powered down.

His brother had told him not to communicate until they were safely settled. There was too much at stake and too much at risk to have their convoy detected and eliminated, should an errant message fall into the wrong hands. But now the time was right, and he was exhilarated and anxious to announce their arrival.

He scrolled through to the end of his apps and found the one he had downloaded just before leaving Syria: Telegram. He pressed his finger on the blue dot and paper-airplane logo. The messenger app, developed by Russian brothers, opened quickly. The Russians had developed the communication app to prevent government surveillance, and ISIS had promptly appropriated it as a means of communicating without detection.

Telegram allowed Abdul up to five thousand contacts, but his account had only one—his famous brother. He couldn't help feeling proud; others would be jealous that he had direct contact with the second in command of the Islamic State.

His brother had instructed him to set the message to self-delete in five minutes to make it that much more difficult to track. Abdul did as he was instructed. Then he began to type.

My brother, journey is complete and we are safely in Hakkâri.

He paused. They hadn't talked about exactly how to communicate. Abdul was afraid to disappoint his oldest brother and didn't want to mess up. When they were children, Abbas always seemed slightly annoyed at him. Even at their father's funeral, Abdul had wanted to cry, until he caught the disapproving look from his brother: *Don't you dare.* Abdul wanted his brother's approval. This was his moment of glory and he was so excited to share the news of their triumphant entry into Turkey.

He reconsidered his message. Abbas did tell him not to use names. Abdul highlighted and deleted what he had typed.

Then, out of the blue, something occurred to him. It was a happy memory, and he smiled. Although Thanksgiving Day was an American tradition, once a year his father had brought home a large turkey, and the entire family celebrated with a bountiful feast. His father had started the practice after seeing an American movie, *An Old-Fashioned Thanksgiving.* His brother vehemently disapproved of American movies and American holidays. But when one of the leading sheikhs came out with an Islamic ruling that it was not prohibited for Muslims to celebrate Thanksgiving, his brother's dissention fell on deaf ears. His father had always argued that it was wise to gather the whole family to thank Allah for his great goodness, and what better way than with a wonderful dinner. Before and after the sheikh's proclamation, everyone in Abdul's family, including Abbas, had enjoyed the annual feast.

Abdul's mouth watered at the memory, but he put his hunger aside. He had found the perfect cryptic message. He started typing again. His message would be short and simple. His brother could ask questions later, if he wanted. Abdul read his message:

Thanksgiving dinner is set. Please send more food.

He sent the message, smiled, and put his phone in his pocket.

"Everything okay?" Akleema interrupted him.

"Yes, just sending a message to my brother through Telegram," he shrugged nonchalantly.

"And?" she asked.

"And I'll tell you when you need to know."

She stared at him, and he forced himself to hold her icy gaze until she turned away to observe the two men on the other side of the room.

The men stood in what Omar had called the "bunker." Eventually, the reinforced brick building that sat away from all the other structures would hold large tanks of medical-grade oxygen, nitrogen and other gases used in a hospital. For now, the team would use it to manufacture an explosive, TATP.

"TATP," Akleema murmured. "The mother of satan."

"What?" he asked.

"That is what my friends in London are calling the explosive."

"TATP." Abdul was sure he understood explosives better than the woman. "You mean triacetone triperoxide?"

She smiled and nodded. "We used it in the London bombings."

They watched as the men carefully added the acetone to the hydrogen peroxide to a glass container and placed the container in an ice bath. One of the men pulled the thermometer out of the water, looked at it, and nodded to the other.

His partner sucked up a pipette of clear fluid from another beaker and released it gently, one drop at a time, into the glass container. His comrade closely watched the thermometer. "*Tawaqquf*, stop," he said and held his hand out.

"What are they doing?" Akleema asked.

"They are adding the battery acid to the acetone and hydrogen peroxide. The reaction begins to produce heat, but they have to keep the temperature below ten degrees Celsius."

"What happens if it goes over that?"

"If that happens, we don't want to be here to see it."

The man watching the thermometer nodded to the other, "*Hasanana*, okay," and the other continued to add the acid, drop by drop.

"What will they do next?" Akleema asked.

"They will finish putting in the acid and keep the mixture in ice overnight, then filter the white precipitate out on a paper towel."

"That's it?" Akleema acted surprised at how easy it was to make.

"Well, yes. But the TATP is quite unstable. Frequently, you hear of people blowing themselves up accidentally. Any shock, friction, or flame will ignite the crystals, and the crystals are nearly as powerful as TNT. You saw what just happened at the airport." He paused and glowered at her. "It is one of our tools to usher in the apocalypse."

The curiosity in her eyes became fear. "Do you really think we are near the end of days?"

"Of course, only Allah knows," he said, "but there are certainly signs. And the only way to know is if we establish the caliphate. My brother believes that we may be seeing the Mahdi, the prophesied redeemer of Islam, within the year."

"And he is to rule Islam for seven years and lead us to victory before the end of the world?"

"Yes, something like that. Then the armies of Rome will attack us in Dabiq, Syria, and that is where we will defeat them."

"The armies of Rome?" she asked. "But the Pope has no army."

"Most believe Rome to be the old Eastern Roman Empire—the capital of which is Istanbul."

Abdul read a look of understanding on her face.

"Oh, the airport," she said.

Abdul nodded. "*Rome* means the Western countries as well. So much of what we are doing around the world is to provoke the infidels to attack us in Dabiq."

"What is supposed to happen after the battle of Dabiq?"

"Our caliphate will expand and conquer Istanbul once again."

"That doesn't sound like the end of days."

"That is when things get interesting." His heart pounded. "The anti-Messiah, the Dajjal, will rise from Iran. A great battle will rage between true believers and the Dajjal and his troops until our brothers are cornered in Jerusalem. Only five thousand will be left. Just as the Dajjal is about to be victorious, Jesus will return, spear Dajjal, and lead our people to victory."

"Jesus?"

He frowned with disgust. *Stupid woman.* "You really need to read your Qur'an."

The White Snake looked at the floor.

Abdul saw her contrition and felt pity for her. He would have to be patient with her ignorance. He took a breath and said, "Now can you see the importance of what we are doing?"

He took his phone from his pocket and typed *Turkey* into the Google search engine. When the map came up, he touched the screen and turned it to Akleema. "Look at the three main roads that go east and west through the caliphate."

Starting at the southern area of the Middle East, he traced his finger over the map. "Just about every major road out of Iran into Iraq goes through Baghdad and then through Ramadi and straight to Jerusalem. The next major route is north of that. It goes through Mosul and then splits into the main thoroughfares of northern Syria and southern Turkey."

He looked at her to make sure she was following.

"Doesn't the Islamic State control Ramadi and Mosul?" she asked.

"Yes. Now you are seeing. The next major route is here, the most northern one," he said, pointing his index finger. "It starts in Tehran and goes through Tabriz, and then here." He paused his finger.

"Hakkâri!" Akleema exclaimed.

"Yes, and on to Istanbul. The Western pigs are using the Kurds to do their dirty work. Most of the Kurds are coming out of Iran and northern Iraq and eastern Turkey to fight our brothers and sisters. As we control this area, we control a major artery for the flow of Kurdish troops and their supplies."

Abdul heard the large generator power down and the air conditioning stop. One of the men working on the TATP told the other to hurry. He could see the man's hands shake as the acid dripped into the glass beaker.

"We should continue this discussion later," he said, opening the door. "It's time to get out of here."

CHAPTER 38

THE MAN IN WHITE

Ali stood at the end of a bed in the children's ward and checked his clipboard, although the child's injury was obvious. The boy with the femur fracture hung in skeletal traction, his fractured thigh suspended by the traction pin. His knee was bent at ninety degrees and parallel to the bed, and his calf was suspended in a sling. The boy stared wide-eyed at him as Ali adjusted the weights hanging off the end of the bed that pulled on the boy's leg and added another pound of weight. An x-ray taken that morning had shown the femur was still too short.

"*Selamünaleyküm*, may God's peace be upon you," the boy said to Ali.

Ali looked at the boy's face. It looked familiar. He smiled and said, "*Aleykümselam*, peace be upon you. You have very good manners, young man. How is your leg feeling?"

"It only hurts when they move me, sir."

"You mean like what I just did to it?"

"No, sir. More like when they wash me or put me on the bed pan."

"I'm sorry." Ali nodded. He sat on the edge of the bed and put his hand on the boy's stomach and began gently palpating. He could feel the boy's colon was full of stool and made a mental note to ask the nurses to give the child a suppository and stool softener. He ran his hand over the boy's chest and could feel his heart pound through bony ribs and wondered how much weight he'd lost.

He realized that in all the chaos, the staff had been in lifesaving mode. Now that things were somewhat under control, it was time to become a physician again and care for the person, not just the bone. He would ask Mr. Bilton to fly in chocolate milk for the kids, something that his own daughters loved.

He picked up the boy's arms one at a time and squeezed down the length of each one, noting that the boy did not wince. "Do you hurt anywhere else?"

The boy shook his head. Ali squeezed the boy's neck and ran his hand over his head, then patted his cheek. His two girls would be about the same age. Maybe he and Astî should try for a boy. *Wouldn't that be wonderful?* The joyous thought crossed his mind only to be canceled by another. Maybe they were too old. His shoulders slumped and he sighed. How he missed his family.

"Are you eating?" he asked the child.

The boy shook his head.

"Tell me your name again."

"Ibrahim," the boy said shyly.

"Oh, yes. Ibrahim." Ali now recognized him. "I have good news for you, Ibrahim. Your friend that you were sitting with in the courtyard opened her eyes today. She still has a long way to go to get better, but that is good improvement."

"Maybe I can ask the man to go visit her," Ibrahim said.

"The man?"

"Yes, the man in white clothes who visits me when I sleep. When he is here, my leg doesn't hurt. Maybe he can go and sit with her too."

He looked at Ibrahim, whose face was so sincere. Trauma could do strange things to people. He remembered a woman with a bad head injury that he had helped care for in the ICU at the MED. As she awoke from her coma, she screamed and screamed for Stacie. When the woman had finally come to her senses, the staff asked her who Stacie was. The woman had no idea. Being a trauma surgeon, Ali was also fascinated by the reports of the blind women who had come out of the horrors in Cambodia. When their eyes had been examined, they were found to be perfectly healthy, but because of the atrocities they had witnessed, their brains had simply turned off their eyes. The women had chosen to no longer see.

Maybe the boy's brain was choosing to see this man.

The boy stared at him with anticipation and Ali smiled at him and said, "That would be kind of you to send the man to see her," Ali said.

Ibrahim smiled but then his expression turned fearful, and his eyes welled with tears. "No one can tell me about my parents. What has happened to my mother and father and my sister?"

He stroked Ibrahim's hair and then his face. "I'm so sorry, Ibrahim. I don't know about your parents. You and I are in the same situation, I'm afraid. I don't know what has become of my mother and father either." He brushed a tear from his own eye, then wiped the tears running down Ibrahim's cheeks.

"*Yarhamuka Allah*, may Allah have mercy on you…on us." He leaned over and kissed Ibrahim's forehead. "Maybe we will hear something soon."

He stood up and made a note on the clipboard across from Ibrahim's name to increase his nutrition and place him on a bowel program.

"I will come back later to check on you, Ibrahim." He smiled and patted the boy's chest. He turned to the next bed, but stopped and turned back. "Did the man who visits you tell you his name?"

Ibrahim answered without pause. "Jesus. He told me his name is Jesus."

***

Vladimir hated needles and was glad he was lying down. Otherwise, he would have collapsed at the sight of the offending instrument. "Can't you use a smaller needle?" he asked the nurse when she removed it from the package.

"Why are you hunky men always the biggest babies?" the stout black nurse asked. "Where are you from?"

"Russia, a little town called Moscow. You ever heard of it?" he said sarcastically and looked away. If he saw his own blood, he would pass out. "And you?"

She hooted. "The big man is funny. Me, I'm from another little town called Atlanta. You ever hear of that?"

Vladimir grimaced as a needle stuck his hand. "Ouch," he groaned.

"Oh, stop it!"

Sweat dripped down his neck and he felt her working on the back of his hand. Trying to ignore the discomfort, he changed the subject. "The Atlanta Falcons?"

"You do know," she said, continuing to work on his hand. "You play any football? It sure looks like you could."

"American football is for sissies. I played Russian rugby."

"Okay, tough guy, you ready for the big stick?"

"No," he said and pulled his hand away. When he looked at his hand, he realized the IV was taped in place. "Wow. You're good, funny lady."

"You be good now, and I'll be back to get you shortly."

Vladimir watched her leave the surgical pre-op room.

Dr. Lee had told him that his wound needed to be washed out in the operating room. He had told the Chinese woman he didn't want that, but after talking it through with AK, he decided it was the right thing to do. Even with antibiotics, the pain was gnawing at him like a toothache, and his shoulder smelled bad.

"None of my business how you got shot," Dr. Lee had said, "but you need to be taken care of."

"I was just trying to find gas after the quake to get AK to a hospital," he had explained.

She had looked at him above her dirty glasses. "You kill someone?"

He reassured her that he had not, and she seemed satisfied, so the subject was dropped. He had been relieved until he realized that he would become a pincushion. The surgeon had told him he would wash the wound and debride some of the dead tissue, after which Vlad would be put on IV antibiotics for a few days until they got on top of the infection.

He was resigned to the fact that he would be separated from AK, even though only by one hospital floor; he was in the men's ward on the first floor, and she was in the women's on the second. He guessed it would be okay. The women and nurses were getting more annoyed with his constant vigil anyway, but he hated that he and AK would be in surgery at the same time in different rooms.

He worried about AK and hoped she was doing okay. The nurses had taken her into the main operating room a few minutes ago. If AK trusted the doctor, he could as well.

***

Nick was in the recovery area to check on the Russian woman, who slept comfortably on the OR gurney after her surgery. He put his hand to his chin, betting she turned heads everywhere she went.

He was relieved her surgery had gone so well. After receiving a titanium nail down the middle of her tibia to reduce and stabilize the fracture, she would need to use crutches only for a few weeks and could bear her own weight as tolerated. The bone would be completely healed in a couple of months.

The rest of the day had also gone well, alternating cases in the main OR with Ali. He was relieved to start on the huge surgical backlog, but was frustrated that the main OR had only completed eight surgeries. At this rate, it would take until next year to finish all the cases. He urgently needed to talk with Jack about getting the third OR up and running, and he hoped the US and Israeli mobile hospitals would soon be ready to accept some patient transfers.

Nick gently lifted the sheet covering the woman's leg and held her toes on the fractured side. Her toes were pink and warm. He bent them slightly backward to check for compartment syndrome, the one possible serious complication after nailing the tibia. The reaming and subsequent bleeding of the bone in the surrounding muscle could increase the pressure in the compartments of the muscle to the point that it cut off the blood supply. When he touched her toes, she didn't react with pain. He knew she was going to be all right.

When he began to pull the sheet back over her leg, she stirred.

"Oh," she moaned sleepily, still in a post-anesthesia fog. "Doctor. How did it go?"

"Hi, AK. How are you feeling?"

"Like someone drove a darn stake into my leg," she said. "Was that you?" She tried to focus her eyes.

Nick touched her arm. "Everything went well today. I know you're pretty sore, but we'll get you up first thing tomorrow and have you start taking a few steps."

"Really? And running a marathon the next week?"

Nick laughed. "Not quite that fast. You ever run a marathon?"

"No, but I expect to, now that I have a bionic leg."

"I guess I should have put a spring in there instead," Nick teased. But she had already drifted back to sleep and missed his joke. He squeezed her arm and began to walk away when he heard her call to him. He turned and saw her eyes were open.

"Dr. Hart?" she said, licking her dry lips. "Can I have some water?"

Nick found a glass of water with a straw on the tray beside her bed and held the straw to her lips. She took a sip.

"Dr. Hart, I have a secret," she said, fighting to keep her eyes from closing. "Come closer so I can whisper."

When he bent his ear to her face to hear her, she planted a kiss on his cheek. "Thank you, Dr. Hart, for saving my life."

He turned, raised his head slowly, and smiled.

"You are so handsome," she sighed.

Although she was flirty with or without the drugs, anesthesia replicated what was once called truth serum and sometimes made patients goofy in recovery.

"We fixed your leg," he said matter-of-factly. "Nothing to it. No lifesaving miracle, but you're welcome."

"Well, if we find what we are looking for, now I can live forever with my good leg."

"A good-looking leg," he tried teasing back, but her eyes drifted closed and then snapped back open like a sleepy drunk.

"I shouldn't tell you this," she said, turning serious. "We were sent here to look for the tree of life."

Nick laughed. "That's just the drugs talking. You need to get some rest."

"Seriously," she insisted with clarity. "Do you believe…do you believe we could live forever?" Then her eyes closed and her voice faded. "Mr. Putin…the tree…" She drifted into sleep before she could say more.

***

"What a day." Ali sighed as he, Nick, and Buck snacked in the cafeteria. The room was lit with candles, and the evening breeze carried the aroma of freshly baked cookies. Someone in the courtyard strummed a guitar. Life was beginning to bloom at King's Hospital.

"How's the new construction for the orphans going?" Nick asked Buck.

"It's amazing what an army of soldiers and the money to back them up can build. We're like the Amish at a barn raising. Couple more days like today, we'll be able to move the kids in and get them out of the elements."

"That's wonderful," Ali said.

"Maggie says hi," Buck told Nick. "And sends her love back to you, too."

"So you did get to talk with her, then?" Nick said. "I bet she had some good suggestions for you."

Buck smiled. "Yeah, like kick your butt for not calling her more."

"Always have my back, don't you?" He smirked. He waited for another smart remark, but Buck just sat there grinning at him until he could stand it no longer. "What?"

"Oh, nothing," Buck said smugly. "But she was helpful. A whole bunch. She's sending an email with all the protocols and procedures she's written over the years in Guatemala."

"Who is Maggie?" Ali asked.

"Maggie Russell is a friend in Guatemala," he said. "My best friend, John, was her husband. They started the Hope Center in Quetzaltenango. John was killed by the North Koreans in that bioterrorist fiasco three years ago," he explained. "When John found out what they were doing, they murdered him. Then they released that stupid virus anyway."

"Oh, yes," Ali nodded. "I knew you were involved in that. I'm sorry about your friend."

"Thanks, Ali. I hope you get a chance to meet Maggie someday. She's something—full of spunk. I don't know if you've heard, but we now rotate our fifth-year residents through the Hope Center."

"I understood they rotated through a mission hospital in Central America. Now I see the connection."

Nick looked at Buck. There was something he wasn't telling him. "Buck, if you don't wipe that smirk off your face, so help me God, I'll do it for you." He raised his fist to Buck in mock revenge and said to Ali, "Buck thinks that Maggie and I would make beautiful music together."

"And?" Ali asked.

The question surprised Nick. Maybe Ali finally saw him as more of a friend. "And...it's pretty complicated. I'm just not sure I can fill John's shoes."

"Someone is afraid of intimacy," Buck added under his breath.

"I'll show you the intimate part of my fist." Nick wagged his fist at him again.

The men laughed together.

"I thought all the surgeries went well today," Ali said.

Nick dropped his fist and turned to Ali. "Yeah, eight down and a million more to go," he lamented. "Did you see any problems on the ward today between cases?"

"I saw a couple of patients for whom we need to step up the debridement and irrigation of their wounds. They may have to go every day to the OR until they turn the corner. I've already told the new guys." Ali paused. "And one of the little boys you put in skeletal traction on Monday told me today that he has been seeing a man who said his name is Jesus."

Nick looked at Buck, surprised not only by the boy's claim, but how easily *Jesus* rolled off Ali's tongue.

"Jesus?" Buck asked.

"The boy says the man named Jesus is dressed in white and comes and visits the children. He told me that his leg feels better when Jesus is there."

Nick decided they were good enough friends to talk about religion. "You talk so naturally about Jesus. What does your faith say about Him?"

Ali laughed, surprising Nick again. "I get it. What does a good Muslim man like me know about Jesus? Did you know that Jesus is mentioned twenty-five times in the Qur'an?"

"Really?" Buck asked, equally surprised. "Who do Muslims believe that He is?"

"That's a difficult question because there are different beliefs even among Muslims, just as all Christians do not believe the same in all matters. But I would say that most Muslims believe Jesus was born of the Blessed Virgin Mary. The Qur'an says an angel appeared to Mary, and God breathed His spirit into Mary while she was a virgin, and Jesus was given the ability to perform miracles by Allah."

Nick was shocked. "I had no idea."

"What you probably won't like," Ali continued, "is that we are taught Jesus never claimed divinity, nor was he crucified. The Qur'an says it was made to appear to unbelievers that he was crucified, but we believe Allah physically raised Jesus into the heavens."

"And that's a big difference," Buck added.

"Most Muslims believe Jesus will return in the end days and defeat the Dajjal—the anti-Christ."

"Well, we can agree on His return," Buck said. "Jesus is coming back. Evil will be defeated."

"Now would be good," Nick said and finished his drink.

Buck and Ali nodded.

"Until then, I've got to get to bed. We have more long days ahead of us," Nick said.

CHAPTER 39

NO FEAR IN LOVE
FRIDAY—POST-QUAKE DAY THIRTEEN

Nick took his time walking down the outside ramp of the hospital from the third floor OR to the second-floor women's ward. Thursday passed in a blur of surgical activity. They had fixed eight patients on Wednesday and ten on Thursday. He and Ali had gotten an early start this morning with the goal to complete twelve cases. It seemed to work best to alternate cases with Ali so the two of them could catch their breath, make rounds between surgeries, and even have the chance to use the bathroom.

As soon as Nick had spoken with Jack, he'd set his crew in motion, and they were putting the finishing touches on the third OR room. It wasn't fancy, but it would be useful as the dirty room for continuing to wash out the open fractures and infections. More volunteers were slated to arrive tomorrow, and once they had acclimated, all three rooms would be put to full use.

A large crow flew by, followed by two smaller birds in hot pursuit. Birds and animals had an instinct for danger. Nick thought of what his young interpreter had told him about the day of the quake. He had been playing soccer in the park with friends when, just before the quake, he'd seen flocks of birds fly off en masse while dogs howled. "It was like they knew what was coming," the boy had said.

He'd also told Nick that, although he was in the middle of

an open field, it had been impossible to stand. The sound of the quake had been so deafening, it was as if thundering trains were coming at them from all directions. He said the worst part had been the mushroom cloud of dust and debris that blocked the sun and blackened the city. "I thought it was the end of time."

Nick shivered, recalling the terrifying image the boy had evoked, and stopped partway down the ramp to let the morning sun burn off the chill. He closed his eyes and stroked his thickening beard. Tomorrow would be two weeks since the earthquake. *Poor Ali. He still doesn't know what happened to his family.* He had to get out to look for them.

Nick opened his eyes, crossed his arms, and sighed. Maybe it was time for him to give it up and go home next week. But what was he going to return to? The MED? A lawsuit? The booze? The one-night stands? No wonder his life was out of balance. Booze and sex were his go-to painkillers.

He wanted to kick himself. Buck was right. From the outside, it must look like he had it all. Why didn't he feel fulfilled? Why was he so blue all the time? Maybe the stress of the job?

He nodded at three UN soldiers pushing a new OR table up the ramp to the third room.

No, not just stress. He'd barely thought about having a drink or a relationship since he'd come to Turkey, and he was under more stress here than back home. He was doing the same work here as he did at the MED—putting people back together, so that wasn't what made him sad.

Nick thanked the men as they passed. It really did take a community, and that's what they were here, working together for a common goal, a greater purpose than slogging at the MED where it was just a job. He wished he could stay in Turkey a little longer.

As the men pushed the table up the ramp, a man and woman coming down the walkway pressed themselves against the wall. When the men passed, the couple in matching scrubs joined hands and strolled by Nick. He recognized them—one of the new anesthesiologists and his wife, an OR nurse.

"Soaking up some sun?" the anesthesiologist asked Nick.

"Yeah, time to get my Vitamin D levels back up," Nick said.

"I heard the cook was making banana bread. You better come getcha some," the wife said.

"Thanks," Nick said.

The couple wrapped their arms around each other and continued on their way.

As he watched them go, a wave of loneliness swept over him. *It must be so comforting to share something like that.* Buck was right; he was not good at intimacy, not with women and certainly not with God. All week Buck's words had echoed in his heart: "You have forgotten who you are." But the gap had widened between what he understood his life as a Christian to be and the reality of what his life had become. He blamed himself for failing—fearing that he didn't live up to any standards he had set for himself to be acceptable in the eyes of God.

Nick rubbed his eyes. There were plenty of people reminding him of his failures; Antonio Scott currently topped that list. *I wonder what terrible things he's saying about me?* Nick hated he wasn't in Memphis defending his reputation and his team. He did not abandon the mayor's son. The kid's poor decisions were his demise. The mayor's anger had to fill some space, but Nick wished it wasn't his. Scott was the real mystery. *Why does that guy hate me so much?* Anger and fear fought for attention in Nick's mind.

"There is no fear in love."

Nick looked around; he did not hear the statement audibly and it seemed to echo in his heart again. *"There is no fear in love."*

Nick took another moment to let the words and the sun soak into his soul and left the ramp for the second floor. He hoped to find his young interpreter, as he needed help for rounds, but the boy was nowhere in sight. *Maybe he'll be with his mother.*

Entering the women's ward, Nick sighed. Maybe he should Skype Maggie tonight. She was one of the few women he could even talk to about love. Any woman that he would consider spending the rest of his life with would have to measure up to Maggie. She was so strong, adventurous, funny and kind.

Nick waved to his interpreter's mother, but he was not there. Nick looked at his watch and decided to go check on the Russian woman. She spoke English and, come to think of it, she had some of the qualities he admired in Maggie.

When Nick approached Antasha's bed, she was asleep. He paused and watched her breathe. Her dark, full eyebrows and fair complexion made her deep-red hair glow brighter. She wore makeup, having drawn with a painter's flair the smoky gray eye shadow accentuated by crimson lipstick. He couldn't help but notice her ample chest rising and falling with each breath.

Without his interpreter and with no way to communicate with anyone else, he decided to wake her. He touched her arm lightly, and her eyes flickered and opened. She smiled. "*Da*...Dr. Hart." She rubbed the sleep from her eyes "I was just dreaming about you. You and I were dancing in the glorious ballroom of the Grand Palace at the Kremlin to the Moscow Orchestra. You looked so very handsome in your black tuxedo."

"I'm sorry to wake you," he said.

"*Da*, let me sleep so I can get back to my dream and see how it ends." She stretched her arms over her head and yawned. "But now that I have the real thing here with me, I'm satisfied." She smiled at him, showing off her pearly white teeth.

"Have you actually been to the Grand Palace?"

"*Da*, twice. Once working and once as a guest. I wore a beautiful satin blue dress that my escort said matched my eyes perfectly."

"Was that Vladimir?" He was surprised to feel jealous.

Antasha laughed loudly, "Oh, no, my dear doctor. Someone much more important than Vlad. My escort was a foreign dignitary."

"And work...do you work for the Russian government?"

"Yes, for one of the agencies."

When he realized she wouldn't elaborate, he changed the subject. "How is your leg feeling?"

"Sore today. But I was able to get up with the crutches and get to the bathroom myself."

"How much weight are you putting on it?"

"I think just my toes. But when I was in the bathroom, I almost fell and grabbed for my crutches. It scared me. I think I put nearly all the weight on my leg. Do you think it's okay?"

"Let me see," Nick said.

When she pulled the sheet off her legs, her lower leg was bound simply with an elastic wrap. "Shouldn't I have some sort of cast or splint on my leg?" she asked.

"No. The metal rod that we put down the bone is now your cast," he smiled. "It's sort of an internal cast."

He palpated up and down her lower leg. There was no bleeding on the bandage. "Move your ankle back and forth," he said, demonstrating with his wrist. "Good." He squeezed her black-and-blue toes.

"They are so ugly." She cringed.

"I'm sorry they don't match the blue of your eyes," he teased. "But don't worry, it's just blood from your fracture that's going downhill with gravity. Your toes will get back to normal. Can you feel them okay?"

"*Da*." She nodded.

"Everything looks great. Try to put more and more weight on your leg. And don't worry about putting all your weight on it, because the fracture will be fine. Actually, the more weight you put on it, the faster it heals."

"Really?" she hesitated. "Okay. You're the doctor. I will trust you."

Nick pulled the sheet back over her legs. "Anything I can get you?"

"Some nice cognac and caviar, if you please. And the next dance."

They both laughed.

Nick felt comfortable with Antasha, and he thought it was a good time to ask her about what she'd said after her surgery. It had been puzzling him. "What is the tree of life?"

She startled and looked away for the first time. Then she recovered and smiled. "What did that blabbermouth Vladimir tell you?"

"Nothing. It was you who told me about some grand search you're on. It was after surgery in the recovery area."

Her smile disappeared, and Nick regretted the question, afraid he had upset her. He waited for her to say something.

"Sodium pentothal?"

He was surprised she knew the name of the truth serum. "Well, no, but something close to it. A more modern version."

"What else did I tell you?"

He hesitated. He thought about teasing her, making up some illicit spy story, but he could tell she was not in the mood for jokes. "Uh, something about being immortal?" He left out her reference to Putin.

Her face turned red.

This was going nowhere, and he was embarrassing her. "It's okay, Antasha. It's none of my business. I didn't mean to upset you."

She glanced at him, then looked away, crossing her arms.

"You okay?"

She hesitated long enough to make him anxious.

"I'm just trying to decide if I should kill you or not."

He fought the urge to take a step back until a smile crossed her face and gave way to a loud laugh. He chuckled nervously with her.

She was nodding, having come to a decision. "Really, Dr. Hart, I was not supposed to tell you, but you are my doctor." She paused. "I'm told everything between patient and doctor is confidential. Is that true?"

"Of course." Nick was relieved she was talking.

"Then…" Antasha hesitated. "Are you a Christian?"

"Yes." He hadn't expected that.

"What do you know about the tree of life?"

"The one mentioned in the Bible?"

"*Da*, the one in the Garden of Eden."

He searched his memory bank. He'd heard the story when he was a kid in Sunday school. He remembered his class illustrating the story, attaching felt figures of Adam and Eve and a snake to a board. "Didn't God put the tree of life and the tree of the knowledge of good and evil in the middle of the garden, then tell them they could eat from any tree except the tree of the knowledge of good and evil?" he said, half telling and half asking.

"Do you know how the story ends?" she asked.

"Not well. The serpent talks them into eating from the tree of knowledge that they're supposed to avoid."

"And…?"

"God kicks them out of the garden," Nick shrugged.

"Yes. It is the last verse of that chapter in Genesis that made the most powerful man in Russia send us on a crazy task."

"And that is?"

"'Man has now become like one of us, knowing good and evil. He must not be allowed to reach out his hand and take also from the tree of life and eat, and live forever,'" she quoted.

It sounded like nonsense, or a riddle at best, and he almost laughed until he saw the seriousness on her face. "And that man believes the tree of life truly exists? What do you think?"

He watched Antasha look away before answering. "There are things I cannot share with you. But I can tell you that the information is…interesting," she said.

He didn't know what to think. "Are you a Christian?" he asked.

"*Nyet*, no. I am good Russian Jew," she smiled. "My parents were Jewish immigrants that lived outside St. Petersburg. I stopped believing in fairytales a long time ago. But who knows?" She shrugged and grinned. "Maybe we find the tree of life and then I'll believe." Her eyes glistened.

CHAPTER 40

JIHAD

Akleema and Abdul were conferring with Omar in his plush office. Tea had been laid, but no one had touched it. An argument was brewing, and the temperature in the room was rising, physically and emotionally.

The White Snake watched Abdul's face flash with color. When he became agitated, his ears turned red and he bounced his legs. Observing his simmering emotions gave her an idea of how to manipulate him.

Omar sat silently clicking his pen and watching the two spar.

"All I'm trying to say," she told Abdul, "is that you might stir up a hornets' nest that we are unable to contain."

"It is my decision, and I am in charge," Abdul said, his voice growing louder. "The men have been preparing for six months. They are ready, and with the festival tonight in Yüksekova, I believe it is perfect timing. Besides, Yüksekova is only an hour and a half away toward Iran. We will not get another chance like this again." He turned to Omar for verification. "This festival is once a year?"

"Yes," the CEO said.

Akleema turned to Omar. "I understand that Yüksekova is one of the main Kurdish cities, but it is so close to what we are establishing, this action could jeopardize our whole operation." She watched his face for confirmation, but, like a shrewd politician, he was not going to take sides.

"How many people will attend the festival?" Abdul asked Omar.

"Ten thousand or more. Maybe even twenty. I hear it is always a huge event. This year they have special cause to celebrate because their city sustained little damage from the earthquake."

"Even more of a reason to strike," Abdul said and got up to pace. "These are our enemies. We cannot let them celebrate in peace while their fighters kill our people. We must pour fear into their hearts and homes."

"But what if our men are caught before they can detonate their vests?" she asked. "They will be tortured until they reveal where we are." She could feel her anger rising. *Foolish, reckless boy.*

"That is a chance I am ready to take." Abdul stood firm. "If that happens, then we will make our last stand here. So be it. Are you afraid to die?"

She glared at him. *How dare you.* "Don't forget who I am!"

Akleema stared down Abdul until Omar broke the tension. "Please sit, Abdul. Akleema, have some tea." He raised his cup to them. "The Qur'an commands us to war against the idolaters, the apostates, and the hypocrites. Do you not agree?" he said. "When I was your age, I did not have your passion. I did not yet have the understanding of jihad."

Omar got up from his desk and handed Abdul a cup of tea. He waited for Abdul to sit. "My parents were pacifists. They believed that jihad was an internal struggle, and the way they understood for us to fulfill jihad was with faith in our hearts, preaching and proselytizing to the unbeliever, and doing good deeds with our hands." Omar sat on the edge of the desk and took a sip of his tea.

"Later in life, as I began to study our holy text, it became clear to me that a fourth way to fulfill jihad was necessary— confronting unbelievers and our enemies with the sword. It became clear to me that Islamic law is the only solution." He paused, taking another sip from his cup. "I found it hard to control my thoughts and actions. But I knew the law, and if I followed the absolutes of the law, I would live righteously, and I would please Allah. I believe as you do that the law has all the answers to our problems—to every situation, both now and in the future."

She nodded with Abdul.

"We not only have to practice jihad in here"—Omar pointed to his head—"but we must wage jihad against nonbelievers. It is our duty. Jihad will help establish Allah's rule on earth by forcing unbelievers to embrace Islam or accept second-class citizenship. If they refuse, they will be eradicated."

Omar returned to his desk chair. Akleema enjoyed watching the man skillfully defuse the situation.

"Whether you decide to send your men now or later," Omar said, "they will be rewarded for their sacrifices with all the pleasures of paradise, and they will be alive with Allah in heaven. Our sacred writings make that clear."

Abdul turned to her, and with his voice subdued he said, "I truly believe that Allah will bless us by doing this. The Kurds do not follow the law. Look how they dress, look how they act. They call themselves Muslims, but they are no better than infidels."

"I agree with all of that," she replied, "I am just concerned." She swirled the last of her tea, looking for wisdom in its leaves at the bottom of her cup. "What if we plant a diversion? What if we engineer a leak that the bombers are coming from Iran? It would turn the attention away from us."

She watched Abdul process the information.

He finally nodded. "That is a good idea. He jumped up from his chair. "Tonight, we strike at the heart of our enemy!"

***

Once Khalid had entered Turkey with Abdul, the White Snake, and the trucks filled with medical supplies and weapons, he understood he could be called on any day to fulfill his sacred vow. He was surprised, however, when Abdul came to him that afternoon to tell him it would be tonight. Of course, it was not unusual to be told at the last minute; his six months of training had prepared him for this very situation.

Khalid glanced at his companion walking beside him. He suspected the man was thinking similar thoughts. After all, the two had trained in Syria for this moment. Khalid had purified himself by refraining from relations with women, abstaining from alcohol, and eating only lawful foods. He washed daily and prayed fervently—clearing his mind of hatred and malice. Before leaving Syria, he had used the money he was paid to retire all his debt, and he told his parents he loved them and made amends with an estranged brother. He had even given up his one addiction, cigarettes. After all, he wanted clean breath when he met Allah face-to-face.

After he had delivered the command, Abdul asked for Khalid's phone. Khalid had given it over, knowing it was a standard precaution against alerting the enemy. But now he chastised himself for not destroying the photographs on his phone. Having photos of himself was a sign of vanity. *Allah, please forgive me.*

As they trudged along, Khalid saw his companion's forehead was beaded with sweat despite the cool night air. He appreciated the chill so their heavy coats did not look out of place. He looked to the sky and saw bright stars and a sliver of the moon. Looking ahead, he saw the lights of the festival. His mind raced, and he forced himself to slow his pace in hopes of slowing his thoughts. He did not want to make any sudden movement that would attract attention.

They had been dropped off in a secluded place on the Iranian side of the city to avoid suspicion, in case anyone saw them walking into town. Finding a vacant location had not been difficult, as much of the town's population of sixty thousand had gone to the festival. The music was getting louder and louder as Khalid and his comrade approached the central park.

Abdul had made it clear that if they encountered any security upon entering the event, they were to detonate their vests immediately. Even if they were unable to infiltrate the largest crowd, he promised that Allah would still bless their efforts. If they gained access, they were to position themselves on opposite sides of the crowd at its highest concentration of people. Khalid's companion would detonate first, and when the crowd ran from the explosion, Khalid would detonate, so the crowd would run right into a second explosion.

During his training, Khalid had worn the suicide vest for days at a time, and it had been comfortable. But it was now tighter and hotter than he remembered. They wore gloves to conceal the detonators in their hands, making his right hand sweat around the small device. It was a challenge to keep his hand still, but if he fidgeted, he could blow himself up prematurely.

The two jihadists split on either side of a mother pushing a stroller with a fussing child, then came back together again. As they entered the city center there was no fence around the festival, and people strolled about freely. The jihadists had no security problem entering.

A huge crowd had gathered around a large, central stage.

Khalid stopped wondering if he would feel pain upon the detonation and turned his thoughts to paradise. Today he would die for jihad. Today he became a martyr. Today he entered paradise and into his special place for Judgment Day. He began to recite under his breath the passages from the Qur'an that said it was the duty of Muslims to bring terror to the enemy.

He and his companion paused to let a family with three children pass in front of them. Two of the children fought over a balloon and their father smiled at Khalid.

His comrade caught his attention with a look and a toss of his head, indicating that they should take their positions on opposite sides of the crowd. As Khalid turned to walk away, anxiety washed over him. What if his friend couldn't do it? What if he lost his courage? *What if it's all up to me?*

He looked over his shoulder to see his comrade disappear into the crowd and turned back just in time to keep from stumbling over a family picnicking on a large blanket. He regained his balance and sighed with relief. That could have been a disaster. He had always hoped to fulfill his divine destiny at a military checkpoint or a police station or some strategic operation, but not over a picnicking family.

He moved quickly into position, only to be slowed by his mind wrestling against his will. He fought to steady his breathing, stay on task, and keep moving. *Allah is the only one that matters. In minutes, he will ask me how many infidels I killed.*

He pushed his body into the left side of the crowd. After the first explosion, the people would run toward him. He turned and the commotion on stage caught his eye. A woman in a multicolored dress danced and sang, and a raucous band thumped behind her. It was a glitzy show, typical of the infidels, and it lightened his guilt and strengthened his resolve. *Hypocrites. Don't they know this cannot be pleasing to Allah?*

The large, boisterous crowd of young and old gaped at the gyrating woman. The music was so loud he couldn't hear himself think, but he could feel his heart beating with anticipation.

Khalid reached what he believed was the correct position and waited for the surge of fleeing humanity. Nothing happened. Why hadn't his partner exploded his vest? Has he lost his courage? Did he get caught? Khalid fumbled with the detonator. *Should I push the button?*

Then he felt something tugging at his leg. He looked down to see his leg clutched in the arms of a small boy. He willed himself not to panic. Obviously, the boy had mistaken his leg for his father's. He shifted, trying to shake off the burden, but the boy looked up at him and smiled.

"*Allah Akbar*, God is great!" A blood-curdling scream rose over the sounds of the festival.

The heat and shock of the blast that followed hit Khalid milliseconds before the sound deafened his ears. People screamed. They ran toward him in a raging wave that knocked him down. A body fell on top of him, and someone stepped on his leg. Khalid gasped for air and tried to push himself up from the crush of the crowd when someone else stepped on his hand, and his world was no more.

CHAPTER 41

THE TRUE VINE
SATURDAY—POST-QUAKE DAY FOURTEEN

Ali directed the UN soldiers pushing his patient in her bed to the second floor. The girl had been on the third floor, where the sickest were kept in a makeshift Intensive Care Unit next to the OR. Because there were only four beds in the ICU, the staff had encouraged him to move the girl to the pediatric ward on the second floor.

Under the circumstances, it was the right decision, but he was concerned for the girl's future. He and his colleagues had weaned her off the ventilator, and she was now breathing on her own. But because she could only move her limbs involuntarily and without purpose, and her only vocalization was a screeching moan, it was obvious she had sustained significant brain trauma.

She was unable to feed herself, so Ali inserted a feeding tube down her nose and into her stomach. There was nothing else they could do for her. Maybe it would have been more humane to let her die. He sighed and banished the thought; after all, as a physician, he had taken the Hippocratic Oath and sworn to do no harm. Would he have done anything differently if she had been one of his daughters lying in the courtyard? Absolutely not. But how would she ever get the specialized care that she required for the rest of her life?

As Ali's entourage entered the pediatric ward, the children ogled the bald girl with the large and angry scalp incision stapled closed. He caught their horrified and fascinated expressions.

He asked the soldiers to rearrange the beds, pushing them closer together to make room for the girl's bed nearest the nurse's desk. Ali hoped someone would always be available to keep a close eye on her. The worst thing the girl could do now would be to inhale the liquid nutrition from her stomach into her lungs and die from a raging aspiration pneumonia—a cruel death.

He gave instructions to a nurse and wrote them down on the clipboard that hung from the girl's bed. "I'll be back to check on her later," he said.

When he turned away, he saw Ibrahim on the other side of the room waving him over.

"Is that my friend from the courtyard?" the boy asked.

"Yes, Ibrahim, it is."

"She does not look so good." He frowned.

Ali hesitated, not sure what to tell him. He had been through so much already. "Ibrahim, she is still very sick. Her brain has been badly injured."

"Will she get better?"

A tear fell from Ibrahim's eye to his cheek. Ali sat on the side of his bed, wiped the tear, and put his hand on his chest. "We will see, Ibrahim. Time is a great healer. We just have to wait and see." He did not want to raise false hopes. "We pray Allah's mercy over her."

***

The hospital team needed some recreational relief in order to function at their best, so Nick suggested a movie for Saturday night. They selected a comedy, and the kitchen crew provided large bowls of popcorn. It was the first time the entire team had taken a break, including the indefatigable Dr. Lee. But when most of the King's Hospital volunteer team gathered around the TV in the cafeteria, what they saw was no comedy.

Before running the DVD, one of the savvy UN information technology workers hooked up the TV to satellite and tuned to

CNN. Nick wished he hadn't been so clever—the news was the last thing they wanted to see on this night of R&R—but now that they were faced with the report of the suicide bombing, no one could look away.

When CNN's anchor Hawk Hudson pointed to the map of Turkey, the news became personal.

"Here is Istanbul at the far western region of Turkey, where the airport was bombed four days ago. There has now been another attack here in Yüksekova, clear on the other side of the country," Hudson said, pointing to a town near the border of Turkey and Iran. The camera zoomed in on the map. "An unconfirmed report points to a terrorist group out of Iran."

The camera zoomed back to Hudson's face. "Yüksekova is thought to be under Kurdish control and recently came off a nearly three-month Turkish military curfew after special forces battled with local Kurdish youth and PKK guerrillas, the Kurdistan Workers' Party."

Hudson held a hand to his earpiece and looked off camera. "We are getting the unofficial number of reported casualties now. Sixty-three people dead and hundreds more injured as the blast rocked the Yüksekova festival. Again, these are unconfirmed reports. When we return, we hope to bring you the mayor of Yüksekova."

CNN faded to an advertisement for reverse mortgages, and Buck leaned over to turn the volume down. "How far is Yüksekova from here?" he asked Ali.

"Um…about three hours."

"Have you been there?" Nick asked.

"I went to that festival many times when I was a boy."

CNN returned, interrupting their discussion and the advertisement. It was Hawk Hudson again, and Buck turned the volume back up.

"We are cutting back in as we have a live feed from the Turkish Broadcasting Network." A grainy picture of a large man with a black mustache stood red-faced in front of what appeared to be a hospital. The man looked angry, and the translation scrolling across the bottom of the screen confirmed it.

"We do not know who did this to our city, whether it was

Iran or the Turkish government itself, but by Allah's will, we will exact our revenge!" the large man shouted.

The picture went black and Hudson returned. "We have lost the feed and will get back to it as soon as we can."

***

Most of the surgical team had scattered, no longer in the mood for a comedy. Nick sat on the wall with Buck and Ali, all holding cups of tea. A cool breeze swept the evening, and a crescent moon hung over the compound.

"My God, I am so sorry for what has happened to your country," Nick told Ali. "And for what continues to happen."

Ali looked down in silence. "It is hard to make sense of all the violence. It seems like it has been this way since the beginning of time, since Cain killed his brother Abel."

"Maybe even before that, when Adam and Eve chose to disobey God in the garden," Buck said.

Ali shrugged.

Nick hesitated. "Ali, you are my friend, so I hope you don't mind my asking." He waited a second. "The men who just attacked the festival, will they be considered martyrs?"

"That question is more complicated than you think," Ali replied evenly. "Our ancient writings do say that a person who dies committing jihad obtains martyrdom. The complicated part is how one interprets the meaning of jihad."

"And what does jihad mean for you?" Buck asked.

"For me, what I was taught by my family, jihad is the internal struggle we all have to go through to become pleasing to God. Like most Muslims, I do not condone the violence." He thought for a moment and asked, "Doesn't Christianity have the concept of martyrdom?"

"Yes, but with a difference," Buck said. "Christian martyrs endure torture and death rather than renounce their faith." He paused. "So, do you think that ISIS is some radical offshoot of Islam, like the media portrays?"

"Unfortunately, the disciples of ISIS don't think so. In fact," Ali said, "rather than an offshoot, they believe they are reclaiming the very foundation of Islam—the true Islam. You find people of my faith all along the spectrum of belief, much like people of the Christian and Jewish faiths. The people who join ISIS are strict in what they believe and feel justified in killing their own Muslim brothers and sisters who do not adhere to the same belief." Ali blew on his hot tea and took a sip. "It is so difficult, because most Muslims believe we are not to criticize our Islamic brothers. I believe that many of those fighting for the Islamic State equate criticism of their belief to apostasy. The penalty for apostasy, for abandoning their belief, is death. That is why you don't see more Muslims speaking out publicly against the violence. They don't want to become a target."

Nick nodded with Buck.

"Maybe it is because we have a hard time discerning Allah's— God's—will," Ali added, "So we live in fear that maybe our own belief is wrong."

"Do you believe that you can have a relationship with God?" Nick asked.

"Dr. Hart, I don't know how that is possible. I suppose I believe like you do, that Adam and Eve walked with God, but since He cast them out of the garden, we have been doing everything we can to get back in His good graces."

"As it was for the Jews in the Old Testament," Nick said, "trying to please an angry God."

"Which brings us to Jesus," Buck said. "As a follower of Yeshua—of Jesus, I believe that is exactly why God sent Jesus, His Son. He wanted Jesus to restore our relationship with Him. The scriptures tell us that He is the vine and we are the branches. Jesus said, 'Abide in me and I in you.' It is this intimate union that has restored our walk with God—that we may know Him."

"But how is that possible?" Nick and Ali said almost simultaneously.

"That my friends," Buck said. "Is our life long search."

CHAPTER 42

THE TRAP
SUNDAY—POST-QUAKE DAY FIFTEEN

Akleema sat fuming in the back of the room, watching Abdul prattle and brag with the men. She hated his youthful arrogance. The two of them had barely spoken yesterday, but every time Abdul had passed her, he smirked as if to say, "I told you so."

She had to admit that after the success at the festival, palpable excitement filled the air. The men were ready for victory. Their team had totaled twenty-one, including the group from Syria, the trusted men who worked at the hospital, and the two men who had just sacrificed themselves. Now there were nineteen.

"Allah be praised!" Abdul was saying. "The mission was successful Friday night. The news has reported that more people have died from their injuries, making a total of eighty-three infidels killed." He smiled proudly.

"Twenty-nine of those were children," Akleema said under her breath.

Abdul didn't seem to hear her or chose to ignore her. He was too busy bragging.

In private he had lamented the fact to her. "Spineless boy," she murmured to herself.

"My brother sends his congratulations and promises more trucks and men in the next few weeks. We are to establish an Islamic State training base here in Hakkâri. We are the tip of the spear to be driven into the heart of Turkey."

Abdul paused to acknowledge a man raising his hand.

"Commander, when is our next mission?" he asked barely able to contain his excitement.

Commander. The White Snake scoffed to herself.

Abdul smiled and replied calmly. "All in good time. All in Allah's time. For now, we should prepare our hearts, minds, and bodies. Each one of us should be prepared to meet Allah any day."

Abdul's phone dinged in his pocket. He pulled it out and checked it. "It is time for *Thuhr,* second prayer," he announced. "Everyone meet me tomorrow in the hospital courtyard after first morning prayer and we will start our physical training. Some of you look like you have been indulging in too many sweets." He chuckled and looked at Omar.

"Yes," the administrator said, patting his belly, "I have been working hard on my costume," and the men laughed.

***

Akleema sat on the twin bed in the room Omar had provided. She was steaming. Abdul hadn't even acknowledged her at the meeting with the team. It was obvious he was pushing her aside, making her insignificant to the mission. She shook her head. Being related to his brother did not make Abdul fit to lead this mission. That was her job; she had earned it. She had lain under his filthy brother to have the right to lead the caliphate in this region. Abbas would never have told Abdul that they had been lovers but he made it clear she was to lead.

Abbas had warned her of Abdul's pride. He did not trust his younger brother. She had coiled her legs around him, listening to him laugh as he compared his relationship to Abdul to that of Cain and Abel's. He'd said, "I'm sure Abdul longs to take my place, but I will send him away instead of killing him."

She looked around the barren room, and her mind filled with regret. She missed her beautiful flat in London and her friends. She even missed her parents. They were both professors at Oxford—her mother taught English literature and her father, mathematics. They were liberals to be sure, but they hated violence and would be repulsed by what she had gotten herself into. They told her she had always been a contrary child. It was probably her adolescent rebellion that drove her to join the Islamic State.

But she had made her bed and now she'd have to sleep in it. She socked the pillow beside her and sneezed. It was the old wool blanket she was sitting on; it smelled of mothballs. She snuffled and gazed absently at the small desk in the corner with a red lamp on top. It was the only color in the room. Maybe she should go home. She pushed the thought from her mind. She wasn't a quitter; too much was at stake and she needed to take charge once again.

The large diesel generator rumbled to life, the bare light bulb in the ceiling came on, and she smiled. At least she could shower. She would have to control Abdul. She would make him her puppet. She knew how to control men—she had done it well all her life.

Akleema gathered her supplies and robe and walked down the hall to the bathrooms. The men's and women's locker rooms were side-by-side, just like the athletic club in London she had attended, although Omar's showers left something to be desired. They were still under construction, and privacy was not yet secure. Since they'd arrived, Akleema had wondered if any of the men had taken advantage of the flimsy plastic sheeting that separated part of the ceiling and upper wall between the two shower rooms.

She didn't care if they had, but it gave her an idea to reassert control over Abdul. She realized Abdul was quick to shower once the generator powered up. He was fussy about his looks; she always caught him checking himself in every mirror they passed.

With the power on, Abdul would be approaching the men's shower soon, and she decided to give him every opportunity to see her beauty bare. Setting the stage, she pulled on the plastic sheeting until some of the tape that held it in place gave way. She didn't want to make the break too obvious, so she freed just one corner. For Abdul's wandering eyes, it would be enough.

Akleema removed her clothes and took a brush from her

bag. She pulled it through her long, straight hair. Her bleached platinum-blond locks were part of the reason they called her the White Snake. Leaning in toward the mirror, she saw that her darker roots were beginning to show and sighed, realizing she had forgotten to bring her coloring for a touch-up.

Examining her naked body in the mirror, she pushed on her stomach with both hands. She frowned. *I could use some calisthenics as well as the men.* When the men's shower began to spray, she stepped into her shower and turned the water to warm. She glanced up to see steam rising in the adjacent shower through the break in the plastic, and she smiled. *Showtime.*

She began to hum, searching for a melody. The only one that came to mind was a Selena Gomez song, "Hands to Myself." *Perfect.* She sang the lyrics softly as she poured a generous dollop of shampoo into her hand and lathered her long tresses. She took her sweet time, finally rinsing slowly, arching her head back in the warm water. Then she caressed her shiny wet skin with fragrant soap, lathering her body and singing with increased volume. She fought the urge to look up at the break in the plastic. If he was watching, she wanted him to have the benefit of the full show.

CHAPTER 43

HEAVEN
MONDAY—POST-QUAKE DAY SIXTEEN

Ibrahim salivated at the sight of a banquet table filled with platters of delicious looking food. The mouthwatering comestibles were piled so high that it took him a few minutes to see all the people surrounding the table—grown-ups filling the seats and children gathering at their feet. *Where am I?* Ibrahim didn't recognize anyone, but he also didn't feel out of place. Something told him he belonged here, something deep inside him.

The massive wooden table contained trays of freshly baked flatbread, a variety of meats and cheeses, pickled vegetables and olives, and fresh fruit of every kind. It made him think of the Ramadan feast that he celebrated last month with his family and friends, but this was more food than Ibrahim had ever seen at one time.

No one was eating. Everyone sat quietly, gazing from time to time at the head of the table, waiting for the host to start. Ibrahim strained to see who it was.

A trumpet blasted, signaling the start of the celebration—the burst of exuberance animated the grown-ups and children. They began to eat and drink and talk and laugh. Their joyful noises filled the great hall and echoed off the walls, ceiling and the floor. Ibrahim looked around in wonder, lingering on the glowing tiles that covered the floor, glistening with precious stones—rubies, sapphires and emeralds. As the talking and laughing rose to a crescendo, so, too, did the echoing harmony from the walls, all in a glorious rhapsody.

He was thrown off balance when a little girl bumped into him. She giggled and gave him a chocolate from a basket she held over her arm, and before he could speak, she disappeared into the crowd. Then he saw other children kissing the right hands of the adults at the table, and the grown-ups, in turn, would place their hands on the children's forehead to bless them, and then reward them with tasty morsels.

Everyone was dressed in clothes of many colors, bright as the beautiful hues of the rainbow. He looked at his own drab rags and was amazed to discover that he was wearing new clothes—a suit of fine linen with gold flecks that shimmered in the radiating light of the room.

Was it the Sugar Feast, the end of the fasting period of Ramadan? He popped the chocolate into his mouth and it burst with flavor, snapping every taste bud to attention. Was it raspberry? No, orange...*not exactly.* Lemon? Maybe all three. *Yes, definitely.* The chocolate was richer and smoother than any he had ever tasted.

The children had formed a line that seemed to snake its way to the head of the table. Ibrahim joined the queue. He saw what everyone was watching—a tall, handsome man, dazzling in an aura of white light—an awe-inspiring sight that made him gasp. But he wasn't afraid and kept moving forward. When he got closer, his jaw dropped. *It's the man in white!* Then, in an instant, as if he was looking through a crazy kaleidoscope, the man would transform into a massive tree and then back to a man. Ibrahim's mind spun with fantastical images from stories his parents had read to him, but this beat them all: *A man who looks like a tree and a tree that looks like a man.*

The man seemed to be rooted to the ground. If Ibrahim held his head in a certain position, he thought he could see massive branches extending in all directions adorned with fruits of every kind and beautiful leaves that danced in the light.

It was as if every joy and every happiness, every hug and

every kiss he had ever received from his mother and father swung from the boughs of this man—like all of life came from this one source.

The man smiled at him, and Ibrahim knew for sure this really was the man in white. He smiled back. It was a moment of incomparable intimacy that made Ibrahim's body vibrate with love. His heart surged with warmth, understanding, and a peace that filled his body until his flesh was becoming light itself. The feeling was so intense it released its glory as the blare of a trumpet.

Ibrahim jerked with alarm. His eyes flashed open. His heart sank knowing he was still in the hospital.

"I'm sorry, Ibrahim," a voice said. "I did not mean to bump your leg."

Ibrahim shook his head and blinked fully awake. He recognized his nurse smiling at him.

She set a tray of food in front of him—a cup of orange Jell-O, a small plate containing a sliced hardboiled egg, and a slab of mystery meat. The Jell-O wiggled, but the egg and meat lay like corpses. He closed his eyes and sighed. He longed to return to the heavenly feast.

***

Antasha and Vladimir shared a cigarette in the courtyard. Vladimir glanced nervously around for Dr. Lee. She had caught them smoking the day before, scolded them severely, and sent them back to their wards. "Smoking worst thing you can do for your leg and shoulder," she had said, shaking a bony finger at each of them. "Better not let me catch you again." She'd pierced them with her eyes. "I have gun, you know," she said, referring to the etiology of Vladimir's wound. To press the point, she'd stuck her finger in the pocket of her doctor's coat, pointed it at them, and made the sound of a toy gun. To Vladimir it had sounded like her usual cackling laugh, but he got the message and put out the cigarette.

AK passed him the cigarette; he inhaled deeply and anxiously.

"My doctor thinks I'm great," she said brightly.

Vladimir glowered at her. "Yeah, I bet."

"Oh, Vlad. You know what I mean," she said, punching his good shoulder lightly.

"I do," he said gruffly and rolled his eyes.

"He thinks I'm doing great with my leg, stupid. See, I can even balance on it." She lifted her crutches to the side and stood on both legs. "Darn good for five days after surgery, don't you think? He said I could go to one crutch when I feel ready."

"I suppose you and your handsome doctor are having a wonderful time while I'm on the first floor, sweating it out with all the stinky men."

"*Da.*" She turned on a dreamy voice to tease him, "Candlelight dinners, warm baths, and, oh, those soft hands of his."

She was just trying to get his goat, but as much as he tried to ignore her, he still felt jealousy steam the back of his neck. "Maybe the doctor will take you back to America."

"Don't think I wouldn't go," she snapped. Then she looked at him and laughed. "Come on, Vlad, I'm kidding."

He wasn't in the mood. He took one long last drag of the cigarette, threw it to the ground, and mashed the butt into the dirt with the toe of his shoe.

"What are you doing? There was one more puff in that. I thought we were sharing. I swear, Vlad, you're impossible."

They stood in silence, looking at nothing to avoid each other's eyes, until AK broke the stalemate. "So, how is your shoulder?"

"My doctor thinks I'm great." He smirked at her, and they both laughed.

"Touché." She grinned.

"The dressing changes hurt like hell, but they tell me it looks good. I never watch." Vladimir shuddered at the thought. "They told me they are going to put some sort of pigskin over it tomorrow and switch me to antibiotics by mouth so I can get this stupid thing out," he added, pulling on the IV attached to his hand.

"Pigskin?" she asked.

"They told me they could take skin off my thigh, but I'd have a big scar there as well. I told them to go with the pig."

"Pig-headed and now pig-shouldered," AK said.

"Ha, ha. Very funny. Maybe I should tell them to take the

skin from your big butt."

AK faked a laugh and changed the subject. "So, what are we going to do?"

"Have you found out any more information?" he asked.

"I found the woman who says she is 169 years old. We could only communicate through an interpreter, but she truly believes she is that old. She told me that the priest from Qodshanes gave her something as a child, and her entire family is very old."

"Qodshanes?" Vladimir asked. "Isn't that the village in some of the reports? The one we were going to investigate?"

"Yes. It was super hard to communicate with the old lady, but her village is outside of Hakkâri, where we were. I asked others for directions, but no one else in the room had heard of it."

"And the priest?"

"I think she said something about the East Church. Maybe I didn't understand because she got very quiet when we talked about her faith. I think she is a Christian. You can imagine what that must be like in a room full of Muslims."

"You know anything about this church?" he asked.

"I don't. You think you can use any of your connections with the soldiers to get to a computer to do a search?"

"You might have more luck with your doctor," Vladimir smirked.

AK blushed and looked away.

"What?" he demanded.

"Um...I'm sorry, but I accidentally told my doctor about our mission." she said.

"What the...are you serious?"

"*Da*, but he sweet-talked it out of me." She looked away.

"And you call me the stupid one."

"I guess I talked when I was coming out of the anesthesia. I doubt if he cares anyway," she shrugged, downplaying her mistake.

***

Nick stood with Buck, Jack Bilton, and Dr. Lee at the compound gate. His stomach growled. He couldn't understand why Buck had been adamant that he shave and why he had to be the one to meet the incoming volunteers before dinner. All Buck had said was, "You can thank me later."

Nick looked up at the evening sky as an ominous dark cloud drifted overhead. He wasn't sure what to make of that, but the sunset had been friendly. He rubbed his smooth cheek with pleasure, glad to be rid of that scruffy beard.

Two jeeps and a large military personnel transport vehicle pulled up to the front gate. One jeep squealed to a stop on bad brakes. He was relieved that more volunteers were arriving. He was exhausted and welcomed the reinforcements. Rumors had it that four new orthopedic surgeons were coming, in which case he might take a few days off or even go home. Nick was especially happy that Ali would be able to get away to look for his family.

In the fading evening light, he saw people pile out of the back of the large troop transport, assisted by two UN soldiers. He saw an older woman struggle with an oversized suitcase and chuckled to himself. So many of the volunteers came with ten too many pairs of shoes and twice that many outfits, only to discover that one sturdy pair of tennis shoes, two pairs of scrubs, and a toothbrush were all they needed.

He was getting annoyed and hungry and frowned at Buck. "I don't know why you're so happy today."

When Buck just grinned at him, he turned back to watch the disembarking volunteers. He recognized a tall, athletic woman with long blond hair walking through the gate. She had chaired a committee of the Orthopedic Trauma Society, of which he was a member. He caught her astonishment when she saw the hospital and the at-capacity tent city within the compound. He had already grown accustomed to the sights, sounds, and smells of ground zero, but it was still a shock to new arrivals.

She recognized him, gave him a quick wave, and threw her arms up in relief that she had survived the long journey. Her exhilaration was interrupted by a soldier who relieved her of her luggage.

Nick shot another annoyed glance to Buck. "Can we go eat now?"

Buck ignored him and stared straight ahead. He followed Buck's gaze to the back of the truck.

Nick's heart leaped with joy. "Oh, my gosh. You knucklehead, why didn't you tell me?" He slugged Buck's arm and took off at a trot. He ignored the outstretched hand of his orthopedic colleague and ran through the gate.

There she was—Maggie Russell—standing beside the truck, looking like she had just stepped out of a magician's box. Nick recognized the canary-yellow dress from the photo she'd texted of her standing by the tractor—it had been his comfort, the image that had allowed him to fall asleep every night since he'd landed here. The dress glowed like a field of sunflowers against her Native American complexion and her long black hair.

He reached her in two more bounds and scooped her up into his arms. "Oh, my God, I can't believe you're here."

She flung her arms around him and squeezed him tightly. "Hi, Nicklaus…surprise." Her warm breath caressed his neck.

"How did you…What in the world?" Nick kissed her cheek and hugged her, looking over her shoulder at Buck, who stood grinning from ear to ear.

"Yeah, yeah, yeah." Nick waved him off and turned back to Maggie, whose radiant smile caressed his face. He pulled her close again and breathed her in deeply.

She tried to ease out of his intimate grasp. "I smell pretty bad after two days of travel." She wrinkled her nose. "I really need a bath."

His eyes welled with tears, and he let them roll freely down his cheeks, holding her at arm's length. "How in the world?" he said with amazement. He searched her eyes to make sure she was real. "I just can't believe you're here."

"When Buck told me about all the new orphans, I had to come," she said. "It only took two minutes to decide, and I packed up right away. I just couldn't stand to wait another day." She searched his eyes. "I guess Buck was able to keep it a secret, huh?" Maggie reached up and pinched his cheeks. "What happened to the Montana mountain man I heard about?"

"That old man got shaved off and flushed down the drain," Nick chuckled.

"Too bad." She twisted her lips. "I was looking forward to seeing what you looked like with a beard…but, I have to admit, I love your clean-shaven face."

He leaned in and kissed her on the forehead. Whatever she worried about smelling like after the long journey, she smelled wonderful. Like Maggie.

CHAPTER 44

MAGGIE

TUESDAY—POST-QUAKE DAY SEVENTEEN

Ali froze in the doorway of the pediatric ward. He was flabbergasted at the unfolding scene—Ibrahim, who rarely smiled, was smiling and talking to the girl with the head injury. Ali couldn't believe it. Three days ago, when he had helped wheel the girl to the ward, he was full of remorse and dread for her future. He thought it was a death sentence to move her to the pediatric ward from the intensive care of their makeshift ICU. But either way, he'd been certain her life would be horrific and short.

Ibrahim waved him over. Ali paused, preparing to come face-to-face with a dying girl whose ghostly white skin emphasized the large, angry scar arching across her shaved head. But when he came to the bed, the girl turned to him, and, to his surprise, her twinkling eyes were full of life.

"*Selamünaleyküm*, may God's peace be upon you," she said to Ali and smiled.

He was unable to make his mouth move to respond.

Ibrahim answered for him. "*Aleykümselam*, peace be upon you." The children laughed at him.

Ali quickly pulled a pen light from the front pocket of his scrubs and turned it on to shine the light into the girl's left eye and then the right, back and forth, back and forth. *Amazing!*

Each pupil was equal, round, and reactive—all signs of a healthy brain. On his last examination, her right pupil had been enlarged and unresponsive, suggesting damage to the left side of the brain. He checked her other cranial nerves, testing for smell, hearing, and facial muscle movement. "Do you know where you are?"

"Yes, of course," she said immediately. "In the hospital."

"Do you know what day it is?"

The girl looked at Ibrahim, who shrugged. Ali laughed. He wasn't sure either. Instinctively, he glanced at his watch and snapped his fingers. "Tuesday," he said a little too loud. "It's Tuesday."

"Tuesday," the girl repeated and looked at Ibrahim. The two children laughed.

"I need to check one more thing," he said and sat on the edge of the girl's bed. He felt her abdomen through the sheet—it was flat and soft. "Do you think you could eat something?"

Her eyes lit up and she nodded enthusiastically.

He hesitated but went with his intuition. "Good," he said, "but there is something I need to do first. Trust me and try to hold still." He pulled the tape covering her nose. "This tape was holding your feeding tube," he said. "Now, close your eyes, beloved child, and hold your breath. This is going to burn, but only for a minute," he promised. She closed her eyes and held her breath. Satisfied, he gently and as quickly as possible pulled the foot and a half of tubing from her stomach out through her nose.

She winced slightly, coughed, and opened her eyes.

"Sorry...but it's all out." He showed her the end of the tube.

She swallowed hard a few times, which caused her eyes to tear up—more good signs of a functioning brain. The girl's eyes were full of life. If he had been a Christian, he would have called it a miracle. But he was a Muslim and didn't believe in miracles. He and the other 1.6 billion Muslims attributed occasions like this to God's will. *Praise Allah*. But he had never seen in Allah's will such a...*miracle*.

Ibrahim seemed to read his mind. "I asked the man in white to come and be with her," he said. "He told me that I should touch her—that I should be His hands. So, I asked the nurses to move my bed next to hers, and I held her hand and asked this man called Jesus to make her better."

When Ali didn't answer, Ibrahim blinked and drew back. "Did I do the right thing, Dr. Ali?"

Ali shook the alarm off his face and smiled. "Yes, my sweet, sweet boy. You did the right thing." He squeezed Ibrahim's shoulder.

***

Nick watched Maggie propose a plan for the orphanage to Jack Bilton, Buck, the UN Commander, and a handful of his troops in the cafeteria. After her arrival, she headed straight for the orphans. Armed with a few words of Turkish and Kurdish she'd learned on the plane, and containers full of treats and gifts, she'd become the pied piper to the kids. Today, she was equally at ease leading the group of men.

He studied the faces of his colleagues and saw how easily they accepted her natural smile, gentle leadership, and inherent strength. For him, just having her near refreshed his soul. He couldn't wait for time alone with her.

"You all have done wonderful things for these children," she said. "You have provided everything they needed—food, water, and shelter—and now, if you would allow me, it's time to move on to the next phase—giving them a home."

Maggie's long black hair was pulled into a bun. She wore a peach-colored blouse and black pants. Her shoulders, arms, and legs were well covered. Nick suspected she was trying to fit in to honor the local culture and didn't doubt she would wear a headscarf when appropriate.

Standing beside the Commander, her five-foot frame should have been dwarfed, but her inspired confidence seemed to make her taller.

"What do you suggest?" the Commander asked Maggie.

"We have gone from fifty-three kids at the King's orphanage to 322, but we should be prepared for more. As you all know, the orphanage director and one of the staff members were killed."

The men nodded.

"Mr. Bilton, you have done a wonderful ministry here. May God richly bless you."

"Jack. Please call me Jack. And He already has." Then he smiled and said, "Maggie, how long can you stay?"

Maggie laughed. Nick loved how her whole face lit up when she smiled.

"I'm sure thankful to be here and I want to stay for as long as I'm needed, but eventually, I need to get back to the Hope Center, to my family."

"Is that the program in Guatemala that you run? How many kids do you have?" Jack asked.

"Yes. Today we have 163 children. My goal for the Hope Center, and something we eventually need to think about for King's, is how we can make the ministry, at least in part, self-sustainable. Jack, I understand you are a generous man, but even you have your limits."

Jack nodded.

"The most important thing we can do right now for these kids is to make this place a home—a place of security that provides love but also gives them a sense of pride and purpose. I appreciate that the children have been helping to distribute food and water. It contributes to their self-esteem. If it's okay with you all, I will act as the temporary director for now, and the two surviving staff members will be my codirectors. I'm sure there are women in the community who have lost their families. We can bring them in to shelter with the children and give them a purpose as well."

"How do you like the new dorm?" Buck spoke up.

"It's great, Buck." Maggie paused to gather her thoughts. "Is there any way I can get you gentlemen to build a staff quarters... and a school?" She bit her lip.

"Whatever you want," the Commander spoke up. "Your wish is my command." He bowed like a French gentleman.

"Ha." Maggie laughed. "You better not let such chivalry go to my head. My wishes can get really big."

The men laughed with her, but Maggie's countenance changed. "You men are something—what you have seen, what you have done. It so blesses me to be here with you." A tear fell to her cheek. "I think we are all orphans in one way or another. I thank God for you all. 'Blessed are those that are merciful as they will be shown mercy.'" The tear slid down onto her blouse. "It's so hard to see what these people are going through, especially the children. It's times like this that challenge our faith, and we must grab hold of God's goodness."

Nick's eyes watered, as did the Commander's. Maggie had articulated the pain and sorrow they all felt but were unable to express in front of their comrades. Jack removed his glasses and wiped his eyes.

***

Ali shook Maggie's hand. "I'm sorry, Ms. Russell...uh... Maggie, for missing your presentation. I have this slave driver boss, you know." He tilted his head at Nick, who stood with Buck and Maggie at the entrance to the hospital. Nick put his arm around Ali's shoulder. He loved the emergence of Ali's sense of humor. It had been hiding for too long under a veil of politeness.

"Thanks for getting all the new guys started," Nick told Ali in all seriousness. "They doing okay?"

Ali grinned. "I enjoy initiating them to the main OR and telling them the story of when you caught the slab of concrete with your head. I love watching them pretend not to look up, expecting the next slab to fall." Ali blushed with the pleasure of telling a good story.

"What?" Maggie exclaimed. "A slab of concrete? No one told me about that. Nick?"

Nick was surprised that Buck hadn't mentioned it. "Just a little mishap with the OR ceiling," Nick said. He was grateful when Ali changed the subject.

"Maggie, Nick tells me you are Native American," Ali said. "I loved studying about the Indians when I was in school."

"I grew up with two brothers and an older sister in Browning, Montana. I'm from the Blackfeet Tribe—Indian through and through."

"I have always dreamed of taking my family to Montana and visiting your culture. You are the first Native American I have met." He smiled shyly and then grew quiet.

"You okay, Ali?" Nick asked.

"Oh, I was thinking about an incident that happened this morning on the pediatric ward. I can't seem to wrap my mind around it."

"Is everyone okay?" he asked with alarm.

"Yes, quite all right, and that is the issue. The girl that I operated on the first night is fully awake, fully functional."

"Seriously? Wasn't she posturing and showing signs of some real brain deficiency a day ago?"

"Yes. I just stopped by to check her again on my way out here. She's eating orange Jell-O. And smiling. And talking."

"That's awesome, Ali. Way to go." He didn't understand why Ali wasn't jubilant.

"That's the thing, Dr. Hart. I had nothing to do with it. That little boy I was telling you about the other night, Ibrahim, the one that says he sees Jesus, he's the one. He told me that he reached out and took her hand...and now she's normal, fully awake." Ali stumbled over the words and what they meant.

Nick looked at Buck and Maggie, who were both smiling. He wasn't surprised they had nothing to say. He was reminded that after he saw his first miracle in Guatemala, words just fell short.

CHAPTER 45

LAMB TO THE SLAUGHTER

Two days had passed since he first saw the White Snake in the shower, and Abdul was beside himself with desire and shame. He had prayed fervently at each of the five calls to prayer, and between the calls, but he could not shake the sight of her naked body. She wasn't the first naked woman he had seen; after all, he'd grown up in the digital age where a benign search on Google could lead to the perverse. After such sightings, he'd confessed his sins to Allah, prayed, and his guilt had gone away. But not this time.

He was a virgin and planned to stay that way. If Allah willed for him to live long enough to take a wife, he wanted not only for his wife to be innocent, but to be pure himself.

But he couldn't stop thinking of the woman. Worst of all, the day after his first sighting, he'd watched her shower a second time.

The third prayer, *Asr*, had ended thirty minutes ago, but he kept his forehead pressed to the ground as the other men gathered their prayer rugs and left. He hoped they had no idea what was on his mind. His head was spinning. Did she know? What if she saw him? Would she turn him in? Probably.

He wished he could talk with the Imam from his mosque. The Imam, a gentle man, had helped him after the death of his father. He wondered if the Imam could help him now. What would his teacher tell him to do? Could he even confess to him his transgressions at night when he thought about her? He inhaled deeply, catching the musky smell of the old prayer rug that had belonged to his father. *Father, how I miss you.*

He had let them down—his father, the Imam, Allah, and himself. He had to do something. Anger flared in his soul. His heart pounded. His legs ached. "It is that woman," he said under his breath. "She did this to me. She made me this way. She must be eliminated. I don't care what my brother says. I must be true to my faith, to Sharia law."

He would force his mind to not think of her…of her body. But then, her familiar image flashed across his mind's eye, soapy water dripping off her silky skin.

Abdul bounced his head on the rug that covered concrete as he tried to pound the image away. It hurt his head, but she had to go. All he wanted was for his life to be acceptable to Allah. But all the good he had done was for nothing because of his stupid behavior caused by that woman. What would Allah think of him now? He shook his battered head. *Not much, not much at all.*

She must be killed. He could order her to jihad. She could not refuse in front of the men. As he formulated the plan, a sense of peace enveloped him, and his shoulders relaxed. He sat up on his heels. His knees were killing him.

He startled when the fluorescent lights snapped on overhead, and the air conditioner rumbled to life. He stood up, thanking Allah for the plan. He rolled up the prayer rug. Having cleansed his soul, he decided it was time for a thorough cleansing of his body. A bath. How long had it been since he took a bath? There was a therapy room at the end of the hallway in the dorm where Omar had given them rooms. A nice hot bath would cleanse him of any temptation to spy through the plastic ever again.

Abdul stretched his legs as he walked down the hallway to his room. His spirits lifted with each step. He allowed himself to wonder what kind of woman he would someday marry. Would she be tall? Would she be short? One thing for sure, she would be a devoted Sunni. *Children.* Would there be children?

He opened the door to his room and switched on the light. He grabbed his towel and bathroom bag, left the room, and turned down the long hallway to the therapy room. It was located around the corner across from the woman's room.

She will be gone soon enough.

As he turned the corner, the hallway was empty. It was unfortunate that she had the whole area to herself. The thought of filling those rooms with real jihadists as soon as she was gone brought a song to his heart, and he began to whistle a very old tune his father had taught him. "The Imam will tell you not to whistle," his father had warned. "But music is good for you. Just be careful not to do it in front of others, lest you be judged as unrighteous."

He slowed his steps when he saw light from the White Snake's room midway down the hall. He stopped whistling and tried to walk softly, but the White Snake stepped from the doorway of her room in a robe and smiled at him. "Abdul, why have you ignored me the last few days? I think you don't like me anymore."

He averted his eyes and tried to step around her, but she stepped in front of him and they almost collided.

"Why won't you talk to me?" she asked.

He stepped back, said nothing and looked past her.

"Abdul, can you not even look at me? I think you will like what you see."

His face flushed with anger. He had to get her out of his sight. He shoved her out of his way, knocking her askew. The fabric belt fastening her silk robe came loose, opening the garment and revealing her naked body. She made no attempt to close her robe and only opened it wider.

"Abdul, I want you and I know you want me."

He froze, unable to move. His body reeled with fierce desire that overwhelmed his devout heart and melted his Sunni will. His mind protested but was unable to fight the temptation. His hands reached out to hold her naked body and he pushed her backward into the room, kicking the door shut behind them.

CHAPTER 46

PILE OF SHOES

They walked together under the evening sky, and Nick was ecstatic to finally have time alone with Maggie. It wasn't exactly a stroll along the Champs-Élysées in Paris, the city of light and love, but he was just as thrilled.

He would have been content to walk through the compound with Maggie, but she had another idea. She wanted to walk outside the walls and see the sights around the hospital. He was wary of danger and didn't relish exposing Maggie to the mass of mangled people still waiting for treatment, but as they left the gate and the security of King's armed guards, he was relieved to see that the long lines had disappeared.

A lighted tent city had arisen from the ash, replacing the dark and ominously quiet streets. The UN soldiers had provided the homeless with tarps, although some rough shelters remained, patched together with cardboard and tin. The Commander had said that most of the homes in the region were destroyed and those that were still intact stood empty because the inhabitants were afraid to go inside, even two weeks after the quake.

Maggie wrapped her hand around his arm as they walked down the street beside the tent city that buzzed with activity. Women were busy fixing evening meals over campfires as children played hide and seek around the tents. While positive changes were at hand and the UN had provided food and water rations, there was one thing that had not changed—the smell of death. It clung to the city like the smoke from the fires.

Turning the corner, a woman stood near the curb behind a large pile of dusty, worn shoes. She called to him in Turkish and spread her arms wide to show off her wares—an eclectic mix of men's running shoes, women's dress shoes, and assorted children's shoes, all in a jumbled heap. He thought they'd be easier to sell if she'd stacked them neatly by type and size. He couldn't even tell if there were any complete pairs.

The woman questioned him in English. "You buy?"

He shook his head and pointed to his feet and his surgical clogs.

She nodded and looked beyond them for another buyer.

They continued past the woman and Maggie adjusted the scarf on her head. "I thought I better cover my head coming out of the compound," she said, acknowledging his gaze.

"It actually looks kind of cute on you. With your dark skin, you look like a proper little Turkish woman."

They laughed and walked to the next corner of the street surrounding the hospital compound, where they encountered a crowd gathered at a newly reconstructed portion of the wall. As they got closer, he saw it was where the UN posted photos of the patients and those that were still missing. People searched frantically for their loved ones—husbands missing wives, wives missing husbands, brothers and sisters missing each other, children missing parents, and parents missing children.

A distraught woman grabbed Maggie's arm and pleaded with her in Turkish, pointing to the wall and sobbing. Maggie squared herself to the woman and held her shoulders. "I am so sorry. I do not understand. I do not speak Turkish."

Undeterred, the woman continued to rant and weep with inconsolable grief.

"I am so sorry," Maggie repeated.

Another local woman intervened. "She's lost her only child," the Good Samaritan told Maggie in English.

Maggie hugged the mother. "I'm so sorry," Maggie said over and over as the woman wailed.

Soon her flood of despair drained, her anguish softened. She kissed Maggie's hands and Maggie reciprocated with a kiss on her cheek. She gave the woman a long embrace. "It's all going to be okay, Mama." Releasing her, she stepped away toward Nick, but returned for another hug and gently guided the woman into the hands of the Good Samaritan.

Nick and Maggie eased away from the crowd that had formed to watch the sad spectacle of the women consoling each other. Nick wiped his tears. "I don't know how you do that."

Maggie smiled at him. Her dark eyes radiated with an inner glow. She put her arm back through his and kissed his shoulder, and they continued their walk in companionable silence.

When they came to the shore of a large body of water, Nick was surprised to see the lake. The last of the golden evening light sparkled on its calm surface. "This must be Lake Van," he said. He hadn't emerged from the hospital compound since he had arrived, but from the top floor of the hospital, he'd caught the scent of a marina and heard the noisy gulls overhead. It was refreshing—the resilience of nature—resting as if nothing had happened.

They walked another block and sat on a wall overlooking the lake. Maggie shivered and he pulled her close to share body heat.

He couldn't stop thinking about how Maggie had dealt with the woman at the lost-and-found wall. "I don't know if I understand what happened back there," he said. He watched a breeze ripple the lake. "What you did. You have such a huge heart." He felt a cold wind blow through his own empty chambers. "I have been searching for that all my life."

"That?" Maggie asked.

"That, what you just did. What you just gave. I don't know… that." He sounded more frustrated than he had meant to, but he was angry. He pulled one leg up and hugged it tight around his shin, trying to wring out the anger. Then he planted his chin on his knee and sighed.

Maggie put her hand on his back and rubbed it gently.

"See…that! That's what I'm talking about." He uncurled himself and stood up, pacing in front of her. "What is that?" He looked at her, waiting. She was about to speak, but he interrupted. "I know what you are going to say. It's God inside of you. It's Jesus. And that is so annoying." He stopped in front of her and put his hands on his hips.

Maggie broke into a loud laugh.

He frowned at her.

She cocked her head, "I'm so sorry, Dr. Hart, but you make me laugh. You think you're so smart. You have it all figured out. You're so grown up. You think you can work this out with your mind. Well, good luck."

His temper was about to flare when she took his hand. "You know I love you, Nicklaus."

Nick pulled his hand away and stomped his foot. "That! How can you love me like that?" His face flushed with embarrassment at his adolescent behavior. He leaned against the wall beside her and crossed his arms to collect himself. "I'm sorry, Maggie. This whole intimacy thing is such a mystery to me."

Maggie didn't respond, and Nick was angry at himself for carrying on. He'd been so happy just walking with her in the cool of the evening, and now he'd gone and spoiled it.

When she didn't respond, he grew edgy. "What are you thinking, Maggie?"

"I'm just praying for you, Nick. That your eyes are opened to the truth."

He crossed his arms, feeling exasperated. "And what is the truth?"

"Do you remember when the Pharisees asked Jesus to name the two greatest commandments?"

She was watching him carefully, but he had no reply.

"To love God with everything you have and to love your neighbor," she paraphrased Matthew, pausing for his reaction.

He had heard the scripture before and nodded.

"Would God ask you to love like that without loving you in even a greater measure?"

He sighed and shook his head. They sat in silence. "I guess not," he said, finally.

"It is almost impossible to love unconditionally until we know our true identity," Maggie said. "The world has us so blinded to who we are and how God sees us."

"And how in the world are we supposed to know how God sees us?"

"Well, for one, the scriptures tell us. And as we experience Him more and more, our eyes become open to Him. Remember your time in Guatemala? I know things changed for you. Think of how your heart grew taking care of the kids with clubfeet."

"True."

"Look, Nick, when Adam and Eve ate from the tree of the knowledge of good and evil, all of mankind fell into darkness. We became separated from God. We became blind. And you know this…Jesus came to restore sight to the blind. To us."

He contemplated her words, looking for answers in the evening sky that was quickly succumbing to darkness. He stood up straight and turned to her. "It's late. We should head back." He reached for her hand to help her off the wall.

She took his hand, pushed away from the wall and they started back to the hospital. "You know, when we feel separated from God, we can be tempted to look for that connection elsewhere."

If only she knew. He caught himself from stumbling over a piece of concrete but couldn't stop himself from stumbling over his thoughts. He wondered if he should tell her about his aberrant ways. She interrupted him before he could decide.

"What are you thinking, Nick?"

He pushed his sin from his thoughts. "Maybe if I just work harder at my faith…read my Bible, get back into church," he searched for the correct answer. "Maybe I should do something like what you're doing…help run a mission."

She just stared at him with astonishment. "Oh, my dear Nicklaus, you just don't get it, do you? It is not what you can do for God that makes Him love you. You can do nothing more… either good or bad…to make Him love you any less or any more. He loves you…period."

Nick frowned, not sure he believed that.

"You know, many other religions are based on works—doing all the right things, doing things just so. The list of rules and regulations just keeps getting longer and longer. It's like trying to sit on a big balloon. The minute you think you have all your life under control, some issue pops out, and you find yourself thinking about something you shouldn't, doing something your spirit knows is not helpful, or even filling yourself with pride that you are doing everything right. On and on and on it goes. You can never be righteous enough. It always seems the more I strive for that, the more distant I feel from God."

He had to agree with that and nodded.

"The fact that God loves us unconditionally is probably the hardest thing for any of us to understand," Maggie said. "Especially if we look through the world's lenses. Do I live up to my parents' expectations, my friends' expectations, and, hardest of all, my own expectations? We look through that lens of getting good-enough grades to be accepted by teachers, dressing and acting to be accepted by friends. It's why we feel like failures so much of the time."

Maggie stopped, turned to him, and held both his hands.

"On top of that, just looking at some of the scriptures can make a person feel like such a failure: Love your neighbor. Love those who hate you, turn your other cheek to those that persecute you. Love unconditionally." Her eyes were full of compassion. "You know, it's hard for me too. Sometimes I find myself loving those that give to the Hope Center and despising those that reject us. It's just not easy."

"So how do you do it?" he asked, at his wits' end.

"By letting go. By surrendering to the fact that God loves you. And to do that, you have to gain a new perspective…open your eyes to a new way of thinking."

They continued walking down the street, and he found himself praying. *Lord, let me see.*

They were back to the woman selling shoes, and as he smiled at her, he felt his heart fill with unfamiliar angst. He looked at the jumbled pile of used shoes and then at the woman, who smiled politely. He turned back to the mismatched footwear.

Just a pile of shoes. He closed his eyes and tried seeing with his heart. He hoped the woman had found the shoes at a collapsed shoe store or apartment building, but what if she took them off the dead? The thought sickened him and anger flashed in his mind toward the woman with the nonchalant affect.

"Nicklaus, look at her through my eyes." The voice in Nick's heart called out.

Nick stared at her and wondered if that was desperation beneath what he saw as smugness.

"Nicklaus, I love this woman. I love each one of the people that wore these shoes."

He closed his eyes again and shook his head, trying to comprehend. Is this all that was left of these people, their shoes? Didn't their lives need to account for so much more? That pile of shoes represented hundreds of lives, each one individual: men, women, children, fathers, mothers, brothers, sisters. Each completely different, each loved by the Father. Compassion for them swept over Nick like a tsunami.

He felt Maggie squeeze his arm, and he opened his eyes. They were still there—the woman's shoes. Maggie steered him down the street back to the compound, but he couldn't stop thinking about it. *Shoes. Just a pile of shoes.*

CHAPTER 47

GRIEF
WEDNESDAY—POST-QUAKE DAY EIGHTEEN

Nick stood at the Russian woman's bedside with x-rays in hand. "I promised I would show you what we did with your leg," he said, smiling at her and the muscle-bound man looming over them with his arms crossed. "I'm sorry, sir. Please remind me of your name," he said, offering his hand to shake.

After a moment's hesitation, the man gripped Nick's hand tightly and nodded. In an awkward moment, Nick tried to withdraw but was powerless in the man's tight grip. Nick nervously smiled at him. The man could easily crush his hand, maybe even snap him in two.

Without easing his grip, a wide smile spread across the Russian's face. "I am Vladimir Molotov." With enthusiasm, he squeezed Nick's hand tighter. "My friends call me the Hammer. You can call me Vladimir." Vladimir continued to squeeze to the point of pain. Then the big man released his hold and laughed loudly. "Thank you for taking good care of my Antasha."

Nick tried to act amused and shook his throbbing hand.

Antasha slapped at Vladimir and almost hit him in the groin. "Don't you dare hurt those beautiful hands."

He smirked at her and bowed slightly to Nick. "Truly, Dr. Hart, we are grateful for everything you have done. I owe you." After a moment of thought, he grinned, "I owe you, at the very least, a shot of Russia's best vodka." When Nick didn't reply, he added, "You do drink vodka?"

"On occasion," Nick said, still nursing his hand.

"*Da*, we share vodka and then you call me the Hammer." He slapped Nick's back hard enough that he fought the urge to cough.

Great. He could just imagine the Hammer filled with booze.

Nick turned his attention back to the woman. He bent over her bed and held the x-ray under the lights over her head. "Antasha…AK, can you see where your leg was broken?"

She pointed to the obvious separation of the tibia with its jagged fracture.

"Yes, that's right." He switched films and showed her the post-operative image. "Here's your leg with the titanium nail down the tibia. You can see how well the fracture is reduced. We locked the nail in place on both the top and bottom with screws."

"You screw me?"

He flushed with embarrassment. He wasn't sure if it was her poor English or if she was flirting again. He felt Vladimir's eyes stabbing him. "Well, uh, yes. We put screws in the bone to hold everything in place."

"You did a wonderful job, Dr. Hart." She smiled at Nick. "Best one I've ever had." She smirked at Vladimir and blew him a fake kiss.

"When do you want to get out of here?" Nick changed the subject to cover his unease.

Antasha shrugged and looked at Vladimir.

For the first time, he saw the big man as more than a muscle-bound gorilla. There must be a brain behind the prominent brow and large nose, because, for all her taunts, the woman seemed to rely on him.

Vladimir's eyes turned thoughtful as he stared Nick down. Finally, he said, "We could have our government fly us out, unless you think flying is not the best option now."

"AK is still at risk for a blood clot, considering the waiting she had to endure, and her recent surgery."

Vladimir nodded. "That is what I thought. Still, we need to

finish our investigation." He looked sternly at Antasha and back at Nick. "I know that big mouth, here, has spilled the apples."

Nick chuckled to himself. *Apples, beans, whatever.* He wasn't going to get into semantics with this man.

"Putin has us chasing ghosts," Vladimir said, throwing up his hands. "AK and I were enjoying a beer on the patio during our excursion to Turkey…and now look at us…prisoners in a hospital, unable to do our duty. And that old-woman patient of yours—what she said is pertinent to our business. We need to get back to work—"

"Like hound dogs on a trail," Antasha finished.

Vladimir flashed her a look of irritation and turned back to Nick. "We started our search in Hakkâri. That old woman says she is from a village close to there, Qodshanes. But here is our challenge, Dr. Hart. After the earthquake struck, we 'borrowed'"—he made air quotes with his fingers—"an SUV from the hotel. Our rental car in the parking garage was buried under tons of concrete. Then, after miles and hours of driving, we ran out of gas and had to leave the SUV and walk. Even if we could find the SUV, it would be useless." He sighed, staring at Nick. "Do you think, Dr. Hart, you could put in a good word with the Commander to get us some help?"

Nick crossed his arms and rested his chin on his hand. Back at the MED, all he had to do was write an order to discharge the patient, and the nurses made it happen. He wasn't sure that he wanted to get involved, but knew the man was right; they were helpless. He had the pulse of all the patients and had been told of Vladimir's gunshot wound. "I guess I need to know about your shoulder injury." It was his turn to stare the big man down. Nick did not flinch.

Vladimir sighed in resignation. "*Da.* It's like this. We were driving through the dark, earthquake-ravaged countryside, desperate for fuel. We stopped at a farm to ask for gas. The farmer caught us and…" He paused. "It did not go well."

"Desperate measures for desperate times," Antasha added.

Vladimir put out his hand to silence her and continued, "I disarmed the farmer, but he got off a shot…and so my shoulder is like this." He moved his shoulder and winced. "That's all there is to it. I may have broken his nose in the process, but nothing else." He held his hands palms up.

Nick stared at him. *He's either a great liar or he's telling the truth.*

"I want to do whatever we can to make it right with the farmer," Vladimir insisted. "I think, given the chance, we could find the old farm again," he added hopefully.

Nick dropped his hands and nodded. "I will see what the Commander says, but I may have to tell him your story."

"Desperate times, Doctor," Vladimir said.

Nick turned back to Antasha. "AK, how is the walking going?"

She smiled, flipped her copper hair back with her hand, threw the sheet off her body, and swung her legs off the side of the bed. Vladimir offered to assist her, but she batted his hand away and stood. Using her good leg, she spun in a circle, letting her loose hospital gown flash the men with her bare backside.

Vladimir and Nick looked at each other and rolled their eyes.

"So, what do you think?" AK asked.

"I think you are doing well," Nick said, "and I think we should get you some clothes."

***

After the doctor left her bedside, Vladimir fumed. "Why do you do that to me?" he complained.

"Do what?"

"You know exactly what I mean." He crossed his arms. "You always disrespect me."

"Vladimir, you know I just joke around."

"I don't think flashing your doctor is a joke. I know you like the man."

"He is handsome and talented. What's not to like?"

It was all he could do to not smash his fist into the wall. Walls, chairs, tables, and other inanimate objects had been targets of his pounding rage. He wasn't called the Hammer for nothing, and most of the knuckles on his right hand were deformed due to his violent urges.

AK was back in bed with the sheet pulled over her. "Why do you care anyway?"

He realized she was irritated. At times like this both their tempers would flare. If they were alone, it would usually result in an all-out battle. He glanced around the room; some of the women, aroused by AK's antics or the loud voices, were eyeing them and scowling. He had never laid a hand on her and never would. With a black belt in judo, he knew how to fight. No man intimidated him. But this woman—this beautiful, sassy woman—made his knees feel weak.

He turned away and stared out the window.

Antasha fluffed her pillow and flung her head back defiantly.

"You know I care for you," he said quietly. "Yet you treat me like a dog."

"Vladimir, we have been partners for over twelve years. I care about you too. You know that. You know I would do anything for you. You are my partner."

"And what about the times we have been intimate?"

She puffed air out her lips. "Probably the vodka."

His heart sank. He looked down at her, frowned, and nodded.

"Vladimir, I really do care for you," she said.

"*Da.*" He turned and left the ward.

***

Maggie stood with Ali at the entrance to the pediatric ward. She swallowed hard, knowing it was time to speak to the boy called Ibrahim. With her encouragement, the Commander had formed a special task force of soldiers to search for clues concerning the children that were unclaimed by their parents—twenty-six of them would soon be added to the orphan list. Ibrahim was one of those. Maggie wanted to meet the boy who had ushered in the miracle for the brain-damaged girl, but not with news like this.

She looked at the paper attached to the clipboard in her hand. She already knew what it said; the UN soldiers had found no surviving members of Ibrahim's family. Maggie adjusted her headscarf, something she was still trying to get used to—something she found claustrophobic today.

She shifted the clipboard to her other hand and touched Ali's forearm. "Thank you for coming with me, Ali. This must be awfully difficult for you, having no word of your own parents."

He looked at her with kind, dark eyes. She could see he was fighting back tears. "I am hoping to get transportation to Hakkâri in the next few days," he said. "We will see. My uncle was here at the hospital yesterday. He has not seen either my parents or my wife's parents, so I fear the reports of them being seen alive are false."

A tear slid down his cheek. "My parents' house is completely destroyed. Asti's parents' place is still standing but abandoned. It depends where they were when the earthquake hit. There has been no sign of them at the government hospital in Van. My uncle told me that some people fled to Hakkâri."

Maggie watched Ali wipe the tear, straighten his spine, and walk into the ward. She understood his resolve. After all, her husband, John, had been a surgeon, and even though he had been more tenderhearted than most, his identity as a surgeon was always intact. When it was time for business, he turned off his emotions and focused on the job. Her eyes welled, thinking of him. How she missed him.

But it was time for business, so she took a deep breath and followed Ali to Ibrahim's bedside. After Ali exchanged greetings with Ibrahim, he introduced Maggie to the boy. Ali spoke to him in Turkish and translated for her.

"Ibrahim, this is Ms. Russell. She is from America, and she is here to help you."

It was all she could do not to throw herself on the floor and weep. The child looked so adorable, so innocent; his dark bushy eyebrows matched his tousled hair, and his thick, beautiful eyelashes blinked with attentiveness.

Ibrahim stared at her, neither smiling nor frowning.

She saw the whites of his eyes were clear, and his dark eyes held a hint of hazel. She sat on the side of his bed and spoke in English as Ali translated to Turkish.

"Hi, Ibrahim. I have heard so much about you. What a handsome boy you are." She hoped she was pronouncing his name correctly, as Ali had taught her. "How is your leg feeling?"

Ibrahim looked at Ali and back at her. Ali reassured him. Apparently satisfied, Ibrahim said, "It hurts just a little."

"I'm glad you are healing so quickly," she said. "Dr. Ali tells me that you will be in traction for another week or two and then they will put you in a cast."

Ibrahim listened to Ali's translation, and his face twisted in confusion. With a wary eye on her, he fired questions at Ali, who explained a spica cast and showed him how it would go around his broken leg, up to his waist, and back down the other leg to his knee. Fear filled Ibrahim's face. Ali sat on the other side of the bed, put his hand on the boy's chest, and gently rephrased his answers.

When the fear ebbed from Ibrahim's face, Ali looked at Maggie and smiled. "He thought he would have to wear the cast for the rest of his life and was asking how he could possibly eat or go to the bathroom. He is very bright. I reassured him that the cast would be on for just a few weeks and that he could eat whatever he wanted and we would make room around his cast so he could go to the bathroom."

Ibrahim asked Ali more questions, and Ali answered them.

This time, when Ali looked at her, his smile was gone. "He wants to know about walking and playing football, uh, soccer. And he wants to know about his parents."

She followed Ali's eyes to Ibrahim's eyes, which were pleading for answers. She touched the boy's cheek, and his lower lip began to quiver. She held his face and could not stop her own tears from forming. She moved closer to him. "I'm so sorry, Ibrahim." She tried unsuccessfully to choke back tears. "The soldiers have looked very hard for your parents, and they cannot find them."

Ibrahim wept—softly at first and then with his whole body. Maggie saw Ali try to steady the leg in traction, so she leaned over the boy and wrapped him in her arms, holding him to her chest. When she felt his heaving slow, she pushed herself up, wiped his tears, and stroked his hair.

"What about my sister?" Ibrahim asked. The shake of Ali's head brought more grief, and once again she enveloped the boy. A song rose from deep in her heart. It was a Julie True ballad she knew well. It had imprinted on her heart when she'd grieved for

John. It had comforted her at times when she thought she would be swallowed up by the pain of her loss. She began to hum the tune and then to sing softly, "I am not afraid of what tomorrow holds…"

As she held Ibrahim, she could feel his head nestle into the crook of her neck while his body shook. She continued to sing and rock Ibrahim to the rhythm of the song. When his weeping slowed, she pressed her lips to his forehead.

Ibrahim's chest stopped heaving. His body relaxed, and he sighed once, then twice before resting. She pushed herself up but continued to sing, gently stroking his eyebrows and cheek. His eyes fluttered closed.

She smiled at Ali, who motioned that he was needed elsewhere. She nodded and mouthed a thank-you between verses.

CHAPTER 48

CONFRONTATION
THURSDAY—POST-QUAKE DAY NINETEEN

Abdul panted in the crisp air. The sun had broken from the towering mountains surrounding Hakkâri and was beginning to warm the hospital grounds. He wondered if his heart would explode and cursed himself for getting so out of shape. He had never liked to run, but he thought he'd affirm his command by leading the men on a short, early morning jog around the compound. As he caught his breath, he knew he had misjudged the distance. He was on his second lap of three that he had ordered his men to complete. He wasn't sure he could make the third in the mile-high elevation.

He took in a deep breath, gathering his stamina. He was content at last. It was a good life. Spending the last two nights and part of the day with Akleema had eclipsed a lifetime of struggle for identity and value. Confidence, which he had struggled to find all his life, poured through his veins. To his surprise, he felt no guilt. Even the grief over his father's death and the loss of his brother weighed less on his shoulders. Being desired by her seemed to fill every void in his life and overshadow any regret.

His heart pounded. He looked back to see some of his men had slowed to a walk or stopped altogether. Maybe it was too much to ask. Maybe he should stop as well. Then he spat in disgust and stood up straight. He was the Commander. He needed to set an example.

He quickened his pace but heard approaching steps behind him—sandals slapping against the asphalt. When he glanced over his shoulder he saw two men, at least twenty years older than he was and in much better shape, running in worn sandals. He wondered why they weren't far ahead of him until he realized they were showing respect to their leader by not passing him. He was, after all, in command. His confidence soared and blew him a second wind as he pushed to complete his third lap.

He jogged past Omar, the hospital administrator, sporting brand new, high-fashion jogging togs and strolling with ease toward the finish of his first lap. When Abdul gave him a salute, Omar feigned the agony of a long-distance runner—grimacing, huffing, puffing, and pausing to pull out a silk handkerchief to wipe his brow. "Just wait until you're fifty-seven."

Abdul laughed and waved him off. Blood pumped through his veins. He was alive.

When he saw Akleema ahead, he quickened his pace and straightened his back. She was wearing sweatpants, an oversized hoodie, and a dark blue headscarf. *Praise Allah.* She did as he had asked and dressed conservatively, as befits a woman.

He turned, ran backward past her, and smiled. "You need some help?"

She scratched her nose with her middle finger.

Abdul laughed, turned, and continued running with even more spring in his step.

Is this what love feels like? Before he could analyze it, his mind raced through images of her body and reprised the warmth of her embrace. He never imagined that sex would be so intoxicating, but it wasn't just the act. It was the way he felt afterward, when they held each other and she stroked his forehead. It was the way he felt now—invincible, strong, and whole. *One more lap to go.*

He heard one of the men with the slapping sandals gaining on him. When he glanced over his shoulder, he saw the other man had dropped back. He faced forward and tried to quicken his pace. His mind was racing, but his lungs and his legs were not cooperating. The shadow of the man behind him grew, and soon the man was running beside him.

"*Selamünaleyküm*, may God's peace be upon you," the man

said.

"*Aleykümselam*, peace be upon you," Abdul panted back.

The man matched his pace stride for stride, and they jogged in silence for another hundred meters. Abdul saw the man glance around before saying, "Commander, I must speak to you."

Abdul studied the man's face and recognized him as one of the hospital guards. He slowed his pace.

"Abdul..." the man said, then hesitated.

"If you need to talk to me, you are free to do so," he said with some irritation. Why was this guard calling him by his first name?

"Commander, I am a man as well. I know what lies at the heart of men and the desires we have."

Sweat dripped down Abdul's back. He stopped, turned to the man, and stared, but the man averted his gaze to his sandals.

"You have something to say to me?"

"Abdul, I am no man's judge. I am not your judge."

He looked around and was grateful no one could hear them. "Then why are you talking to me?" he asked with rising anger.

"It is my duty under Sharia law to confront a brother in sin."

"How dare you?" His anger was boiling. "Don't you know who I am?"

"Yes, Commander, but we all are in danger of sin."

"And what sin are you accusing me of?" Abdul squared his body to the man and clenched his fists at his sides.

The man lifted his face and stared at him. "*Zinā*, fornication."

"And who is your witness?" he demanded. He knew that to prove *Zinā*, four witnesses had to testify to the actual act of penetration. He stepped closer to the trembling little man who stood almost a foot shorter. Abdul was furious and not intimidated by his accuser.

"It is only I," the man said softly but with conviction. "I saw you coming out of the woman's room in the night. I was one of the guards on duty last night walking the hallways—"

"So, I was in the woman's room. What does that prove?" His agitation grew as the man's confidence increased.

"Young man, beautiful woman," the guard said.

"You better watch your mouth." He spat out the words. "And

more important, you better watch your accusations," he shouted, shoving the guard, who stumbled backward but regained his footing and moved toward him.

"You need to step down as our leader and confess in the name of Allah," the guard shot back.

"Who else have you told about this?" Abdul grabbed the guard by the shirt.

"As Allah is my witness, I bring this only to you." He tried to pull himself free.

Abdul saw other men jogging around the corner of the complex. His rage peaked, and he raised his fist. He swung hard and fast with his right hand and hit the guard square in the jaw. The guard staggered but recovered quickly and charged him.

He tried to sidestep the attack, but the guard grabbed his shirt and pulled him forward, knocking him off balance and pulling them both to the ground. Abdul fell on top of the guard and frantically clawed the guard's face and gouged him in the eye.

When the guard hollered, Abdul swung his left elbow to smash his nose. He tried to turn the man's head and smash it facedown into the asphalt. But the guard twisted violently and Abdul reeled as if he were in a car rollover. His world spun and he found himself trapped between the guard and the asphalt. The man grabbed his throat and squeezed.

The guard yelled a primordial scream and slammed his fist into Abdul's right eye, all the while choking his neck. Abdul was crazed. He heard loud voices and flailed his arms and legs and fought for breath as the guard squeezed his neck. Struggling for air, he realized he was losing the fight. He tore at the guard's hands, fighting to stay alive. Adrenaline kicked in and he pushed up his knees and legs to throw the guard off, but the guard had locked his own legs around him and didn't let go of his death grip.

A black curtain fell over Abdul's vision. "Air, I need air." He called for his father. "Father!" he gasped, believing it was his last utterance.

***

He was not dead. Abdul heard the rasp of his breathing. He reached for his aching throat and touched his face. He opened his eyes and was horrified to see his hands covered in blood. *I'm bleeding. I'm dying.* His heart pounded, and he gasped for breath. It came easily. *I'm alive.*

He looked around in panic and saw faces above him, reflecting his own terror in their eyes. His men were standing over him.

Then he saw Akleema. She was mouthing something and he strained to make out the words. "Abdul. Abdul, are you okay?" He looked at his bloodied hands. He couldn't speak and tried to understand what had happened. Then he remembered the guard attacking him. *Where is the guard?* He moved his head from side to side.

He felt something heavy on top of him. He looked over his chest and saw a head. The guard! He steeled himself, waiting for another attack, but the guard did not move.

Abdul took a deep breath and, with difficulty, pushed himself onto his elbows. He saw blood gushing from the guard's throat and Akleema holding a knife dripping with blood.

"Abdul, are you okay?" she asked again.

Abdul reflexively pushed the dead guard off and recoiled. His men and Akleema stared down at him, waiting. *Do they know? Do they all know?* He made himself nod to answer to her question.

"He is okay!" Akleema shouted. The men cheered.

Abdul wiped at the blood on his face.

"Our Commander has survived," a chorus of voices cheered. "Allah be praised."

"The Commander has survived the attack of this spy," Akleema shouted and spat on the dead man.

The men cheered again, and one of them kicked the dead man clear of Abdul's body. Another kicked the dead man's head, splattering blood.

He tried to smile in gratitude and watched the sweating administrator push into the group, look at him and then at the corpse, and shake his head.

CHAPTER 49

THE TREE OF LIFE

"The tree of life?" Buck laughed and bit into his tuna sandwich.

Nick shrugged, "That's what the Russians are telling me." He looked to Ali for help but found none. "The only reason I bring it up is that they want to go back to Hakkâri, and that is where Ali is headed."

Nick glanced across the table at Jack and Maggie, who committed to nothing else but their sandwiches. He turned back to Ali beside him. "Ali, you were telling me about the rich history of this area. What do you think?" When Ali still didn't respond, Nick poked him lightly. "Earth to Ali."

"I'm sorry, Dr. Hart. My mind was elsewhere…as for what the Russians told you, I may not be much help. My culture believes that this ancient area of Mesopotamia is at the heart of the beginning of time. As for the tree of life, Muslims believe it existed in the Garden of Eden, but we believe the Garden of Eden is in heaven, not on earth. Our ancient manuscripts tell us that when Adam and Eve were in the Garden of Eden, Allah forbade them to eat from the tree, and when they disobeyed, they were banished from heaven to earth."

Nick nodded and shrugged. "The thing is," he said to them all, "the Russians won't share all the information they have, but from what I'm putting together, it seems like a search for the Holy Grail."

"Maybe they're searching for the fountain of youth," Jack said, and the others chuckled.

Nick bit into his peanut butter and jelly sandwich. He sat back, chewed, and mused, "I have to admit, ever since the Russian woman mentioned it, the idea of searching for the tree of life has been intriguing. I hadn't thought about the Garden of Eden since Sunday school. It always seemed like a nice story for little kids."

Buck gulped lemonade and nodded. "The tree of life was kind of hard to wrap my mind around, and I always got a headache trying to figure it out. I guess it's just one of those things I accepted on faith. But, for sure, I always understood the Garden of Eden was a real place because it says so in the scriptures."

Everyone turned to Jack, who was reading from a pocket-size Bible he'd pulled from his shirt. "'God saw all that he had made, and it was very good. And there was evening, and there was morning—the sixth day.'"

He flipped to the next page, adjusted his glasses, pointed his index finger at the text, and continued reading. "'Thus the heavens and the earth were completed in all their vast array...'" He scanned the page with his finger. "'Now no shrub had yet appeared on the earth...the Lord God formed a man from the dust of the ground and breathed into his nostrils...Now the Lord God had planted a garden in the east, in Eden; and there he put the man he had formed.'" Jack peered over his glasses at the team. "Sounds to me the scriptures say that the garden is... er, was, on earth."

One of the older orphans interrupted them to ask if anyone wanted more lemonade. Maggie and Buck raised their glasses to take her up on the offer. Maggie stroked the girl's long hair, and with her newly acquired handful of Turkish phrases, she asked the girl what her name was. "*Adın ne?*"

"*Benim adım Elif,*" the girl replied.

Ali translated, "*Elif* means 'slender' or 'the girl who spreads light.'"

"How do you say, 'You are beautiful'?" Maggie asked him.

"*Çok güzelsin,*" Ali said.

Maggie stroked the girl's cheek with the back of her hand and repeated Ali's translation, "Çok güzelsin."

The girl said something in return, and Maggie looked to Ali for help.

"She says you are pretty as well."

"Teşekkür ederim, thank you, Elif," Maggie said, patting the girl's arm.

Jack smiled at Maggie and continued to read. "'The Lord God made all kinds of trees grow out of the ground—trees that were pleasing to the eye and good for food. In the middle of the garden were the tree of life and the tree of the knowledge of good and evil.'"

Maggie interrupted. "Have you guys ever wondered what those magnificent trees really looked like?"

No one had an answer. They chewed and sipped in thoughtful silence.

Finally, Buck sighed. "I'm getting a headache trying to picture the dang trees."

Everyone laughed.

"I found something," Jack said. "Listen to this. 'A river watering the garden flowed from Eden; from there it was separated into four headwaters. The name of the first is the Pishon…the name of the second river is the Gihon…the name of the third is the Tigris…and the fourth river is the Euphrates.'" Jack closed the Bible, put it on the table, and opened his hands to discussion. "What say you, my friends?"

"That's definitive," Buck said, grinning. "It's the GPS of the scriptures."

Nick wondered what Ali would say to that. Apparently the others wondered too, because they all looked at Ali.

Ali surveyed them with amusement. "I have never heard of the Gihon and Pishon, but we are certainly at the headwaters of both the Tigris and the Euphrates. Who knows?" He shrugged.

"It's kind of fun to think about," Maggie said. "Can you imagine actually walking with God in the garden in the cool of the day?"

"Naked?" Nick said without thinking. He blushed and then said, "Maybe they didn't have any thorns then."

Maggie smiled and patted his hand. "When Eve first appeared in the Garden of Eden, she was innocent, as was Adam, and their bodies were bare and beautiful. There was no shame, and fig leaves were not needed."

Buck reached for the Bible. "You mind?" he asked Jack.

"Help yourself," Jack said.

While Buck was paging through the book, Jack asked Nick, "What makes you think the Russians have any evidence of the garden or the tree of life? I'm not sure I want to expend any resources on some wild goose chase."

"Well." Nick swallowed. "I can't speak for them, but it sure wouldn't hurt to help them on their way. One thing's for sure, if we got them out of here, it would free up some bed space."

"What if I went with them?" Ali said. "I was hoping to talk with you, Mr. Bilton, to see if there was any way I could use one of the hospital vehicles for a couple of days to go look for my parents."

Jack nodded. "Getting you to Hakkâri is a given, son, but I'd have to think long and hard about the Russians joining you. I'm not sure I want to get involved in any political mess, especially when Putin is involved." He paused and tapped his fingers on the table. "The scriptures tell us that the tree of life gives immortality. Is that true in the Islamic tradition as well, Ali?"

Ali nodded. "The Imams don't call it the tree of life but rather the tree of immortality."

Jack's eyebrows raised, and he crossed his arms over his chest. "I'll tell you what, I think it's all a bunch of baloney, but I'll tell you something else: if the Russians really did find the garden, or the tree, or some branch of the tree, and the immortality thing turned out to be true, I sure wouldn't want Putin to have it and live forever."

Buck looked up from the Bible. "Putin would love to rule the world forever."

"That's neither here nor there," Nick said. He didn't want the discussion to divert to politics. He'd promised the Russians he'd try to help them. "The fact is that people are living longer and longer these days. Maybe there really is something to this. What if our patient truly is 169 years old? I know that's not forever, but that's old. Didn't some of the biblical patriarchs live hundreds of years?"

"The scriptures say that Noah was over nine hundred years old," Maggie said.

"And fathered his three sons when he was a mere youngster at five hundred," Ali added.

"How old was Abraham?" Nick asked.

Ali and Maggie answered simultaneously, "One hundred and seventy-five."

Jack laughed and looked at Ali. "Whether it's the tree of life or the tree of immortality or any of it is real, I guess we do share the same history."

They all nodded except Buck, who found what he was looking for.

"Listen to this," he exclaimed. "So, after Adam and Eve disobeyed God…this is what the scripture says: 'The Lord God made garments of skin for Adam and his wife and clothed them. And the Lord God said, "The man has now become like one of us, knowing good and evil. He must not be allowed to reach out his hand and take also from the tree of life and eat, and live forever."'"

"So, there is the immortality piece," Jack said.

"Yeah, but listen to the rest: 'So the Lord God banished him from the Garden of Eden to work the ground from which he had been taken. After he drove the man out, he placed on the east side of the Garden of Eden cherubim and a flaming sword flashing back and forth to guard the way to the tree of life.'" Buck closed the Bible and pushed it back to Jack. "Doesn't exactly make it sound like God would allow us to find it."

"Us?" Maggie asked.

"Well…the collective us through the ages," Buck said. "Sounds like anyone who tried to find the way to the Garden of Eden would encounter a giant angel swinging a flaming sword to warn them they'd lost their passport to paradise." He swung his huge arm above his head as though he were wielding a heavy sword.

Everyone laughed at the absurdity of it all.

"Step right up, folks." Buck mimicked a carnival barker. "Try your strength against the angel and win the prizes of the Garden of Eden, apples and oranges and all the good stuff. Who dares to defy the flaming sword?"

They cheered and clinked lemonade glasses.

Nick's laughter faded. "I know this all sounds farfetched," he said, mostly to Jack, "but I want you to at least meet with the Russians. I know they look terribly out of place here, but they are both sincere people. I've seen Vladimir help the soldiers lift and move heavy equipment. And as for our old patient, maybe she just thinks she has lived that long, or if it's true, her age may have nothing to do with the scriptures. Maybe she's lived 169 years because of the water or the food in her village. It might be interesting to find out. It might even be beneficial to modern medicine."

Jack sighed. "All right. You have my attention, Dr. Hart. Let's talk with the Russians this evening. I'll speak with the Commander, see if he'd care to join us."

***

It was late in the afternoon as Nick sat on a bench under a fig tree at the edge of the hospital compound. Gazing into the branches, the leaves reminded him of the conversation they'd had at lunch, about the Garden of Eden and Adam and Eve. A ripe fig fell from the tree and smacked his thigh. He rubbed his thigh and scooted to the end of the bench, away from falling fruit.

He wished Maggie was with him, but she was busy with the staff preparing the evening meal for the kids. He looked at his watch. It wouldn't be long before the entire hospital team would sit down for dinner. He'd spent most of the afternoon in the OR, but with all the new volunteers and only three operating rooms, he was beginning to feel like a fifth wheel. The visiting surgeons wanted to operate, and it would be unfair to limit their time in the operating room. He understood they were eager to make the trip worth their while. After all, like him, they'd flown here at their own expense and taken a loss of income from their regular practices.

He scanned the compound. The only activity was in the far corner where Buck had organized a lively soccer game. Buck, at the center of the joyous pandemonium, sported shorts, showing off his bright blue, high-tech prostheses. He still marveled at how well the big man moved.

It was nice to see happiness filling the space where hundreds of hurting patients had waited. By now, most of them had been moved inside the hospital or treated and released to the tent cities. His mind spun with images of the chaos and devastation that had crowded the courtyard just days ago. *How things change.*

He couldn't believe that almost three weeks had passed since the earthquake. There was so much more to be done for the people of Van to restore their bodies and to rebuild their lives. Just thinking about it exhausted and overwhelmed him, and he wasn't sure how much he had left to give. Maybe he should just head home. But then he'd be stuck on call and right back on the treadmill. Worse, he'd have to face the Mayor's attorney. He craved a drink for the first time since leaving Memphis.

He looked at the opposite end of the compound and saw Maggie carrying a huge bowl of salad across the orphanage patio into the cafeteria. A brood of little girls tagged along behind her like chicks following a mother hen. He watched Maggie with longing and shook his head. This was not exactly the place to kindle a romance. She didn't seem ready and probably never would be.

"How am I ever going to find balance in my life?" He sighed, leaned back against the bench, and clasped his hands behind his head. "Too tired to go, too tired to stay." The familiar weight of depression pressed against his sternum.

He planted his feet firmly on the ground, but before he could stand, he saw Jack limping toward him, leaning on his cane.

"Hey, friend, mind if I sit a spell?" Jack asked.

"Of course, but you better sit close to me or you're liable to be conked by a fig. This tree is shedding."

Jack sat by Nick on the edge of the bench. "Dang arthritic hip," he moaned. "I hate being old and decrepit."

"Man, Jack, I wish I had your energy," he said. "You ever think about getting that hip replaced?"

Jack huffed. "I'm waiting until I get ancient. Besides, I try to stay away from doctors." He smiled and peered over the top of his glasses at Nick. "No offense."

"None taken. I feel the same way."

They laughed.

"Nick, I know you've heard me say this several times, but I appreciate what you have done for these people, for King's, so much. You'll be heading back to the States one of these days, and I want you to know"—he paused to catch his breath—"if there is anything I can ever do for you, you have only to ask."

"Thank you. You have already done so much for so many." His eyes began to water. He pushed on his sternum and blinked back a tear.

Jack put his hand on his shoulder.

Nick shrugged it off. "Sorry. I'm just exhausted is all. Thank you for the offer and all you have done."

Jack nodded and sat forward, leaning on the top of his cane. They sat in silence.

Finally, Jack turned to him and asked, "How old are you?"

The question surprised him. "Forty-five." He watched Jack stare beyond the soccer game and tear up.

"I'm eighty-two." Jack shook his head. "I'm not sure where the time goes, or how I got so old so fast." He adjusted his cane. "I think I was just a little older than you are now, Nick, when my business was experiencing a huge growth. I was opening new dealerships and making a ton of money. I was blessed, but my life was sucking me dry. My wife left me, and my best friend betrayed me. Two years later I was diagnosed with colon cancer." His tears fell without shame. "I thought I was doing life right. I was going to church and led a Bible study in my home. I was not just giving ten percent to the poor…I was giving twenty. After my diagnosis, I got so mad at God I lost my temper and yelled at him, 'Don't you see what I'm doing for you?'"

Jack pulled a handkerchief from his pocket and blotted his tears.

"My life went into a death spiral—my business began to fail, and I started having a hard time paying the bills. I was like…if this is following God, I don't want anything to do with it. One day I was sitting in a bar, nursing my fifth rum and coke, when a voice in my heart whispered, 'Jack...I don't want your stuff. I don't want your money. I don't want anything you can do for me...I want you. I love you.' That just about knocked me off the bar stool. It certainly knocked me off my mountain of self-pity. God was telling me I didn't have to prove anything." Jack paused to mop more tears. "He would love me for me."

Jack looked thoughtfully at Nick. "It wasn't a magic pill, mind you, but it changed my life. Of course, it wasn't easy. I'd take one step forward, only to falter and take two steps back. But as I let go of my expectations of God and my expectations of myself, I began to experience real life. Little by little, I found more peace, more joy, and more love. I think this is what Saint Paul meant when he said we have to 'die to self.'"

Nick was stunned. His relationship with Jack had been cordial but superficial; now Jack was reading him like a book. He thought he was better at hiding his emotional angst.

"I hope you don't mind an old man's advice, but I see myself in you—driven, determined, self-sufficient. Not that those things are bad, but they can get in the way of knowing who we really are."

"Jack, honestly..." He took a breath. "Sometimes I don't even know who I am anymore, and I certainly don't know how to be loved like that...to have God love me like that."

"The only way I know how is to surrender."

"Surrender?"

"To let go of who we think we are and to let go of who we think God is. It's the moment when our intellect gives way to the faith in our heart." Jack wiped his brow. "I've been thinking a lot about our conversation at lunch. I'm actually looking forward to talking to your Russian friends. I think we need to learn to step back into that garden, to walk intimately with God in the cool of the day."

Jack stabbed at the ground with his cane and gathered his thoughts. Nick appreciated that the man not only walked with a physical limp, but he had a full life of experiences and it hadn't all been easy. Jack was someone he could trust.

"When I grew up, I put my identity in material things and

discovered I'd lost myself," Jack said. "I came to a point where I was so miserable I had to let go of my worldly identities. When I let go of my material striving, I discovered I already was who God wanted me to be." Jack patted Nick's knee. "When I realized God loved me the way I was, I found I could love myself that way. Love trumps fear."

"That's what Maggie and Buck have been telling me."

"It's why the scriptures tell us we are complete. We don't need to become more than who we are. All we need to do is open our eyes to see ourselves as Jesus sees us." He paused to wipe his upper lip. "Jesus came to restore sight to the blind. We are all blinded in some manner by our distorted beliefs."

It was almost exactly what Maggie had said. They didn't speak for a while, giving Nick a chance to process what he'd just heard.

Jack reached for Nick's arm and broke the silence. "Look, Nick, to fully discover who you are—your true identity—you have to let go of everything you think you are, all your identities—doctor, surgeon, friend, whatever else you call yourself." Jack chuckled. "Of course, our lesser identities are fierce warriors, and, given the pressures of life, they keep pulling us back into their camps."

"Jack, can I ask you something?"

"Anything," Jack said.

"When you let go of all those identities, what was left? Who are you?"

Jack whistled through his teeth and looked as though no one had asked him that before. "Well, Nick, when I surrendered everything else, I became a child of God...His son. That is my true identity."

"Maybe I'm making this harder than it is," Nick sighed. "I guess I'm a work in progress."

Jack smiled and squeezed Nick's arm. "It's okay. You'll see." He glanced at his watch. "Looks like it's time for dinner. I am feeling a bit peckish, and you've earned a hot meal."

CHAPTER 50

STORIES

Abdul winced as he flexed his shoulders. He was still sore from his encounter with the guard, but he had to do this. He extended his chest, opened the door, and entered the secretary's office adjacent to the hospital administrator's inner sanctum. He was grateful the secretary was away. Omar's massive wooden door was closed, but voices came from inside. He put his ear to the door to hear them better.

Why hadn't Akleema told him she was going to talk to Omar? Rage boiled in his belly when he learned about it from one of his men, who claimed to have seen her ascending the large staircase in the hospital entryway.

He listened through the door and heard her unmistakable laugh. Sure enough, she was there. He heard them laugh together and became incensed. He wished he could hear what they were saying, but the rumbling diesel generator and the roaring fountain echoing off the marble made it impossible to understand their words.

He heard Omar emphasize something to which Akleema laughed again.

"May I help you?" a woman's voice startled him.

The secretary. Abdul straightened his spine and spun around. "Uh…I was just checking to see if Omar was in. I was about to knock." His face betrayed him, and he turned back to the door, flung it open and entered Omar's office.

"Abdul," Omar said with neither alarm nor welcome. "We thought you'd be resting after the terrible incident. How are you feeling?" When he did not reply, Omar opened his arms. "Please come in. I was just telling Akleema a story." He rose from a chair that was cozily placed next to Akleema's. "Please fetch another cup," Omar said to his secretary, who stood in the doorway behind him. "Please come in, Abdul." He took three steps forward trying to encourage him into the room. "Sit down. You must take it easy."

He didn't move. He stared at Omar and then at Akleema, whose white skin flushed as she looked away.

"I don't want to interrupt your little get-together." He glowered at the White Snake.

Omar took his elbow. "Not at all, my door is always open."

Always open except for now.

Omar scowled at the agitated secretary and waved her away, indicating that she should do as he had asked. Then he attempted to pull Abdul forward.

He resisted. He crossed his arms, stood his ground, and glared at Akleema. He wasn't about to be agreeable, and he didn't care if it showed.

His anger grew when Akleema turned away from him, and he frowned at Omar. "What is so secret that the door was closed and I knew nothing of this meeting?"

"Oh, my," Omar apologized. "Commander, please. Akleema was just enduring stories told by an old man. We simply shut the door because of the noisy waterfall. By Allah, I swear. Please forgive me."

Omar's double chin shook like a turkey wattle. Abdul watched the irritating fat man grovel, allowing the jealous storm inside him to subside. When Omar's eyes focused beyond him, Abdul turned to see the secretary standing in the doorway with a cup and saucer and a small decorative box. He stepped aside to let her enter.

"Aha." Omar patted his hands together and met her halfway, taking the cup, saucer and box and dismissing her with a nod. He handed the tea cup to Abdul. "Look here," he preened, holding up the box and lifting its lid. "I have Turkish delight for you. It's so fresh, it practically melts in your mouth." Omar plucked a jellied candy covered in powdered sugar, licked his lips, waved it front of Abdul and plopped it in his own mouth. When Abdul refused a piece, Omar shrugged and put the box on the table.

Akleema finally turned and frowned at Abdul, her face flushed with anger. He was angry too, but he wanted her alliance in more ways than one. Maybe he was making a big deal out of nothing. He relinquished his glare and tilted his head in apology. Her expression softened, then she puckered her lips and smiled playfully.

He accepted the tea that Omar offered to pour for him.

With a grin that made his greasy mustache flex, Omar insisted Abdul take a candy. "Is delicious, no? Sit down. Join us. We are so glad you are feeling better. You have been through so much," he said nervously. "Join the conversation. We were just talking about the dead."

Omar offered him the leather chair he'd been sitting in and took a chair across from them.

"The dead?" He looked at Akleema as he sat, squirming in the chair's leftover warmth from Omar's large body.

Akleema looked at Omar to explain.

"I was telling Akleema an amusing story about the thirteen *stelae* that were found in Hakkâri."

"*Stelae?*" Abdul asked.

"Yes, stone carvings of men. I mentioned these on the day of your arrival, yes? There are thirteen of them that range from three feet high to more than ten feet. They were discovered only twenty years ago when a local man was digging for mud at the base of the Ottoman castle ruins on the edge of town. The locals go there for the clay to repair their roofs damaged by the harsh winters. The *stelae* are chiseled from hard, local stone and appear to be over three thousand years old."

"And the dead?" he asked, still not understanding what was so funny.

"From what I understand," Omar said, "The archeologists believe the *stelae* are associated with graves and cults of the dead. Apparently, they are similar to the Bal-Bal of the Philippines.

These carvings represent undead monsters that steal corpses and feed on them."

"Like zombies," Akleema smiled. "Omar was telling me that they have a keen smell for dead bodies, and they have huge claws and sharp teeth that they use to dismember their prizes."

"Yes, and because they feast only on corpses, their breath is rather foul." Omar pinched his nose with one hand and sipped his tea with the other.

Abdul noticed the administrator's hand shake. Looking at Akleema he said with sarcasm, "Yes, I can see how funny that story is."

***

When the Russians arrived to have coffee and fresh-baked cookies with the team after dinner, Nick was relieved that Antasha was wearing pants. She had shed the hospital gown for a pair of baggy scrubs a new nurse from Alabama donated to her. AK's bottom was covered, but the scrubs couldn't hide her tall and shapely figure.

He introduced them to Jack, Buck, Maggie, and the UN Commander. He was thankful the Commander had come. The Russians nodded to Ali, whom they had already met. When Buck shook Vladimir's hand, Nick watched with amusement. Buck rarely looked small next to anyone, but next to the giant Russian, he did.

"Would you like some coffee? Cookies?" Maggie offered.

They both smiled but declined.

"Do you have cognac?" AK asked.

Vladimir glowered at her, and she caught his look and apologized. "I'm sorry. Just kidding of course. It has been a long few weeks."

Except for Vladimir, they all laughed, including the UN Commander.

"I believe I'll have coffee after all," Antasha said and Maggie poured her a cup.

"Thank you," AK said and sipped. "Excellent." She turned to Jack. "Mr. Bilton, I understand you built this hospital. I must thank you...we must thank you for everything you have done for us. We are forever grateful. I don't know how we will repay you, but I promise we will not forget. We thank all of you."

Nick was relieved that she had put on her best behavior along with the pants.

The UN Commander cut to the chase. "I understand you want to go back to Hakkâri."

AK looked at Vladimir. Nick was surprised when Vladimir spoke directly to the Commander in fluent French. He was amazed at the sound of such an eloquent language coming from the big Russian's mouth.

The two conversed for a moment. Then Vladimir turned to the rest of the team and spoke in English. "Forgive me, but before I became part of the Foreign Intelligence Service, I was part of the Russian delegation to the UN for three years. I was just complimenting the Commander's soldiers and his leadership. It has not been easy, I'm sure. I thank you all for your good work. Спасибо," he added in Russian.

"Dr. Hart has been telling us a fantastic tale," the Commander said.

"I expect he has been telling you about the tree of life," Vladimir said and opened his hands like a book on the table, as though about to reveal its secrets. "Obviously, under normal circumstances, I could tell you nothing. This"—he waved a hand over the room, indicating the hospital and the compound—"is not normal. Still, you must forgive me if I do not tell you everything I know; I would be thrown in the gulag if I did. Yes, we were sent to Turkey to find information on immortality. Or maybe I should say longevity. I can honestly tell you there is absolutely no report of anyone becoming immortal." He looked at the team with sincerity.

"No reports of angels with flaming swords guarding the entrance to the Garden of Eden?" Buck said, not hiding his sarcasm and disdain.

Vladimir did not seem to be intimidated and smiled at Buck. "I see you know the Bible. No, we know of no such thing. In fact, you can read what I have to say in any history book. I will not be telling you national secrets." He paused, took a breath, and continued. "The Russians had much presence in this area throughout history, not all of it pleasant. I'm afraid we have not been good friends of the people who live here." He said this to Ali, who nodded. "In the last few centuries, the Russians partnered with Slavic and Christian minorities against the Ottoman rule. Since the mid-1500s and until the First World War, the Russians and minorities in the area fought many battles against the Ottomans. That is when the Assyrians and the Armenians joined together against the Ottomans."

"This is part of the violent history over this land," Ali interjected. "This area was the homeland of the Assyrians and the Armenians...and of my own people, the Kurds. The Ottoman Empire was all about establishing the Islamic caliphate." Ali paused and lowered his voice. "Much like what ISIS is doing today to reestablish the Islamic State."

"*Da,*" Vladimir agreed. "This all came to a head during the First World War. The Assyrians and Armenians, with the help of the Russians, fought bravely and fiercely for three years, even though they were at a great disadvantage. They controlled this whole area of eastern Turkey, northern Syria, Iraq and Iran. I know this because my heritage is Armenian." Vladimir added the biographical note as if letting them know that he, too, had a stake in the land.

The Commander looked at his watch. Nick could tell he was growing impatient. "And this has to do with...?"

"Sorry, forgive me," Vladimir said. "I know you are busy. The Russians betrayed the people of this area and abandoned them, but not before secrets were passed from the local church to the Russian church. When Russia withdrew support, the Assyrians, the Armenians, and the Christians were mostly killed or driven off by the Ottomans and their allies, the Kurds."

Nick looked at Ali, who did not react.

"This was early 1900s," Vladimir continued. "Most of the information on longevity that I have comes from the Russian Orthodox Church—mostly anecdotal stories of priests that lived to be hundreds of years old, and hints and whispers of ancient secrets protected by the church. Of course, they're only stories and difficult to prove...but difficult to dispute."

"And difficult to ignore," Nick added. "I guess we'd all love to live longer, healthier lives." Many of the others nodded.

"Some of the very old documents point to this area of ancient Mesopotamia," Vladimir said, "but the connections are not clear."

"Which is why the Russian government gave us this wonderful trip to paradise," Antasha said sarcastically.

Vladimir shot her an irritated look and continued. "I didn't understand the connection between the Russian Orthodox Church and the Christians in this area, Dr. Hart, until Antasha talked with your elderly patient. Now I will let her tell you about that." Vladimir nodded to Antasha to continue the story.

"Dr. Hart's patient, a very old woman, told me that she was a disciple from the East Church. I wasn't quite sure what she meant, and I wanted to look it up, so I asked one of your soldiers if I could use a computer"—she smiled apologetically at the Commander—"and he did me the favor."

Yeah, wonder how she got that favor? Nick speculated.

"So, I searched Internet for hints about what the old woman had said, when suddenly it hit me. It wasn't the East Church; it was the Church of the East. The church she was talking about is the Assyrian Church of the East. The Assyrian Church of the East had close ties to the Russian Orthodox Church, and like all of Christianity that spread east from Israel, the Church of the East stretches back to the Apostolic Age. I read that the Church of the East was established by the apostles Thomas, Bartholomew, and Thaddeus of Edessa."

"Are you Christian?" Maggie asked.

Antasha laughed. "*Nyet, n*o. I was raised as a Russian Jew… and now I'm not exactly a practicing Jew. I'm just telling you what I read." She took a folded sheet of paper from the pocket of her scrubs, opened it, glanced at it, and said, "Your Saint Peter, chief of the apostles…" She paused and looked at Maggie, who nodded and urged her to continue. "Your chief of apostles blessed the Church of the East when he visited the people of Babylon."

Vladimir took back the conversation. "Christianity spread rapidly through the Middle East, Russia and Asia—including China and India. Like many religions, the Assyrian Church of the East had some divisions, but in 1692, the patriarch of the church moved the seat of power to an Assyrian village called Qodshanes." He paused for effect. "It is in the mountains above Hakkâri."

Buck rolled his eyes and said, "I don't know about the rest of you, but I've got a doozy of a headache." Everyone but the Russians laughed. Buck stared at Vladimir. "And what does any of this have to do with the tree of life?"

"I'm coming to that." Vladimir smiled a steely smile. "The priest who moved the Church to Qodshanes in 1692 was born in—?" He held out his hands for everyone to guess.

AK didn't wait for an answer and blurted out, "The priest was born in 1450, and he died around 1700."

Nick and everyone else did the math.

"He was two hundred fifty years old." Vladimir said. "And look at this." He dug into the front pocket of his pants, pulled out a folded sheet of paper, and unfurled it with a snap of his wrist. "The priest's coat of arms."

Nick and the others looked at the paper. The design was simple—a large tree surrounded by Cyrillic script. Vladimir translated. "This is the priest's name, here at the bottom. The script at the top says, *'The tree that gives life.'*"

Nick saw that the Russians finally had the Commander's attention.

"The river that flows past Qodshanes is the Zab River," Vladimir explained. "The ancient manuscripts from the church call it the Pishon, one of the four rivers of Paradise." He paused to look at each member of the team. "The old priest would occasionally sign his letters, 'from the Garden of Eden.'"

"Have you been to this village of Qodshanes?" the Commander asked.

"We were headed there the day the earthquake struck. We have no idea what we will find," Vladimir said.

The Commander leaned back in his chair, crossed his arms, and sighed. "I have to admit, it's captivating." He looked at Jack and then at Nick and Ali.

Everyone was smiling.

"Sounds like a historical and archeological adventure more than a political one," Buck added.

The Commander nodded. "I think this warrants investigation. Ali, we need to get you to Hakkâri. You mind some company?"

CHAPTER 51

LISTENING
THURSDAY EVENING—
POST-QUAKE DAY NINETEEN

It was almost impossible at King's Hospital to find a quiet, secluded spot, and Maggie was not convinced that climbing up the construction ladders from the third floor to the roof after dark was a great idea in earthquake country. When Nick insisted that no one had felt a tremor for several days, she relented. Once they got to the rooftop, they were rewarded with a dazzling display. The night sky was brilliant. With only a sliver moon and no city lights, the stars lit up the darkness, glistening and winking with majesty and mystery.

Even though they were exhausted from the long day, they needed to seize this time together. Alone at last on the rooftop, they found a rickety crate to sit on. It wasn't the Ritz, but it would have to do. Besides, it beat the incessant chaos in the hospital below.

They sat speechless, in awe of the night sky. A cool breeze blew off Lake Van, and Maggie pulled her sweater tightly around her neck.

He gazed into the glittering canopy. "It's amazing to see the same stars I saw as a kid in Montana."

Maggie nodded. "It always gives me comfort to know there's one constant in this crazy world."

"There's Polaris, the North Star." He pointed. "Look how well you can see the Big and Little Dippers. The stars are so bright you can make out the Great Bear in Ursa Major. See how the Big Dipper's tail makes up the tail of the bear." He laughed. "Which is kind of funny, since bears don't have long tails."

Maggie followed his finger pointing to the constellations but only sighed. He looked at her; she didn't seem interested in talking about stars. "Sure reminds you of sitting at Mollman Lake in the Missions, doesn't it?" he asked.

He thought he detected a faint smile, but she didn't answer. He decided she must be thinking of John. The first time Nick had met Maggie was at Mollman Lake, when he thought he was surprising John, who was camping there. But he was the one who'd been surprised when this beautiful woman from the Blackfeet Tribe came out of his friend's tent pointing a .44 Mag pistol at his chest.

John had married Maggie the following year. Now three years had passed since John's murder in Guatemala. "I miss him too," Nick said.

Maggie nodded and moved closer to him, and he was happy to feel the warmth of her body as they sat in companionable silence.

Maggie shivered and finally spoke, "I miss him every second of every day." She gazed at the sky. "When we would sit like this and watch the stars, John would tell me that he loved me more than there are stars in the sky. Then, he'd add, 'That's a lot, you know,' as if I didn't. He'd say it every time. It became our standing joke, and I'd repeat the answer with him."

A brilliant shooting star arced across the sky.

"Wow!" Nick said. "That was big enough to make a couple of wishes on."

"Then I wish for homes for all these kids," she said and leaned her head on his shoulder. "Thank you for being my friend, Nicklaus. I'm not sure I would have survived without your help when John left."

Left. He put his arm around her shoulders. He understood what that meant. To her, John had not died, he had left. Gone to heaven, where he would wait until they were reunited...so she would wait as well. He kissed her forehead.

"I think it's actually the other way around," he said. "I think you're the one who saved me…from myself. You and Buck. And Jack."

"Jack?" Maggie pulled away enough to look into his eyes.

He grinned. "I feel like I have the counsel of the Three Wise Men. Well, two wise men and one wise woman." His grin faded into the night. "Jack sat with me this afternoon. He told me about his life and his struggles. And he told me about surrendering to God. Jack said the things you and Buck have been trying to get through my thick skull."

"And?"

"And…I guess you can only get hit over the head by a two-by-four so many times until you start to get the idea."

They laughed.

"It's just that I'm not sure how to do it…to let go and surrender."

"Then the wise men…and this wise woman…will keep praying for you." She kissed his shoulder.

They sat without words, watching the stars dance. The blinking lights of two jets passed slowly through the celestial ballroom.

"It's amazing how life goes on while we sit in all this mess," he said, following the jet trails. "I bet the news reports back home have moved on to the next crisis, even though these people are barely surviving."

"Sad, but true," Maggie replied.

"So, how are things in the orphanage?"

"Kind of organized chaos at this point. I'll be so glad to get more beds. Once we have more beds, we can move into the new dorm and start bringing some stability to these kiddos. I hate having so many of them still sleeping on the floor."

"You're so good with them, and they love you. I watched you earlier. You looked like Mother Goose followed by her goslings."

Maggie held her face in her hands, ignoring his jest. "My Lord, what are we going to do with all these orphans? I don't think the people in this region can afford to take them in, they'll be so consumed rebuilding their own lives. Maybe people in other countries can help. I need to check Turkish laws for international adoption regulations. These children are so very precious."

Nick squeezed her shoulders. "You're a good mama."

"What about you? What are you going to do?" Maggie asked.

"You mean about my miserable life or in the next few days?" he joked.

She smiled at him. "I was thinking more the latter. I don't think your life is miserable. Do you really feel that way?"

"I guess I just dread going home." Nick looked back at the stars. "I'm going home to face the chief of staff of the MED; my judge, jury, and executioner." He looked back at Maggie and frowned.

"Huh?"

"Right before I left, a guy on meth came into the ER and shot up the place, killing two. My team took him to the OR and he died from the anesthesia. I wasn't there," he said and looked back at the stars. "The kid's dad is the mayor of Memphis and has filed suit. I guess there is a real fire storm brewing and the chief of staff has it out for me."

"That's too bad. You feel like you did anything wrong?"

"No, but you know how these things work."

"John never was named in a malpractice case, but he'd be the first to admit that working in Guatemala and out of the suit happy environment of the States was a relief," she said.

"I really do like helping people. It's just that when I'm back at the MED, I feel like I'm slogging through quicksand and getting nowhere. Always rushed, always stressed. I finish one case, and it's on to the next. Or I put out one fire, and the next one flares up. I feel like I have a thousand people pulling me in a million directions, every one of them wanting a chunk of me. I can't seem to find a healthy balance in my life. Honestly, sometimes I feel like saying screw it and walking away from it all."

"And what if you did?"

"You mean walk away? That probably scares me more than anything. You remember how many years it took me to get here?" He instantly regretted his condescension. She had helped John through his training. "I'm sorry, Maggie, I know you know that."

She smiled gracefully at him.

THE TREE OF LIFE

"It's these things called bills that seem to keep rolling in. I could sell my condo and my car, but then what?" He sighed deeply. "This is the point I always get to. Hate what I'm doing and too afraid to jump off the cliff into the unknown. So, I just keep medicating myself with…other stuff."

He was glad she didn't ask. She probably knew anyway.

"You will always be a physician. You could be a doctor anywhere or anyhow," she said. "What about going back to Montana?"

Nick nodded. "I've thought about that, but honestly, Maggie, I was reading the other day in a medical journal that docs are leaving the profession by the droves. The dissatisfaction rate among all doctors, especially surgeons, is way up there. The burnout is high, and even the suicide rate has increased."

"Sounds like you're not the only one feeling trapped."

"You don't know the half of it." Nick shook his head. "It's just awful—insurance companies telling you how to practice medicine, hospital corporations taking over everything and using doctors as pawns. You're told how much time you can spend with a patient, no matter the situation. 'Gee, I'm sorry, Mrs. Smith, I know your husband just died, but I only have five more minutes to spend with you.'"

He took a deep breath. "I'm sorry, Maggie. I didn't bring you up here to complain."

"That's okay. Venting is good. Besides, I like being with you." She hugged his arm.

"Me too…like being with you," he said, relaxing into her embrace. "But I sure wish you could tell me what to do," he added, half-seriously and half-joking.

"Yeah, I'd probably mess that up." She paused, squeezing his arm. "What are you hearing from God these days?"

Nick puffed air out his lips. "I guess if He is talking to me through the three wise men, it would be to let go…to trust Him."

"And?"

"And I wish the big guy would write it all down for me. Maybe I'm just thick-headed."

"Why don't you write it down?" She pulled away from him and looked at him. "You remember John's journal that you read in Guatemala? Why don't you write your own?"

Nick remembered John's journal. It was key to solving the mystery of John's death but contained so much more. It was like love letters to and from the Father. "You don't understand. I have no idea if God even speaks to me."

"He does and He will," she said with absolute assurance.

"How do I know I'm not just making up crap as I write?"

"It is a bit of a challenge at first. You have to quiet your mind. Some people start with a prayer like, 'God what would you say to me right now?' Real complicated, right?"

"You mean even an orthopod could do it?"

"Even a bone doctor." She laughed and poked him in the ribs. "The more you ask, the more you will hear His voice in your heart. You will be amazed at the things He says to you. Let's try it right now."

Before he could protest, another shooting star flew by as Maggie started to pray. "Father, speak to us. We silence the voice of the enemy and even our own voices, for that matter. Father, what would you say to us right now?"

He saw that her eyes were closed, and he closed his. Almost immediately, he heard words coming from his heart: *You are my son.* Nick was unable to speak; all he could do was squeeze his eyes tighter to preserve the sound. Then he heard: *You are my son, whom I love.* His eyes opened in surprise.

"Anything?" Maggie asked.

"He said that you should marry me."

"Oh, Nick, you're impossible." She laughed and slugged his arm. "Are you going to tell me what you heard?"

He swallowed the lump in his throat. "Uh…He said I am His son…that He loves me."

Maggie caressed his arm. "That's beautiful, Nick. That sounds like God. What a beautiful place to start that journal. Write it down." She studied his face. "He saying anything else to you?"

Nick pursed his lips and listened. "I don't know if this is me or God, but I think I'm supposed to go with Ali to help him search for his parents. I keep hearing *Hakkâri*, but Hakkâri was on my mind so much tonight that I don't know if I'm just making it up. We should be gone just a few days, and the hospital volunteers have everything under control." He paused. "I could go home, but you already know how I feel about that."

Maggie looked down, but not before Nick saw sadness cross her face. "I don't know, Nick," she said. "The last time you went off on an adventure was in Guatemala, and you almost didn't come back." She looked up and smiled. "But if that is what God is telling you to do, that is what you should do. I think you are always the safest abiding in God's will."

Nick nodded. "I think I'll talk with Buck tonight. See what he thinks."

***

Nick stood at the edge of his bunk looking at the dreadful army cot. He had just left Maggie, who patted him on the shoulder as they said good night. "No reason to get the rumor mill started," she told him. *Not very satisfying.*

The men's quarters were dark and quiet, except for some light snoring.

"You look like it's going to bite you," Buck whispered from the cot beside his.

He glanced at Buck, who lay on his back with a small reading light attached to his book, then glared at the cot. "You should see the bite this damn thing has taken out of my back and my shoulder and my hip. I don't know how you can sleep on it."

The light of Buck's lamp cast ghoulish shadows over his face, but Nick could see he was smiling.

"Just clean living, man," Buck chuckled.

"Yeah, whatever. Well, anyway, I'm glad you're still up," Nick whispered. "I need to talk. You got a minute?" He tilted his head toward the door.

Buck sat up and reached for his leg prostheses. "You bet. I was about to head out to take a shower anyway. Gonna try it out. I helped the UN soldiers put the finishing touches on the shower stalls today." He eyed Nick and sniffed. "Looks like you could use a long hot shower yourself."

"Maybe a cold one."

Buck looked at him, confused.

"I'll tell you as we walk," he said.

After Buck quickly slipped on his legs, they left the sleeping quarters and walked into the night air. They passed the cafeteria, where a small group huddled over coffee.

When they were out of earshot, Buck asked, "Didn't go so well with Maggie?"

"That woman drives me crazy in all sorts of ways."

"Welcome to the hu–man race," Buck joked. "Hang on. Got to adjust one of my dang legs. I think I managed to get a blister tonight playing with the kids." He leaned against a tree in the courtyard and slipped off his right prosthesis, removed the stocking covering his stump, and rubbed the end of his missing leg. "I think you need to be patient with her."

"I thought three years was giving her time."

Buck smiled. "I had to court Katy for five years. Man, did she play hard to get."

"How are Katy and your boys?" Nick asked, feeling a little guilty he hadn't asked before.

"Missing me of course, but I've decided to head back to the States next Wednesday. My youngest is getting his Eagle Scout award on Friday, and I don't want to miss that. Speaking of which, when are you headed home?"

"That's why I need to talk—"

"Dr. Hart?" interrupted a woman's sharp voice from behind.

Nick turned to find a short, stocky woman in scrubs marching toward him. Out of breath, she adjusted her glasses and put her hands on her wide hips. "Are you Dr. Hart?"

Nick was concerned. "Everyone okay?" He was thinking there was a crisis on one of the wards.

"Well...er...yes. Actually, I just got here this afternoon. I'm Ms. Simpsun from Quebec. I was getting debriefed in the cafeteria when I was told you'd just walked by. I wanted to meet you." She thrust out a hand and pulled it back to her hip. "I am the head of nursing for the Royal Canadian Hospital in Quebec, and I have never seen such a mess."

"Me as well," he said with relief that it wasn't an emergency. "It's terrible, isn't it?"

The head nurse glanced at Buck, who was replacing his leg. "Dr. Hart." She cleared her throat. "There are certain hospital standards that need to be met, and, quite frankly, you are not meeting them."

The accusation forced him to cross his arms defensively over his chest. "I'm sorry, Ms...."

"Simpsun...*s,i,m,p,s,U,n*," she said with an emphasis on the *u*. "I run the surgical programs at a Level I trauma center, and you are way out of compliance here. I have written the manuals on protocols and compliance, and I'm here to tell you that you need to get your house in order."

"I beg your pardon?" he said. Surprised, he glanced at Buck, who was on his feet and had taken a step away from the woman.

"My God, I examined your charts, and I have yet to come across one surgical release form, and some of them don't even show patient history or a physical exam report. I mean, not even the basics. Dr. Hart, where are your medication records, vitals records, nursing notes?" She ticked off the list of his failures on her fingers and then planted her hands squarely back on her hips. "Our compliance attorneys would have a field day with this...this...mess. I just can't wait to see your operating theater in the morning. Who is keeping track of the surgeons? Are they board certified? Are their credentials up to date? I can tell just by looking that the local nurses have not been properly trained."

"Just by looking at them, eh?"

Nick glanced at Buck, whose mouth gaped open. A sharp pain stabbed the center of Nick's chest, and he coughed reflexively. He felt his heart skip a beat, and for a split second, thought he was having a cardiac event. He tapped his chest with his knuckles, and the pain left as suddenly as it had come. He rubbed his forehead and blew a long breath through his lips.

The woman paused and he looked into her eyes. During the last three weeks, he had seen people react to the horror of the earthquake devastation in all sorts of ways—fear and trembling, anger, compassion, grief, kindness—he, too, had reacted in all those ways. He had been in her shoes. A battle raged inside his head. Should he respond with anger or kindness? When he put a hand on his chest, he thought he knew. He took a chance.

Nick reached for the woman's shoulder. She flinched as if to ward off a blow, but he held it firmly to make his point. "You're right," he said.

She looked at him in shock.

"You're right. We are a mess right now, and I'm glad you're here. How long can you stay?"

Nurse Simpsun was still in shock, either from his hand on her shoulder or from his conciliatory tone. "Uh…three weeks."

"That's great. We do need to start bringing order to the chaos. I want you to do me a favor. I am going to be away for the weekend. While I'm gone, I would like you to write up a report on the protocols we will need to implement. We'll go through it together when I get back, and we can talk to Mr. Bilton and the UN Commander about putting them in place."

The woman took her hands off her hips and her eyes welled with tears. "I've never seen anything like this…these poor people." She threw her arms around Nick and hugged him, stepping back quickly, turning, and retreating to the cafeteria, wiping her eyes.

Nick watched her hustle away and looked at Buck, who was shaking his head.

"Who are you and what have you done with my friend?" Buck exclaimed. "Dude…that was beautiful. After all you guys have been through, I wanted to tear into that woman."

Nick laughed. "Honestly, me too. But I was just too tired to fight." He patted his chest. "Can I get that hot shower now?"

As they turned toward the dorm, Buck asked, "So, where you headed this weekend?"

"As a matter of fact, that's what I wanted to talk to you about. I'm thinking of going with Ali and the Russians to Hakkâri tomorrow and wanted to know what you had to say about it."

Buck laughed. "I think *I* should go, and you should stay with Attila the Hun and get your butt-whoopin'."

"I think Nurse Simp*sun* helped make the decision."

"Honestly," Buck said seriously, "if you hadn't brought it up, I was going to. I think Ali could use your support, and you could use the break. Needless to say, I'm coming too. Somebody's got to look after you. Besides, you know how I love adventure, and this could be a doozy. Can you imagine if we actually found something?"

The men walked into the freshly painted bathroom shining with new tile and a line of seven pristine shower stalls.

"Welcome to the Turkish bath," Buck announced. "The hot water is on me."

CHAPTER 52

THE SEARCH
FRIDAY—POST-QUAKE DAY TWENTY

Ali found a box of Hershey's chocolate bars among the supplies that the UN had received to stock the kitchen. He didn't think anyone would mind if he pocketed a bar to give to Ibrahim. He remembered the first time he'd enjoyed the rich chocolate in America—he was well into his thirties. Ibrahim wouldn't have to wait that long.

At Maggie's suggestion, the medical staff had moved Ibrahim from the hospital to the orphanage. Sharing a room full of other boys would be good medicine, and she was right.

Walking into the boys' room at the orphanage, Ali smiled and waved to Ibrahim, pulling the candy bar from his pocket. All the beds had been neatly made and lined up in rows. Ibrahim and another boy about the same age were alone in the room, sitting on his bed playing a card game and laughing.

"Hi, Ibrahim," he said. "How do you like your new surroundings?"

Ibrahim gave him a broad smile and asked his friend for a two.

"Go fish," the boy said.

Ali waved the chocolate bar in front of the boys' faces. "Have you ever tasted chocolate from America?"

The boys threw down their cards and clapped their hands, carefully watching him break the bar. He offered each boy a half. Ibrahim's friend immediately grabbed his half, ripped off the wrapper, pushed the chocolate into his mouth, and nodded with satisfaction. Ibrahim broke his half in two and offered a chunk to Ali. He wanted Ibrahim to have the whole piece, but he was touched and accepted the offering. "You are a thoughtful young man."

Ali slid the chocolate into his mouth and thought about how to break the news of his departure. Best be straightforward and simple.

"Ibrahim, I am going away for a few days."

Ibrahim's smile turned upside down. "Are you going back to America?" he asked.

He swallowed hard, thinking that would soon be the case, but for now he could truthfully say, "Oh no, Ibrahim. I am going to a nearby city to look for my parents…for our parents." He bit his tongue and regretted the addition. There had been no indication that Ibrahim's parents might still be alive. If they were, they would have been frantically looking for their precious son and would have found him by now. He regretted giving Ibrahim hope, because now, when he returned, he would have to tell Ibrahim all over again that his parents were nowhere to be found. His heart ached.

Ibrahim teared up, and Ali figured it was for his parents. "I don't want you to go, Dr. Ali."

He leaned over and kissed Ibrahim's forehead. "My dear boy, I will be back in a few days."

***

Ali was surprised to see Buck and Nick, along with the Russian couple and Jack standing next to the white van with large UN letters imprinted in black on the side. He appreciated that they'd come to see him off, as he was anxious about the trip and wasn't sure why. Maybe it was the Russians that made him uneasy. He hadn't originally planned on traveling with them, even though he'd suggested it to Jack, and the Commander had agreed.

"Good morning," he greeted them all. "Sorry I'm late. I was just saying good-bye to Ibrahim."

"You're right on time, young man," Jack said, looking at his watch.

"Dr. Hassan, thank you for allowing us to hitch a ride," Antasha said.

She and Ali shook hands.

"Yes, Doctor, thank you," Vladimir said.

Ali smiled at Nick and Buck. He was puzzled by the sight of duffel bags beside their feet and looked at Nick, who grinned at him.

"You think we would let you go on this adventure without us?"

Ali shook his head. "Seriously, Dr. Hart…Sergeant. I will be fine."

"Of course you will, but I need a break for a few days, and lughead here won't let me go without him."

Buck smiled. "Hope you don't mind the company."

Ali had to laugh. "Not at all. Thank you. You are true friends." Truth be told, he was relieved, and some of his anxiety drained away.

The three of them and the Russians turned to Jack and took turns shaking his hand.

"Kind of wish I was going with you," Jack said, "but you don't need an old man slowing you down." He chuckled and scanned each face. "I hope you find what you are searching for." Then he turned to Ali and embraced him with a hearty hug.

CHAPTER 53

SUFFERING

Abdul was trapped. He paced back and forth in his room. He felt trapped by the hospital compound, trapped by the turn of events in his life, trapped by the constant clicking of the new fan Omar had installed, and especially trapped by the woman. Anxiety made him sweat. The fan was supposed to provide airflow in this stagnant space, but it wasn't helping. He mopped his brow and cursed Omar. He frowned and sniffed. The staff had cleaned his room, but he hated the smell of the cleanser. It reminded him of the smell of the morgue where he and his family had gone to claim his father's body. He felt caged by the smell of death.

Things were not turning out the way he'd planned. Yes, two men had been sent to jihad last week, but this week was a waiting game. The last message he'd received from his brother said that new recruits and supplies would arrive in a couple of weeks. His brother had told him to hold tight on any additional operations. It had been three weeks since the earthquake, and with the terror attacks, the border was tightening up. His brother didn't want any further incidents to provoke the Turkish government to close it. They had only a small window for unhindered access.

He found it hard to understand. Why were they not sending recruits sooner? He shrugged. Maybe there were logistical problems getting supplies, or the Americans had stepped up airstrikes. Either way, he hated the waiting.

When he left for Turkey, he had decided he was willing to give his life for Allah. He was ready to be a hero and a martyr for the cause. But now…it was just calisthenics and doldrums and that damn clicking fan. His confidence increased when he was with the woman, but even there he was losing ground. She seemed to turn off and on like a flickering light. The physical intimacy no longer seemed to fulfill the deep desire inside of him to belong. He had the feeling she would make love to him whenever she wished, and when she was done, she'd send him away.

He was trapped.

***

Vladimir had wanted to take the wheel of the van, but the Commander insisted upon a UN driver, so, as a gesture of courtesy, Nick offered the giant Russian the front passenger seat. Ali and AK volunteered to sit in the far back, while Buck sat with him in the middle.

"So, a Muslim, a Christian, and a Jew walk into a bar…" AK joked from the back.

He had to agree. "Aren't we a motley crew?"

Buck laughed. "You can say that again. I guess if we all die in a fiery crash at least one of us will be right."

"Except for poor Vladimir," AK added. "He just gets dirt and worms."

Vladimir harrumphed. "I believe in the good old USSR and the truth of Communism. As for you, AK, you'll be right there with me and the worms. You don't believe in God either."

"I don't know, Vlad," she mused. "There might be something to this crazy God idea. Who knows? He might have mercy even for you." Vladimir rolled his eyes. She said to the others, "In any case, Vladimir is also Jewish. Maybe we're safe somehow."

Buck was about to say something, but he pursed his lips and turned to look out the window. Nick let it pass and scanned his traveling companions. *We really are an eclectic group.* He looked at Vladimir, with his prominent brow and even larger nose, staring straight ahead. His nose looked like it had been broken a few times and his left ear was cauliflowered. It was the kind of image that made children shudder at night and check under their beds for the boogey-man. He glanced back at Ali, who was looking out the window, and to AK, who flipped her flowing copper hair back and smiled at him.

The driver filled the silence with an announcement that they would have to go north through the city of Van to get to the highway that led to Hakkâri.

Nick saw a sign for the airport where he'd landed what seemed like a lifetime ago. Nothing looked familiar. He had arrived under the cloak of darkness, and now, weeks later in the light of day, all he saw was devastation. It was disorienting and disheartening. UN workers had shoved debris to the sides of the main thoroughfare to allow passage, but chunks of flattened cars covered in brick and concrete still lined the street. Occasionally, Nick saw a building standing upright, empty and abandoned with extensive damage. Other unrecognizable buildings—stores, offices, houses, apartments—had been crushed into piles of dust and debris.

"Look at that." Nick pointed, surprised to see people shuffling on top of the wreckage. He saw men and women lifting and discarding chunks of concrete rubble. "They can't still be looking for survivors." Search and rescue had stopped two weeks earlier. The last survivors to be found were a young mother and her baby, and that was seven days after the quake. Miraculously, the baby had survived on breast milk.

A shroud of solemnity fell over the group. The destruction was even more severe when the vehicle came over a rise that overlooked the city of Van.

"My God," Nick gasped.

He was the only person who hadn't seen the city, and no one could have prepared him for the horrific scene. No graphic description or photograph could have revealed the extent of the devastation. It reminded him of pictures of Hiroshima after the nuclear blast. Utter destruction.

"The Commander told me the UN brought in heavy equipment with its huge helicopters, but the airport runway is out of commission and the road to Ankara is still closed," Buck said. "It just hasn't been enough."

Nick could see now that their patient load was the tip of the iceberg. Thousands upon thousands of people were buried forever under the rubble. It was clear that, for the most part, the survivors of the quake and the rescue teams had used only their hands to remove the debris. He imagined them standing by helplessly, listening to the sounds of life slowly fade into silence—voices disappearing in their tombs. "Buried alive… what a terrible way to die," he said.

"Maybe in God's mercy, most were already dead," Buck said.

"If you believe that sort of thing," Vladimir added.

The van passed a structure that remained intact but leaned against another, as if a giant had lumbered through the city knocking over the building. A large fire from a broken gas pipe still burned.

"I am so sorry about your city, Dr. Hassan," AK said.

Ali did not reply. He just stared out the window.

***

It took only half an hour to drive to Çavuştepe. Dark and gray earthquake devastation gave way to eerily unscathed green fields, serene and fertile, until the group came into the small town that was badly damaged. Nick was thankful to pass through the ruined town and back into the peace of the countryside.

After leaving Van, Nick and the others fell into an uneasy silence that continued through Çavuştepe, into the Hoşap River basin, and east into desolate and wild country. The UN van sputtered slightly as it began its long ascent into the thin air of the high mountains. Sheer cliffs rose on each side of the road that had been carved into the bedrock and snaked beside the river.

Up ahead, a huge concrete structure stretched across the valley and their path. It seemed that the road would be swallowed by a giant wall until the roadway switched back into the granite and up and over the manmade structure. They realized they were driving on top of a mammoth dam that held back millions of gallons of mountain water.

The group looked at Ali. "Zernek Dam," he said. "It supplies most of the fresh water for this area."

"Look at those men hanging by ropes inspecting the side of the dam," Vladimir said. "That takes some nuts."

Nick grinned at Buck, enjoying the Russian's take on the English vernacular. But when he looked back at the dam, he saw the gravity of the situation. At one corner of the dam was a large crack. If the dam gave way, the voluminous expanse of water behind the reservoir could flood the entire valley. The people in the tent cities below wouldn't stand a chance. As they drove along the reservoir, Nick held his breath, willing the dam to hold the cold, green water.

Buck echoed his thoughts. "Lord, hold back the waters."

"Allah, have mercy," Ali said.

Throughout the journey, Nick wondered if they all had the same thought, but it was AK who said, "Where is this *God* in all of this?"

No one replied.

Finally, Vladimir turned and faced them. "Before I left Russia, I read a story from America about a man who was on that airplane that landed in the Hudson River in New York City. The one where everyone survived. You know it?"

"Sully was the heroic pilot," Nick said, and the others nodded.

Vladimir continued. "*Da.* The story I read said that the man survived the plane crash but was then killed a few months later in a train crash." He paused for effect. "What the hell? That man was a devoted Jew. How do you explain that?"

"I have a friend whose three-year-old daughter died a terrible death from a brain tumor," AK added. "How do you explain *that*? And just look what we've come through…all those innocent people…dead."

"Why do bad things happen to good people?" Buck murmured.

"What?" AK asked.

"Why do bad things happen to good people?" Buck repeated. "It's the title of a book written by a Jewish rabbi many years ago, after his son died of an incurable genetic disease."

No one said anything. AK's original question waited to be answered.

Vladimir didn't let it go. "You religious people talk about this all-knowing, all-powerful, all-loving God, but why would a divine entity like that let people suffer like they do?" His face flushed, betraying his anger.

"Yes, it's a hard question to answer," Buck said. "People have been asking it for a long, long time."

Ali finally spoke again. "It is a question that has been wrestled with since the beginning of time, but you have to remember that our all-powerful God has also created natural laws that have irrevocable consequences on earth."

"As a Christian, I agree with you, Ali," Buck said. "When God created the earth, he made it perfect. It wasn't until humans messed it up that it began to fall apart."

"Yes," Ali said. "The Qur'an indicates the same. The natural disasters we see are, in part, due to our own sins. Look at the flood during Noah's time, or the volcanic eruptions over Sodom and Gomorrah, or the people during the time of Lot. Are these natural disasters or divine punishments?"

The van lurched and the team grabbed door handles and seat arms to steady themselves as the driver swerved around two large cracks in the asphalt. The vehicle bounced clear.

"I would agree with you, Ali...up to a point," Buck said. "The Old Testament is full of God's judgment of sin. But the New Testament gives us a new covenant to live through Jesus... and Jesus never blessed a storm. He rebuked them and turned them away. God does not cause suffering."

"But there is still all this suffering," AK said. "How do you explain that?"

"Then for me, maybe the better question to ask is 'why is there suffering?'" Nick added.

AK turned to him. "And what is your answer?"

Buck jumped in before he could reply. "Our all-powerful, all-knowing God must allow suffering, like He allows all sorts of things, because we have the freedom to choose. Our scriptures make it clear that our faith does not guarantee an easy life, but He does promise to be with us in the midst of suffering."

"I read something interesting before we left Memphis," Ali said. "In the one thousand years before 1900, there were eleven massive earthquakes. In the last one hundred years, there have been thirteen. It makes you wonder."

"You guys may have heard the scripture on the end times," Buck said. "'You will hear of wars and rumors of wars, but see to it that you are not alarmed. Such things must happen, but the end is still to come. Nation will rise against nation, and kingdom against kingdom. There will be famines and earthquakes in various places. All these are the beginning of birth pains.'"

"You think we are in the end times?" AK asked Buck.

"Man, who knows?"

"I think that's scary," AK told the group.

"It would be, without faith," Buck said. "I love the writings of C. S. Lewis. He talks about life on earth as the land of shadows. He says that real life hasn't even begun."

Vladimir took a swig of water. "Are you talking about heaven then? But why would your God allow us to suffer now?"

"I guess if you believe in a good God, then you have to believe there are reasons for suffering," Nick said, surprising himself.

"Exactly," Ali and Buck answered simultaneously. They looked at each other and smiled. Buck waited for Ali to speak, but Ali extended his hand to Buck.

"I would have to go back to C. S. Lewis," Buck said, "and one of my favorite quotes: 'But pain insists upon being attended to. God whispers to us in our pleasures, speaks in our conscience, but shouts in our pain: it is his megaphone to rouse a deaf world.'"

"I'm often reminded of this in surgery," Ali added. "Sometimes I hate doing it. It pains me to cut. I know I'm hurting that person. But Allah tells me pain is necessary, and the patient will get well and be grateful. We find healing through pain."

Nick smiled at Ali. His fondness for the man continued to grow. Maybe Ali and Buck were right, that pain awakens us to God somehow.

Buck spoke up. "I suppose...and I don't mean this disrespectfully"—he looked at Vladimir and then at Antasha—"to the atheist, when you die, that's it...it's done, over...you're food for worms, as you said. For those of us of faith, death is not the end, but the beginning."

"Amen, ya'll," Ali said in a southern Memphis accent, sounding more like a Baptist preacher than a Shia Muslim. It made everyone laugh.

CHAPTER 54

TIME BOMB

Akleema studied the clock on the wall. The second hand crawled from minute to minute. Sometimes it hit the numbers and at other times the spaces between. He would be done soon.

This was just as it was when she was six years old, when her uncle came to her room and entered her bed. She'd stared at the friendly image on the blue face of her bedside clock—Belle dancing with the Beast. Its second hand had the same unusual cadence. Her uncle had given her the clock for her second birthday. How appropriate: Beauty and the Beast. Even at six, she understood the irony.

Did her parents ever know or even suspect? They were probably too busy climbing the social ladder at Oxford and focusing on their tenure. *Good for them.* Who would have guessed that her mother's brother was a pervert—after all, he was a successful lawyer in a large firm. They had no idea.

Just as the police had no idea that she had killed him. She smiled to herself, remembering his face as she thrust the knife just under his solar plexus and into his heart. According to the police report, the man had been stabbed more than one hundred times. They believed it was obviously a crime of passion, but they had no suspect. Akleema was not even questioned; everyone assumed she was away at university. At the funeral, she mourned dutifully with the rest of the family, but she was glad she had her life back. She was glad that she was in control; she craved being in control.

Abdul rolled off her. "You seemed to enjoy that," he said, out of breath and sweating.

"Yes, every minute," she lied.

He leaned over and tried to kiss her mouth, but she pulled away and sat up. "You should get dressed. It's almost time for *Asr*, third prayer. The other men will wonder where you are."

"Damn, I hate this place. I feel like the walls are closing in on us. I'm going to ask Omar if I can go into town this afternoon. Do you want to go with me?" He pleaded with his eyes.

She looked into his dark eyes and saw his need, and it irritated her. He was like a lost puppy, so weak and pathetic. She could get him to do anything she wanted. Bile rose from her stomach. She remembered throwing up into the wastebasket next to her bed after her uncle had left her room and how her mother accused her of being bulimic.

She forced down the contents of her stomach. "Yes, I think I would like that, if Omar says it's okay."

"He will say it's okay because I say it's okay," Abdul announced triumphantly and pulled on his pants.

She smiled at the boy.

***

Autumn seemed to have come in an instant. Walking through Hakkâri, Akleema wished she had her camera to capture the seasonal splendor. The jagged mountain peaks surrounding the city thrust up into the brilliant blue sky. With a fresh dusting of new snow, their majesty seemed magnified. The first week of September opened the curtain to a spectacular contrast between the last days of summer and the first days of winter. The emerald-green fields enclosing the city and the trees glowing in golden yellows and dazzling reds would soon give way to a cold, white canvas.

The afternoon sun was quickly disappearing behind the mountains crowning the city, casting long shadows and subdued, gilded light over the market. The days were becoming shorter, and the temperatures were dropping. Fifteen minutes earlier,

Akleema had been sweating in her jacket and headscarf; now she was thankful to be wrapped in both. She inhaled the cold wind that swooped down the mountainside, carrying the chill off the crystal snow.

"Glad to be out?" Abdul interrupted her autumnal solace. She had almost forgotten he was at her side.

She smiled at him, remembering she had a role to play. "Yes. Thank you for breaking me out." She laughed playfully.

Omar had tried to convince them not to go out to the city, especially unaccompanied, but when he realized he was not going to succeed, he talked them into wearing their vests bearing the Red Crescent emblem. "You will stand out anyway, why not stand out in a good way?" he told them. "And speak English. People will be wary of you if you speak Arabic."

He had been correct. Many people stopped the pair and, in broken English, Kurdish, or Turkish, thanked them. Akleema carried a growing bouquet of flowers women and children had given her.

The city was bouncing back from the turmoil of the earthquake. Unlike many of the surrounding communities, the most extensive damage had occurred in isolated pockets of the city. Even though power was not yet restored, the town was self-reliant on local agriculture and the abundance of water from the mountain streams. That was evident in the makeshift market they strolled through. Farmers and ranchers had a wealth of fresh vegetables and meats and were happy to capitalize on the needs of the people—supply and demand.

Akleema stopped in front of a booth manned by an elderly woman in a bright floral dress with a wool sweater and no headscarf. It was still hard for her to see so many of the women without their hair covered. The woman's booth was full of beautifully ripened carrots, beets, onions, and assorted fruits.

She dug into her pocket and pulled out a stack of Turkish lira that Omar had given them. The lira was worth only a third of a euro, but she was certain that the marketers would have overinflated prices, so she picked up a bundle of carrots and handed the woman a twenty-lira bill. The woman did not take the money and said something she didn't understand. Thinking the woman wanted more money, she peeled another twenty from her stack of bills and offered it to the woman. The woman stepped back and waved her hands.

Akleema looked at Abdul and then back at the woman, unsure of what to do. She wondered if she should peel off another bill, but at the same time, she was getting angry, fearing she'd been taken advantage of. When she began to put the carrots down, the woman came from behind her produce stall, gently touched her arm, and pushed the carrots back to her. The woman held her other hand palm up in a negative gesture, smiled, and said something in Kurdish.

Abdul understood. "I think she wants to give you the carrots," he told Akleema.

She did not want to take the carrots. *How can I accept this gift?* But before she could set them down, the woman reached for a small paper sack, filled it with apples, and handed it to Abdul. In broken English, the woman said, "Thank you," and patted her on the arm.

Abdul pulled her arm and whispered, "Have you never received a gift?"

"Um..." she said, unsettled by the encounter.

"You were about to start a scene. What's wrong with you?"

"I guess I did not expect that." Her cheeks flushed with embarrassment.

"Maybe you've had too much freedom and too much fresh mountain air," he said. "Let's head back."

They crossed the plaza between vendors toward the main square and their car as a flock of pigeons parted for them. Groups of young adults gathered in the square, handing out flyers. Two girls wearing modern clothes, jeans and tight sweaters approached them. The shortest took the lead.

"Hello," the girl said. "You from the Red Crescent?" She spoke perfect English.

The other girl held back and giggled.

"You speak very good English," Akleema said. "Where did you learn?"

"School, of course." The girl shrugged and rolled her eyes like a Western teen.

"What grade are you?"

"Tenth," she replied nonchalantly. "Where are you from?"

"I'm British. From London," she said.

The girl's attitude changed and her face shone with excitement. She smiled at her friend. "Do you know Harry Styles from One Direction?" The girls giggled.

Akleema remembered how her hormones raged at that age. "I'm afraid I only know of him," she said, trying not to sound too disappointing. "I did see him once in a concert in London."

The two girls grabbed each other's hands and squealed. "I bet he was wonderful."

She glanced at Abdul and saw him steal a glance at the girl's breasts stretching her sweater. Her last boyfriend had cheated on her, and the first sign of his infidelity had been checking out her girlfriends. Even if she had no use for Abdul, she wasn't going to stand for him cheating on her. The unabashed Turkish girl must also have noticed Abdul's leer. She smiled at him and pulled her shoulders back to improve his view.

Akleema's rage swelled. She remembered finding her boyfriend in her best friend's bed. It was the one time that her violent temper had nearly ensnared her. She took her wrath out on her friend, whose body was found in the River Thames. This time, Akleema was questioned by police. Fortunately, no evidence connected her to the crime. Her ex-boyfriend, to save his own life, swallowed any signs of betrayal.

She shot Abdul a cold stare, forcing him to turn away from the young Turkish girl.

"Would you like to come to our festival?" the girl asked, handing her a flyer.

"Uh, what?" Akleema took a few seconds to get her bearings. She looked at the yellow flyer and saw a large graphic of two people dancing over the words *Hakkâri Festival.* She could not read the words under the picture.

"On Sunday," the girl explained, "we are having a dance at the high school to raise money for the orphanage in town. We would love for you to come. We will play good music. Maybe even some One Direction."

Akleema couldn't help but smile. Maybe it was time to strike. "Yes, maybe we can have a presence there."

CHAPTER 55

MIRE

FRIDAY EVENING—POST-QUAKE DAY TWENTY

Nick was nauseated. He wasn't sure if it was the altitude or the incessant hairpin switchbacks up the Cilo-Sat mountain range. The mountains were part of the Toros chain. Ali had told them that these monstrous peaks formed the westernmost section of the Himalayan mountain belt. Feeling short of oxygen, he took a deep breath and concentrated on the heights. *What majesty.* It seemed as if they were climbing up to the heavens.

Ali had also told them that the drive from Van to Başkale normally took an hour and a half, but in the aftermath of the earthquake, it was going to take all day. When the quake hit, the natural response was to flee, and the people of Hakkâri province fled to Van province, where they found themselves at the epicenter. As soon as they realized that everything there was worse than in their own community, they headed back home, once they could find more gasoline. The combined chaos of the devastation and the migration back and forth from Van to Hakkâri made for bumper-to-bumper traffic, plugging up the steep mountain pass.

As the UN van neared the top of the pass, the team saw that further progress was impeded by the consequence of a landslide—a large portion of the mountain road was covered with a thick, slimy mud.

"What do you all think?" the driver asked them.

"Keep moving forward," Vladimir ordered. "If you stop, the mud will suck us in like quicksand."

Nick saw that he was right. Cars were stalled in mud up to their frames, and some teetered on the edge of the steep road. A single policeman tried to bring order to the bedlam and waved frantically for the UN van to come forward through the sludge.

The van eased into the mire, the worst of it twenty yards long.

"Steady, steady," Vladimir warned the driver. But as soon as the words left his mouth the van jumped and stalled against a rock. The driver made the irrevocable error of gunning the engine. Instead of propelling them forward, the tires cut into the mud, and the van was stuck. The driver threw the gear into reverse and floored the accelerator, only to dig them deeper.

"Nyet!" Vladimir shouted, reaching for the driver's arm. "Stop! You will only make it worse." He glanced back at Buck. "You ready for action, Marine?"

Nick watched Buck's brow furrow in answer to the challenge. Buck and Vladimir jumped out of the van into the ankle-deep mud. Nick looked at Ali, stuck in the back of the van, shrugged, and followed the musclemen into the fray, instantly regretting his decision.

The thick mud grabbed his feet like a demon from hell and wouldn't let go. He staggered, certain he was being sucked into the quagmire. Buck and Vladimir pulled him upright, and, locking arms, the three men trudged together through the sludge to the back of the van to push.

Ali had moved up to Vladimir's seat and was hanging out the window. "How does it look?"

"Well, it's not going to move itself," Vladimir declared, putting his back to the van and shoving. "What do you think, Marine?" he taunted.

"Ooh rah! Let's move this thing," Buck yelled, planting his prostheses in the mud and his back against the van.

Nick stood watching, feeling inadequate next to the strong men and not sure if he'd do anything more than get in the way.

Then Vladimir yelled at him. "Doctor! On three, tell the driver to ease on the gas, but for God's sake, don't gun it."

He turned and yelled instructions to Ali.

"You ready, Marine?" Vladimir asked.

"Born ready."

"Odin, dva, tri," Vladimir counted off in Russian, and on three, he let out a primordial scream.

"Give it some gas," Nick yelled to Ali.

At first the van sputtered and shuddered pathetically, and he thought it was all for naught. Then the van moved. They were lifting it out of the mud. It inched forward as Vladimir and Buck grunted and pushed.

The van gathered momentum, spitting mud every which way like a big wet dog shaking. Nick tried to stay with the van, but after a few yards he lost traction and fell to his hands and knees. Slopping in the sludge, trying to stand, he saw Buck was also stuck up to his knee hinges. All they could do was watch in awe as the big Russian single-handedly pushed the van all the way out of the mire. When the vehicle lurched forward onto solid ground, Vladimir stood tall, flexed his arms, and let out a whoop. "Come on, men, we did it," he yelled, waving them to come out of the mud.

Nick looked at Buck and laughed. "He looks like Ivan Drago, Rocky's big Russian nemesis."

"I must break you," Buck imitated the character.

Nick laughed and tried to shake the mud off his hands and arms. He struggled to his feet and took exaggerated strides over the mud to move forward. He was almost free of the mire when he turned to see that Buck hadn't moved. His friend was stuck tight, unable to control his prostheses in the thick, gloppy mess.

Nick started back to help Buck but saw that Vladimir was already on the way to the rescue. When the Russian reached Buck, he tried to help him walk, until it became clear that Buck wasn't going anywhere on his own power. The Russian turned his back toward Buck, pulled Buck's arms around his neck, hefted him up, and dragged him to safety.

"No man left behind. Right, Marine? Isn't that what you say?"

Semper fi, " Buck grinned. "Thanks, man."

The three of them laughed and high-fived. As they inspected each other, covered in thick, wet, brown muck, they howled.

"You look like you fell into vat of chocolate," Vladimir told Buck.

"Chocolate was not what I was thinking," Buck retorted.

They tried to clean off the mud, but the more they wiped, the more they smeared it all over themselves and each other, and the more they laughed.

***

Driving down the pass was easy, and they pulled into Başkale at dusk. The first stop on the agenda was the farm where the Russians had stolen gas after the earthquake. Vladimir was intent on making amends to the farmer for the altercation that had ensued.

"I think this is the turn?" He looked to Antasha for verification, and she nodded.

"You think the farmer is going to be happy to see us?" Nick asked, looking at their disheveled condition. He and the others had cleaned up as best they could, but the mud had dried into cracked body casts.

"I don't know about you guys, but he probably won't recognize me," Vladimir lifted his mud-caked arms and laughed ghoulishly. Vladimir peeled mud from the top of his bald head and added with sincerity, "I hate to have unpaid debt. I hope he will accept my apologies and the money."

Two more turns and the headlights of the van illuminated the familiar scene—the barn and the fuel tanks. There was no sign of life. They wondered if the farmer had fled.

"I wish we had arrived before dark," Vladimir said. "It would have been easier to face the farmer in daylight." He rubbed his shoulder and rolled down his window. They sat in silence, listening. The only sounds they heard were the chirping of the evening crickets and the clicking of the van's cooling engine.

In the distance, they saw lights come on in the farmhouse.

"I'll go check at the house," Ali volunteered, moving past Buck and stepping out the side door. As soon as his feet touched the ground, the team heard an unmistakable sound—the chambering of a shotgun shell. Ali reflexively put his hands in the air and said something in Turkish.

A dark figure lurked from the barn and said something gruffly. When the figure came into the beam of the headlights, they saw an angry man with a shotgun. Ali spoke in an even tone and explained their situation, even lowering his hands in a gesture of trust. Nick wasn't sure he could ever do that with a gun pointed at his chest.

The farmer moved closer into the headlights, and the team saw his face with remnants of purple bruising across his cheeks, eyes and forehead, and a nose still swollen to twice its size.

"Nice one," AK whispered to Vladimir.

Vladimir winced and shot daggers at her.

The farmer aimed his gun at the van and fired off a volley of words. Ali held his palms up in surrender to keep the peace and then spoke into the front passenger window to Vladimir. "He wants you to step out of the car."

Vladimir did not hesitate. Pulling a stash from under the seat, he opened the door and stepped out. He held his hands high holding a bottle of vodka and a wad of cash. "I'm sorry," he said. "I'm so sorry."

"Where in the world did he get those?" Nick whispered to AK.

"He can be very resourceful." She smiled.

"I see that."

The farmer stood his ground, and a long discussion ensued between him and Ali. Nick realized he was holding his breath. Just when it looked as though the conversation was going nowhere, the farmer lowered his gun and waved Ali and Vladimir toward the farmhouse.

Vladimir and the others inside the van stared at Ali, who smiled. "It's all good," he told the team. "He has invited us all to come in for some soup."

***

The farmer's wife was a stout woman with rosy cheeks. She bubbled with cheer and served them potato soup, home-baked bread, strong coffee, and fresh fig cake for dessert. Nick declined the fig cake but thought it was one of the best meals he had ever tasted. Maybe they all had died and gone to heaven.

He was in the farmhouse attic in a featherbed that belonged to the farmer's oldest child. It was a little snug for his height, but he scrunched up under the thick quilt that enveloped him. He wasn't sure he had ever experienced such hospitality.

As soon as the farmer's wife had seen them, she insisted the muddy men clean up in the stream that ran beside the barn. She provided soap and towels, and afterward she gave them clothes to cover their essentials, except for Vladimir. All she could find that fit him was a blanket. He accepted it with a bow and a smile and wore it proudly around his waist like a gladiator. She then filled their bellies with tasty food and proudly showed them the house and tidy bedrooms where they would sleep.

After dinner, they'd all relaxed and visited. In short order, the farmer and Vladimir had become fast friends, sharing the vodka and telling stories of the Russians fighting the Ottomans. As it turned out, the farmer's father had fought alongside the Russians and taught him some phrases in Russian that he still remembered.

The UN driver and Antasha had retired, and Nick excused himself shortly after dinner. Now snug in his featherbed, Nick heard the others laughing below, with Ali translating for the former adversaries and Buck joining the frivolity. Nick was exhausted and so happy to be horizontal. The smell of kerosene lamps wafted through the air, encouraging his drowsiness, and the thick quilt cocooned him into slumber.

He thought he was dreaming when he heard a creak on the wood floor and felt a presence at his bedside. He opened his eyes slowly, but in the dark he could see only the outline of a figure lift the edge of the quilt and slip into the bed beside him. His eyes popped open. It was no dream. He knew immediately who it was. He had fantasized about it and dreaded it at the same time.

He felt the warmth of AK's skin against his.

"I thought you might like some company," she whispered, draping her leg over his and planting a kiss on his mouth.

Reflexively, he kissed her back. His body stirred with

excitement, but his head sounded alarm bells that he tried to ignore. She pressed her body into his, and he wrapped his arms around her. Her scent and the softness of her skin were intoxicating.

"I want to pay you back for your kindness."

Yes, kindness. This is okay, she's not married. He needed this. He wanted her.

She kissed his neck and rolled on top of him. He kissed her again and let his hands caress her skin, luxuriously working their way to the small of her back when suddenly a voice thundered in his head: *Remember who you are.*

He tried to ignore it, burying his face in her silky hair, but it thundered even louder, REMEMBER WHO YOU ARE.

He let his body go limp.

AK rolled part way off him. "You okay?"

He smiled wearily at her. Even in the darkness, he knew her beautiful aqua-blue eyes were searching him. He ran his fingers through her hair. It was fine and soft and slipped effortlessly through his fingers. "My God, you are so beautiful, AK. God must have looked at Eve and wanted another just like her."

She smiled back at him. "That may be the nicest thing any man has ever said to me."

"Believe me, AK, it is not that I don't desire you. Every cell in my body wants you...but I can't. I won't," he said, trying to convince himself as well as her. "You better head back to your own bed." He held her at arm's length and eased her out of his bed. She'd better go before he changed his mind.

"Okay," she said, "but you don't know what you're missing." She slid off his bed and crept out of the room.

CHAPTER 56

GABRIEL

"Ibrahim."

He was far away when he heard his name.

"Ibrahim. You want to play cards?"

The sound came closer as the dream slipped away. He reluctantly opened his eyes. He recognized the room in the orphanage. He saw the boy standing next to his bed shuffling a deck of cards. He didn't want to play cards. He wanted to go back to that special place. He shut his eyes, willed himself back to sleep, and tried to catch the dream.

All he knew was that when he was dreaming, he was happy. His leg that ached all day no longer hurt, and he was no longer afraid. In this dream, there were no flashbacks of the terror he had endured—no visions of crumbling concrete buildings tossed like rocks, no heart-racing sounds like trembling aftershocks, no rumbling hospital supply trucks or thumping helicopter blades—all of which made him afraid and his body flush with heat. In this dream, a cool, gentle peace stilled the air, and he was soothed by a sense of belonging and security. He was no longer alone.

He opened his eyes and gazed upon a scene of splendor. He'd caught the dream and was back. He stood at the edge of a thick carpet of wildflowers beside a glacial blue lake crowned with snowcapped mountains of silver granite. The blue sky matched the lake's brilliance. A cool breeze floated from the summit, but he wasn't chilled as the sun caressed his skin like lamb's wool.

Ibrahim looked at his bare feet and wiggled his toes against the flowers. There were so many different kinds and colors—more than his old box of crayons contained. The flowers propelled his steps forward, genuflected, and then joyfully rose back toward the sun.

This new world pulsed with energy. The exotic fragrance of each flower made him giggle and rub his nose. Sparrows, bluebirds, robins and birds of every size and shape gathered above him to sing in harmony like a choir of angels.

The pathway was a floral quilt that led Ibrahim to the edge of the lake. He was surprised to see a boy about his age skipping rocks across the crystal waters. The boy turned to him, smiled warmly, and said, "Hi, Ibrahim."

How did he know him? The boy's blue eyes matched the lake and the sky, and his floppy blond hair was laced with strands of gold. Without embarrassment, the boy put his hands on his shoulders and hugged him tight. So close, Ibrahim thought for a moment their hearts intertwined and danced together in joyous union. It was an acceptance he had never experienced, and he liked it.

As the boy stepped back from the embrace, Ibrahim's world oscillated in and out of focus and his head spun. He heard the mountains awake with music. "Holy, Holy, Holy," they sang. He staggered and felt the boy catch his arm to steady him. He laughed, and the boy laughed with him—their spontaneous joy intensified the colors and sounds of this wonderland.

"It's okay, Ibrahim," the boy reassured him. "You will get used to it."

He inhaled deeply, and peace poured into his lungs and flooded his body from the top of his head to the tips of his fingers and toes. It was like a bubble bath, and he giggled. His five senses intermingled—smells became tasty flavors, sights became colorful sounds, and sounds became bright colors.

"Here," the boy offered, "have some of this." He handed him a piece of fruit. It was royal purple and emerald green and looked like a fig, but a fig unlike any Ibrahim had ever seen. He bit into the fruit's soft skin, and its honey-flavored nectar exploded in his mouth. The effect was like medicine calming his overstimulated brain, turning down the volume of his boisterous senses. He took another bite and his vision focused on the magnificence of his surroundings and his new companion.

"My name is Gabriel," the boy said before Ibrahim could speak.

"The archangel?" he asked, surprised at the melodious sound of his own voice.

"Yes, Ibrahim, Gabriel the archangel. I probably don't look like what you imagined, but I have the ability to appear in different ways to different people at different times and places." He smiled.

"Am I in *Jannah*…heaven?"

"Yes, my friend. One aspect of heaven."

"Am I…dead?" he asked without fear.

"No, Ibrahim," Gabriel laughed. "It is not your time. The Father has each one of your days numbered."

"The Father?"

"Yes, you call Him Allah…God."

The world began to spin once more, and he felt his hand moving of its own accord. But it was Gabriel lifting Ibrahim's hand that held the fig to his mouth. He didn't hesitate to bite the fruit.

"Your earthly senses have a difficult time here," Gabriel said.

He chewed the fig, and his world stopped spinning. He looked around and saw trees of every kind—maple, elm, oak, fir, dogwood, willow, and cedar. But one tree stood out above the rest. It was magnificent, like a regal throne, thrusting its trunk into the blue sky while the mountain breeze flashed its leaves gold and silver, emitting a song like a singing dove. The tree's majestic branches hung with the delicious figs that Ibrahim was eating.

"Is this the Garden of Eden?" Ibrahim asked.

Gabriel's only answer was a wide smile.

Ibrahim heard the mountains again: "Holy, Holy, Holy."

"Ibrahim," the boy said, "in the beginning, the Father put man into the garden. Now He puts the garden into man—into you."

"I don't understand."

"You will, Ibrahim, you will. Because of the gift of Jesus, God's Spirit now lives within you."

A recent memory came to him. *Could it be?* "The man in white?"

"Yes. Jesus."

As Gabriel said the name, *Jesus,* Ibrahim looked down at his body. It seemed to grow and expand, gaining strength and healing. *The man in white,* his heart rejoiced.

"Holy, Holy, Holy," the trees harmonized with the mountains, and the birds joined the heavenly choir.

Ibrahim's body swelled until he thought he would burst, and then it eased back to its normal size.

Gabriel laughed. "You have been filled with God's Holy Spirit," he said. "The Spirit, the Father, and Jesus are one. You are one with the Father. You now have the choice of walking with the Father—day by day, moment by moment, with Him in the garden."

"How do I do that?" he asked.

"The Holy Spirit now lives within you. You will learn to exercise this…like exercising your other senses. Think of it as having the eyes of your heart opened. See now through the Father's Spirit. Close your physical eyes, Ibrahim, and let the Spirit take you to where you want to go."

He looked around. He liked where he was and wasn't sure he wanted to go anywhere else. He had never felt so much peace before. He looked at Gabriel, who patiently waited for him to choose.

Ibrahim settled his heart, closed his eyes, and thought. In the next moment, he was transported from the high mountain meadow to his bedroom back home in Van. He lay in his own bed. With his eyes still closed, he heard the curtains rustle in the wind through the open window, and the sounds of the city below. He heard his friends playing soccer in the street. He searched through his other senses. He found the aroma of sweet bread wafting from the kitchen, and his mouth watered. Then he heard the sweet trill of his mother's voice singing his favorite song.

He tried to leap from his bed, but his legs were wobbly. When he regained his balance, he found himself standing by the lake and supported by Gabriel.

"Your earthen vessel can only take so much, so I must send you back," Gabriel said. "Once you are filled with the Holy Spirit, you will never be the same."

A strong wind swooped Ibrahim into a whirl of dreams. He was falling, somersaulting through time and space, over and over, blinded by dazzling lights and deafened by a loud, clattering sound.

He jerked awake and his eyes popped open. His card-playing friend and a nurse stood next to his bed, laughing. His breakfast tray was splattered on the floor.

"Oh, what a mess we've made," the nurse exclaimed.

His friend was giggling and picking green Jell-O off the top of his head.

Ibrahim looked around and was perplexed. Where was Gabriel? Then he saw his leg hanging from the traction bow, and he knew where he was. He was disappointed to see he was still at the orphanage.

"It's okay, Ibrahim," the nurse said. "Sorry to wake you with such a clatter. I'll go get another tray while your friend changes his shirt." She smiled at his friend, directing him to the bathroom.

Ibrahim looked around the room, wishing he was in his own bed or back with Gabriel, but any sadness was replaced with the sweet fragrance of the flowers and the melody of the mountains lingering in his heart. He smiled. Then he noticed something even more wonderful: he may be back in his bed at the orphanage, but his leg no longer ached.

CHAPTER 57

QODSHANES
SATURDAY—POST-QUAKE DAY TWENTY-ONE

Abdul sat on the edge of Akleema's bed with his head in his hands. "I don't know if it would be the right thing to do. My brother told us to lie low."

The White Snake, lying beside him, lazily lifted her hand to his neck and gently raked her fingernails down his back. "Yes, but your brother is not here." She yawned. "You are the leader of the movement, and you are the one who is here in Turkey." He relaxed into her touch. How easy it was to manipulate the boy.

"Don't you think we should wait a few more weeks until the others get here?" he asked. "What if the commotion closes the border?"

"I think that's a risk we should be willing to take. Remember, one of our main objectives is to destabilize the area, and there's nothing like killing a bunch of children for doing that," she said coldly.

Abdul turned to face her, and she pulled up her legs to sit cross-legged. "I think this festival is the perfect time to strike." She turned to the bedside table, picked up the flyer the girl had given her, and pushed it at him.

He took it and studied the graphic of children dancing. "I hated the girl that gave this to us." He said with contempt. "She was so...American." He crumpled the flyer. "I believe it is the perfect time to strike," he said with decisive authority, as though it had been his idea. He threw the crinkled flyer across the room and turned to her. "Should we send two of our men with suicide vests?"

Did she have to spell everything out? Such a stupid boy. She wanted to rebuke him, but she didn't want to provoke his anger, so she swallowed those thoughts and gave him something he could grasp. "What would you think of providing boxes of food and water for the party? We could place boxes of explosives among them, and put them where they would do the most damage."

"But wouldn't they know the explosives came from us?"

She sighed at his naïveté but recovered quickly. "They'd be more likely to accuse the Kurdistan Workers' Party that has attacked this area before."

"Yes," he said as though he'd just thought of it, "and we could make it look like the PKK planted the explosives."

"Exactly. The Turks will fight our enemy…the enemy of our enemy is our friend."

He caught the riddle and claimed it as his own. "The Turks attack the Kurds, the US threatens the Turks, and we are left alone and blameless."

"And," she said, "we will be called to aid in the rescue."

He cocked his head, not understanding.

She continued. "Of the children that don't die, many will be injured, and the Red Crescent will be welcomed with supplies. That's us. We will be looked on favorably. You will be the hero."

He beamed at her and smiled, seeming to grasp the wisdom in the plan. "How many kids will be at the festival?"

"Who knows, but for terror's sake, one dead child is all it takes." She lifted her water glass from the bedside table and drank. She handed Abdul the glass and he took a sip.

"We have to plan how to make it look like the PKK," he said.

"And do you have some suggestions?" she asked, knowing he didn't.

"I'll have to think about it," he said, sounding like he was already losing his nerve. He returned the glass to the table. "Maybe we should go check with Omar."

She leaned toward him and put her hand on his back. "We

might never have this chance again to strike terror in the hearts of these pigs. Remember…they killed your second brother!" Her words went deep and she thumped him on the back with her fist, mocking the thrust of a knife.

**

Nick's group said their good-byes to the farmer and his wife with great fanfare. He smiled to himself as he watched the big Russian kiss the hosts' cheeks in the traditional Russian farewell, then almost lift the farmer off the ground in an embrace.

"You are my brother," Vladimir said. Ali translated.

Nick was beginning to appreciate the Russian for more than his physical strength. Aside from his intelligence, it was his ability to engage people that fascinated him. Everyone's initial reaction to the Russian, including his own, had been fear. Yet Vladimir could disarm their anxiety and win them over. How could someone seem so intimidating and yet be so friendly? It was a quality he admired.

While piling into the van, Nick held the door for Ali and Antasha to climb into the back seat. AK smiled at him but showed no glimmer of their nocturnal encounter. For a moment he thought he had dreamed the whole thing.

With everyone in place, the team waved to the farmer and his wife and continued their journey. As they settled into their seats, a sumptuous aroma wafted from the bread the farmer's wife had packed for the team.

The UN van descended from the peaks of Başkale into a basin with a raging river.

"This is the Zab," Ali told them.

"Ah…the Pishon," Vladimir said. "We are headed back to paradise."

Ali pointed to the east. "We are now very close to Iran." As the words left his mouth, both his and Buck's phones chimed with messages. They had been charging their phones in the van and hoped to receive a cellular signal on their journey.

Buck grabbed his phone, scanned his messages, and grinned.

"News from home?" Nick asked.

"Yes, from Katy and the boys. Wishing us well and praying for us," he said, talking and reading simultaneously. "And a note from Katy…" He stopped and his face flushed.

"Everything okay?"

"Just a little love note," Buck said shyly.

Nick slugged his arm and looked back at Ali, who was also reading his messages. "Any news?"

"Notes from Astî and some from work. Unfortunately, no news about our parents."

The group rode in silence. They quickly regained the altitude they had lost coming into the Zab Valley. The Zab River tumbled and roared over huge boulders alongside the road, and once again they began to climb a steep mountain pass, barren and wild.

Nick noticed that Buck was still glued to his phone. Buck tipped his head, looked at Nick, and smiled. "Man, I missed the Internet. I was just looking at the map. It looks like we pass by Qodshanes before we get to Hakkâri. Should we stop there first, to save gas?" he inquired, turning to Ali.

"I would agree, Sergeant," Ali said.

"Have you been to this…Qodshanes?" Buck stumbled over the pronunciation of the word.

"*Ko-can-is,*" Ali pronounced slowly. "I'm afraid I have not. The first I ever even heard of it was from Vladimir and Ms. Antasha. I have only been to Hakkâri once or twice. My father took us there to visit my aunt and uncle when I was a young boy. It was not a journey people from Van could afford to make often. Also, it is an area that has been prone to much violence, so it has not always been safe."

As Buck continued to study his phone, he said, "I was just googling Qodshanes. Listen to this: in the late 1800s, Isabella Bird, the eldest daughter of a British clergyman, made a trip to this area and wrote about her travels. 'Qodshanes consists of a church built on the verge of a precipice, many tombs, a grove of poplars, a sloping lawn, scattered village houses and, nearly on the edge of a precipitous cliff, the Patriarch's residence. Everything is singularly picturesque…looking across the tremendous ravine of the Zab upon savage mountains, the lower slopes of which are clothed with the tawny foliage of scrub oak, the upper heights with snow.'"

"Yes, I know about this Isabella Bird," Vladimir said. "Friedrich Schultz, a German archaeologist, discovered the Assyrians there in the early 1800s. The Assyrians formed an official liaison with the Anglican Church. In the late 1800s and early 1900s, they sent a British missionary, Michael Browne, who lived in Qodshanes for twenty-five years."

"Amazing," Nick said. "I've never even heard of this area before."

"Look here!" Buck exclaimed, still working his phone's Internet search engine. "There's a book written about this area by a guy named William Wigram. It's called *The Cradle of Mankind.* It was written in 1922."

"*Da,* I have read that book," Vladimir said, "but I didn't know anyone outside my country was interested. So much for Russian secrets."

Buck laughed. "Thank you, Google," he said and continued to read off his phone. "Here is Wigram's description of Qodshanes: 'The village of Qodshanes, which is the residence of the Nestorian or Assyrian Patriarch, Mar Shimun, and the headquarters of his Church, has a marvelous situation. It lies on a sloping alp of rugged pasture, between two mountain torrents which spring from the towering snow-fields to the west of it; and which descend in gradually deepening gorges, enclosing the tongue-shaped plateau on which the village stands. They meet beneath the point of the tongue at the base of a lofty wedge of rock; and thence the united stream flows on, joined by others on its way, till it falls into the Zab.'"

"Does Google have my name, address, and phone number?" Vladimir asked.

"Give me a minute," Buck teased. "Here they are—your bank account info and passwords." He turned the phone toward Vladimir, who fell for the joke and stared at the blank screen.

"Ha, funny man."

Buck continued. "Wigram says more. Listen: 'The village is dominated by the large, but simple residence of the Assyrian Patriarch and the Patriarchal Church that stands on a precipice, like a guardian over paradise. The Church is an impressive stone structure that rests as a windowless castle on the rock. Its multiple interior arches give it a simple, but elegant design. Multiple wooden beams span the space in which curious batches of drying fruit hang from the rafters.'"

AK spoke for the first time in quite a while. "I guess that would make Qodshanes a Christian village. Ali, no wonder your parents would avoid taking you there."

Ali nodded.

Buck scanned another article. "This one's current," he said and read to them, "'The modest patriarchal church, devoted to Mar Shalite, is one of the only buildings still standing in Qodshanes...the place is still uninhabited, except for some guards of the landowner. Most houses have crumbled away.'"

Buck paused and looked up from his phone. He frowned at Vladimir. "Did you know the village is abandoned?"

"Yes, for the most part. Abandoned, but not forgotten."

CHAPTER 58

PARADISE

The driver pulled the UN van into a small hamlet of twenty modest, earthen homes built into the crook of the Zab River, where a steep canyon opened. The team figured they were close to the turnout for Qodshanes, but they couldn't verify it because they had lost the Internet miles back as they'd traveled deeper into the Zab gorge. Fifteen minutes earlier, when they had passed the turnoff to Yüksekova, Buck reminded them that Yüksekova was the site where the bomb had exploded at the festival last week.

As the van came to a stop, the team saw three stern-looking men standing outside a small roadside shop. Nick sensed that Ali was reluctant to exit the van to ask directions. The three men leaned on rifles and wore large, ancient knives tucked into their belts. Summoning courage, Ali stepped warily from the van and approached the three men. Nick was reminded of pulling into the isolated high mountain villages in Guatemala, but these three did not display the warmth and hospitality of the Maya descendants.

The three men stood their ground, staring at Ali and the van. Nick thought their suspicions focused on Vladimir and wondered if, in the future, he should sit in a rear seat. The three men received all of Ali's questions with stone-faced silence.

Nick thought the men looked like characters out of the pages of *Arabian Nights*. Their clothes were both odd and splendid.

Each man wore striped baggy pants and weathered knee-high, leather boots. They all wore fine silk shirts of various colors under ornate vests. Two of them sported thin mustaches, while the third had a full gray beard. Each wore a matching hat, a peculiar combination of felt cap and turban. The man with a beard had crisscrossing bandoliers across his chest.

As if he'd read his mind, Buck joked, "We're not in Kansas anymore."

Indeed, the landscape had been changing ever since they'd left Van, but now he sensed anxiety surging within his companions as they watched Ali get nowhere with the strange, silent men.

Buck gasped when Vladimir opened his door and stepped into the fray. Before Nick or Buck could speak, the Russian was outside the van wielding his weapon of choice—a bottle of vodka.

"This could get interesting," Buck murmured.

The three men did not flinch at the sight of Vladimir, nor did their expressions change as he approached them.

"That guy is fearless," Nick said.

Vladimir spoke to the men, with Ali translating. After what seemed to Nick an endless sea of syllables, the man with the beard extended his hand and took Vladimir's offering, which also included a wad of cash the Russian had extracted from his coat. The bearded man still said nothing, but using the hand that held the loot, he pointed to a rutted dirt path adjacent to the roadside store.

Nick had to look twice to see that there was a passage wide enough for the van and was relieved when he saw it. "They're going to let us go," he said to Buck.

Buck nodded. "That must be the turnoff to Qodshanes," he said and laughed. "Can it also be the road to paradise? Maybe these guys are the guardian angels with the flaming swords."

Ali and Vladimir were already back in the van, and Ali told the driver to head up the rutted road. Vladimir waved to the three men, and the bearded one waved the bottle, and, for the first time, his stone face cracked into a toothless grin.

"I assume Qodshanes is up this road?" Nick asked Ali.

"Apparently."

"Why were they so hesitant to help us?"

Ali frowned. "Please, no offense…it is a little difficult to explain to outsiders. These lands and these people are as rugged and untamed as the mountains surrounding us. This is all tribal land. You might find one village of Kurds and the next one of Ottoman Turks, or Assyrian Christians, or even some more ancient tribal group…"

"Or the Armenians," Vladimir said, once again reminding them of his heritage.

"Yes, of course," Ali smiled. "Each group is trying desperately to carve out a life and survive in this untamed wilderness. And, as in every society, there are constant squabbles and fights over everything imaginable—land, water, sheep, wives, religion. Whatever you can think of, they have fought over it. So, when an outsider arrives, they are always suspicious."

"I see that women were thrown in with the sheep," Antasha said, making the men laugh.

"He actually listed women *after* the sheep," Vladimir shot back.

"Baaaa," AK bleated.

"I meant no offense, madam," Ali said, "but at one time, sheep were more valued than women. Sheep could be used not only for food, but their wool could be used for warmth."

"Oh, I can keep a man warm at night." AK laughed.

None of the men took the bait and Nick tried not to react. He was certainly not going to look back at her.

Ali quickly changed the subject. "Vladimir, thank you for your help back there. But I must say, that trick may not work out so well with Muslims."

"*Da*, I understand."

The team all reached for handholds as the van bounced up the steep mountain road made for mules more than modern vehicles. The rutted path followed a tributary of the Zab.

Still trying to forget AK's remark, Nick studied the scenery and was surprised to feel very much at home—as though he were back in his beloved Glacier National Park in Montana. The dirt road took them through flowing pastures crowned with sharp peaks that thrust their snowy caps into the brilliant blue heavens.

Driving for another mile, the pastures collapsed into a deep gorge, and the road etched its way through rocky crags, emerging into a high mountain meadow dotted with shelters that were almost indistinguishable from the landscape, some of them extensions of the terrain outcroppings, with natural turf serving as roofs. *These must be their houses.* He wondered if the old woman he had operated on lived in one of them.

"Anyone have any idea how far we are from Qodshanes?" he asked.

"Isabella Bird's journal said it took them six hours from the Zab to reach Qodshanes." Buck said. "Of course, that was around 1889...and on horseback. Can you imagine? Her diary said they traveled about a mile an hour. So, six miles?"

"Six miles? From what I'm seeing, not much has changed since Isabella's time," Nick said. Just then the van jolted, bounced, and scraped over a rut. "It might have been easier on a horse," he added.

***

The road grew more perilous and Nick was about to suggest they had been misled, but before he could utter the words, the van came over a rise and onto a montane plateau. The vista of a brand-new world was so high in elevation, it seemed to be birthing the clouds.

"It's just as Isabella described," Buck and Vladimir said in unison.

Indeed, they had entered a land that time forgot. It was truly an awesome sight. An emerald-green pasture sloped down to a cliff that yielded a view of the Zab River. Fresh snow blanketed the giant mountains that stood guard over the valley. Each side of the alpine meadow was sliced by jagged ravines, highlighted with trees adorned in autumn colors—golden yellows, fiery oranges, and crimson reds. The newly birthed cumulous clouds danced around the mountain peaks and tumbled and swirled down the cliffs, gathering into puffs of vapor, cascading to the valley below.

"Where to now?" the driver asked.

The team looked at Vladimir, who shrugged. "I don't see the

church, but I see something over there that looks like a farm." He pointed toward the base of one of the towering mountains. "And there. I think that's a road. Turn here."

"Might have been a road at one time," the driver said and turned in. The van sank slightly into the fresh dirt that had known only the hooves of cattle, but then gained traction, and they motored on.

As they came closer to the mountains, Vladimir's guess proved correct. What he'd seen was clearly a farm, with a farmer plowing a small field next to two crumbled stone buildings. The farmer stood on a hand plow pulled by a large ox. The turned soil was as dark and rich as any Nick had ever seen.

Without having to be told, the driver stopped the van alongside the field, and Ali slid out the side door to wait for the farmer to come near. But the farmer paid no attention to him and didn't acknowledge the van. He continued to drive the ox forward.

Vladimir rolled down his window and was about to put fingers to his mouth to whistle, when Nick grabbed his arm. "Let him finish his row."

Vladimir glanced at him and nodded. But when the farmer finished the row, he simply turned and started another. Vladimir looked at him again.

"Give him another minute."

They watched and waited, mesmerized by the working rhythm of the farmer in his natural state, blissfully tending his land, oblivious to the rest of the world. Nick couldn't help but think of the first farmer, Adam, cultivating his garden.

AK interrupted the tranquility. "I don't know about you gentlemen, but that road jiggled my bladder so much it's about ready to burst. If you'll excuse me, I'm going to step into the powder room." Before anyone could say a word, she'd scooted past Buck and Nick and was out the side door and behind the van, where she emptied her bladder. When she finished, she walked to Ali, who smiled quickly and looked back to the field.

Maybe it was her auburn hair that caught his attention, but as soon as AK joined Ali, the farmer looked up from his plow and stopped. He tied the reins of his ox to the plow, slapped the dust from his hands, and ambled toward the van.

AK turned to the men in the van. "Baaaaa," she smirked.

When the farmer caught up, he smiled at Antasha and nodded to Ali and the others. He was a short, jolly man with a keen smile, dressed plainly in work clothes and leather boots. His face was weathered, and his build was thin and muscular.

Nick got out of the van with the others. The farmer smiled warmly at each of them, showing no fear or anxiety. They could have been old friends out for a drive stopping to say hello.

The team deferred to Ali to make the introductions. From what Nick gathered, Ali told the farmer they were doctors—it was one of the few words he understood in Turkish. After a lengthy discussion, the farmer looked at Nick, bowed slightly, and said, "*Teşekkür ederim*, thank you." He spoke in Turkish and then, surprisingly, in good English.

Ali translated anyway, just to make sure there was no misunderstanding. "He is thanking us for our service to the people."

Nick smiled and asked, "Was the earthquake felt here?" He looked at Ali to translate, but the farmer understood and replied in English.

"Oh yes, it hit very hard and suddenly." He clenched his fists and thrust them out. "Boom, boom, boom. It shook the earth," he said with a strong Turkish accent.

"Was anyone hurt?" he asked, still amazed the man spoke English.

The farmer smiled again. "You can see there is not much to shake here." He spread his arms over the valley. "But one woman was thrown to the ground and broke her hip. I heard she was taken to Van for care."

Nick's patient. He smiled at Ali. Then he turned to the farmer. "You speak such good English."

The farmer smiled proudly. "Yes, we have had missionaries visit our area from time to time, and they taught me."

Nick glanced at Vladimir, who looked poised to ask questions.

Nick beat him to it. "Would you mind showing us the church?" he asked the farmer.

"Yes, I would be happy to. Unfortunately, there is not much to see."

"We'd still like to see it. Did it survive the earthquake?"

"Oh, yes. Always. We have had many quakes here, and still it stands." The farmer looked past the van and pointed to the edge of the plateau. "It's over there. It is hiding in the clouds today. But we can go there. It's too far to walk. Maybe we can take your van."

"Of course," Nick said, and the team piled in, offering the farmer the front passenger seat. The farmer introduced himself to the driver and directed him down the road, across a beautiful lush green field and over an ancient stone bridge to the other side of the expansive plateau, where foundations of stone houses appeared, barely distinguishable from the earth that swallowed them. There were thirty or forty such structures, with an occasional intact stone wall or chimney. The mist grew heavy as they approached the edge of the precipice and the beginning of a grove of trees that fell into the plunging ravine.

There, at the cliff's edge, was the structure that so many travelers before them had so vividly described—the Church of the Patriarch. It seemed to grow out of the rock on which it stood. The stone structure was disappointingly plain and not massive by any means, but there it stood—the survivor of wars and conflicts, earthquakes, and thunderous mountain storms.

The farmer got out of the van and headed to the church, and the team followed in solemnity to gaze upon the holy structure.

Buck broke the silence. "When we had signal, I downloaded Isabella Bird's description of the area. Here's what she said, 'The church has nothing especially ecclesiastical in its appearance. It has some resemblance to a keep with outbuildings.'"

"A keep?" AK asked.

"A keep was a fortified tower in a castle in the Middle Ages," Buck explained and continued, "'Its irregular form seems to have been dictated by the configuration of the rock. It has no windows, and the cruciform slits at a great height look like loopholes.'" He looked at AK to explain. "The cruciform slits are cross-shaped holes, and loopholes are openings from where defenders shot invaders."

"Would you like to go inside?" the farmer asked.

"Of course," Buck spoke for the team. The driver declined, saying he'd wait and keep watch.

The farmer led the team to one side of the stone wall where a rickety, ten-foot wooden ladder led to the small entrance.

"Is this the only way in?" Vladimir asked, not liking the look of the ladder or the mouse hole.

"Yes," the farmer said cheerfully as he stepped on the first rung and began the steep climb.

The team followed, one by one, entering the church through a primitive doorway only three feet in height. Ali was up like a shot. Nick saw that it was going to be a challenge for Buck and Vladimir and not a piece of cake for himself either. He saw that AK, mindful of her healing leg, viewed the ladder with anxiety. He helped her up and through the entry. He scrunched through the doorway, and Buck managed to do the same. Vladimir brought up the rear, squeezing through the entry like a bear wiggling through a doggy door.

"Vlad, that is the only way you will be able to approach God," AK said. "On your hands and knees."

"Shut up and help me through." He extended a hand for assistance.

Buck didn't hesitate to pull him through.

"Thanks, Marine," the Russian said, stretching to full height.

"It's hard to imagine all the old people getting up that ladder and through the door," Buck said. "I wonder why it was built that way."

"To keep the riffraff out," AK laughed and jerked her thumb at Vladimir.

They entered a small courtyard, its roof long gone, and saw two stone stairways and another small, stone doorway.

"That goes to the sanctuary," the farmer said. "Shall we enter?"

"Lead on," Buck said.

The farmer led them to the doorway, bowing low, and went through followed by Ali. AK also slipped through, but it wasn't as easy for Nick, Buck, and Vladimir, as they prostrated themselves entering the inner sanctum.

AK teased Vladimir again, assuming an evangelical voice and intonation. "Get down on your knees, sinner." She laughed while Vladimir scowled.

When Nick entered the pitch-black, disorienting sanctuary, he had some difficulty retaining his balance in the darkness. The only light was the glimmer that filtered in from the doorway. He grabbed Buck's arms for stability. Ali was prepared and pulled a Maglite flashlight out of his pocket, turning it on.

"Let there be light," AK marveled.

The visitors looked around. The sanctuary appeared to be about thirty-five feet long and just slightly narrower. It smelled of dirt and musk. Large stone arches spanned the nave and supported the ceiling. The team walked to the far end of the church and saw a massive stone wall burned black by candles. There were no pews, benches or chairs. The room was completely empty, catacomb-like.

Nothing. Nick was disappointed there was not a single clue to longevity or immortality. The tree of life. Yeah, right. Some grand adventure.

As he chastised himself for getting his hopes up, he heard a voice in his heart: *Why do you look for the living among the dead?*

It startled him and he bumped into Buck, who was staring at the ceiling.

Buck turned and caught him. "What?" he asked.

He composed himself. "I'll tell you later. What do you see?"

"I was thinking about Isabella's description again. She talked about bundles of fruit hanging from wooden rafters. I was picturing that." Buck looked around the room. "I guess there were three altars somewhere," he said, reciting what he'd read about the sanctuary.

"*Evet*, yes," the farmer said and indicated the now empty place.

"The first was the altar of prayers, where the anthem books were laid. The second was the altar of gospels that held the Book of Gospels wrapped in cloth, and the third was where the Cross of Christ lay," Buck said. "The worshippers kissed it after receiving the sacraments."

Ali shone his light at every nook and cranny, searching for some long-lost mystery or secret passage, but their hopes were dashed. The room was dark, dank, and empty.

The team stood in silence, waiting for a revelation as Ali's light bounced off the walls. Nick hoped that something mystical would happen—an angel, a vision, a visitation—but there was nothing. A great sadness washed over him, and he sighed. That's all there was. This church with its long-forgotten saints and prayers was empty, just like his own life.

Then he heard the voice again: *Nicklaus, why do you seek the living among the dead?*

His heart beat quickened, and he consciously had to control his breathing. The shadowy walls of the church seemed to close in on him. He shut his eyes to steady his nerves.

"I guess we have seen enough." Vladimir broke the silence this time.

With nothing to see and a growing sense of anxiety, Nick was relieved that the team was ready to leave. They squeezed back through the doorways and down the ladder. Once at the bottom, they looked at each other and shrugged.

Antasha turned to the farmer. "Are there other buildings?" she asked hopefully.

"No, not from the ancient days," the farmer said as though he heard the question often. "Only the tombs that are on this side of the church. I'll show you." He led them to the far side of the church into a primeval graveyard. Only a few headstones remained. Carved on two of the grave markers were weathered cuts that looked like symbols—circular marks—circles within circles, multiple overlapping circles of the same size.

"Those marks, what do they mean?" Antasha asked the farmer.

"They are symbols for the seed of life," he replied.

"The seed of life?" the team asked simultaneously.

"Yes, of course. Would you like to see the seed of life?" the farmer's eyes brightened.

Five jaws dropped.

The farmer waved for them to follow as he strolled down a short path to a grove that was filled with a variety of trees bursting with blossoms and fruit. The farmer walked directly to a medium-sized tree and picked a fruit. The fruit was purple and green and grew in large, round clumps that made Nick think of the symbol on the grave—circles within circles, bunches of circles.

"What kind of fruit is that?" Nick asked the farmer.

"It looks like a fig," Vladimir said.

"You are correct," the farmer said and proceeded to push his thumbs into the butt of the fruit. It split open easily. He showed the joined halves to the visitors. "The seed of life," he said, smiling broadly, letting them see that the fruit was packed with tiny seeds.

Vladimir was excited. "Look at how the seeds are arranged. It's the same pattern as the fruit on the tree. The seeds and the fruit are both arranged in clumps...circles within circles."

Nick joined his excitement. "It's a fractal," he exclaimed.

"Spot on," Ali said, and Vladimir nodded enthusiastically.

"Amazing," AK chimed in.

"Wait a minute," Buck said. "Hold everything. I hate to be the only one who doesn't know, but this Marine needs help. What's a fractal?"

"Fractals are quite fascinating, Sergeant," Ali said. "I studied them extensively when I was taking mechanical engineering as an undergraduate. Essentially, a fractal is a pattern or a geometric figure where each part of the structure has the same characteristics as the whole. It's like the same pattern recurs at progressively larger scales—like repeating shapes on every scale."

"Why haven't I ever heard of this?" Buck asked.

"Maybe you haven't heard the word, but you see fractals everywhere," Ali answered, "like in snowflakes and fern leaves and broccoli buds."

"Broccoli buds?" Buck frowned.

"Buck," Nick added, "think of the architecture of our lungs and our blood vessels, how they branch out and continue to branch out in repeating patterns."

"That's correct, Dr. Hart," Ali said, "even down to our DNA."

"Scientists have even explained galaxy formation as fractals," Vladimir added.

Buck studied the recurring pattern in the split fig the farmer held. "Kind of hard not to believe in a higher power when you understand fractals."

AK was excited. "Do you think this is what we've been looking for?"

The team looked at Vladimir, but he simply shrugged.

"Who knows?" Nick said. "Maybe it's like that old prescription: 'An apple a day keeps the doctor away.'"

"More like a fig a day keeps death at bay," Vladimir laughed. Then he turned to the farmer. "Is this the only fig tree here?" he asked. Nick heard hope resound in his voice.

The farmer laughed. "Oh no, many, many figs." He waved his arm. "Look around."

Nick watched Vladimir study the farmer. Finally, he asked what he was wondering himself. "Can I ask you—how old are you?"

The farmer smiled, laughed, and shrugged.

The team waited for an answer, but it was clear, the farmer didn't know how old he was or, if he did, he wasn't about to tell them.

"Would you like to take some figs with you from my garden?" Without waiting for an answer, the farmer reached into the tree, separated the figs from the clusters, and gave the team all they could carry.

Nick looked toward the west as the sun fell behind one of the jagged peaks. The mist continued to swirl around them, and without the sun, the temperature had dropped five to ten degrees. He looked at his watch: three o'clock. "I guess the sun sets early in paradise. We should be going. We need to get Ali to Hakkâri."

They walked single file on the trail back to the van with their arms full of figs. Nick wasn't sure he'd ever had a fig, but the present circumstances compelled him to try one. He took a bite, hoping that, just as he had hoped in the church, he would feel some sort of transformation. The fig was sweet and meaty, but he felt no different for eating it.

Once back at the van, the team thanked the farmer. Nick watched as Antasha paused at the van door to look back at the church.

"Why did the patriarch build the church on this rock?" she asked the farmer.

"Why do you ask?" the old man's eyes seemed to light up.

"It's such an unusual place to build a church—on a huge rock, on the edge of a cliff. Not exactly the most inviting of places—"

"—or the most accessible," Vladimir finished.

The farmer didn't answer immediately. He seemed to study the red-headed woman. Finally, he said with a heavy Turkish accent, "It is because of the econ."

"Econ?" Antasha repeated.

"Like economics?" Nick asked.

The farmer looked confused. He turned to Ali for help and questioned the word. "Econ?"

Ali nodded and explained. "*I* in Turkish is pronounced *E*. What he is saying is icon."

"Icon?" Vladimir said. "I did not see an icon in the church."

"It is not in the church," the farmer said.

The team waited for an explanation, but the farmer just smiled.

Nick thought the farmer was teasing them with his secret.

Finally, Ali spoke to the farmer in Turkish. After a brief conversation, the farmer spoke to his visitors in English. "Would you like to see the econ?"

"Yes," they said in unison.

"The econ is not in the church. It is in the rock on which the church stands," the farmer said. "I will show you." He waved for them to follow.

He led them to the cliff side of the church and carefully picked a path along the precipice. "The rocks are slippery and the way is narrow," he said, glancing back at his followers.

"Isn't that scriptural?" Buck murmured.

Nick peered over the precipice at the treacherous drop. Clouds swooped down the cliff's edge and nudged him to go ahead and free-fall. With no desire for a swan dive, he turned to his fellow travelers. He noticed AK contemplating the rocky, slippery path. She must have been exhausted. After all, she had limped her way through the church without her crutches. "I'm not sure you want to do this," he told her.

"Are you kidding me? I will not miss this," she said defiantly and limped toward the crag. Nick steadied her from the front, and Vladimir assisted from behind. The team inched along the scarp, clinging to the rock until they reached a small ledge leading into a cave.

The farmer entered the cave without hesitation. Once again, the opening was small, just like the doorway of the church. Because of the position of the aperture, everyone was required to squeeze through on their hands and knees. Ali was first to follow the farmer, and once inside he shone his flashlight so the others could see as they emerged into the cave. The chamber was just big enough to hold the group. Beyond reach of the mountain mist and wind, the temperature inside was surprisingly comfortable. A low-pitched moan came from the opening of the cavern.

"Econ," the farmer said and pointed to an antechamber at the far end of the cave, recessed into the ceiling. As soon as Ali's light hit the recess, an image carved in the stone was visible—a tree.

"*Мой Бог!* My God!" Vladimir exclaimed. He looked at AK and back at the carving. He began to recite, "'And there you will find a tree of stone that transforms.'" He paused to catch his breath "'I will give you a new heart and put a new spirit in you. I will remove from you your heart of stone and give you a heart of flesh.'"

"That sounds like the Old Testament," Buck said.

"Yes, the last two sentences from Ezekiel…and"—Vladimir hesitated and looked at Antasha, who shrugged—"the first statement is from writings of a ninth-century Russian priest."

They all stepped closer to the carving. Almost six feet high, the branches of the tree spread out in equal dimensions, each limb branching equally into two limbs and branching again and again.

"Is that a fractal?" Buck asked.

Nick and Ali nodded as they stared in wonder.

Ali leaned in closer with the light. "There's an inscription. What does it say?" he turned to the farmer. When the farmer did not immediately reply, Ali shone his light on him. The farmer stood behind the group with a wide smile. He looked directly at Antasha. "Do you know?"

Antasha pushed through the men to get a closer look and Ali

handed her the light. She shone the light at the ancient script. It was written in such a way that it seemed to hang from the tree like fresh fruit.

Nick watched her examine the writing, each delicate stroke.

עושי ירצנה דלמו סידוהיה

He had no idea.

Antasha reached out, touched the script and gasped. She collapsed and began to weep uncontrollably. Nick reached down to support her, but she resisted. Her chest heaved and she fell to her hands and knees, causing her to drop the flashlight into the dirt. The chamber went nearly dark and the cave's moan echoed Antasha's angst.

Ali reached for the flashlight and restored the light. AK continued to wail until her strength gave way, and she collapsed into the dirt. Through her sobs and tears, she mumbled something in Russian. Nick looked at Vladimir for translation, but he appeared shocked and horrified. Nick looked at the farmer, expecting similar dismay, but the farmer was smiling.

Unsure of what to do with the grieving woman, Nick and Ali, half dragged and half carried Antasha from the cave and along the cliff wall, back to the van. Vladimir found a bottle of water and put it to her lips. She coughed and continued to weep, much longer than the men were comfortable with, but they managed to settle her into the van.

Dusk was descending on the alp, and the UN driver reminded them of the harrowing journey down the mountain. Nick, Ali, and Buck looked at Vladimir, who stuck his hand out to the farmer.

"Thank you for showing us the church and the icon. Who else knows about the carving?"

"The patriarchs, of course."

"Anyone else?" Vladimir pressed.

"Me, of course," he grinned.

"And?" Vladimir's face flushed with exasperation.

"I showed Isabella," the farmer confessed, almost embarrassed. He looked at Antasha. "She had red hair as well."

"Isabella Bird?"

"Oh, yes…and Mr. Browne," the farmer blushed.

Nick did the math and looked at Buck and Vladimir. Red hair aside, Bird and Browne had visited more than a hundred years earlier.

***

The team was on the road again. The farmer had graciously invited them to stay with him overnight, and even though they'd been tempted, they declined, knowing they needed to search for Ali's parents. The unfolding mystery of the tree of life would have to wait a few more days.

They sat in silent reflection as they bounced down the rough mountain road. Antasha slept, stretched out on the back seat. Ali joined Buck and Nick in the middle seat.

They rode in silence until the van was back on pavement, when Buck asked, "What do you all think?"

Nick was examining one of the farmer's figs. He turned it around in his fingers and sniffed it. "Discoveries of natural cures are found all the time in nature," he said. "Maybe these little guys hold the key…maybe they're packed full of vitamins or antioxidants. Maybe they carry antimicrobial or anticancer properties. Who knows?"

"But people eat figs all the time," Buck shrugged.

"Yes, especially in my culture," Ali said. "But, Sergeant, you need to remember, most foods we eat today are so very far from the original, what with all the genetic modifications that the food industry has done…like wheat that produces its own pesticides."

"I always thought of figs as a natural laxative," Buck joked. "Like prunes."

"Yeah, good for what ails you," Nick said. "That's what my grandmother used to say about foods that made your bowels move. I guess it's part of healthy living."

The team laughed.

Vladimir's face turned serious. "What if the fig and these fig trees are as close as one can get in this modern world to the original? It's something we must consider."

"Well, if we find a new cancer drug, we'll have to name it after King's Hospital," Nick joked.

"Now that would be appropriate...the King's Cure," Buck added.

Vladimir turned in his seat to face them. "Thank you for allowing us to go up there." He paused, looking thoughtful, and went on. "But I must say, it was one of the most intriguing and disappointing places I have ever seen. I guess I knew we wouldn't find a marvelous, glowing tree standing in the middle of a field, but I thought there'd be something more. Unfortunately, except for the old farmer—and God knows how old he is—the place is all but abandoned." He shook his head. "I don't know what to think of the icon and what happened to AK."

"Yeah, the church seemed more like a giant tomb than a house of God," Buck said.

"Why do you look for the living among the dead?" Nick murmured under his breath.

"What did you say?" Vladimir asked.

"I don't know." Nick had surprised himself. "It was just something I heard in the church. Why do you look for the living among the dead?" he repeated.

Ali and Vladimir frowned, but Buck smiled.

"Of course," Buck said. "Why the heck didn't I see it?" He turned to his companions. "Do you see it? It was like when Mary went to Jesus's tomb after he was crucified. She was weeping in the empty tomb, and two angels appeared to her and said, 'Why do you look for the living among the dead? He is not here; he has risen!'"

"What does that have to do with the tree of life?" Vladimir asked.

"I don't know," Buck admitted, "but even your leaders apparently believe that eating from the tree of life can bring immortality. Isn't that what Jesus has already promised us... eternal life? That whoever believes in Him will have eternal life?" Buck paused to look at his band of brothers. "My spirit is just leaping. It's something I've never really considered before. Think about all the scriptures that tell us about being 'grafted in.' Saint Paul talks in the book of Romans about us being grafted into Christ. And even Jesus said, 'I am the vine; you are the branches. If you remain in me and I in you, you will bear much fruit; apart from me you can do nothing.' Maybe we really are looking for the living among the dead. Maybe…the true tree of life is Jesus?"

"But what about the carving, the icon?" Vladimir asked. "You think it holds some mystical power? Look what it did to AK. We have icons in Russia…нерукотворные…what is the word in English? *Acheiropoieta*, 'made without hands.' There are reports of miracles surrounding those icons."

Buck scratched his neck. "Yeah, but icons and even miracles are not God. They are meant to point the way to Him."

The van hit a bump in the road and jostled the men. Nick looked back at Antasha, who stirred and moaned. He watched as she slowly pushed herself up to sit. Her eyes were not yet focused and mascara was smudged on her cheeks. She held her head in her hands, then pushed her hair from her face.

"Where are we?" she asked, looking out the window.

"On our way to Hakkâri," Nick answered. "How are you feeling?"

She furrowed her brow.

"You passed out or something in the cave. You remember?"

She nodded slowly and rubbed her face.

"You reached out and touched the script and *wham*," Nick said. "What happened?"

"I don't know. It was like electricity hit my body." Antasha's lower lip quivered and tears flowed from her eyes once more.

Nick offered her a bottle of water, but she waved it off.

"Do you know what the script said?" he asked.

"Yes…it is written in Hebrew." She paused and struggled with the words. She looked out the window and back at the men who stared at her, awaiting an answer.

"It said…*Iesvs Nazarenvs Rex Ivdaeorvm*." She spoke in Latin and wept so hard she found it difficult to speak. Finally, she caught her breath and said in English, "Jesus of Nazareth, the King of the Jews."

CHAPTER 59

SADNESS
SATURDAY NIGHT—
POST-QUAKE DAY TWENTY-ONE

Abdul watched the bomb makers package the "mother of satan" explosive, TATP, into Ziploc baggies. Its bleach-like odor stung his nostrils. The concrete bunker was cool, but the two men wiped sweat from their brows. Both men were chain smokers. Having gone over an hour without a cigarette was part of the reason their hands shook, but mainly it was the fact that if they made one mistake, their lives would be evaporated in an instant.

He didn't need to oversee the operation. He realized he was risking his life being there, but it made him feel alive and in command. His men seemed to have lost confidence in his leadership, and he hoped his indifference to the possibility of death would reaffirm their respect. He noticed that his men seemed more distant and less inclined to obey him. Perhaps he was just imagining their disaffection, or maybe they were just bored with the lack of activity and uncertainty. Or worse, he wondered if they knew about his relationship with the White Snake and had lost respect for him.

But maybe it was something else, and it was possible his men saw beyond all that. It was possible they surmised he was not convinced in his heart of hearts that this act of jihad was the right thing to do—that killing a bunch of children was wrong, even if they were Kurdish children who would grow up to fight their own brothers and sisters. He had a sense this was a line Allah did not want them to cross. He would have preferred fighting against an armed enemy. Kill or be killed. Like his brother fighting in Jobar. He was one year younger than his third brother and they constantly competed in everything. Abdul carried a picture of his brother shooting a rocket-propelled grenade. He pulled it from his pocket and gazed at it again. With war-soiled clothes, full beard, and a black beret, his brother looked so important as the RPG burst from the launcher toward an unknown target. Abdul often wondered what was on the deadly end of the rocket.

He shook his head slowly. Killing children was not right. One of the bomb makers coughed, and Abdul jerked back to the moment. It was too late to cancel the mission. He had already given the command. It would have to be done. He had been surprised and a little disappointed that Omar had approved. *Allah have mercy.* Abdul sighed. He didn't want to be here. He wished he were back at the university with his friends.

He swallowed, resetting his mind on the explosives. He had designed the bombs—a box within a box. Typically, TATP worked well in pressure-cooker bombs, but the hospital's kitchen didn't have a pressure cooker and going to town to buy two of them would have raised suspicions. The boxes would have to do. But maybe they'd work just as well, and—who knew—maybe even better.

The space between the box within a box was filled with nails, bolts, nuts, and whatever small pieces of metal his men had found that would penetrate for a hundred feet or more. The inner boxes contained propane tanks, four hand grenades—one in each corner—five packets of TATP and a detonator. The result would be a series of explosions, each one building on the next. They would happen in milliseconds and appear to be one massive explosion. The small detonator would ignite the TATP that would explode the grenades that would rupture the propane tank, resulting in a combustive explosion so violent that it was likely the gymnasium would implode. The metal pieces, shooting with the velocity of bullets from a high-powered rifle, would rip through flesh and bone.

He watched his bomb makers. Whoever he chose to carry the boxes into the gymnasium would have to be rock-steady, as the task required extreme care. The TATP was extremely unpredictable. Typically, heat, friction, or shock would explode the powder. That was why his men were taking great pains to secure the plastic bags in bubble wrap to prevent the package from exploding prematurely. Once secure, only the small detonator would start the chain reaction and the devastation.

***

It was dusk when the team pulled into the driveway at a small farm outside of Hakkâri that belonged to Ali's uncle and aunt. Even though it had been many years since he'd visited, Ali said the place was unchanged. The headlights of the van illuminated the large oak tree with the tire swing hanging from a branch. The paint on the small farmhouse was faded, and the porch needed repair.

"You okay?" Nick asked.

Ali wagged his head side to side. "I'm afraid, Dr. Hart, that I have not had much hope since the day we heard about the earthquake in the OR lounge. And we have been so busy the last couple of weeks, I honestly haven't allowed myself to think much about it. But now that I'm here, the weight of it all seems to have pinned me to my seat."

"Ali, I will be honored to go with you, my friend."

"It appears, Dr. Hart, that my aunt and uncle have come out to greet us instead."

Nick turned to see an elderly man and woman standing on the rickety porch. The man looked like an older version of Ali—thin and wiry with large ears. He wore faded blue jeans and a dusty white tank top. The woman was just as thin but shorter, with cropped gray hair pulled back and held in place with a red bandana.

Seeing his relatives freed Ali from his seat, and he bounded out of the van with Nick in tow. He'd told the team it had been over twenty-five years since he'd seen his aunt and uncle, and he wasn't sure if they'd know him. But his aunt recognized him immediately and embraced him tightly. His uncle looked wary until his aunt spoke to him and his face lit up with excitement. He threw his arms around his wife and Ali, hugging them both, lifting them up and down, dancing with glee.

Ali's aunt untangled the embrace and took Ali's face in her hands. She gazed deep into his eyes and brushed her fingers through his hair as though he were still a child. She tenderly touched the scar on his cheek, then kissed his face over and over.

Ali's uncle peppered his nephew with questions. Ali gestured with his hands, trying to slow the verbal onslaught. Several times he pointed to the van and explained his traveling companions. Finally, Ali's uncle paused to take a breath, turned to the van, and waved the rest of the team to join the reunion.

Ali made introductions. His uncle welcomed everyone effusively and shook their hands with gusto. After the greetings, Ali and his relatives chatted in Turkish, and while Nick didn't understand, he felt the tension hanging in the night sky like a full moon when Ali's uncle must have asked about his brother and sister-in-law, Ali's parents.

Nick read the disappointment on their faces—Ali's, when he realized his parents had not come here, and the uncle's, when he realized Ali had not found them. Ali and his family talked among themselves, but the timbre of the conversation had turned from major to minor. The joy of their reunion was gone. Ali's aunt gasped and cried, softly at first, then worked up to a wail. Nick and the others looked at the ground, understanding but unable to intervene. Pain and grief were palpable, a universal language, but the emotions they stirred were personal.

***

Despite their grief, Ali's aunt and uncle invited the team to spend the night and they wouldn't take no for an answer. As far as they knew, all the local hotels were closed due to damage from the earthquake. The couple had raised six children, all grown and living on their own, so they had many empty bedrooms. Ali's aunt gave Buck, Ali, and Nick the boys' room, and, assuming the Russians were a couple, she gave them the girls' room. Both rooms had small twin beds, which suited Antasha, who still seemed to be recovering from her encounter with the Hebrew script. The UN driver insisted on sleeping in the van.

By the time the team had taken turns washing up, Ali's uncle had butchered a lamb, skewered it, and had it roasting over a large open fire. The savory aroma was mouthwatering. They all enjoyed a meal fit for a king—which, they joked, was fitting as they'd come from King's Hospital. The lamb was the most tender and juiciest meat that Nick had ever tasted, delicately seasoned with fresh rosemary, sage, and thyme. Ali's aunt served an assortment of vegetables along with fresh baked bread and hand-churned butter. The gustatory celebration tempered the sadness of their loss.

Sated and sipping Turkish brandy, they lingered at the table in the glow of thick wax candles. Ali's uncle wanted to know everything from information about Van to the world news. He mostly wanted to hear about Ali's wife and daughters. Ali blushed with embarrassment when his aunt asked him why they were stopping with only two children. But Ali took it all in good stead; after all, it had been a quarter of a century since he'd seen his aunt and uncle, and there was much to tell.

But as the hours wore on, Nick noticed that Ali was exhausted. The realization that his parents were still missing, plus translating every conversation, and at times multiple conversations, had worn him out. Ali's aunt recognized it too, because it wasn't long before she scolded her husband to stop the interrogation and shooed them all off to bed.

The beds were small and uncomfortable, but Nick had no complaints.

"Man, your aunt and uncle are great people," Buck said to Ali.

"It always amazes me that sometimes the people with the least have the most generous hearts," Nick commented. "I'm not sure why that is."

"Maybe it's because they know what it's like to do without," Buck said. "Just like the people we met in Guatemala."

"My uncle is my dad's older brother," Ali said, "but he is cut from the same cloth—generous and kind. They would do anything for anyone, regardless of religion, race, tribe, whatever… none of it ever mattered."

"I can see where you get your gentle nature, my friend," Nick said. "I'm so sorry about your parents. I had hoped it was going to be a different scenario today."

"Thank you, Nick. I as well, but like I said, I have had the feeling it would turn out this way. I don't know, it's kind of hard to explain, but I have been filled with a deep sense of loneliness, as though my parents have gone and I am an orphan." Ali sniffed and his voice cracked.

Nick sensed God's tenderness drift into the room, and he began to pray silently for his friend. He thought of his own parents and how he might feel on the day of their passing. A great longing and homesickness welled up within him, and his eyes teared in sympathy for his friend.

"It's crazy," Ali said between sniffs. "All I can think about is that little boy with the femur fracture that we have been caring for—Ibrahim. I wonder what his tender little heart must feel with all of this. How afraid and lonely he must feel." Ali's voice cracked again.

CHAPTER 60

HEALINGS
SUNDAY—POST-QUAKE DAY TWENTY-TWO

Nick jumped at the sound of the ringer in his backpack. The travelers sat around the dining table with Ali's aunt and uncle, drinking strong Turkish coffee and eating a hearty breakfast of eggs and lamb sausage patties. Nick had forgotten about the emergency satellite phone the UN Commander had given him before they'd left Van.

He rummaged through his backpack and pulled out the oversized phone. He stared at the illuminated face but wasn't sure how to use it. Buck leaned over and pushed a button. He directed him to put the phone to his ear.

"Hello. HQ." Nick clowned to disguise his embarrassment that he didn't know the protocol for answering a military sat phone.

"Nick?" Maggie's voice came through the phone.

He was relieved to hear her voice but continued to joke, rattling off a volley of military jargon: "Uh, Roger that, HQ... tango, forty-niner."

His companions rolled their eyes and chuckles came from the phone.

"Hey, Nick." It was Jack.

"Nick, I have Jack and the UN Commander with me." It was Maggie again. "You're on speaker phone."

"Everything okay?" He asked with concern.

. "We were just about to ask you the same," the Commander said.

"Yes," he said. "We're okay. We're in Hakkâri. We're doing fine. We are at Ali's aunt and uncle's home. Unfortunately, his parents are not here." Nick glanced at Ali, who looked down. "But we haven't given up hope. We are going into town today to look around. Ali has a few more distant relatives, and there are two hospitals here. We thought we'd check them as well."

"Tell Ali we are all thinking about him and praying for his family," Maggie said.

"I will for sure," he said. "And everything there?" he asked, still concerned that something was wrong.

When there was no response, Nick's heart began to race.

"There has been a bit of a situation that we need to run by you and Ali."

Nick turned toward Buck. "How do you put this darn thing on speaker phone?"

Buck pushed another button and nodded. "Can you hear us?" Nick anxiously asked. "What is happening?" he said into the phone.

"Ali." It was Maggie. "We are so sad that you have not found your parents yet. We have been so hopeful."

"Thank you, Ms. Maggie," Ali said solemnly.

"Ali, Jack Bilton here. We have assigned a team specifically to search through the remains of your parents' house and the home of your wife's parents."

"That is very kind of you, Mr. Bilton. Thank you."

"Well, it's the least we can do…I am so sorry, son, that you have not found them yet."

"Thank you, sir."

"Ali and Nick." It was Maggie. "We need to ask you about one of your patients."

"Yes, of course," Nick said. "Who? Is everything all right?"

"It's little Ibrahim."

Nick's heart sank. He looked at Ali and worried about piling more grief upon his friend. "What has happened?"

"Well, that's the problem, he is more than all right. This morning, I went into the boys' wing at the orphanage, and he was sitting up in bed...out of his traction."

"What?" Nick asked with surprise and annoyance. "How did that happen?" He was frustrated that someone could let it happen. With the fracture only being three weeks old, the bone would have barely begun the healing process. Out of traction, it would easily deform or shorten. "Did one of the volunteer surgeons put him back in traction?"

"Well, not exactly," Jack said.

"Could you ask one of them to do that, please?" He said stronger than he meant to.

"When we found the boy sitting on the side of his bed, we immediately made him lie back down, and we held his leg straight and called one of the surgeons right away. Ibrahim told us he had untied the traction rope from the bow across the pin in his leg."

Nick cursed to himself for not making sure the rope was better secured and covered in tape. This would not be the first child who had wiggled out of an apparatus. "I hope he learned his lesson. It must have hurt like a son-of-a-gun when that traction let go."

"Well, here's the thing," Maggie continued, "Ibrahim said it didn't hurt at all. He was sitting happily on the side of the bed talking with his friends. The surgeon from Arkansas came in, and we x-rayed his leg right away. I'd have the surgeon on the phone as well, but he is in surgery. Anyway, he looked at the x-ray and just shook his head and said he had never seen anything like it. He said that kids heal fast, but not this fast. He said that there is a huge healing callus around the fracture. This surgeon only does joint replacements at home and thought I'd better run it by you two."

"Yeah, it's way too early to take off the traction," Ali said.

"I have the x-ray right here. I'm no surgeon, but guys, it looks pretty healed."

"Any way you can snap a picture of it and send it to my cell phone?" Ali asked. "I've had one bar of signal since we got to Hakkâri."

Nick could hear a discussion between the Commander and someone else, possibly a member of his communications team. "Stand by," the Commander said. "We're working on it."

Nick watched Antasha get up from the table and walk to the bathroom. He was slightly embarrassed when he saw Buck staring disapprovingly at him. Buck probably thought he was watching her cute derriere, but it was her gait that he was observing. She had been using her crutches, or for short distances, limping and hopping. But now she walked unaided and without a limp. Nick was stunned. Before he could speak, Ali's phone beeped.

Ali pulled the x-ray picture up on his screen and stared at it. Nick grew impatient. "Well?"

Ali shrugged and gave his phone to him. "See for yourself."

He stared at the image. Then, using his fingers, he zoomed and unzoomed and zoomed again.

"You guys get it?" the Commander asked.

"Yes," Nick said slowly without commitment.

"And?"

"Are you sure this is Ibrahim's leg?" he asked.

"Ha. That's exactly what the surgeon here said. You guys are all skeptics," Maggie said. "Just tell me what you see."

He answered her slowly. "I see a child's fracture that has a huge amount of healing around it, like it has been in traction for four weeks and a spica cast for another four."

"Right," Maggie affirmed. "So, you think it's healed?"

He looked at Ali, and they both shrugged. "I would have to say yes," he said. "Impossible, but yes."

"Did the surgeon examine the leg?" Ali asked.

"Yes. He said it feels like the fracture is as solid as a rock," Maggie said. "He'd like to take the traction pin out of the leg and keep Ibrahim out of traction, but he wanted the final word from you two."

"This is all highly unusual," Ali said.

"Or a miracle," Jack added.

"There is something miraculous about that little boy," Maggie said. "In Guatemala, we often see children usher in miracles. It's something about their innocence."

The team in Hakkâri went silent.

"You all okay?" Maggie asked.

No one answered.

"We lose you guys?" the Commander's voice boomed through the sat phone. "I think we lost them," he said to Maggie and Jack.

"Hang on," Buck said into the phone.

Antasha was back at the table, standing beside her chair. This time they all watched her walk back from the bathroom. She was crying. She had been teary all morning, but now she was weeping.

The team was speechless with wonder.

"I didn't say anything this morning when I got up," she said through her tears, "but something has changed in my leg. It feels as if it was never broken." She held her arms up for balance and put all her weight on the fractured leg. Then she hopped on it. "No pain," she said. "I thought it was just a fluke until I heard you talking about the little boy. I think I, too, have received a miracle." She cried tears of gladness.

"A miracle?" Vladimir said. "She's not a child and she's certainly not innocent," he added sarcastically.

Antasha sniffed back her tears. "Something happened yesterday. I can't explain it." She covered her face with her hands, unable to stop crying.

Buck put his arm around her shoulders. "I say thank you, God." He helped her to her chair, although she no longer needed the assistance.

"Nick?" Maggie asked.

"Uh…yeah, sorry. We are kind of having a moment here ourselves. Antasha was translating some ancient writing on a carving at the church and…" he paused, not knowing how to explain it.

"She was touched by God," Buck said. "She's been healed as well."

"Thank you, Jesus," Jack said.

Vladimir handed AK his cloth napkin. He seemed ill at ease and slightly embarrassed by the fuss being made over her.

"What did you find yesterday at Qodshanes?" the Commander asked.

"Well, honestly, we're not sure," Nick said. "A really, really old man and an abandoned church."

"Is that it?" Jack asked.

"Not exactly," Buck said. "The church was built on a huge rock. In the rock is a cave and in the cave is a stone carved with a picture and ancient writing—an icon." He signaled to Nick to finish the story.

"The picture is a tree," Nick said. "On the tree hangs a sign. It is in Hebrew script, and it says, 'Jesus of Nazareth, the King of the Jews.'" As the words left his mouth, Antasha's sobs increased. "It has...uh...AK a bit undone."

"Amazing," Jack said. "What else did you find?"

"Figs," Buck said before anyone else could answer.

"Figs?" Maggie asked.

"Yes. It's a long story," Nick said. "We'll tell you about it when we get back. I'm thinking the figs may have something to do with the longevity of these people."

"Never really thought of the tree of life as a fig tree," Maggie mused, "but now that you say it, it kind of makes sense. After Adam and Eve disobeyed God, they covered themselves with fig leaves. Maybe fig leaves from the tree of life are meant to heal our sins."

"We're bringing some of the figs back," Nick said. "That is, if I can keep Buck from eating them all."

"Hey, they're delicious...and good for what ails you," Buck grinned, reminding the team of Nick's prescription for figs.

"Yeah, we're regular guys," Nick said sarcastically and turned from Buck to Vladimir. He spoke to Maggie, Jack, and the Commander. "Since it was a joint discovery, we can send the figs for analysis in both of our countries. If there's something to be learned, we need to share it with the Russians."

Vladimir nodded.

"And what do you want me to do with Ibrahim?" Maggie asked.

Nick looked at Ali. "Yeah, I guess you can go ahead and have the guys take his pin out. But just to be on the safe side, see if you can keep him in bed until we get back so we can see for ourselves."

Ali nodded. "Yes, please," he added, realizing they couldn't see him.

"When will you be back?" Maggie asked.

"Uh, we haven't exactly talked about it," Nick answered for the others. "We want to give Ali as much time as we can." He didn't know what else to say.

"Well, you gentlemen be careful," the Commander said. "We will check with you in the next day or so."

The phone clicked several times and went silent.

Nick found himself staring at AK. She was still wiping tears from her eyes. "You going to be okay?" He couldn't help but notice that her tears seemed to deepen the aqua-blue of her eyes.

She finally smiled. "I just don't have the words to say what happened to me. When I touched the tree…the Hebrew words… it was like being struck by lightning. It shocked my whole body. This will probably sound crazy, but it felt like I was standing with God. All my life I have been afraid of being judged by God, even though I have professed not to believe. Something always nagged me: what if there is a God and I must stand in judgement before him? At the moment when I read those words, I believed I was standing before God, but what I'd expected to be a look of disappointment and anger was instead—" Her bottom lip began to quiver. "I don't know how to describe it. God looked at me with acceptance and love. Like my *babushka*…my grandmother…She just loved me. Not for anything I did or didn't do. She loved me just for me." AK looked at Nick and the others. "My God, you are all looking at me like I'm crazy."

Buck shook his head. "Not at all, Antasha."

"I am," Vladimir smirked.

Everyone looked at him, unsure whether to laugh or disapprove.

Buck came to the rescue. "So often, God takes us out of our comfort zone. I love the story in the scriptures, I think it's in Numbers, where God speaks to one of his prophets through a donkey." Buck looked at Vladimir. "These signs and wonders, these miracles are His way of pointing us toward Him."

"I think if God speaks through an ass, he would be speaking through Vladimir all the time," AK said and blew him a kiss.

They all laughed, even Vladimir.

"What do you think you and AK will do now?" Nick asked the Russian.

Vladimir looked at Antasha. "I think this crazy woman needs to go home," he teased. "Get some strong medication."

"Or figs," Buck added.

"Oh, you men are hilarious," she said. "I'll put your figs where the sun doesn't shine."

"Oh good, there is the AK I know." Vladimir laughed. "I was afraid some alien abducted you, the way you were carrying on." Then he turned serious. "What I would like to do is spend some more time in Qodshanes, maybe even visit the surrounding villages. Of course, we must see if we can rent a vehicle. And I would appreciate if we could stop at the hotel we stayed at before the quake. If any of it is still standing, we might recover our belongings."

"We can certainly do that," Nick said.

"But first, if it is okay with you, we would like to help our friend, Dr. Ali, any way we can. Can we hang with you until you return to Van?" Vladimir asked.

CHAPTER 61

AISHA

Akleema knew she should be praying but didn't feel like it. Abdul told her that the men resented her attendance at their daily prayer, so for the last few days, she had participated in prayer alone in her room. Abdul had told her they could build a barrier to separate her from the men so she could remain in the same room. But she had rejected his suggestion.

Why must women always accommodate men? Maybe instead of women wearing hot, black burqas the men should wear blindfolds.

Lying on her bed, she glanced at the clock on the nightstand. Five minutes after twelve. She wasn't sure how much longer the men would be in noon prayer, but she didn't really care. All she cared about was that they would leave for the festival in three hours. The dance started at four, so it would give them plenty of time to set up. As the Red Crescent, they were bringing soda pop, water bottles, cookies, and other snacks…and the entertainment. She chuckled.

One of Omar's men knew the school's gymnasium well. He figured most of the children would be near the music close to the stage. He was confident he could easily move one of the box bombs under the stage without being detected. One of the bomb makers suggested that they put the other bomb in the atrium near the exit and have a time delay of thirty seconds between detonations. That way, the first explosion would push the herd of children into the second blast.

Akleema reached for the book she'd brought with her. *Aisha: The Wife, the Companion, the Scholar.* She'd lost track of how many times she had read it. She loved it more than any book she had ever read. Aisha, whose full name was Ā'ishah bint Abī Bakr, was one of Muhammad's wives and one of the most preeminent women in Islamic history.

Akleema smelled the musky pages of the book and thought about the one thing she had in common with Aisha. In accordance with Islamic tradition, Aisha was married to Muhammad when she was six or seven, and the marriage was consummated when she was nine or ten, and the prophet was fifty-three—the same age as Akleema's uncle when he started his visits to her bedroom. Aisha and the prophet were married for only nine years when he died. She lived another forty-four years of prominence.

As the prophet's third and youngest wife, Aisha was rumored to be his favorite, and legend says that he took his last breath in her arms. Her importance in history was due not only to her marriage, but to the fact that she was the daughter of Abu Bakr, the first caliph to succeed Muhammad. Akleema had learned that the division between the Sunni and Shia came at the time of the succession. The Shia believed that Abu Bakr was not the proper successor; they argued that the prophet had anointed his cousin, Ali, to lead.

What Akleema loved about Aisha was that her true significance came later in her own right and without the accord of any man. Aisha became one of history's early female politicians, holding honor and influence in the first three caliphate reigns— Abu Bakr, Umar, and Uthman. Abu Bakr's reign lasted only two years and Umar's ten. When Uthman took over the caliphate, Aisha disagreed strongly with aspects of his rule and was ordered to stay at home.

Thinking about it, Akleema laughed to herself. *That sounds familiar.* She fanned herself with the book pages.

Uthman's reign lasted twelve years, ending when a thousand rebels surrounded his house and murdered him. It was then that the Shia sect got their way, and Ali, the prophet's anointed heir, became the fourth and new caliph.

Although the book did not point the finger at either Ali or Aisha for the assassination, Akleema had to wonder. *She was such a bad-ass!*

Flipping through the pages of the book, she paused at one of her favorite chapters and began to read to herself. "When Aisha marched her army into Basra to confront Ali's army and demand the prosecution of Uthman's killers, her forces captured Basra and she ordered the execution of six hundred Muslims. Ali rallied his supporters and a great battle ensued known as the Battle of the Camel, from the fact that Aisha directed her forces from the back of a large camel."

She admired a drawing of the woman atop a camel, leading her army to war. She traced the illustration with her fingertip and longed to see a detailed picture of Aisha, wondering what she really looked like.

She hated that Aisha's army had been defeated and ten thousand Muslims had been killed in the battle. The battle was considered the first war where Muslims had killed Muslims. But Akleema took heart because, despite her defeat, Aisha had gone on to write more than two thousand *hadiths*—teachings of Islam—and was highly esteemed for many different subjects, including poetry and medicine.

"Aisha," the White Snake said aloud with defiance, "it's time for another woman to rise up and take control." She slammed the book shut. "And I am that woman."

CHAPTER 62

RULES

Ali said tearful good-byes to his aunt and uncle with a promise that they'd stop by before returning to Van. He also promised to contact them if he heard any news about his or Asti's parents. As soon as Ali's uncle had given them directions to locate the other relatives in Hakkâri, the UN van pulled away from the farmhouse and headed into the center of the city, only to be assaulted by a booming voice coming from a minaret.

Nick was startled. It didn't sound like a terrorist alarm, more like a prayer. Was this the famous call to worship? He'd heard of it, but in Van, there wasn't a mosque near King's Hospital, or it was no longer standing. He looked at Ali for an explanation.

"That voice is the *ezan*, the Islamic call to worship. It's recited by the muezzin five times a day at the prescribed time as a call to prayer." Ali checked his watch. "This one's for noon prayer."

"Do we need to do something for you, Ali? Take you to a mosque or something?" he asked, trying to be cognizant of his friend's faith.

"You are kind to ask, Dr. Hart. I ask Allah for mercy, but I'm afraid my medical training has long ruined my standing as a good Muslim. It's kind of hard to stop in the middle of surgery and throw down my rug to pray...especially in Memphis." He chuckled.

"Yes, I guess that would be complicated," he smiled, picturing the image of Ali dropping his scalpel and getting down on his knees. At the same time, he was saddened by the fact that so many people in the US disregarded him because of his faith. He wished everyone recognized that Ali was a good person and a fine physician.

Without understanding, he listened to the haunting Arabic prayers broadcast from the mosques throughout the city. The sound echoed off the rugged peaks, amplified by the mountainous bowl in which Hakkâri was located. Scanning the city and the wild, undeveloped Turkish countryside and recalling the harrowing roads, Nick marveled at the modernity of Hakkâri. But the city had reached its boundaries; it had grown to the edges of the cauldron, where steep, rocky crags shot up to the jagged peaks of the encompassing mountain range. The city had nowhere to grow but up, and tall apartment complexes comprised one neighborhood after another.

Unlike Van, the earthquake hadn't flattened Hakkâri, and only pockets of the city seemed to have been affected. For blocks, there was no sign of damage—then he'd see an area of collapsed buildings. Ali's uncle had said that even though many people had survived, most of them relocated to tent encampments outside the city, fearing more buildings would collapse. Nick thought the morning's thickening frost would soon move people back to the apartment complexes in search of better shelter, despite the risk.

The call to prayer grew louder as they approached a large green and orange mosque covered with a silver dome. When Nick looked at the large minaret standing erect next to the mosque, he noticed several large loudspeakers and saw men filing into the building.

"Are you required to go to prayer every day?" Buck asked Ali.

"Well, not required, as in your meaning of the word, Sergeant, but prayer is one of the five pillars of Islam."

"Do Muslims believe in the Ten Commandments?" Buck wondered.

"Yes, we do. All of them are in the Qur'an, except the one concerning the observance of the Sabbath. But the commandments are not listed exactly as in your scriptures. We have many, many rules to follow." He smiled at Buck. "Sometimes I can't follow all of them. I probably wouldn't be considered devout, but I try the best I can."

"Me and you both, my brother," Nick put in. "I'm afraid I haven't been good at following all the rules, either."

"That's why Jesus said He came…to set us free," Buck laughed, then turned serious. "He set us free from the law of sin and death. For me, it all boils down to the simple commands Jesus gave. First, 'Love the Lord your God with all your heart and with all your soul and with all your mind and with all your strength.' And the second: 'Love your neighbor as yourself.'"

"Oh, that's easy," Nick said sarcastically.

They'd passed the mosque and drove by a row of apartment buildings, many over ten stories tall. Nick was surprised at how well they'd survived the earthquake. The buildings were painted in bright oranges, yellows, reds, and greens, the sort of color combinations you'd expect to see along the canals in Venice. He couldn't help but notice satellite dishes sprouting from the balconies of each apartment and the tops of the buildings. "I guess we have one thing in common," he said, "we all like our TV."

The road beside the apartment buildings ended at a large soccer field covered with a carpet of lush, green grass. Ali asked the driver to turn and head north up the main boulevard. At the end of the thoroughfare, they arrived at a five-story medical complex.

"This is the government hospital," Ali said. "My uncle said there is another private hospital across town that is supposed to open its doors any day. He wasn't sure whether they are accepting patients. He thought if my parents were hospitalized, they would be here. He did tell us to be careful, because the government hospital was bombed last year by the PKK."

"The PKK?" AK asked.

"The *Partiya Karkerên Kurdistanê*, in Kurdish. Everyone knows it as the Kurdistan Workers' Party. It's a left-wing organization that has waged an armed struggle against the Turkish government for control of this area."

"Man, no wonder this land is so volatile," Buck said.

Ali nodded. "Now you are beginning to see why the people have such a difficult time trusting outsiders when they can hardly trust their neighbor."

"Love your neighbor as yourself," Nick repeated.

Ali directed the driver to park on the side street next to the hospital. Vladimir and AK offered to stay with the van, and Ali, Nick, and Buck went into the modern-looking building.

They were accustomed to the noisy chaos at King's, but the lobby of this hospital was eerily quiet. A young woman sitting behind a desk looked suspiciously at them. Nick was thankful that Vladimir and AK had stayed in the van.

Ali was not deterred by the chilly reception. He spoke respectfully to her in Kurdish, disarming her wariness. After a lengthy conversation, the woman left her post and walked down the hallway and through a set of double doors.

"She's going to see if she can find the Medical Officer on duty," Ali told them.

Moments later, she returned with a very young man in eyeglasses wearing a white coat. A stethoscope hung around his neck, and he clutched a clipboard in one hand. Ali and the young doctor greeted each other. Then Ali introduced him to Nick and Buck.

Ali asked the young doctor a question in Kurdish. "Yes, I speak English," he replied with a strong accent.

Nick was relieved, and Ali addressed the doctor in English. "I am looking for my parents and my wife's parents," he said and handed over a piece of paper with their names written down. The doctor took the paper and held it next to the clipboard. "I have a list of patients right here." He scanned multiple pages and shook his head. "I'm very sorry. Neither set of parents appear on my registry." He tucked his chin and looked over the top of his glasses. "I'm truly sorry."

Ali nodded, as though he was not surprised by the answer.

"You are welcome to walk with me through the wards, just in case any of the names were written in error," the doctor suggested.

"That is kind of you," Ali said.

"Do you have any orthopedic surgeons here in Hakkâri?" Nick asked.

"Yes, we have three. Forgive me, I should say two. One of our surgeons died in the quake." The doctor's face saddened.

"I'm sorry. It's been awful," Nick said. "Are any of the other surgeons here today?"

"They were. You just missed them. They have worked their fingers to the bone for the last three weeks, to the point that we have very little left in the hospital to care for our patients. We have been hoping that the other hospital would open soon, or at least share some supplies. We heard that the Red Crescent brought some but took them all to the other hospital."

Nick caught Ali's eye and looked at Buck, who understood. "Maybe we can get some supplies for you all," he said.

"We would be so grateful for any help. I wish the surgeons were here to meet you, but it is their first afternoon off in weeks. They're taking their families to the festival at the high school. I'm sure if you stop by there, they would so appreciate meeting you," he added, scribbling on the paper Ali had given to him. "Here's the address."

Nick took the paper and turned to Ali. "We'll wait for you in the van." He and Buck would not be helpful in identifying Ali's parents and didn't want to create a spectacle in the wards and corridors as foreign visitors.

***

Ali was pale when he returned to the van, shaking his head. The team sighed a collective sigh, their hopes dashed again.

"I'm sorry," Ali said. "I feel like I've been wasting everyone's time."

They shook their heads slowly, as if to let him know it was not a waste of time. Nick gave words to the sentiment. "We will do whatever it takes," he said.

Ali climbed back into the van. He sat back in his seat and dug in his jacket and found the map his uncle had given them, marking homes of distant cousins. Ali gave the driver directions to one of them.

Noon prayer had ended, and the streets were filled with people headed back to work. The tent cities were not so densely populated, and many shops had reopened their doors. With an occasional traffic light blinking yellow, Nick could see power had been restored to portions of the city.

The road turned sharply upward, and they climbed to the east and the towering mountains. The van crossed a flowing stream tumbling from the higher elevations and flanked with colorful autumn foliage. Ali checked the street signs against his map. He directed the driver to some apartment complexes nestled below a rocky outcrop. They had no sooner approached the complex than it became apparent that this visit would not be fruitful. Part of the mountain had collapsed, avalanching over half the complex and blocking off the entire area.

"This definitely is a dead end," Ali said. There was nothing else to say. He glanced from one Russian to the other. "But I think your hotel is close by." He pointed to the map.

The driver found a place to turn around, and they drove south, noticing that this section of the city had been greatly affected by the quake. Many buildings had collapsed or were badly damaged. When they arrived at the hotel, it was apparent that Vladimir and AK's survival had been miraculous. AK gasped.

Half of the five-story, four-star hotel had imploded, and the other half leaned at a forty-five-degree angle.

"Our rooms were on the third floor. On that side," Vladimir said, pointing to the crumbled portion.

Nick's jaw dropped. "How in the world did you escape?"

Vladimir looked back at AK.

She threw up her hands. "Okay, if you must know. Someone wanted to fool around, and I said to that someone, 'Only if you buy me drink first.' So, we were out on the back patio drinking beers when it hit. The patio was spared." She sobered at the gravity of the situation. "How do you explain that?" she shrugged. "Just dumb luck? What about the people that weren't so lucky?"

The men shook their heads, not having an answer.

Vladimir spoke. "We're obviously not going to find any of our belongings. We should move on."

Ali took the cue. "I have one more relative to check on, and then I suggest that we go to the festival. It sounds like most of the town will be there. I would like to connect with the orthopedists the young doctor mentioned. Maybe we can see about getting supplies for the government hospital."

CHAPTER 63

GLANCING BLOW

Ali directed the driver to his cousin's apartment complex. It was intact, but no one was home. A watchful neighbor had seen the van stop and suggested they check the festival.

As they drove back into the city en route to the school, it became clear to him that he would have to call Astî soon to tell her the news, and it wasn't going to be easy. He was racked with guilt. Astî had often encouraged him to take her and the girls for a visit to Turkey. "You just don't know how much time we have left with our parents," she'd told him. "They should get to know their granddaughters."

It had been the biggest point of contention in their marriage. His switch from general surgery to orthopedics added five years of training and another five years of terribly low wages. He didn't think that she minded the loss of income, but she resented the fact that they had not seen their parents since before the girls were born. "They do not even know their grandparents," she often said, crying herself to sleep. He had planned to take the family to Van when his fellowship was completed—it was to be a delayed but joyous homecoming, but now it would never happen.

Allah's will. He had said it so many times that it rolled off his tongue without emotion. He said it to himself when he dealt with the suffering of his patients, or when he saw images on TV that had no reality for him. This time he was angry. How could this be Allah's will? Was it Allah's will that he would never see his mother and father again? That his wife would be furious at him? That he was an orphan? That the time he looked forward to sitting and talking with his father, man to man, was never going to happen?

He was overcome with emotion and gasped, "Can you please turn up the air or open a window?"

The driver turned up the air conditioner, and Buck and Nick pointed the van's ceiling vents toward him.

"You okay? Nick asked.

"I'm afraid I'm feeling a little carsick."

"Pull over in that driveway," Nick told the driver.

As soon as the van stopped, Ali jumped out and ran to the back, where he fell to his hands and knees and gagged. He knelt at the back bumper and tried to collect himself. His head spun, and he was sweating profusely though the alpine air was cool. He cleared his throat and spit. On top of his guilt and nausea, he felt embarrassed.

He turned and saw Nick standing behind him.

"I am so sorry, Dr. Hart." Nick's hand was on his shoulder, and he took the bottle of water Nick was offering. He took a swig and then another. "Thank you." He rolled over to sit on the asphalt. He leaned against the back tire of the van and took another drink.

Nick sat down beside him. "I am so sorry about your parents, about Asti's parents," Nick told him, waiting in silence while he finished drinking.

"Dr. Hart, do you ever wonder if it's all worth it?"

"You mean medicine?" Nick asked and laughed. "Only about every second of every day."

He smiled at his mentor's honesty.

"I don't know, Ali, it's like there has been this unknown force pushing me forward. Wanting to be a better surgeon, to be respected…and yes, to help people. It's weird…it's like we are in this grand battle. Maybe with death. Maybe it's just against our own ego, I don't really know."

"Me, too," he said. "I thought once I was done with my training, my life would begin. I felt that only then would I earn the right to live my life."

"Only to find out it starts all over again," Nick said.

He waited for Nick to explain.

"Look, I hate to burst your bubble, Ali, but you just get off one treadmill and step onto another." He paused. "I'll be totally honest with you. I have been thinking about walking away."

Ali was shocked. "But, Dr. Hart, you are one of the best there is. My friends were so envious of me when I secured my fellowship with you."

"Well, then, maybe the thing that I'm really good at is being a poser."

The men heard a honk on the other side of the van and Vladimir leaned out the window. "Sorry gentlemen, we need to pull up. We are blocking an entryway."

He and Nick stood, stepped away from the UN van, and watched it back out of the driveway and park on the side of the road. A large green military transport truck was waiting to exit. They stepped back and two men in the truck glared at them as the truck cleared the driveway. The diesel gunned its engine, blowing black smoke, and drove into the street. A black Mercedes sedan with dark tinted windows followed the truck into the street.

"The Red Crescent?" Nick asked.

Ali watched the truck drive away. Large white panels with a blood-red crescent moon covered each side and the back of the green military transport vehicle. "I guess so."

They turned at the sound of a loud ratcheting noise behind them to see an iron gate clank shut. A strand of razor wire laced the top of the wrought-iron gate, and two guards armed with AK-47s stood inside. Nick and Ali peered through the entry to see a complex of several buildings, the largest four stories tall, cream-colored with red trim.

"A military installation?" Nick asked.

Ali stepped closer to the gate so he could read a sign on the building. "No. It's *Merhamet Hastanesi*, Mercy Hospital. It must be the private hospital that my uncle was talking about, but you're right, it does look more like an army base."

"Not exactly inviting," Nick said.

Ali nodded.

Nick put his hand on Ali's shoulder. "You going to be okay?"

"Yes, Dr. Hart. Thank you."

"Ali," he said, putting his other hand on his other shoulder, "maybe I haven't been a very good mentor to you. I think medicine is so challenging, and I think we're all afraid to show how much we struggle…afraid to show our own humanity. I'm trying to figure it out myself. But there's one thing I do know," he paused, "I know I am so glad you are my friend."

***

"They are just standing there," Abdul said, turning in his seat to look out the back window. "What the hell is the UN doing here and sitting outside our gate?" He directed his anger at Omar, who was driving the Mercedes. He turned to Akleema, who sat in the back. "Did you see who else was in the van?" He turned back to Omar. "What do you know about this? If you betray us, I will gladly slit your throat."

"Commander…please. There must be some explanation." Omar followed the truck down the street, sweat beading on his forehead. "We do have the Turkish military come through from time to time."

"Have you ever seen the UN here?" Abdul asked.

"I am afraid not." Omar turned to Abdul but refocused on his driving as the car swerved, almost running off the road. "Please, Commander, I know nothing about this. Perhaps they are here to lend support?"

"They were not in uniform," Akleema said.

Abdul was further enraged. She had said what he hadn't even noticed. He cursed himself silently. "Did you see their nationality? I only saw the shorter man, and he looked like a local."

Akleema hesitated, knowing how close he was to panicking.

"Well?" Abdul flashed.

"The other man was Caucasian."

"What is a white man doing here in the middle of the caliphate?" Abdul grabbed Omar by the collar, making the Mercedes swerve.

"Commander, please," Omar said, attempting to regain control of the sedan.

The White Snake squeezed Abdul's shoulder and spoke gently. "Abdul, you are going to get us all killed. Do not jump to conclusions. We have a mission to do. Stay focused."

"I think we need to abort this mission until we know what is happening," he said defiantly. "Maybe there is a whole UN battalion here."

"On the other hand," Akleema soothed, "maybe it is nothing, and if we abort, we lose a brilliant chance to strike."

"I will do whatever you command," Omar said, clutching the wheel with trembling hands.

"Please, Abdul," Akleema said calmly. "Do not be afraid. If we get to the school and there are more UN soldiers, or something doesn't seem right, we will abort."

It was the tone of her voice more than her words that released some of the tension in his shoulders. He turned to her, gazed into her eyes, and lingered on her seductive smile.

CHAPTER 64

FESTIVAL

The high school was built at the edge of the city overlooking the Zab Valley. The building had been completed two years earlier, and Omar spoke fondly of the project and how his hospital foundation had donated close to one million dollars toward its construction. It was the only high school in the city of sixty thousand people, and four thousand students attended.

Akleema smiled to herself as Omar maneuvered the sedan around the transport truck through the traffic and the growing crowd of pedestrians. The festival was not scheduled to start for an hour, but it was clear that the inhabitants of the city were ready to celebrate, after surviving three weeks of heartache caused by the quake. People parked their cars blocks away from the high school and walked down the boulevard to the event. To Akleema, it was reminiscent of the huge crowds moving through the streets toward Wembley Stadium to watch the Arsenal football team play. The same festive atmosphere filled this Turkish city.

Omar signaled to the truck to follow him. "I think we should have brought more drinks," he said with worry.

"We'll be fine." Akleema tried to keep him calm.

Omar pulled up to the gymnasium that was attached to one corner of the modern, four-story school. The school took full advantage of the view. Instead of the typical Quonset-style gymnasium, the facility was a modern building with a portion of the roof jutting out over the building resembling an arrow shot over the Zab valley. The entrance to the gymnasium was a large glass atrium—two stories of windows.

Omar backed up and parked the Mercedes in front of the entrance to the atrium and stepped out. Like a proud politician, he waved to the crowd and shook the hands of those who stepped near to greet him. What a chameleon, the White Snake thought, one minute cowering to Abdul and the next minute grinning with confidence as though he's the king of the world.

The brakes of the Red Crescent truck squealed loudly as it stopped behind the Mercedes.

"No UN presence," Abdul whispered to her as they exited the sedan. He had been tapping a foot and drumming his fingers incessantly. *He'd better not give it all away.* She looked forward to the delicious carnage that lay ahead.

Akleema heard a familiar voice behind them and turned. "You came, you came! Thank you so much for supporting us." The girl who had given them the flyer in the park ran up to them with a flock of girls in tow. She wore a short cheerleading skirt and, once again, a tight sweater with the image of a lion stretched over her chest. Many of the other girls wore matching outfits.

"These are the people I was telling you about," the girl said to her followers. "She saw One Direction in London, didn't you?" She turned to Akleema to confirm the story.

"Yes, last year, and they were wonderful," she said, realizing that she, too, was a chameleon.

The gaggle of girls sighed and giggled. She wasn't sure if it was all for the boy band or for her handsome Arab companion that many of the girls ogled. She had to admit, he did look kind of cute in his Red Crescent vest.

"We brought you as much soda pop as we could find and some snacks," Akleema said.

"And something else that you haven't seen for weeks—ice." Abdul added.

The girls looked surprised that the handsome Arab had spoken to them. They elbowed each other, blushed, and snickered.

"I will show you where you can set up, if that's okay." The head cheerleader took Akleema's arm and pulled her toward the atrium entrance. Akleema looked back at Abdul and indicated he should follow.

As they entered the atrium, Akleema was impressed with its beauty. It reminded her of the entry to the hospital or a miniature version of an entrance to one of the grand British soccer stadiums. The atrium's glass wall allowed for an abundance of light and led to the multiple double doors of the gymnasium.

Just inside the atrium, the head cheerleader stopped and turned Akleema toward a statue of a huge roaring lion. "We saved you this area to set up drinks and snacks, if that's okay."

Women were setting up tables nearby with an assortment of edible treats, including homemade cookies, cupcakes, fruits, and candies. The girl called to a woman standing in front of a table of baked goods, "Mom, this is my friend from London." She squeezed Akleema's arm. The girl's mother, who looked like an older version of the girl, smiled and waved. "My mother is head of our Booster Club," the girl said and leaned her head against Akleema's arm. "I'm so glad you came. Would you like to see our decorations?" Without waiting for an answer, she pulled her through the doors to the gymnasium.

Akleema followed her into a kaleidoscope of color and light—red and white stringers, rotating lights, and mirrored disco balls, swirling polka dots that changed with the pulsating, loud music. The gym was already filled with noisy high school students, anxious for the party to start and a young DJ at the center of the stage was spinning the music.

"This is wonderful," she shouted, feeling the girl staring at her, waiting for affirmation. "I'd better go back and get set up before everyone gets here."

"You need help?" the girl hollered back.

"That's okay," she said. "We'll be just fine."

***

The team from King's could see the large school in the distance, but it was impossible to get close. Four or five blocks away, traffic had slowed to a crawl, and people had started to park along the road. The van's driver glanced in his rearview mirror, wanting instructions. "Not sure I can get us much closer," he said. "What do you all think?"

"I don't mind walking," AK said cheerfully, now that her leg was pain-free.

"There's a place in front of that building," Vladimir said, pointing to a spot where a car was backing out. The driver pulled the van into the spot. As they piled out, a man quickly came out of the storefront and aggressively spoke to their driver, who looked at Ali for help. Ali slid out, calmly spoke to the man, and listened to his plea. Then he turned to the team. "It seems we're parking in front of his restaurant, and he asks that we either pay him for the spot or come in and eat a meal. Anyone hungry?"

"I thought you'd never ask," Vladimir said, patting his belly.

"I'm famished," Buck added.

"You're always hungry," Nick slapped him on the back. "But actually, it sounds good to me too."

The restaurant owner broke into a big smile. "Yes, yes, please. Come in," he said in broken English. "I just reopen today for festival, so everything fresh." He grabbed Vladimir's elbow to lead him in. "You have great appetite, no?"

The small diner held six empty tables. It wasn't a stunning commentary on a grand reopening, but it was clean and the aroma wafting from the kitchen smelled delicious. The man pushed two tables together and held the chairs for each team member to sit. "My wife has cook fresh today—*köfte, kuzu tandır,* and *börek,* and for dessert, baklava."

"I like baklava," Nick said, "but as for the rest…" He looked to Ali for translation.

"*Köfte* is a Turkish staple," Ali said. "like meatball stew. *Kuzu tandır* is lamb that is slow-roasted and served over rice, and *börek…*" Ali paused, inhaling the kitchen aromas. "I didn't think I was hungry, but my mouth is watering. *Börek* is a pastry filled with minced meat or spinach and cheese." He spoke to their host in Turkish and smiled at the man's response.

"The *börek* today is spinach and cheese. My favorite," Ali told the team.

"My wife makes best *börek* in Turkey," the man added.

"And how are we going to pay for this feast?" Nick asked. "Anyone have lira?"

"No worries, no worries," the owner smiled. "I take Visa and MasterCard."

"Of course you do." Nick smiled.

"And I happen to have my Visa right here," Vladimir said, waving his card. "Let's eat."

**

Omar moved the Mercedes forward, and Abdul waved to the driver of the transport truck to back up to the curb at the entrance of the gymnasium. They had brought three stainless-steel tanks designed to be used in the hospital's physical therapy department for water rehabilitation. The tanks made excellent tubs for the ice, soda cans and water bottles that would be sold for one lira each, about the same as a quarter of a euro or an American dollar. It was a fraction of what the drinks cost, but they would tell the people that the hospital was generously donating it all. The profit would go toward the orphanage. In reality, it didn't matter what they charged; once the bombs went off, there would be nothing left.

Abdul ordered his two men to arrange the tubs around the statue of the roaring lion in the atrium entrance. He thought the statue was appropriate—it wouldn't be long before the bombs roared like lions. He smiled noticing the atrium's glass, realizing that once it shattered, the pieces would create as much harm as the projectiles shot from the explosive device.

They unloaded the cases of drinks and snacks, including the two boxes packed behind the bags of ice—the ice that was keeping the volatile TATP at rest. He nodded to one of the guards and carefully handed one of the heavy bomb boxes into his arms. The guard understood to put the package innocently among the other boxes at the foot of the lion.

Abdul turned and carefully lifted the second bomb box out of the truck. It would be positioned under the front corner of the stage. He handed it to one of Omar's recruits that had worked as a janitor at the high school before coming to work at the hospital. The man promised he could deliver the package undetected.

Abdul closed the truck's tailgate and smiled.

The detonators in the bombs would be activated by his cell phone. He glanced at his phone and was relieved to see that his signal had three bars. The network had been restored after being down for so many days.

They had discussed placing items associated with the PKK in and around the bombs, but when Abdul had calculated the explosive force of the blast, they realized it would not be necessary. The explosion would be so massive that there would not be anything left of the bombs; it would create a blast zone of fifty to sixty feet in all directions. The projectile metal fragments would blast another hundred yards, and any structural damage to the building would add to the devastation. There would be nothing left to investigate. They had already prepared a note from the PKK taking credit for the killing field. It would be discreetly delivered to local government offices under the cover of darkness.

He got into the black Mercedes with Omar and began to work on his phone's touch screen. He glanced at the clock in the car—it was almost four o'clock.

"What time are you setting it to go off?" Omar asked.

"I will detonate the bomb under the stage at five o'clock. The second will detonate thirty seconds later, just in time to catch the stampede of people at the door."

"Allah have mercy," Omar said, wiping his brow with his handkerchief.

***

The food at the restaurant was as delicious as Ali had described. Nick's stomach had long ago reached capacity. Even so, he forked a sliver of lamb and popped it into his mouth for one more lingering taste.

"My gosh, that was delicious," Buck said, leaning back in his chair. "And thank you, Vlad. You should let us square up with you somehow."

"My treat." Vladimir waved his hand and loudly belched so that everyone laughed. He looked around to see that the owner was back in the kitchen. "And thanks to the Russian government."

"Well, tell Mr. Putin thank you from us." Buck grinned and raised an empty glass.

"Speaking of Mr. Putin, what will you tell your government about the tree?" Nick said, putting air quotes around *tree*. Vladimir and Antasha only looked at each other and waited for the other to answer.

Finally, AK spoke. "We have been arguing over that very thing. Vladimir wants to spill the beans. He wants to tell them all about the icon. I want only to give them figs."

"Figs or beans," Vladimir shrugged, trying to make light of the subject.

AK frowned at him. "If we tell the government about the ancient carving, they will do something stupid, like bring in a big helicopter and take the icon back to Russia. Then they will destroy it, like everything else they touch."

Vladimir reprimanded her in Russian, but she waved him off. "Don't be an idiot." She looked back to the rest of the team. "As you can see, we haven't decided. Vladimir is afraid he will be sent to the gulag if he withholds information." She blew air through her lips. "As for me, I have no fear."

Nick was fond of the pair. They were never afraid to say exactly what was on their minds.

"Why don't you just tell them the angel with the flaming sword would not let you near the tree?" Buck laughed.

"*Da*, do not pass go, do not collect two hundred rubles," AK joked, then turned thoughtfully. "That is a whole three US dollars. See what I mean…they ruin everything?"

Ali dug in his pocket. "Speaking of currency, I've been meaning to give you this." He handed a coin to Vladimir.

Vladimir took it and held it to the light. "What's this?"

Nick looked at the coin. He saw a man's profile on one side and on the other, an image stamped with the number five.

"What is it?" Vladimir asked again.

"It is the Turkish *kuruş*—our nickel." Ali smiled and added, "But do you know what the image represents?"

Vladimir shook his head.

"It's the tree of life. Now you can never say that you didn't find it," Ali laughed, and everyone joined him.

Nick still didn't know what the Russians planned to tell their government, but there was plenty of time to find out. He looked out the restaurant's window, caught the late afternoon sun, and looked at his watch. "It's four fifteen," he said. "The festival has started. Maybe we should get going."

CHAPTER 65

THE BLAST

The crowd at the festival was eager to buy beverages and snacks, and their spirit of generosity surprised Abdul after they had suffered so much tragedy. The cash basket on the table was full to overflowing. While the children put in one lira coins, many adults put in paper lira in denominations of tens and twenties. He couldn't help but think it was a shame that so much money would go to waste, incinerated in the explosion.

Jubilant families streamed into the gymnasium. The loud music and boisterous conversation echoed throughout the atrium, which made individual conversation difficult. Omar's man came through the door and gave him a thumbs-up after placing the bomb under the stage and returning without incident.

Abdul glanced at the man that would remain at the beverage table to be sacrificed in the name of Allah and for the sake of the Islamic State. The man had willingly volunteered, knowing he would soon be in paradise. Abdul was in awe of the man's serenity. He was about to die, yet he was happily selling drinks.

Abdul realized there was one thing he hadn't considered when they had planned the mission—the volume of the music. What if the loud music prematurely detonated the TATP? He had never been close to ground zero of a detonation but had seen the grizzly pictures on the news. What if it went off before they got to safety? His stomach churned at the thought.

"You okay?" Akleema held her hand to his ear and shouted.

Abdul showed her his phone and the time—4:45—and cocked his head toward the door. "Time to go," he mouthed. He saw Omar glad-handing everyone like a politician running for office. He managed to catch Omar's attention to let him know it was time to go, then turned to shake the martyr's hand. He looked directly into the volunteer's eyes and saw no fear. The man simply smiled and went back to dispersing drinks and snacks.

Abdul followed Akleema and Omar out of the atrium. They would detonate the bomb from the safety of the hospital compound.

But they were halted by a familiar voice.

"You're not leaving, are you?"

The three turned to see the bubbly cheerleader and her friends running toward them.

"We were just coming to get you," the girl caught her breath and looked at Akleema. "We have a special presentation for you." She turned to include the men. "For all of you. Please come back into the gymnasium."

Abdul shook his head at the girl.

"Please," she pleaded. "We have been working on it all week."

Abdul shrugged and sighed, realizing they would have to comply. At least the explosives were not set on a timer. But what if the thumping bass set them off?

Omar's arm encircled his waist and pulled him back into the atrium. "This won't take long," he whispered. "Allah's will."

***

The UN driver stayed with the van while the team walked to the school. They could hear the music when they left the restaurant, and now that they got closer to the event, it was much louder. Nick looked at the others, and they all nodded in agreement. This was, indeed, a party—a celebration of life. The joyous feeling was palpable and well-deserved after what the country, the city, and every individual had endured. It was time to honor the resilience of the human spirit.

"You are ambulating so well," he complimented Antasha as he watched her walk with a normal stride.

AK skipped playfully like a teenager, then turned to walk backward. She smiled and raised her arms in triumph. "What can I say, Doctor?"

"'Therefore, strengthen your feeble arms and weak knees. Make level paths for your feet, so that the lame may not be disabled, but rather healed,'" Buck quoted from Hebrews. "Thank you, Jesus."

As they arrived at the school, Nick was amazed at its architecture. It looked like a school in an affluent Memphis neighborhood. It was a grand achievement and he wondered how this mostly agricultural area could afford such a modern building. Music blared through the doors while a crowd of adults stood outside. He chuckled to himself at the universality of the situation—young people playing their music at top volume while adults protected what was left of their hearing by staying as far away as possible, but close enough to keep an eye on what was happening.

"Why do kids always have to blast their music?" he asked.

"They just want to express themselves, to feel the vibrations," AK said. "The louder it is, the more tangible. I'm sure you were young once. They just want to feel something."

Nick grinned at her.

Walking into the crowd, even the sight of foreigners did not seem to dampen the mood of the locals, and soon a group of men gravitated toward them. Men approached Ali and asked him questions. The locals were keenly interested in the huge man and the woman with the fiery red hair.

"The circus has come to town," AK whispered to Nick. "I'm the trapeze lady and Vlad is the elephant in the room." Nick laughed with her.

Ali turned to them. "I'm telling them who we are and that we are here to find my cousin and the two orthopedic surgeons from the government hospital."

The word spread quickly and men scattered to locate the doctors and Ali's family. Those who remained continued to stare at Vladimir, fascinated with his size. A brave few approached him to shake hands and to measure their grip against his. Vladimir seemed to enjoy the attention and complied easily when they asked to take photos with him. He put his giant arm around each man as they snapped selfies.

It wasn't long before some of the men returned with Ali's cousin and his wife, who embraced Ali.

Watching Ali's face as the two men spoke, Nick realized that the cousin was only confirming Ali's premonition. There was no question about the fate of Ali's parents and in-laws, and the cousins embraced again in condolence.

The family reunion was interrupted when the other men brought the two surgeons to meet the team. Nick watched Ali swallow his sadness to greet the doctors. One surgeon was an older, portly man in his sixties, and the other was young and muscular, probably early on in his career.

Ali introduced everyone from King's. Neither of the Turkish doctors spoke English, so Ali translated for them all. The four surgeons agreed that they had never seen such trauma in their lives.

"The doctors tell me that they are completely out of external fixators," Ali told Nick. "They have a huge backlog of patients waiting for nails and fixation devices. Any help we can provide them would be greatly appreciated. Even basic things, like gloves and IV fluids, are nearly gone. They can't take any more patients until they get some supplies. They feel like the Turkish government has forgotten them."

Nick thought of Jack Bilton. "If there is a way, Jack will make sure it happens for them," he told Ali. He was sure Jack could talk the UN Commander into flying some supplies to Hakkâri. "We will certainly do all we can," Nick reassured the doctors through Ali. "What about the new hospital, can you use it?"

When Ali translated the question, Nick watched the younger doctor look at the older one.

"We certainly hope to," the older doctor finally said. "In fact, I noticed that the administrator is here today. I am hoping to talk with him about it."

Ali looked at his mentor. "It is always a little complicated. These surgeons are probably paid by the government. Sometimes they can work in a private hospital to supplement their income, but it can be tricky."

Nick shook his head. "Yes, the politics of medicine. No one is immune from it. Let them know we will do everything we can to help them."

Ali translated and they all smiled and shook hands.

"Tell them it was nice to meet them, and please excuse me for a moment, I need to find the men's room," Nick said, sensing his bladder was about to burst after the huge lunch.

***

The honorary presentation to Abdul, Omar, and the White Snake was a dance number with cheerleading moves, choreographed to a recording of "Drag Me Down," a song by One Direction. As far as Abdul was concerned, the performance was embarrassing and disgusting. It affirmed why the caliphate had to be established. *Curse the infidels.* America's filth had penetrated clear to the wilderness of Hakkâri. Any remorse he'd felt about the bombing evaporated, and he was only too glad when the gyrating ended.

The girls bowed to the applause and ran to hug Akleema.

"Thank you for your thoughtfulness," she said. "Now, continue to enjoy your festival. We must go, but we will be right back. We have to make a trip back to the hospital for more drinks and snacks because everything is selling out so quickly."

Abdul looked at the phone in his hand. "We need to go," he said to Akleema and Omar.

The music powered up, louder than ever. The gymnasium was packed with adolescent and pubescent energy. Teens were on the dance floor near the stage, and at the back of the gym children played games and visited booths set up by the older kids.

As they left, Abdul glanced back. When it was over, there would be hundreds if not thousands dead. It might be the bloodiest attack in the history of the modern Islamic State. He hoped his brother would be pleased.

They exited the gym into the atrium. When they approached the beverage table, Abdul saw he had left his backpack behind the table. He knew that nothing, certainly not his wallet, would survive as evidence, but he was angry because he should not have been so careless. A leader must be aware of all things at all times.

The martyr seemed unsettled to see them. Abdul reached behind the table, grabbed his backpack and nodded to his man, who stared back blankly.

Two men approached Omar to shake his hand, delaying their exit. The White Snake glanced at Abdul and frowned. "We need to get the politician out of here," she said.

***

Nick found the bathroom in the hallway of the gymnasium foyer. After emptying his bladder, he made his way through the crowd. He was all too aware of being a foreigner as people pointed at him and whispered. He was anxious to get back to the team and away from the music and the throng.

As he headed into the atrium, he noticed a concessions table. Water bottles packed on ice in stainless steel tanks reminded him how thirsty he was from the salty meal.

"Sorry, excuse me," Nick said, reaching between two people wearing vests with Red Crescent patches on their backs. He grabbed a bottle from the ice and pulled out his wallet. The people turned to move out of his way, and as they did, he felt their glare. The young man glowered at him. He had been in places in Memphis where he had not been welcome, but he was taken aback and wondered if he should return the bottle to the tank. He hesitated and looked at the other person. He was relieved to see a Caucasian woman.

"I'm sorry, maybe I shouldn't," Nick apologized to the woman, whose headscarf framed her penetrating blue eyes. Her expression was one of shock.

"American?" she asked Nick.

"Yes. I'm afraid I only have US dollars," he said. He smiled meekly at her and caught the facial exchange of disgust between her and the young man. Never in his life had he felt the object of so much hatred.

Heat rose up his neck. "I'm sorry," he said, put the bottle under his arm and reached into his wallet. He pulled out a twenty, realizing he had nothing smaller. "Here…keep the change," he tossed the bill into the basket and quickly exited the building.

***

"What the hell?" Abdul watched the white man walk out the double doors. "An American?" He was practically yelling. The White Snake glanced at the people around them and shushed him. She grabbed his arm and pulled him to the window to see if they could see where the American was going.

"Who do you think he is?" he fumed.

She frowned. "He was the man standing next to the UN vehicle back at the hospital."

They watched the American join a group of locals and three more Caucasians—a large man, an even larger man, and a redheaded woman.

"What do you think?" Akleema asked.

"So much for anonymity," he said. "Worst of all, the American saw us standing here. If the locals were to investigate the blast, they would probably never discover us. But with the UN here, I don't know what to think." He looked at the large crowd in the atrium and thought about the larger crowd in the gym, and his shoulders slumped. "We have to abort."

Akleema nodded. "I think, in view of this new development, that is the prudent thing to do. But what about the bombs?"

"Well, we can't leave them here, especially this one," he indicated the box at their feet. "And we need to get the one under the stage. What if the cleaning staff found it?"

Omar turned toward them with his palms face up, questioning the situation.

"The UN is here," Abdul said. "We are aborting the mission. Go tell our man in the truck to retrieve the package under the stage. I will send this box back to the truck now." He turned to the martyr dispensing the drinks. "I'm sorry, my friend. It is not your time. Take this box back to the truck and wait for the other one. Return with the truck to the hospital. We will stay here and finish up."

The puzzled volunteer did as he was told. He picked up the bomb box and walked carefully through the doors to the truck.

***

"What a waste of time planning and preparing," Abdul said in disgust, as he watched the transport diesel drive away with the two bombs. A large black cloud of diesel came from the exhaust. The truck moved through the parking lot, rocking slightly as it drove over the gutter and into the street. Then it happened—in an instant, a blinding flash of light followed by the explosion and shards of shattering glass splintered down upon them like an icy rain.

The mother of satan had detonated.

CHAPTER 66

CHAOS

Abdul lay on his stomach, pinned to the floor, covered with fragments of glass, wallowing in blood, screaming in disbelief. So much blood. Was it his? *Akleema.* Where was Akleema?

Dazed, he tried to push himself into a sitting position, but wherever he put his hands for leverage, he sliced them bloody on the shattered glass. Bloody terror coated his tongue and his head spun. Light flickered and died. He was passing out. He was falling, tumbling head over heels, into a deep, dark void. Nothingness. *Allah have mercy.*

***

No sooner had Nick left the building to join the team than he was hurled to the ground. He pushed himself up to his knees, trying to make sense of whatever had happened. His ears rang as if he were inside a big brass bell. Someone was on the ground beside him. It was Ali. His lips were moving, but Nick couldn't make out the words.

There was a presence over him. It was Buck, shielding him with his body from the hot pieces of metal falling around them. A piece landed on Nick's leg, and he reached down and rubbed his thigh, making sure it hadn't pierced the skin. He tried to stand, but Buck kept him shielded. Nick glanced to his left and saw Vladimir doing the same for AK.

The strong acidic smell of explosives heightened his senses, and the clanging in his ears changed from a robotic blare to shrill screams of humanity.

The metal shower ended as quickly as it had begun, and Buck yanked Nick to his feet, clutched his shoulders, looked him over, and scanned the horizon.

"Car bomb!"

That's what Nick thought he heard Buck yell. He concentrated on the next words.

"We need to get the hell out of here!" Buck shouted and pulled Nick away. "There may be more!"

Buck's natural legs had been taken by a roadside IED, and he was an expert at recognizing dangerous situations. Still, Nick resisted Buck's pull and bent to help Ali to his feet. When Ali stood beside him, Nick took his bearings and thought at first that the explosion had come from inside the school. The large glass front of the atrium had shattered, but inward instead of outward.

People all around them were yelling and screaming. One man bumped into them as he ran toward the school. Others pointed at the street where the road had become a large, smoldering crater. If it had been a car bomb, little was left of the vehicle, and several cars surrounding the blast zone were engulfed in flames.

To Nick's right, a woman lay on the ground in a pool of blood that flowed from her head. A man stood over her, screaming for help. Buck had resisted the instinct to flee and bent down to examine the woman.

"It's a scalp wound," he yelled to Nick and told the man to hold pressure on the wound.

All was chaos.

"We need to triage," Ali screamed, "to get the most critical to the hospital."

"We need to get into the school to assess the damage," Buck shouted.

Nick opened his jaw wide to try to clear his plugged ears and saw the UN van squealing around the blast zone into the parking lot. Their driver searched for them. "Ali, we can use the van for transport," he yelled. "The docs said the government hospital was full. We'll have to head to that new hospital. They'll have to open their doors. It's our only hope."

Nick sensed Vladimir at his side, awaiting orders. He looked past the Russian at AK, who stood beside him. "You guys okay?"

AK nodded in affirmation.

"AK, go tell the driver that we will bring the most critical victims to the van. Tell him we will take them to that new hospital down the road."

She nodded again and ran to the van.

He yelled to his team, "Let's go!"

***

Screams snapped Abdul back to consciousness and he staggered to his feet. The lion statue had saved them from the collapsing wall of glass. He turned to see Akleema staggering, shaking glass shards from her hands. Her face filled with horror and he followed her gaze to see Omar, flailing on the floor with large pieces of glass embedded in his forehead and a large wound pumping blood from the side of his head.

"Abdul! Help Omar," she screamed.

Together, they dragged him forward. Abdul turned and kicked out the remaining glass panel behind the lion and they pulled Omar through the opening and out to the sidewalk. People stampeded in and out in every direction. He saw the people from the UN running into the building.

They held Omar under his arms and hauled him to the Mercedes that was still parked close by.

Car keys. Abdul dug into Omar's front pocket and found the keys. He pushed Omar onto the back seat and slammed the door. Akleema was already in the front passenger seat. He jumped behind the wheel, gunned the engine, and sped away.

***

There was an impasse at the atrium entrance. No one could get in or out, and Nick was afraid he would be crushed by the mob.

Then, like air released from a tire, the pressure deflated, and Nick saw children tumbling out through the shattered wall like water over a dam and running to parents rushing to meet them.

Entering the atrium, he stood stock still, frozen at the sight of bodies, blood, and smashed glass.

"Come on, let's go!" Buck yelled shoving past him and charged into the fray.

***

"What the hell happened?" the White Snake screamed at the top of her lungs, as Abdul sped down the boulevard. "How did they go off? What did you do?"

"Shut up!" he yelled back. "Just shut up. I didn't do anything." Spittle, sweat, and tears smeared his face. "The TATP must have become unstable."

Akleema saw he was crying. *You stupid, stupid idiot.*

"I've ruined it," he cried. "I've ruined everything."

Akleema sighed, knowing she had to stabilize him. "It will be okay. We will figure it out. Just calm down." She was afraid that in his condition he would crash the car. "Did you see if anything was left of the truck? Maybe no one realized it was our truck that exploded," she added hopefully.

"I've ruined all that we have done. My brother will kill me." Abdul sobbed.

"Calm down. Just drive. It's going to be all right," she tried to reassure him, while thinking of their next step. "We need to release the PKK statement right away, before anyone has any other suspicions."

***

It was nothing short of miraculous. As Nick and the team worked their way around the room, they found only four dead and two critically wounded. The rest would survive with minimal treatment. Buck and Vladimir helped the injured out of the sea of glass shards. Scalp wounds bled profusely and looked severe, but most of the injuries would be manageable with pressure and a few stitches. It was clear that the dead had died instantly and likely without pain when large, jagged sheets of glass had sliced through vital organs.

"Let's get these two to the hospital," Nick yelled at Buck and Vladimir. He was holding pressure on a spouting femoral artery while Ali held an upper arm brachial bleed. They removed their belts and used them to cinch around the affected limbs to stop the bleeding. Vladimir picked up Ali's patient, and Buck took Nick's. They carefully picked their way out of the devastation toward the waiting van.

***

Abdul cursed, pounded his fist on the steering wheel, and blared the horn when the sedan skidded to a stop in front of the hospital. The guards looked surprised to see Abdul driving the Mercedes and ran to open the gate.

Once inside, Abdul jumped from the sedan and flung open the back door. "Get him out," he yelled. The guards pulled Omar from the back seat as blood splattered on their shoes.

"He needs a doctor," the guard said.

"Then he may die," Abdul said. "Do I look like a doctor? Get him a doctor."

The White Snake jumped out of the sedan and screamed at the guards. "Let's get him inside."

***

As the UN van squealed around the corner, Nick was relieved to see that the gate to the new hospital was open. A black Mercedes was parked inside the gate. It seemed familiar, but he didn't have time to think about it. A large red sign at the side of the hospital read ACIL SERVIS. Nick hoped it was Turkish for emergency room, and he pointed the UN driver to it. As they steered closer to the entrance, three armed guards raced toward them with AK-47s readied.

The UN driver pulled to a stop in the circular drive under the red sign. Nick and the others jumped out of the van as the guards caught up to them. Ali stepped between the angry guards and the team with his hands held up. One of the guards yelled loudly in Turkish and waved his gun from the van to the gate. The meaning was clear—they should leave. Ali, remaining calm, told the guards there were two patients in the van who needed help and opened the door to show them.

One of the guards looked at the team and the patients, took two steps back, leveled his AK-47 at their chests and began yelling and waving them back to the gate. Nick had no idea what the other guards and Ali were saying, but the dialog was heated. Then he heard a word he knew: *doktor*. The guard lowered his voice but not the barrel of his gun.

"Doktor?" he pointed the gun at Nick's chest. Nick nodded instantly. The guard said the same to Vladimir and Buck, *"Doktor? Doktor?"* He waved the gun from one to the other. They looked at Ali, who nodded because there was no time to explain. They followed his lead and nodded forcefully.

The guard turned his gun on Ali and accosted him with a rush of Turkish.

Ali translated for Nick. "They have an injured patient as well and want to know if we will help him."

"Of course," Nick said and took a step toward the guard.

The guard started to yell again and shouldered the rifle at Nick's head. Instinctively, Nick raised his hands and stepped back. "Okay, okay."

Ali managed to calm the guard until he lowered the rifle and waved the team into the emergency room.

Vladimir and Buck carried their patients through automatic sliding doors and into a pristine ER. It was similar to the emergency department at the MED, but immaculate, modern—and totally unused.

It was strange that such a beautiful facility sat empty after the carnage of the earthquake. Nick looked at Ali and wondered if he thought the same. Buck and Vladimir laid the patients on stretchers in what appeared to be a fully stocked trauma room, complete with monitors, suction, crash cart, an x-ray machine, and all the life-saving equipment one would find in a Western emergency department.

Ali and Nick began to attend their patients when the guard started to yell again. Nick looked at Ali for explanation.

"He's demanding that one of us go with him to see their injured friend," Ali explained.

"You stay here with these two, and I'll go see what's happening," Nick said. "AK and Vladimir, you stay with Ali and protect him from these crazies. Buck, you're with me." He motioned to the guard to lead the way.

The rest of the ER was dark and empty. No one was in sight, not one staff member. He thought it was eerie. No doctors, nurses, or techs. *No one.*

He followed the guard down a dark hallway to a large foyer where people and several armed guards gathered around a man on the floor. He was surprised when he recognized the young man and the Caucasian woman from the water bottle incident. When he got closer to the patient, he saw a large pool of blood near the man's head and was shocked that the group stood frozen around him.

The guard leading Nick yelled and the people jumped at his bark. *"Doktor,"* the guard yelled, grabbing Nick's arm and shaking it. *"Doktor, doktor."*

Nick shook off the guard and dove to the injured man, kneeling to feel for a pulse at his neck. It was there, but barely. He saw the injury and put his bare hand over the scalp wound that extended from above the right eye to the right ear, possibly severing the temporal artery.

"We need to get this man to the ER," Nick said, staring up to blank faces.

Finally, the woman in the Red Crescent vest stepped forward. "Are you a doctor?"

"Yes, a surgeon," Nick barked. "A little pressure on the wound would have been helpful," he said with irritation. "Help me get him to the ER."

Buck began to pick the man up and two guards set their rifles down to assist. The three of them carried the man to the ER, while Nick held pressure on the wound; the man could not afford to lose any more blood.

They put him on a stretcher in the second trauma room,

adjacent to Ali's. Then he grabbed the angry young man in the Red Crescent vest and forced his hand onto the bleeding man's head wound. "Press hard," Nick commanded, having no idea if the kid spoke English.

"You guys okay over there?" he shouted to Ali.

AK appeared from the other room. "Ali is trying to find supplies for you," she said.

Her appearance created a buzz among the guards and the Red Crescent pair, caught off guard by her red hair and Russian accent. "Don't you have nurses or doctors or any staff?" Nick asked. He rolled his eyes and looked to the ceiling. "My God, we need some help here."

A full-bearded guard stepped forward and said in broken English, "I am EMT."

Nick stared in disbelief at the man. "EMT?"

"Ambulance," the guard said and spun his finger in the air imitating a flashing red light.

Nick nodded. "IV," he said and poked at the bleeding man's arm to imitate inserting a needle.

With a nod, the guard understood. "IV. *Akışkan*," he said, handing his weapon to another guard and taking off his green uniform jacket.

AK, who had been listening to the exchange, darted into the adjacent room and returned with an IV setup. "We are doing the same," she said.

Nick grabbed the packet containing the IV needle. He was disappointed it was only a small 20 gauge. "Got anything bigger, Ali?" he called to his colleague. "I need to dump a ton of fluid into this guy."

"No, that's it," AK answered for Ali.

Improvise. Nick grabbed a cuff of the injured man's shirt and tore it open, splitting the fabric up the arm. Without taking time to clean the skin, he opened the IV needle and plunged it into the antecubital area at the crook of the elbow. "Thank God," he said when he saw the flash of blood. He slipped the catheter into the vein with ease. The EMT inserted one end of the tubing into the IV solution bag and handed him the other end. Nick attached the tubing. The EMT opened the valve and fluid ran into the man's arm.

"AK, see if Ali has any tape," Nick said. He held the catheter in place with one hand and made a squeezing motion with the other toward the IV bag. The EMT understood and placed both hands around the bag and squeezed.

"Here's some tape," AK said, pushing her way through the gawking crowd. "Ali also handed me these. He said you would know what to do."

Nick looked at the large needles. They weren't IV cannulas, but they would do. "Ali, you are a genius, my friend," Nick called. "Scissors, I need scissors," he said to one of the guards standing nearby, who looked very confused.

"Don't know...s c i s s o r s," he said slowly, trying to mimic Nick's pronunciation of the word.

Finally, the woman in the Red Crescent vest stepped forward and translated the word. The guard rummaged through the drawers and pulled out a pair of trauma shears. Nick took the shears and slid them up each pant leg, slitting the fabric. AK brought more IV setups from the other room. "Ali said you would need these."

Buck scavenged through the drawers, found some gloves and alcohol wipes, and gave them to Nick. Buck then handed a large stack of gauze dressings to the young man with his hand clamped on the patient's scalp. He pantomimed using them to help hold pressure on the wound. The wound would start to hemorrhage again once the man's pressure normalized.

Nick quickly pulled the gloves on, wiped the skin just below the man's knee, and plunged the needles deep into the bone, provoking moans from the patient and triggering the click of a gun safety behind him.

"I put large needles into the bone so we can dump more fluid into him," he said. "His heart will stop soon if we don't give it something to pump. Tell your men to put away the damn guns. We don't need any more injuries."

The EMT assembled the rest of the IV setups, and Nick hooked the tubing to the needles sticking out of the bones. He handed one bag to Buck to squeeze and the other to the woman.

She hesitated.

"What? Were you just going to let the man die?"

Her face flashed with anger. "No. It was not like that," she said.

Nick was surprised by her accent. "You a Brit?"

She nodded.

"No one ever teach you first aid?"

Nick could see he was irritating her, but didn't care. "Who is this man?" he asked, looking down at the patient.

"His name is Omar. He is the Hospital Administrator."

"No wonder you were going to let him lie there and die—most doctors feel the same way about their administrators." His joke went over her head. He focused on the patient, pulling down the lower lids of his eyes. They were pale and poorly perfused.

"AK, you guys have any luck over there finding oxygen tubing? This guy could use some *Os*."

"I'll ask Ali," she said and ducked into the other room.

The patients they'd brought from the school needed him as well, and he glanced at the clock on the wall. If it was correct, it had already been forty-five minutes since they had put the tourniquets on the other patients' limbs. They had another hour before irreparable ischemia would set in.

Nick rummaged through the drawers, leaving bloody handprints from his gloves. He opened a large cabinet by the sink. "Yes," he said when he saw a stack of disposable suture kits, a large box of different types of suture, and the best timesaving device of all—a surgical staple gun.

"Buck, did you see any disinfectant or betadine?"

"There are bottles of something in that cabinet," Buck said, pointing to the cabinet by the door.

Nick opened the cabinet. It was going to be messy, but it was going to save much-needed time. He grabbed a bottle of the brown, sticky disinfectant and snapped open the top. He pushed the man in the Red Crescent vest out of the way and poured the betadine over the patient's scalp. Blood gushed from the wound and mixed with the betadine. Nick put fresh gauze on the wound and turned to Buck.

"Buck, open those suture kits."

Buck handed the IV bag to one of the guards and began to rip the tops off the sterile packs. He held one to Nick, who grabbed the hemostats and said, "The instruments are probably all from Pakistan, like the suture kits back home—cheap and disposable—but they'll have to do."

He dabbed the wound with sterile gauze, then put the hemostat into the wound to search for the bleeding arteries. There were two severed vessels, and Nick found the ends of both. He pulled open the suture pack that he had set on the man's chest. "Not exactly sterile technique, but time's a wasting." Then, skillfully, he tied off each end of the detached arteries and cut the remaining suture. He chuckled to himself, imagining he was roping a calf, throwing loops of rope around its legs, racing the clock for the rodeo prize. He picked up the staple gun. "Someone hold him down," he called. "Your administrator is not going to like this."

Nick pinched together the edges of the skin wound and pulled the trigger to shoot the staples into the thick hide of the scalp. He fired them rapidly, one at a time, closing the wound like a zipper. Halfway through the stapling of the six-inch wound, the patient became conscious and started to move. Buck dove across his chest, and two guards held his legs. Nick stabilized Omar's shaking head and finished the closure.

He let go of Omar's head and looked at the clock. The procedure had taken only five minutes, but those were five minutes his other patients didn't have. "The scalp is so vascular that severed arteries can be simply tied off, and the scalp will reperfuse from the other side," he explained to the British woman, still wearing her blue scarf. "But arms and legs don't have that benefit, so I gotta get next door. I've got patients there whose arteries must be repaired or their limbs will have to be amputated."

Omar moaned, turned his head and stared wild-eyed at Nick.

"Hey, Omar. Welcome back," Nick said. Satisfied he'd done all he could under the circumstances, he snapped off his gloves and tossed them on the floor. He turned to Buck. "You mind supervising a dressing to his head? Go ahead and pull the needles out of his legs after the IV bags empty." He turned back to the British woman. "He may live to fight another day."

Nick didn't wait for a reply and headed for the adjacent trauma room, thinking he'd made a mistake bringing the festival patients to this hospital. It had the equipment, but no staff. There was no way to take patients to the OR without anesthesia and support staff. They no longer had enough time to relocate the patients to the government hospital. In the best of circumstances, immediate transfers saved lives and limbs. By this time, the government hospital probably had an ER full of patients. With only an hour left for the tourniquets, it was unlikely the patients' limbs would survive the transfer.

Fortunately, Nick's dour calculations had missed an important variable. He realized his mistake as soon as he entered the adjacent room and saw that Ali had everything under control. Nick smiled at his colleague. *Such a good critical thinker.*

Ali smiled at Nick. "We don't have the luxury of an OR, but we've got it covered." He bobbed his head from side to side. Then he looked down and injected local anesthetic into an arm. "The leg is ready to go, if you want to take that," he told Nick, moving his head to indicate the other patient.

CHAPTER 67

CAPTURED

Both tourniquets came off in under two hours, and the patients' fingers and toes instantly turned from dark purple to pink. Nick and Ali high-fived each other, then Buck and Vladimir. Buck had assisted Nick, and Vladimir had helped Ali with AK as the circulator. With a clean slice to both arteries, the vessels could be repaired primarily, end to end, with no need for a graft.

Nick was thankful he had the femoral artery to repair because the artery was nearly as big as the pinky finger, easy to see and easier to stitch. Ali, on the other hand, had to extend the wound slightly to make it possible to repair the much smaller brachial artery. But once he had the full exposure, his repair had gone smoothly as well.

Nick glanced around the room and shook his head. It looked like a battle zone with blood, betadine, used gloves, and packaging scattered all over the floor. But that was of small concern because the patients were alive and would keep their limbs—as long as they could stave off blood clots and infection.

"Sorry for the mess." Nick smiled at the young man and the British woman lurking at the door with a handful of guards. The man and the woman had shed their Red Crescent vests. "How is your administrator doing?" Nick asked.

"He will live," the young man said. Nick was surprised to hear him speak English.

"So, you truly are doctors then," the British woman said.

Nick chuckled. "No, I just play one on TV."

His sarcasm escaped the young man, who turned to the woman for clarification. She did not return his look. Nick was chilled by the lack of empathy coming from the pair.

"We invite you to please follow us," the woman said.

Alarm bells rang in Nick's head. It didn't feel right. He searched his team and didn't see Antasha. "Where is AK?" he asked.

No sooner had the words left his mouth than Nick heard her scream. Vladimir rushed toward the man and woman but was dropped to the floor by a blast from a guard's gun.

"What the..." Buck jumped to help Vladimir when a second shot blasted, missing its mark but stopping Buck in his tracks.

The guards leveled their guns at Nick, Buck, Ali, and the fallen Vladimir.

"Stop!" the British woman yelled. "There is no room for heroics."

Nick and Ali ignored the threat and jumped to Vladimir's aid. He had been shot in the leg. Nick held pressure while Ali opened a large gauze bandage and an elastic wrap and wrapped it tightly around the limb.

Nick turned to the young man and the British woman. "What the hell are you doing?"

Vladimir cursed loudly in Russian, and Nick turned back to help Ali keep him from charging the guards. Nick had no doubt the next shot would kill him.

More men in green uniforms burst into the room and dragged them into the hall. When Buck fought back, a guard smashed the butt of his gun into Buck's head, subduing him.

For an instant, Nick thought of breaking free from the guard's grip and running for the door, but he wouldn't get five steps before he was dropped. He looked back at Vladimir grimacing as three guards hauled him from the ER, leaving a trail of blood.

As they were pulled down a dark hallway, Nick heard AK screaming and cursing somewhere ahead of him. The guards pushed and shoved him down the corridor until they turned and passed through a set of double doors into what appeared to be the surgical area. Nick hesitated at the entrance until a gun butt slammed his shoulder blade. Another guard yanked him by the arm into the first operating room and swept his legs out from underneath him. He fell and smashed his elbow onto the cold, tile floor.

One guard jerked him into a sitting position while another guard grabbed his arms and zip-tied his hands together behind his back. AK was sitting on the tile a few feet from him, unharmed but mad as hell. The bright ceiling lights in the OR were off, but surgical spotlights illuminated the room.

The guards arranged the members of Nick's team in a semicircle on the floor. Vladimir writhed in pain and the guards quit trying to make him sit and let him lie.

Nick was livid. "What do you think you're doing? Do you know who we are? Who the hell are you?"

No sooner did he see the young man nod to a guard than he felt a sharp pain hit the back of his neck. Agony zipped down his spine, dropping a black curtain over his mind only to be snatched back to consciousness when someone yanked his hair.

"You will speak only when I give you permission," the young man barked at them.

AK spit at the man, yelled obscenities, and tried to stand, only to be shoved back down.

"Shut that woman up," the young man ordered.

The guards covered AK's mouth with duct tape, but not before she had landed a well-placed kick to one man's groin. The guard recovered quickly and caught AK with a hard right-cross, cutting a gash on her forehead.

"Anyone else need a lesson in submission?" the young man jeered, pausing to glare at each of them. When he was satisfied, he smiled and said, "Welcome to the Islamic State."

Nick's heart sank. He never imagined he would hear those words and understood they were all in deep trouble. He wondered about the fate of the UN driver. He wanted to believe he had escaped and was safe, but something told him the man was dead.

Nick saw black hoods dropped over the heads of each of his companions until the room went dark as his head was covered. The hood was tightened around his neck to the point that he could barely breathe. It smelled of gasoline that stifled the air even more.

Buck sat beside him, and he heard his friend curse and fight the guards. Then he heard Buck howl in agony when a gun blast silenced the room.

CHAPTER 68

TORTURE

"Who wants to speak first?" the young man asked.

Nick could not see him but heard him pacing back and forth.

"What is the UN doing here?" the young man asked. "Who do you work for?"

Nick was dizzy from the trauma and smell of the gasoline, but he was concerned for his friend and whispered, "Buck?"

Nick's whisper was audible to his captors, but Buck replied, "Just a warning shot." He responded boldly without lowering his voice, which got him a punch in his gut.

"You Americans do not follow instructions well," the young man said. "The UN soldier you left in the van is already dead. No one else needs to die but you must talk. What are the Americans and Russians doing here together?"

Ali spoke for the first time. While the others had asked questions or verbally protested, Ali kept quiet. "We are doctors," Ali said. "We truly are doctors. For Allah's sake, please do not harm us."

"You are all doctors—is that what you want me to believe?" the young man sneered. "Are you a doctor?" he asked Nick and slapped his head hard.

Reeling from the blow, Nick heard him ask each team member the same question, followed by a hard slap. "I doubt you are all doctors," the young man said.

"I am a doctor," Ali pleaded, "and Dr. Hart...you watched us work. You have to know we are surgeons."

"You from the CIA? KGB?"

Vladimir yowled. Nick surmised the man was squeezing his wounded leg.

"Who is going to tell me?" the young man asked.

"Yeah, I'm from the CIA, you idiot," Nick yelled, steaming with anger. "Ever see a CIA agent fix a femoral artery?"

Nick's head almost exploded from the side blow that knocked him over. His head hit the tile and bounced. Someone pulled him back to a sitting position.

"And what about you? You look like some sort of soldier. You CIA as well?"

"No, not me." Buck answered. "I'm just a medical equipment rep helping the good doctors here." Buck said calmly, trying to defuse the situation. "The doctors have been putting people back together in Van after the earthquake."

"That is not what you were doing here," the young man said. "I think you are snooping where you should not be meddling."

Buck grunted as he received a crack over his head.

The young man was quiet for a moment. Nick heard the British woman whisper, then the OR door opened and closed, followed by silence.

Finally, Nick heard Buck's voice. "Everyone okay—?"

He was stopped midsentence by another blow and the cock of a gun.

"No speak," ordered a man with a heavy accent.

***

"How is Omar?" Abdul asked the White Snake.

"He is talking. Not always coherently, but it looks like he is going to survive. Those people saved his life."

"Whatever," Abdul snapped back.

Akleema saw the wild look in his eyes. Was it fear or blood lust? "You okay?"

"What are these people doing here? We have to find out or they could ruin it all," he said manically. "We should kill them and bury their bodies."

Akleema watched him fidget from one leg to the other. He was not thinking clearly. "Abdul!" she barked. Then she realized a softer approach was more likely to work. "Abdul, it's going to be okay. We will figure this out. We will find out who they are and maybe even use them to our advantage." She stroked his cheek and felt his warm face flush. She glanced around to make sure they were truly alone, leaned in and kissed him on his forehead.

Her touch made his shoulders soften and his eyes clear. "What do you think we should do?"

"We should send a man out to deliver the letter from the PKK, and we should wait."

CHAPTER 69

עוֹשִׂי

SUNDAY MIDNIGHT—
POST-QUAKE DAY TWENTY-THREE

Nick slumped to the cold, tile floor. His body shook. His mind spun in and out of consciousness. At least the beatings had stopped. Every time one of the captives had slumped over, they were kicked, punched or pistol-whipped, and again if they cried out, and sometimes for no reason at all. But all was quiet now. AK, who had been hysterical, was silent. He prayed that nothing worse happened to her. The guards had beaten her unmercifully.

He had no idea what time it was or if any guards were in the room. His body tremored from the cold as he lay in his urine and blood. Air. He needed air. The moisture of his own breath created a water-boarding effect in the hood, and he felt as if he was drowning.

He tried to think about his love for Maggie but thoughts of love were inundated by grief.

Concentrate. Try to concentrate on a medical procedure. Yes. Medicine wouldn't fail him. What were the steps to fix a humerus? He pictured his hand holding the scalpel and guiding it through the skin. He saw the shiny, white fat bulging out the subcutaneous layer. *Separate the muscle.*

The muscles in his own hand spasmed, snapping him back to reality. He winced as the zip-ties cut deeper into his wrists.

He hyperventilated, gasping for air. Was this how he was going to die?

He tried forcing his mind back to the surgery, but memory took him back to college. He was sitting for an organic chemistry test. The pressure was unbearable. If he did not ace this test, his chances of getting into medical school were dashed. He glanced at the instructor's desk and saw the answer key. He couldn't read it clearly but saw it well enough to know the position of the correct answers.

His present mind cringed at his dishonesty. *Father, forgive me.* Where else had he cheated in life?

The answer was quick. *Relationships, of course. Past and present.* He had cheated on his college girlfriend by sleeping with her friend. He thought of his indiscretions with his nurse colleagues and those girls in the bar. Why had sex turned into such a drug for him? He realized that sex relieved the stress from his workaholic existence and acted as a pain reliever. He moaned in pain as quietly as possible. His shoulder ached, plastered against the icy tile. He tried to roll off it but only trapped himself with his face to the floor.

With all the energy he could summon, he forced himself onto his back, apologizing to his sore elbow and painful wrists for having to take the pressure.

Angst pumped through his mind as if mainlined through a vein to his brain. *Things done, things left undone.* So many things he hadn't noticed. He had been so blind. Blind to the pain he'd caused others and himself for not seeing. The sins of omission, the sins of commission. But nothing made sense. He hadn't meant to cause harm. He'd been raised right. He'd grown up with loving parents and good friends. *Why so much pain?*

It felt like life had betrayed him. *Betrayal.* The word pounded in his head. He'd always believed that if he worked hard, if he treated people right, if he believed the best in people…his life would be fulfilled and his desires satisfied.

But he was in a constant fight for identity. The voices of accusers throughout his life echoed in his mind: *What's wrong with you? You're not good enough. You'll never be good enough. You're a cheat. You're a liar.* The vicious voices cracked his core. *You are unacceptable, a failure. God cannot love you.*

Nick's chest heaved with sorrow. He tried to be a good person; he tried the best he could. His thoughts fired like bullets, and he tried slowing his breathing. He wasn't sure his heart could take much more. Maybe this was it. Maybe he was going to die anyway.

The story of his life spun to the months after returning from Guatemala, when he thought he had found hope. But his optimism had slipped away bit by bit, like a man standing on a hill of loose gravel and the Chief of Staff's accusations were pushing him further to the edge. Scott was wrongly accusing him of abandoning a patient. To save his own skin, Scott would lie about him and won't hesitate to betray him.

Then another lie grew in Nick's mind. *Maybe it was You, God...maybe You're the one who betrayed me.* Anger rose with the thought. *If I only fully believed. If I had fully sold out to Him.*

God, is that true? Did you betray me?

All the bad things that had ever happened to Nick began to smother him. He tried to fight it away, but the pressure of his life pinned him to the cold, tile floor so he couldn't move. Silence screamed at him and darkness blinded him.

He wanted to die, but reflexively he gasped for air. *I should die. I should let go.* Just let go. Then he heard voices, the voices of Maggie and Jack—*You must learn to let go.*

Nick wrestled with the thought. His eyes tried to penetrate the darkness. *God, where are you?*

"I am right here Nicklaus. Do not be afraid, my son."

Instantly the pressure began to lift, and the pain dissipated from his body and mind. Nick didn't know what was happening, but he felt comforted. Maybe he was dying, and dying was a pleasant experience. Soon he could stand beside his body and observe his sorry life.

Then he saw Jesus standing before him with His arms open wide, beckoning him to an embrace. He saw blood dripping from Jesus's palms, and he remembered that He, too, had known pain. When Nick looked up, he saw a magnificent tree standing behind Jesus. He studied the tree and saw Jesus's crucified silhouette imprinted on the tree, burned into the bark of its trunk.

"I laid down my life for you, Nicklaus."

Jesus knew betrayal. Nick instinctively threw himself down at Jesus's feet. He looked up into the eyes of Jesus and saw compassion and love. Then he looked at the tree and saw the encryption in the trunk. It was the same that was on the tree carved in stone under the church they had visited in Qodshanes, the Hebrew writing Antasha had translated.

עושי ירצנה דלמו סידוהיה

Jesus of Nazareth, the King of the Jews.

CHAPTER 70

AFRAID

MONDAY—POST-QUAKE DAY TWENTY-FOUR

Nick woke with a start. Was he dead or alive? He listened. Nothing. Was he alone? What about his friends? Did he dare call out?

He cleared his throat and waited for a brutal reprisal. Nothing happened. *Thank God.* He heard Buck clear his throat and someone else do the same. Still believing violence was imminent, Nick cringed, tightening his body to ward off a blow. He held his breath and waited for what seemed a long time.

When the blow didn't come, he took a chance and whispered, "Buck? Ali? Vlad?" He tightened his core and waited for a response, friendly or not.

"Nick?" Buck moaned.

"Here, bud," Nick said. "Is everyone here?" He heard whispered acknowledgements.

"AK, are you all right?" Nick asked. He heard her moan.

Buck shushed them. "We may be alone at this moment, but I just heard voices outside the door."

"Who the hell are these people?" Nick whispered.

"Al-Dawla al-Islamiya al-Iraq al-Sham," Ali moaned. "Daesh …you know them as ISIS."

No one spoke.

"We need to try to keep them calm." It was Buck taking

charge. "Whoever these psychopaths are, they are quick to anger and quicker to kill. Don't give them a reason. Short answers, nothing to upset them. Our only chance of survival is to appear to be no threat to them. Let's try to stay together. If they separate us, we are dead."

Nick flinched as the OR door slammed open and a gunshot went off.

"Silence!" one of the guards yelled.

Nick let his body go slack against his restraints. His friends were alive and in the room. He clung to that relief as his mind eased between conscious and unconscious.

***

The small wooden boat rocked violently against the waves. Thunder and lightning roared overhead. *Pain.* Fraught with pain, Nick struggled to stand, only to be knocked to the bottom of the boat, hitting his head, and spinning his mind. The boat fell to the bottom of a huge swell, only to be raised up by the next wave, swirled, and dropped back down, filling the boat with water. His body was inundated up to his waist. He couldn't move, and he gasped for air.

"This vessel is everything you thought would keep you safe."

Nick startled, his eyes searched for the speaker. *Is it Jesus?*

It was. It was Jesus, sitting in the bow of the boat.

Nick was violently tossed down again against his ribs. He thought he heard one crack. "Jesus, save me!"

Jesus remained seated, at ease and smiling.

"Save me," Nick pleaded. Another wave washed over the boat, soaking him in ice-cold water. His body trembled.

He struggled to push himself up. He wanted a closer look at Jesus. When he faced him, Jesus smiled. *"Why are you afraid?"*

"I can't breathe. I'm dying." Nick felt his body pulled into the vortex of death. His body and spirit were being ripped apart. Split—a veil rent from the top—revealing a different dimension. He didn't protest and, strangely, he was no longer afraid. He could breathe easily. He let go. He gave into a welcoming warmth. He welcomed a peaceable kingdom.

But another cold wave slammed his body, and a bright light blinded his sight. Water hit his face. He licked his wet lips and took a deep breath. His vision cleared. His hood had been removed. But the pain returned and with it, the recognition that he was still a prisoner in the operating room.

He tried to wipe his face to clear his eyes but couldn't lift his arms. His head drooped with pain, shock and exhaustion, until he saw he was naked. Where were his clothes? He squirmed to discover he was sitting in a chair, and his hands were tightly bound behind him.

What had Ali said? He tried to remember. They were in the hands of ISIS.

Trying not to react, he watched the guards trying to strip the clothes off Buck. He resisted, and the guards threw him to the ground and ripped at his clothes. When they saw his prostheses, they laughed, yanked them off his stumps, and tossed them into the middle of the room with the rest of their clothes. Then they hauled Buck up and hurled him into a chair. They taped his hands behind him and sprayed him with a hose. They jeered as the water hit the black hood. Nick could see Buck fight for air, gasping into the wet fabric. Nick tried to tell them to stop, but he was unable to utter a sound. As Buck began to collapse, a guard ripped off Buck's hood and howled with laughter. He and the other tormentors laughed, watching the legless man rise to consciousness as they sprayed his face.

Nick averted his eyes and glanced around the room. He saw his team, each one tied to a chair, naked, with hoods removed. At least they were alive and together. It was some consolation. Then he saw Ali slumped over, and his heart sank. Was he dead? He studied his friend and thought he saw the rise and fall of his chest.

The door to the OR opened and the Red Crescent pair walked in. It angered Nick to see the woman smiling. He thought she might be shocked to see the state of the captives. Instead, she looked delighted. She spoke to the young man, who looked like he could be no more than twenty years old. The man barked out orders to the soldiers, who finished duct taping Vladimir's arms to his chair. With their belongings and Buck's legs piled in the middle of the circle, a soldier with a push broom swept the rest of the water on the floor down the OR drain.

"Today, we find out what you are doing here," the young man said to his prisoners. "Tell the truth, or you die." He turned to the woman, who waved their military satellite phone at them.

The young man pulled a pistol from his pants and stood in front of Buck. "You, soldier, where did you fight?" With the tip of his pistol, he traced the large scars over Buck's chest and abdomen, and with the barrel, he shoved Buck's head from side to side. "This looks like an IED. Where did you fight? Afghanistan? Iraq? How many of my brothers did you kill?" He pistol-whipped Buck hard on the side of his head. Buck lost consciousness.

"Why do you have a military satellite phone?" he screamed at Buck, who was limp and unresponsive.

Then he turned to Vladimir, glowering at the Russian. Nick noticed that Vladimir's leg had stopped bleeding. He could see it was swollen and hoped it was a through-and-through wound sparing bone and artery. Vladimir was conscious, but he looked ashen from the injury.

"What is your story?" the young man sneered and forced Vladimir's head back by pointing the gun at his forehead. "Russian?" he demanded.

"*Da*...yes, of course."

His straightforward answer seemed to surprise the young man, who looked at the woman. Nick wondered if she was the real leader of the cell.

Vladimir's voice was raspy and weak. "My wife and I were here in Turkey for vacation." He coughed against the pressure of the pistol. "You can see she was hurt in the earthquake...her leg." He nodded toward AK who sat across from him. "The doctors here," he tried to indicate Nick and Ali, "fixed her leg."

"Here in Hakkâri?" the young man demanded.

"No, in Van."

"Then what are you doing in Hakkâri?" he accused and raised his free arm to strike Vladimir.

"It was for me," Ali shouted. Where he got the strength, Nick didn't know, but his shout was so alarming the young man spun to face him.

"*Selamünaleyküm*, may God's peace be upon you," Ali said, looking at him.

"*Aleykümselam,*" the young man replied reflexively.

"This is all my fault," Ali said. "I will tell you everything. Please, do no more harm. In Allah's name, I swear to you."

The young man stood in front of Ali and crossed his arms, holding the pistol in his hand.

"In Allah I swear, we have been working in Van since the earthquake," Ali explained. "Dr. Hart and I are surgeons. We came to help."

"From America?" the woman asked. She stood behind the young man.

"Yes," Ali continued, "but I am originally from Van." Ali lowered his head in exhaustion.

"What is your name?" The man brought the pistol across Ali's face, snapping his head back and causing blood to ooze from his nose.

A guard entered the OR. "Commander, come quickly. It is what you have been waiting for."

Commander? Nick mused and watched their captors hesitate for a moment. The young man looked at the woman, who whispered into his ear. Then, without waiting for his reaction, she threw their satellite phone on the pile of the team's belongings and left the room. The young man followed her.

Nick watched the interaction. *My God...she really is in control.*

CHAPTER 71

DECEPTION

Abdul and the White Snake smiled at each other as they watched the television report from the Turkish broadcasting station. The newscaster was reading the letter that they had drafted: "The PKK demands the sovereignty of their land from the oppression of the illegitimate Turkish government. Further bombings will continue until our demands are met."

The broadcast showed footage from the bombing site. All that remained of the cargo truck was its twisted frame. Since the truck was full of diesel, the fuel tanks doubled the power of the explosion.

"It appears that the Red Crescent was the target of the attack," the newscaster reported. "The Red Crescent had recently brought relief supplies into Hakkâri. At least two relief workers were killed in the attack, along with four people at the school."

The scene changed to the school, where a reporter was interviewing a man. "Yes, yes, I saw everything that happened," the man said. "As the Red Crescent truck was leaving, a car pulled up beside it, and there was a huge explosion. Thanks be to Allah, that the car bomber did not make it to the school."

The White Snake nodded with satisfaction. The man had performed perfectly. Planting a spokesman at the school after the bombing had been her idea too.

The reporter interviewed two more people who confirmed the planted spokesman's story.

"The power of suggestion is a very compelling thing," she smiled. She knew that others, having heard the spokesman tell the story with such authority, would follow his lead. It would be all over the Internet that the PKK was responsible.

"What should we do with our prisoners?" Abdul asked.

"With that report, it appears we are safe for now," she said. "Our captives say they were helping with relief efforts."

"We should not trust what the American pigs and the Russians tell us," he said, trying to negotiate his leadership. "I believe there is more to their story."

"Yes, this perhaps is true," she nodded, "but there is no denying that two of them really are doctors. At this point, I think they are more valuable to us alive than dead. Who knows? Maybe the Russian and the American governments will pay for their release."

She reminded Abdul that ISIS had made millions of dollars on ransoms. Some prisoners made it home, others didn't. She didn't care, even if the ransom was delivered. "The next twenty-four hours will tell. For now…let them live."

***

Shivering and scared, Ali focused on Astî's beautiful smile. He pictured himself with her and their two girls, playing in the park near their house that they loved so much. By US standards, their Memphis home was modest, but to them it was a palace. Their girls had even talked them into getting a puppy, an impossible dream when he and Astî were kids in Van.

Ali had dodged a bullet when the man had asked him his name and was interrupted before Ali could answer. *Lucky break.* Ali Hassan was not a good name to have in the hands of the Sunni led ISIS. The ancient Sunni-Shia split had been caused by the seventh-century Ali and his son, Hassan, whom the Shiites viewed as the first of the twelve imams or holy leaders. The Sunnis had vehemently disagreed.

Ali suspected these men were Sunni. They would consider him an infidel at best, and at worst, if they discovered he was Kurdish, a wretched animal of the lowest species. He was certain they had found his wallet. But maybe they hadn't, or they would have killed him by now.

Ali tried to think of a plan to get out of this situation. He was aware of the custom of *Taqiyya*. Ali thought the Sunnis called it *Ikraah*—to lie in order to protect yourself. It was even in the Qur'an. Yes, that was what he must do. It might be the only way he would see Astî and his beautiful daughters again. Figuring out how to do this would take his mind off his aching face.

***

Nick had never felt so cold. His body shook uncontrollably. It was a healthy response, but when the shaking stopped, signaling severe hypothermia, death would soon follow. He was worried about AK. She was slumped unconscious in her chair, with her hands blue from the cold and the tight binding.

He saw Buck measure the room with one eye, the other swollen shut.

"What are they doing? What are they waiting for?" Nick whispered to Buck.

"Probably trying to decide what to do with us. Are we more valuable dead or alive? The longer we are alive, the better for us. We must get help for AK. She doesn't look well."

The OR door opened and Buck dropped his head in silence.

Nick pretended to close his eyes, but squinted enough to see the guards wheeling in a table. *Now what? More torture?* He was relieved to see the table piled with blankets. The guard draped a blanket over him and the others and held water bottles to their lips. He was so thirsty, he desperately sought the mouth of the bottle to gulp the water.

As he rested after swallowing as much as he could, he heard Ali speak to one of the guards. Ali and the guard spoke in Turkish. He guessed they were talking about AK as Ali kept nodding to her. When Ali stopped talking, the guards talked among themselves. One of them took a large knife out of his front pocket and sliced the tape from Ali's wrist. Ali's legs wobbled as he stood, but he made his way to AK's side and gently lifted her head. He said something to the guard who cut her free from the chair, and she collapsed into Ali's arms. He adjusted the blanket the soldiers had draped over her and wrapped his own blanket around her. Then he laid her on the floor.

She moaned softly.

Thank God, Nick thought. He watched Ali lift AK's head and put the water bottle to her lips. She gagged and coughed, but then took a large drink. The guard ordered Ali back to his chair. He quickly obeyed and the soldiers retaped his arms to the sides of the chair. His naked body shivered in the cold.

Before they left, the guards covered the prisoners' heads with the black hoods, cloaking Nick with the dread of continued isolation from his friends.

***

The guards stopped coming into the room. Their rotation had provided Nick a reference for the passing of time. But now, time had no meaning. How long were they to sit there, naked and shivering and sightless?

Nick flexed his toes. The muscles in his legs cramped from either dehydration or an electrolyte imbalance or both. He thought it must be night. No hint of nearby light penetrated the darkness. But, truth be told, they had been there so long that night could have given way to day and then night again.

If he was grateful for anything, it was that the hood had not been tied around his neck, so he could still breathe. Thank God he could breathe. But the ability to breathe didn't keep his body from aching fiercely. He was too cold and in too much pain to scream. Only his thoughts were free to roam.

How could these people treat other human beings like this, like animals, like nonhumans? Nick understood there was evil in the world. He had experienced it. How could a person's ideology get so distorted? He remembered when Buck had told him about the two kingdoms—the kingdom of light and the kingdom of darkness—the kingdom of love and the kingdom of hate. Buck said, "*The Kingdom of Heaven is here,*' Jesus declared. To enter the Kingdom of Heaven requires an awakening to Jesus, and entering requires a new birth—an opening of our eyes."

Father, open my eyes, Nick prayed.

Fear shook his body. He had seen the videos of the beheadings and the graphic video of ISIS fighters jeering and laughing as they burned a Jordanian pilot alive. Nausea washed over him. He thought of his burn rotation as an intern; it had been the worst four weeks of his life. He had never seen such suffering.

Terror consumed him, eating at his mind and body. Could they end up like that? What was going to happen to them? He tried to push the images away.

Fear. His mind and body were full of it and yet it was strangely familiar. *Yes,* he had always lived in fear. Fear of dying, fear of pain, fear of loss, fear of failure, fear of not being good enough, fear of letting someone down, fear of saying the wrong thing, fear of rejection. *Fear, fear, fear.*

His fear was overtaken by the memory of an incident in med school. A patient had told him about a near-death experience. He was skeptical, but as he listened, the patient was convincing. The man told him that he had coded during a minor surgical procedure, and his heart had stopped for thirty minutes before he was resuscitated. The patient said prior to it happening he had been afraid to die. But during all those minutes his heart had stopped, he had felt no pain and no fear. He said he was at peace. He said if that was death, he would never again fear it.

Words echoed in Nick's head. *"There is no fear in love."*

"Father, how can I live without fear?"

"By loving. By letting go of everything that you think keeps you safe, Nicklaus." The words filled the darkness of his mind.

Nick's chest heaved and he wept. "I don't know how."

"Today is the day of new sight."

CHAPTER 72

NIMROD
TUESDAY—POST-QUAKE DAY TWENTY-FIVE

Abdul sat on the edge of Omar's desk.

One of his men marched into the room. "Commander." He snapped a salute and stood at attention. Abdul observed the man who was twice his age and gloated. Since he'd captured the foreigners, he'd noticed his men carried themselves with a renewed sense of purpose. Most of all, they treated him with respect. He was, after all, their Commander.

"Yes?" Abdul said with disdain.

"Commander, a platoon of Turkish soldiers was just at the gate."

Abdul's confidence ebbed. He looked at the White Snake and back at his man.

"And?" He tried to hide the anxiety in his voice.

"They asked to speak with the administrator of the hospital and want to know if everything here is in order."

"And what did you tell them?" Abdul studied his fingernails.

"I told them that the administrator had gone into town and would be back later and that everything within the compound was satisfactory."

He crossed his arms and looked at the ceiling. "Were they satisfied?"

"Yes." The man hesitated. "But they said they would come back later to speak with Omar."

Abdul stood, put his hands on his hips, and frowned. "What are their capabilities?"

"A platoon of fifty men, four Humvees, and two transport trucks. They seem to be patrolling the neighborhoods."

He sighed and nodded. "Okay, you may go."

The man saluted again, turned on his heels, and left the room.

Abdul stared at the floor.

"I think—" the White Snake began.

He waved her to silence. "I think you have kicked a hornets' nest," he accused her. "I told you we should wait." He couldn't contain his anger. He wanted to hit something. Instead, he dropped himself back down into Omar's leather desk chair.

"Just because the government sent some soldiers on patrol doesn't mean we should worry," she said. "It's normal under the circumstances."

He glared at the white woman. "I think you forget who you are." He paused to stare her down. "And who I am."

She sighed. "Abdul, please." She moved to soothe him, to touch his arm, but as soon as she got near, he pushed the chair back and held out his hand for her to stop.

"That's enough," he spat. "You've done enough."

She waved her hand nonchalantly. "You shouldn't worry, Abdul. It's nothing. We simply stall the army…we tell them Omar went to visit a friend…or got waylaid by a potential donor…or—"

He wasn't listening and cut her off. "We should prepare to leave. I am issuing the order for the Red Crescent team to return to Cizre."

She sighed. "Do you think that's really necessary?"

His face flushed. She dared to contradict him? Her Commander? "We will stay in Cizre if it is safe. If we hear that the army has departed Hakkâri, we can return."

The White Snake folded her arms. "You can't run away every time there is danger."

"I have made my decision," he snapped.

"Or maybe you have lost your taste for jihad," she said. "Are you afraid to die?"

He shot up from the chair and shoved her with both hands. She lost her balance, fell against a small table and landed on the floor, hitting her back hard. She fought for her breath, scrambled to her feet, and reached into her sleeve.

Abdul knew that was where she kept a concealed blade. He pulled his pistol from his waist, cocked it, aimed at her chest, and said with a steely voice, "Tell me if this needs to go further."

The White Snake winced, pulled her empty hand from her sleeve, and held it palm up. "I'm sorry, Abdul. You are right."

He slowly released the pistol's hammer and tucked the weapon into his waistband. "We must find out the real reason the Americans and Russians are here together in Turkey. Then we will use them for propaganda to strike fear into the West—taking them with us as our hostages for ransom or killing them if we must."

***

When the soldiers removed their hoods, Nick could see AK was cognizant but dazed. The soldiers gave them water, and he thought their situation might be improving. Then their captors entered.

"The Turkish army has brought troops to this city, and a mandatory curfew is in place," the young man shouted. His voice and eyes held fear. Even the British woman's countenance had changed, her eyes downcast. "This is your final hour. Tell me why you are here or die."

Ali began to speak in Turkish. The young man listened with interest and told the guards to cut him loose from his chair. But when Ali stood and begged for their lives, the guards kicked his knees. Ali collapsed but immediately pushed himself to his knees and continued pleading for the lives of the team.

The young man pointed his pistol at the crown of Ali's head. "If you are from Van, are you Sunni or Shia? Or are you a Kurdish pig?" He pulled back on the hammer.

"In the name of Allah, I swear, I am your brother."

"Show me how you pray," the young man said.

Ali's body shook uncontrollably. He folded his arms and with a trembling voice, he recited the prayers.

Nick could tell that whatever Ali was saying and the way he was praying was pacifying the terrorist, who removed the gun from Ali's head.

"Why are you with these infidels?" the young man inquired. His voice had softened.

"My brother, these are good people. They are not your enemies."

The comment incited the young man, and he pointed the gun at Ali's head again. "All infidels are our enemies."

"Yes, of course," Ali pleaded for calm. "As a righteous man, you surely know the story of Cain and Abel. The Qur'an tells us that their story is a message for all of mankind and teaches us about the consequence of murder—that killing one righteous person is as if you have slain the whole of mankind."

"Are you telling me these are righteous people?"

"Do you remember Abel told Cain that by murdering him, he would not only carry the weight of his own sin, but the sins of his victim, and that his victim, suffering injustice, would have his sins forgiven? My brother, do not take on the sins of these people and, therefore, spend eternity in the fires of hell."

"Don't lecture me." The young man stuck his foot in Ali's chest and pushed him backward, causing him to crash into the chair. A guard picked up Ali and put him in the chair.

Vladimir was sitting next to Ali, and the young man turned his attention to him. "Is that right, are you a righteous man?" He pointed the gun at Vladimir's forehead. "Are you a Jew? A Christian?"

"Me, sir, I am a Russian. I'm afraid that does not make me a righteous man."

"Maybe an honest man." The young man smirked. He pulled the gun from Vladimir's head and looked at Antasha.

"And how about you, Russian woman. You a good Russian?"

Nick watched AK's eyes focus on her tormenter. A tear ran down her cheek. She spoke to him in Russian and then in all clarity, spoke forcefully in English. "I believe in Jesus." She left no doubt that she was speaking from her heart.

Nick was shocked, and Vladimir looked just as stunned. The young man slapped her face. Vladimir tried to go to her defense, jumping to his feet, the tape still binding his arms to the chair. He lunged at the Commander, but the two guards standing behind him quickly forced him and the chair back down. The larger of the two butted him in the chest with his rifle.

"And you two?" the young man spun around to face Nick and Buck.

Buck did not hesitate. "I believe in One God—the Father and His Son, Jesus, and His Holy Spirit."

The young man stared at Nick. His eyes were black with hatred. For the first time in Nick's life, he felt no fear; in fact, he felt the opposite of fear—he felt peace, more peace than he had ever experienced. "Yes." He stared into the young man's eyes. "I, too, am a follower of Jesus."

Nick won the stare-down when the young man's eyes turned to the British woman.

With trepidation, Ali interrupted. "It is only Allah that gives life or death. Do you remember the story of Nimrod and our prophet Ibrahim? Peace be upon him."

Ali's comment seemed to enrage the young man. His gun hand shook as he spun to Ali. "Shut up!"

His black eyes stared daggers at each of his prisoners. "Your governments will pay for your lives, but first you must renounce your faith or you will die. I will give you three hours to decide."

CHAPTER 73

MARTYRDOM

TUESDAY AFTERNOON—

POST-QUAKE DAY TWENTY-FIVE

"What's going on?" Nick whispered to Ali. Their hoods were still off, and there seemed to be considerable discussion among the guards who came and went.

"I…" Ali stopped and cleared his throat as a guard came through the OR doors, grabbed supplies from one of the cabinets, and left.

Nick looked at his friends. If he looked as terrible as they did, they were all in trouble.

Ali waited for a few seconds after the guard went out before speaking. "I overheard two of the guards talking about packing supplies. They may be moving us."

"That's not good," Buck said.

"*Da,*" Vladimir echoed.

"Where would they move us to?" AK asked hoarsely.

"Or…they may leave us here," Buck said.

Nick understood what he meant.

"Look," Buck continued, "we might not have much time, so I'm just going to say it…"

The door swung open again, and two guards brought in a tripod and video camera. They set up the equipment in the middle of the room and left.

Nick looked at Buck and Ali. They nodded with understanding. Nick thought of the pictures of ISIS militants beheading twenty-one Christian Egyptian men on a shore in Libya.

"You all are way more valuable to them alive," Vladimir said. "Stay that way."

Nick realized that Vladimir was suggesting they renounce their faith.

Buck spoke with unwavering confidence. "I have been ready to die since I signed up to be a Marine, but maybe more importantly, since I accepted Jesus as my Savior."

Nick and the others would have to decide for themselves.

Was he ready to give it all? He closed his eyes and prayed. *Father…forgive me. Forgive me for my weakness. Forgive me for my unbelief, my doubt. Oh, God.* His body shook and tears ran down his face.

He jumped when the OR door slammed open. The British woman appeared first, dressed in a full burka. Five guards followed and, finally, the young man, pistol in hand.

The young man nodded toward AK, and two of the guards grabbed the back of her chair and pulled her to the center of the room. A guard adjusted a surgical light at her face, while another turned on the video camera. The British woman pulled the veil over her face and drew a long knife from her sleeve. She stood behind AK.

The young man stepped behind the camera. "You will renounce your faith and tell your government that they must pay for your release. One million euros is your value."

The British woman grabbed a hunk of AK's red hair and placed her knife next to AK's neck.

"Tell them," the woman demanded.

AK's voice was hoarse and weak as she spoke in Russian to the camera. Nick had no idea what she was saying, but knowing AK, it was not what the captors wanted her to say, and he figured the captors recognized that, also.

"Now in English," the woman yelled at her, pressing the knife to her neck, drawing blood. "Do you renounce your faith?"

AK mumbled incoherently. She cleared her throat, and her

voice and will grew stronger. "I am Antasha Katrina Volkova. I am a Russian citizen. I am being held against my will. I was born a Russian Jew." She paused.

The British woman twisted AK's hair, nearly pulling it from her scalp. "Do you renounce your faith?" she screamed.

Nick could see AK swallow against the blade and try to shrink away from the cutting edge.

"I have no faith. I am atheist." AK swallowed again. "I did not believe in a god...until He touched me." AK began to whimper. The whimper turned into weeping, then to joyous tears. "He touched me. I saw Him," she exclaimed.

The room was still except for the blinking red light of the video camera. Nick held his breath, waiting for the evil British woman hiding behind the burka to cut AK's throat. He could see her eyes behind the veil staring at the young man, who appeared to be frozen behind the camera, unable to give the command.

AK spoke. "You may take my life; you may let me live. For to me, it makes no difference. I know now what I know."

"Who touched you? What did you see?" the British woman pulled back tightly on AK's copper hair.

Nick watched AK fearlessly turn her head against the blade to look up at the woman's veiled face. "I saw Jesus."

"Are you a Christian then?" the woman demanded.

"I don't even know what that means. I only know what I saw. What I experienced...that He reached out and touched me."

The British woman looked at the young man, who shrugged and indicated to a guard to put AK back in place. When the British woman pulled her knife away, Nick saw blood trickle down her pale neck onto her chest. Two guards dragged her from in front of the camera.

Nick's heart sank when he saw the young man nod to him. The guards obeyed and pulled him in his chair to the front of the camera under the surgical light. He remembered how many times he had used it to bring life to patients. He imagined reaching up to the light to bring focus onto the patient's injured body, often at the most critical time in the procedure, trying to see, trying to focus, his bloody hand leaving its mark on the sterile light handle.

"Now do you see?" a voice in his heart said. *"Focus. Do you see the life-giving blood? Do you see, Nicklaus?"*

In a vision in his mind, he looked down at an opened body on the operating table, its chest split wide, the heart rhythmically pumping, the pink lungs filling with air and then releasing. It was beautiful. Everything working in harmony, delicately balanced. Nick looked at the patient's face and saw it was his own. *"It is beautiful,"* the voice said. *"I made you perfectly."*

The patient's face transformed into the face he saw in his vision. Jesus. *"This is my body that I have given for you. This is my blood, it is poured out for all, for the forgiveness of your sins."*

Nick's head snapped back and he felt the cold blade on his throat.

"Dr. Hart…there is no reason to die today. It is time to beg for your life," the young man said.

He felt the sting of the blade cutting his skin. But he wasn't afraid.

"Why?" he asked, looking up at the woman. Behind the veil, her eyes stared coldly back at him. He felt her hatred.

She grabbed his hair and forced him to look at the camera.

"Tell us who you are," the young man ordered.

"I am Dr. Nicklaus Hart." He swallowed hard. "I am Dr. Nicklaus Hart, son of Thomas Hart, defender of the broken, son of my Father in Heaven." The words flowed from his heart.

"Do you renounce your faith?" The woman jerked his hair and pressed harder on the knife.

Nick smiled. What a stupid question. It didn't matter. It was as if she was asking him to renounce his skin. He couldn't remove something that was part him. He in Christ, Christ in him, they in the Father.

Suddenly, a voice shouted, "You don't have to do this." It was Ali. "Abdul…son…you don't have to do this. This is not the way of Allah."

Nick felt the pressure on the knife relax as the pair turned their attention on Ali.

"This is not the way of Islam. This is not the way of Allah," Ali pleaded, tears running down his cheeks.

"How do you know my name?" Abdul backhanded Ali across his face. "And do not call me son."

"I'm sorry, I heard the guard talking—"

"I know you as well," Abdul cut him off.

Nick watched Abdul pull a wallet from his front pocket and throw it into Ali's lap.

Abdul grabbed Ali by the throat with one hand, and with the other, he cocked and pointed his pistol at Ali's head. "I don't believe you are a Sunni brother, Ali Hassan. Your name betrays you. You will be the first to die."

"Don't you want to kill me first, you raghead?" Buck screamed. "Like I killed all your cowardly brothers in Iraq?"

Abdul loosened his grip on Ali's neck and straightened his spine. Buck had hit the mark—he was going all in.

The British woman stepped between Buck and Abdul. "Abdul, no! Do not let this pig incite you," she yelled. "They are more valuable to us alive. The Americans will pay millions for him. Abdul, please."

Abdul stared at the woman, then grabbed her and violently tossed her aside, sending her crashing to the floor.

He pointed his pistol at Buck's head and grinned. "You think you can control me like that?" He turned and aimed the gun at Nick and said to Buck, "What if I kill your friend?"

Nick closed his eyes, not wanting to see death. Then all hell broke loose.

CHAPTER 74

LIFE AND DEATH

Leaving Vladimir's legs unbound to the chair turned out to be a deadly decision. Despite his taped hands and his injured leg, the huge man charged Abdul and hit him like a stampeding bull—head to chest. It sent both Nick and the captor flying. Nick heard the familiar sound of breaking bones when Vladimir hit the man. Two shots rang out and ended in deadly thuds.

Still strapped to his chair and on the floor, Nick thrashed around to see the mayhem. He saw Abdul sprawled in front of him, dazed and gasping for breath. Nick contorted his body to see Vladimir standing over them, his arms and the chair hanging behind his massive frame. He grinned at Nick, then coughed. Blood dripped from his mouth. He staggered, struggling to stay on his feet.

Nick looked beyond Vladimir to see the British woman holding a smoking pistol. With her other hand, she pulled off her veil and headscarf. Her bleached-blond hair fell over her shoulders. "That will be enough," she said.

Vladimir turned to step toward her, but she took a step back and smiled. Nick saw the bloody entry wounds through his back. The big Russian staggered backward and like a large oak fell, crashing to the floor, taking the camera with him.

He landed beside Nick, coughed up more blood, and smiled. "Thank you, my friend." Vladimir's eyes locked with Nick's. Nick wrestled to release his arms from his chair, but he couldn't move.

"Let me help him!" he screamed at the woman. She did not budge and Nick looked back at Vladimir. "Aaaaa," he screamed and fought against the tape that kept him immobile. "Vladimir, breathe." He could see Vladimir's life escaping.

"I have decided, Dr. Hart," Vladimir said, coughing up more blood. "I've decided that worms do not sound so good." He smiled. "Will you pray for me?" Nick watched Vladimir's eyes flutter as he gasped his last breath.

"Vladimir. No!" Nick screamed and strained against his restraints. Vladimir did not move. His chest ceased all movement. The only breathing he heard came from Abdul lying behind him, gasping for air.

"Help me," Abdul wheezed.

The woman went to Abdul and squat to put her hand on his chest.

"Help me, I can't breathe," Abdul pleaded.

The woman stood and pointed her gun at Nick and ordered one of the guards to cut him loose.

The stunned guard pulled a knife from his front pocket, clicked open the blade, and cut the tape, freeing Nick. He rolled toward Vladimir and lifted the big man's head, feeling for a carotid pulse. There was none. "Jesus," he cried. "Jesus, have mercy."

He looked at Buck and then at AK, who hung her head and wept against her restraints.

"He is dead," the British woman coldly pronounced. She grabbed Nick by his hair and held the gun to the back of his head. "Now, you must play doctor again." She forced his head toward Abdul.

He resisted and came to his knees with her pull. "I would rather die." He gritted his teeth and stared coldly at her.

"If you insist." She straightened her arm and pushed the barrel into his hair.

"Help me," Abdul gasped, stretching his arms to the woman, causing her to loosen her grip on the trigger.

"Help him!" she screamed, waving her gun.

He looked down at Abdul and saw evil. He saw the evil creature that had captured and tortured him and his friends. The one that was about to put a bullet through his head. He should die. He deserved to die.

He looked at the woman and her gun and was ready to accept his own fate for refusing to help. Then he heard a voice in his heart as clear as day.

"Look again, Nicklaus," the voice said.

Nick looked down at Abdul's face.

"I shed my blood for all."

Abdul looked at Nick and pleaded with his eyes, filled with anxiety only known by a person slowly suffocating.

"Remember who you are."

The young man looked more like a scared adolescent than the monster he was moments earlier.

Abdul's breathing was rapid and shallow. Nick could see the tachycardic carotid pulse bounce in man-boy's neck and his distended jugular veins. Abdul reached for Nick's arm. Nick looked at his hand—the one that had struck him earlier, the one that held the gun to his head, maybe even the one that had detonated the bomb. It was a hand just like his own.

"Remember whose you are."

Abdul's lips were turning blue, and he was losing consciousness.

"Nicklaus, choose love over hate."

"Do something," the woman screamed.

Abdul's trachea had shifted to one side—he had a tension pneumothorax. Vladimir had hit him with such brute force that it had created a tear in his lung, which had created a one-way valve, letting air flow between the chest wall and the lung, building pressure on that side of the chest and collapsing the lung. His body was smothering itself.

Nick turned to the pile of clothes on the floor. He shivered at the hard, cold steel of the pistol at his back.

"What are you doing?" she shouted.

"Do you want me to save him or not?" Nick yelled as he dug through the pile. He found his trousers and took what he needed from the front pocket.

Nick pushed himself up and stepped toward Abdul. "I'm doing this for myself." He glared at the woman. He unsheathed the large needle that he retrieved from his pocket and plunged it into the boy's chest.

There was an audible rush of air from the needle, like opening a valve on a tire. The young man gasped, then breathed in deeply.

CHAPTER 75

RESCUE

"What have you done?" the woman screamed.

Nick looked at Abdul, still fighting for breath and life.

"I saved his life," Nick said, "for the moment."

"He does not look well," she said.

"He has a collapsed lung, and the pressure in his chest will keep building until a chest tube can be inserted. The needle relieved the pressure temporarily, but he is only breathing with one lung. The other side needs to be reinflated." Nick looked at Abdul and saw the anxiety of suffocation torturing the torturer's mind. He grimaced at the irony.

Nick watched the patient's heart pound in his neck, trying desperately to pump more of the oxygen-depleted blood to his brain. His heart kept up with the demand only because of his youth, but it wouldn't be long before that advantage would wane. He would have only thirty minutes before the lack of oxygen would injure his brain or stop his heart.

"If he dies, you all die," she said, pointing the gun at Nick's chest and spinning around to the other captives.

"He needs a chest tube," Nick told her.

"Then do it," she turned back to him and thrust the pistol at his chest.

"Look, lady, why should I do anything to save him? Who are you?" His face flushed with anger. "Why are you doing this to us? My God, you have tortured us and killed our friend, and now you want me to save this murderer?"

"You are in no position to ask questions."

"Neither is he." Nick glanced at Abdul, who was fighting for every breath.

"We are doing Allah's work," the woman declared.

"What? To harm people? To kill them?" he challenged her. "To murder them in cold blood?"

"You are an infidel. You would not understand. Your mind and heart are deceived."

He looked at her blue eyes and blond hair. "How can you even think like this?"

She composed herself. "Dr. Hart, in my belief, we would ask, 'How can you not think like this?' The Qur'an orders believers to fight against those that fight against us...the oppressors and aggressors. My country and yours have been the oppressors and aggressors. Throughout history, my country and yours have killed innocent men, women, and children."

Nick hated his captors but she was right. So many people had been killed in the name of freedom or God. It was a never-ending battle. Murder begets murder; war begets war. "An eye for an eye, a tooth for a tooth," he murmured.

Nick glanced down and saw the young man's gun at his feet, hidden from the woman by Vladimir's body. If only he had that gun. He wanted to put a bullet in the woman's forehead, right between her blue eyes. He wanted to put a bullet into every one of the ISIS fighters. He wanted them dead and gone, and he wanted to savor watching Abdul suffocate and die. Let him suffer. Let them all suffer.

Hate wooed him. It was the easier path. Nick could feel the rending of his soul.

The weight of human existence fell on him, with its aggression, greed, and violence. His legs buckled and he slumped to his knees. He saw his opening.

He looked at the woman and said, "Then take my life...but let my friends go." He raised his hands in surrender and dropped his head in submission.

The gun was right at his knee. He slumped over with his

hands on the floor, his hand finding the grip of the pistol. It burned in his hand. Could he draw it fast enough to catch the woman off guard? His head was spinning. Could he kill? The weight of this decision sickened him.

"*Where does the hatred stop?*" It was the voice in his heart again.

Abdul coughed with labored breathing. He was dying. Nick looked up at his companions. AK was battered and bruised and sobbing. Ali hung his head in defeat or prayer. But Buck stared back at him with one eye. His right eye was swollen shut. A large gash bled across his forehead. Buck, who could read him better than anyone else, straightened his spine.

"Nick," Buck croaked hoarsely, causing the woman to turn.

Nick tightened his grip on the pistol and felt for the trigger.

"Nick, no!" Buck yelled.

Buck's words caused Nick to hesitate.

"Nick, I am not afraid to die. They can take our life, but not our identity. You are a healer. Nick…blessed are the merciful, for they will find mercy."

Nick loosened his grip on the gun. Buck was right. He looked at the woman, then back at the dying boy. He knew what he had to do and removed his finger from the trigger.

"We need to get a chest tube in him, and I'm going to need Ali's help"—he nodded toward Ali—"and my pants."

The woman turned to the guards and ordered them to free Ali. When she turned back, she saw Nick standing with his arm extended, the pistol dangling from his finger through the trigger guard. "I'll trade you this for a chest tube."

One of the guards, seeing Nick's weapon, aimed his rifle against Nick's head and yelled at him to drop the gun. The woman spoke sharply to the guard, who took the pistol from Nick and backed off.

"Get dressed," the woman said to Nick and Ali.

"We are going to need supplies from the emergency room," Ali said, pulling on his pants. "I remember seeing some chest tubes in the supply cabinets."

"I'll get him onto the OR table," Nick said, pulling on his shirt and nodding toward the new operating table in the corner.

"I'll have him ready by the time you get back."

The woman barked orders and Ali sprinted through the OR door with two guards in tow.

***

Akleema watched the two surgeons work. Her guards had moved the operating table back to the center of the room and lifted Abdul onto the table under the same lights they had used to torture the prisoners.

The surgeons quickly made use of the supplies from the ER. They lifted Abdul's shirt up to his neck and slipped on their surgical gloves. Dr. Hart painted Abdul's skin with disinfectant, while the Turkish doctor injected a swath of skin midway down his side over his ribs.

Although she appreciated their effort, she didn't care if Abdul lived or died. In fact, she hoped he died. But for the sake of the guards, she had to put on a show of wanting to save their leader. She thought maybe these doctors would pull it off, as they were capable. Maybe too capable. Better to let the weak, stupid boy die on the operating table in their care. She was in charge now, and she intended to keep it that way.

She pictured Aisha leading her army into battle on top of her camel. Would future generations read stories about the White Snake? Great Britain had embraced a woman Prime Minister, and America tried to elect their first female President. Maybe it was time that the Islamic State was run by a woman. Men were too stupid to rule.

She watched the surgeon run the scalpel between the ribs. She was surprised when he crudely inserted an instrument between the ribs and spread it open, separating the muscle. As he entered the chest cavity, a gush of blood splashed from the wound and onto the floor. What shocked her was that the surgeons seemed to take it all in stride and thrust a large, clear tube into Abdul's chest, pushing it in for seven or eight inches.

She couldn't believe the procedure that looked as if it should kill Abdul was saving him. But it was. She saw his breathing become less labored and his blue lips turn back to pink.

Dr. Hart turned to her, while the other doctor sutured the tube in place and closed the skin around it. "There is a plastic box called a Pleur-evac that this tube hooks into. It pulls gentle suction to reinflate the lung. I have no idea if this hospital has one, so we will try to improvise one out of suction canisters...if we can find some in the cabinets."

Ali snipped the last of the sutures. The woman nodded and said something to one of the soldiers to help Ali search.

"We have kept our end of the bargain," Nick said, "now cut my friends loose and let them dress." He squared off with the woman. She kept him at arm's length at the end of her pistol.

"You were mistaken, Dr. Hart. This is not a negotiation." She aimed the pistol at his head.

Nick stared into her blue eyes and saw ice-cold hatred. He looked down the barrel of her 9mm. She held the gun steady, without tremor, without fear, without remorse. She was more comfortable with a gun than he was with a scalpel.

Nick startled when someone grabbed his wrist. He turned. It was Abdul. Blood still dripped from the chest tube. He was trying to speak. He mouthed something until his lips couldn't move. His hand fell away from Nick's wrist.

"Look what I found," Ali called from the supply cabinet in the corner. He held up two suction canisters.

The White Snake turned to look at Ali but kept the pistol pointed at Nick. When she turned back to Nick, he saw a red laser dot on her forehead and a bullet hit its target. The room erupted with noise and light and chaos.

***

Three deafening explosions—blinding flashes of light—crackling bullets—screams—smoke—hellacious cries.

Nick heard shots hit flesh and men yell. He was knocked off his feet and hit the floor hard. The room went dark.

"Stay down! Stay down!" someone yelled.

Nick heard a short blast of rapid fire, followed by a body hitting the floor.

"Clear!" someone yelled.

"Clear," someone else echoed.

Silence. The raging storm was over in seconds.

Nick struggled to move. Someone grabbed him around the shoulders. Fearing an aggressor, he tried with all his strength to break the grip, but had no success. The arms held him tight.

"Dr. Hart?" someone asked.

"Dr. Hart. We are Maroon Berets…Turkish Special Forces."

The cavalry. Nick smiled in delirium.

"I've got you, Dr. Hart. You are safe now."

The arms that gripped him loosened, and Nick felt his body relax. He looked for the person that belonged to the voice. His eyes were open, but he saw only blackness.

"Dr. Hart," the voice said, "are you with me? Are you okay?"

Nick reached for the body that held him and felt body armor.

"Yes, thank you. I think I'm okay…I just can't see you, I can't see anything."

CHAPTER 76

BLINDNESS
TUESDAY EVENING—
POST-QUAKE DAY TWENTY-FIVE

Thump. Thump. Thump. The rotors pulsed overhead through the night air. The headphones over Nick's ears crackled with chatter between the pilot and copilot flying the Black Hawk helicopters. He wasn't sure what time it was. He had lost all track of time in captivity, and after his world went black, he lost all orientation too.

He ran his fingers over his face and the gauze wrap that covered his eyes. He sighed and leaned his head back.

"You okay, my friend?" It was Buck's voice through the headphones.

Nick felt Buck's hand on his arm. He'd always recognize that big, meaty paw that had pulled him out of so many jams.

Nick nodded, and Buck squeezed his arm. "Hang in there, bud."

Hang in there... Nick remembered the piercing pain. He had never experienced such excruciating pain. He remembered how he'd screamed when it felt like nails had pierced his eyeballs. Ali had reassured him there were no punctures, the fight was over, and that he was rescued. *Rescued?* The rescue was a blur—a swirling tangle of pain, chaos, anxiety, morphine... *Thank goodness for morphine.*

Nick remembered being flung over someone's shoulder and rushed to what he thought was the ER, but that turned out to be the helicopter. Ali had examined him, telling him he was shining a light into his eyes. He didn't remember seeing a light, only dim shadows. But he did remember a shot in the arm. Was it in the ER or the helicopter? He couldn't remember where or when, but he remembered when the searing pain subsided. Was that the morphine?

Nick lifted his head in the direction of Buck's voice. "Did they get everyone?"

"We are all here, Nick. Everyone."

THURSDAY—
POST-QUAKE DAY TWENTY-SEVEN

When he heard her voice, Nick touched Maggie's face. He felt her concern. He ran his fingers over her forehead and felt the frown lines.

"What time is it?" he asked her.

"It's noon."

Nick nodded. "What day?"

"Thursday."

Nick's mind tried to make sense of it all. "Maggie, what has happened?"

He felt her pull back slightly. "Nick," she said, "Buck and Ali are here as well."

Nick felt someone take his hand. "Hello, Dr. Hart." It was Ali. "We have kept you comfortable for the past twenty-four hours or so. As soon as they got us back to King's, we took you to surgery. We gave you an anesthetic so I could examine your eyes. I called an eye surgeon friend back in Memphis, and he talked me through the exam." Ali paused.

Nick waited for him to continue. His mind searched for an answer, even though he suspected it wasn't going to be good.

"Dr. Hart, unfortunately our capabilities here are quite limited for eye surgery."

With great effort, Nick lifted and turned his head, hoping a change in position would reveal some light, physical and metaphorical. But everything was still dark.

"You need to keep your head down, Nick." It was Buck.

"Hey, Buck." He reached his hand toward the sound of Buck's voice, until he realized his arm was tethered by an IV.

Buck took Nick's hand. "I'm right here, man."

"What happened?" he asked.

"The good guys came to get us. The bad guys lost," Buck said.

Nick felt a stab of pain as he shifted his body. He wrenched a smile. "Why doesn't it feel like we won? How did they find us?"

"We tracked you through the GPS of the sat phone." It was Jack. Nick was surprised to hear Jack's voice.

"Hey, Jack," he said hoarsely. His throat ached from the tube put in his trachea for the anesthesia.

Someone put a straw to his lips. "Drink some water, Nick." It was Buck who held Nick's hands on a glass of water.

He sipped long and deep. "Thanks, Buck," he said, turning toward Jack's voice. "Jack, thanks for sending the cavalry...or should I say Calvary?" He tried to laugh, remembering their joke when Jack stepped from the helicopter for the first time at King's. But the joke only provoked a cough against his dry throat.

"Glad they didn't steal your sense of humor, young man." Jack laughed. "Even with the sat phone off, we could pinpoint your precise location. When you didn't call, and we couldn't get a call through to you...and when we heard the news about the bombing, we realized something was up. If only we'd been smart enough to listen to Maggie. She'd been telling us for hours that something was wrong, but we knuckleheads didn't listen until it was almost too late."

Nick hesitated. "AK?"

"She's fine," Buck said. "Pretty banged up, physically and emotionally. We brought Vlad's body with us. The UN Commander is working with the Russian government to get them both home."

Nick thought of Vladimir. In a different life, in a different world, he would have enjoyed knowing the big man. As it was, a great light had been snuffed out. He remembered what Vladimir had said. *Thank you, my friend.*

Maybe they'd both been shown the way. He remembered Vladimir asking for prayer at his final moment. *Lord, have mercy on his soul.*

"And the young man…Abdul?" Nick asked.

"They have him here at King's for now, but they're moving him to a secure location soon," Buck said. "His full name is Abdul Awwal Fadhil. He is the brother of Abbas Fadhil who is the first in command under Abu Bakr al-Baghdadi."

Nick's foggy mind tried to comprehend the information.

"Abdul's brother is the second in command of all of ISIS," Buck explained. "I'm sure the military will make very good use of Abdul."

He understood and nodded.

"And the woman?"

"Her name is Akleema Mohammad…the colonel told me that she is called the White Snake. Every intelligence agency in the world has her on their radar."

He remembered what it was like to stare into her hate-filled eyes—her evil eyes. A cold shiver ran down his spine. "And?" Nick asked, hoping he was remembering correctly about the laser dot and the bullet blasting her to hell.

"She is dead…very dead," Buck assured him. "It appears that ISIS was setting up a base in Turkey. The hospital was just a cover. They may have succeeded if not for us. We may never understand the blow that we inadvertently dealt to them."

Silence fell over the team.

"And my eyes?" Nick finally asked.

Ali took his hand. "Dr. Hart, I'm afraid I do not have good news. They were damaged by a flash grenade…I wish I were an eye surgeon."

He envisioned Ali bobbing his head from side to side. He waited to hear the rest of the bad news.

"You have sustained considerable damage to both eyes," Ali continued. "The eye surgeons, of course, need to evaluate you, but you may require surgery on both eyes. There is no one here in Van that can do that type of surgery."

Nick was trying to adsorb the news. The answer was simple, no one here knew what was wrong and no one here could help. An overwhelming sense of grief welled up inside of him about how so many people in the world must feel. He thought of the family in Guatemala whose daughter's feet were deformed by a congenital irregularity. He thought of those whose loved ones had medical problems that couldn't be treated where they lived, made hopeless by their lack of resources. He could feel his chest heave in sorrow.

Maggie seemed to read his thoughts and laid her head on his chest. "It's going to be okay, Nick. I just know it is."

He held her close, grieving for others and himself.

Nick heard footsteps and felt the others turn to the intruder. Maggie lifted her head.

"We are ready to go." Nick recognized the voice of the UN Commander.

"Son, we are flying you to the nearest...and best, I might add...eye hospital in Europe, the Moorfields Eye Hospital in London."

Nick didn't know what to say.

"Your chariot awaits," the Commander continued. "A short helicopter ride to Ankara, and then we have a jet ready to take you to London. You will be there this afternoon. They are awaiting your arrival."

"Great...another helicopter ride." Nick joked, breaking the tension in the room. He searched for Jack's hand. "Jack, thank you for all you've done."

He didn't wait long to feel the old man's hand on his chest.

"God's speed, son," Jack said and patted the top of Nick's head.

"Maggie? Buck?" Nick stretched his arms for one or the other.

Maggie hugged his chest tightly. She said nothing. She was crying.

"Ali? Buck?" Nick called.

Ali grabbed his hand. "I will stay for a few more days to make sure there is a smooth transition, Dr. Hart."

"Thank you, Ali…my friend," Nick said, squeezing his hand. "Buck?"

"You ain't going nowhere without me," Buck said, slugging Nick's arm. "You'd probably find some way to fall out of the helicopter if I wasn't there watching out for you."

The team laughed.

Nick felt the stretcher he lay on starting to move, making his head spin with vertigo. He realized they were on the top floor of King's when the stretcher was pushed around the spiral ramp down to the bottom floor. Memories of the last few weeks flooded his mind—the vast devastation, the horrific conditions, the lines of maimed and injured, the baby born amid the chaos, almost losing his life when the ceiling collapsed. Patients' faces flashed through his mind—the small orphan who wrapped his arms around his back—a true kiss from God. Flashbacks of fear, anxiety, love, and triumph. *Yes, ultimately triumph.* Life was already returning to King's…God was the God of restoration.

He was sad to leave the comfort and affection of his friends, especially when he had no idea what would happen to him. But he didn't panic and felt no anxiety. Instead, he was filled with a sense of peace.

His gurney came to a stop, and he felt a warm pair of hands around his.

"You thought you would escape without saying *Da-svi-da-niya?*"

Nick smiled and wished he could see AK. He reached up to touch her face.

"AK, I'm so sorry about Vladimir."

"*Da*, he was a good man."

"He gave his life for us. I can't help but think God is smiling upon him."

"*Da*, I hope as well."

She kissed his forehead, and he reached around to hug her.

"*Bud'te zdorovy*, bless you, Dr. Hart. Be healthy." She kissed him again and hugged him around the neck.

When Nick hugged her, he felt the bare skin of her back and imagined she was wearing a hospital gown. He smiled and whispered in her ear, "Hope you are wearing pants, AK."

"Wouldn't you like to know?" she teased back. "When you are better, you need to come see me in St. Petersburg. I still owe you that dance." Then she kissed him tenderly on his bottom lip.

The sound of the helicopter increased as they moved him closer and he waved to the blackness, unsure of who he was waving to. He had a sense that he was waving good-bye to his old life.

"God," he said out loud, "I thought you were going to open my eyes."

"Nicklaus, I have."

EPILOGUE

SIX MONTHS LATER

Nick wondered if he'd been forgotten. He thought it was strange that because he had lost his sight, he had also lost his value in the eyes of the world. Maybe he had. After all, everyone related to him as a surgeon, but he could no longer practice surgery, a skill he had worked for his whole life, an ability that gave him so much pride and comfort. People knew him as a driver of a beautiful sports car, and he was no longer able to drive. Actually, he wasn't even much good at walking these days. He could barely get himself to the corner grocery store without stumbling over something or someone.

Still, it was strange. There were so many things he could no longer do, but did that mean he'd lost value? If others judged him to be without value because he couldn't see, he thought it was peculiar because, as far as he was concerned, he valued himself more now than ever in his entire life.

After departing Van, he'd spent two weeks in London undergoing surgeries on both eyes. He'd been under the watchful care of one of the world's leading eye surgeons. The surgeon and his team had been hopeful when he started to see shadows, until scarring covered his corneas and the shadows disappeared. At first, Nick had faithfully followed instructions, inserting eye drops multiple times a day, but when he saw no changes or improvements he became less compliant. He hung his hopes on his surgeon's words: "Sometimes these things reverse themselves."

After a second and third opinion back in the States, he learned that a corneal transplant might be an option in a few months, but "there is no guarantee." He realized with irony that it was the same disclaimer he had told many of his own patients with difficult bone deformities.

Nick, Buck, Ali, and AK had received certificates of appreciation from the government of Turkey for what their team had done for the Turkish people. The devastation at the school could have killed or maimed hundreds more if not for their unwitting involvement, and no one could say what dangers had been averted had ISIS gained a stronger foothold in Turkey. Knowing that their contribution had been appreciated helped Nick through some of his darkest days of depression.

He turned off the radio. Before his blindness, he'd been accustomed to watching FOX news and admiring the leggy stable of newscasters. But without being able to see them, listening to TV did not hold his attention. Listening to radio had become more interesting. The words seemed to matter more, and he enjoyed picturing events and personalities, although he never imagined he'd become a fan of NPR. He'd always found National Public Radio a bit stuffy. But as interesting as NPR had become with its constant and reasoned updates on current events, he discovered that, to keep his sanity, he could only listen in short spurts. The world had gone crazy. Crime, hate, injustice, inequality ran rampant. The latest US election almost tore the country apart with everyone pointing a finger—typically the middle—at everyone else. ISIS had been dealt significant blows, but there was another lone-wolf terrorist attack on US soil just two days ago. Whenever ISIS was beaten down, a different jihadist group rose up to perform unbelievable acts of violence, usually against women and children, the elderly, and the sick. Even hospitals had been destroyed in Syria.

"Father, where is the love?" Nick said out loud.

"Nicklaus, you are my love. You are my expression of that love… through you I have glorified my love, revealed my love." God spoke to Nick's heart.

"Yeah, a lot of good I can do being blind." Even though he valued himself, he was not sure how he would regain a sense of purpose and significance.

"But now you can see," God told him, as He had many times. *"You can help others see."*

There was one thing Nick understood in his unseeing reality, and that was growth in his deep and trusting relationship with God. He truly did hear from God, and his Father was not afraid of his questions, his grumbling, his complaining, or even his anger. Nick had cried before Him, screamed at Him, pleaded with Him, and even cursed Him. But his Father's response was always the same...love.

"Thank you, Father," he said, as he had said many times.

Nick's partners and coworkers at the MED had been kind in sending flowers and cards, but, for the most part, Nick thought he might as well have leprosy or some other highly contagious disease, because few people had come to visit him. He had been treated with a distant sympathy. It was easy for him to feel forgotten.

With Nick's notoriety and accolades from the Turkish and US governments, the malpractice suit brought by the mayor of Memphis was settled in arbitration. Nick's attorney was sure they didn't want to put a blind doctor being hailed as a hero on the stand. The case was settled for two million dollars with no admission of wrongdoings. Nick's heart bled for the mayor; no amount of money would lessen the pain of losing his son.

Dr. Antonio Scott, the chief of staff at the MED, had never called. Nick doubted he ever would. At first, it made Nick angry. Nick understood he was no longer bringing economic value to the hospital as a practicing surgeon or coverage of call or whatever it was administrators wanted, but he thought he could still offer some value, and Dr. Scott should have been smart enough to know that. After all he'd done for the hospital, Nick didn't think he would be so easily abandoned.

He began to understand the way of the world from a new perspective. In the game that was played, the kingdom of the world against the Kingdom of God, the currency was so different. Nick's value in the Kingdom of Heaven was simple—he was the value. He was valuable for just being himself. Even blind. Nick understood that when people let him down or betrayed him, and when life seemed like it might crush him, God was there—always faithful, always loving.

Nick's parents and true friends had rallied around him—loving him despite his flaws, and he had reciprocated their love.

"Speaking of which," Nick said aloud as he reached for a clock on the table near his recliner, picked it up, and felt for its hands. It was almost two, and Buck would arrive any minute. Not only that, Ali and Astî were coming over with their two girls and their newly adopted son. It was a big day, and Nick's heart leaped. He wished Maggie were here as well.

Maggie had stayed in Van for an additional month until she got the orphanage in tip-top shape. Then, knowing she'd left King's Orphanage in good hands, she returned to her responsibilities in Guatemala. Shellie, the mouse of a nurse, had become a capable leader and convinced her firefighter husband to bring their kids to Van to join her as the director of the orphanage. When she told Nick of her decision, she'd told him it would only be for a short time, but he had to smile. Even the redoubtable Dr. Lee was staying at King's for another year. He hoped she finally got some sleep…and washed those glasses.

Maggie had come to Memphis three times already to help Nick, but those visits had always been way too short. Her faith and prayers were such a source of strength for Nick. He knew she truly believed that everything was going to be okay. He loved her so much, enough to release her to be free to serve God in Guatemala. He just wished he could be there to help her.

Nick startled when his phone dinged. He felt for it on the table and after finally finding it, he pushed the one manual button on it and spoke, "Open message."

"Message from Antasha Katrina Volkova," a mechanical voice said.

AK. He smiled. She had figured out how to send him voice messages with her computer and sent them frequently. Sometimes the messages were appropriate and sometimes not, but whether it was a subtle or a not-so-subtle proposition—it always made him laugh.

Even though Vladimir's death and funeral had been extremely difficult for her, she seemed to throw herself back into her work, assignments about which she could only hint. She often threatened that one night he might find her at his door with a smile and a bottle of cognac.

He knew without asking that the discovery of the icon of the tree of life was a secret that she would take to her grave. They were both relieved that the Russian and US scientists were working together on what they called the "King's Cure." The figs did, indeed, have an anticancer property, but it would take years to develop a new cancer drug and years beyond that to complete clinical trials. Nick realized with a sigh of resignation that once big pharma got involved, any cooperation between the two countries would be a thing of the past. He wondered how many thousands of dollars a corporation would bilk out of a patient fighting cancer to line its own pockets.

Nick forced his mind away from the negative and said into the phone, "Listen to message."

"Hi my love, Nicklaus." It was Antasha's voice.

Nick loved how she said his name with her Russian accent—*Neak-a-los.*

"I am in country that rhymes with *dance*, looking at lighted and very large tower…thinking of you, of course."

Nick could hear traffic in the background as she laughed.

"I hope you are good boy and not meeting too many beautiful nurses these days. I am sending you a picture of me I thought you might like." She giggled again. "Don't forget me."

"Oh boy," he grimaced.

"I miss you terribly, darling."

Nick heard her kissing the phone over and over.

Then the message ended.

She might be the death of him. AK loved nothing more than to tease him and often sent photos. She knew he couldn't see them, and the only way he could find out what they looked like was to ask someone to describe them. Most of the photos were decent, but others, when he heard about them, just plain made him blush.

Nick heard a knock, a key inserted, and the swish of an opening door. It was Buck. He had given his friend a key—and he was always welcome.

"Hey bud, you in here?"

"Hey, Buck," Nick called from his chair.

"You mind if I turn on a light for the living?" Buck chuckled.

"Just doing my bit for global warming," Nick retorted. He sometimes forgot that his apartment was in the same darkness that he lived in. He heard Buck walk past him and open the drapes.

"AK send you another love note?"

He brought the phone to his chest. "Yeah, and a picture. You ready for Russian roulette?" he said, holding the phone toward Buck's voice.

Buck laughed. "The last one took me a while to get out of my mental Rolodex."

He felt Buck take the phone from his hand. "And?" he asked.

"Well, it's AK all right."

When Buck grew silent, Nick figured he was zooming in and out on her image.

"Geez, Buck, give a guy a break."

As Buck cleared his throat, he sensed Buck was fighting back tears.

"It's a picture of AK," Buck said. "She's getting baptized."

"Is she fully clothed?" Nick laughed.

"Fully."

The men laughed together. "Good for you, AK," Nick said.

There was another knock at the door, and Buck hooted, "Ali…Astî…come on in."

Nick could hear Ali's voice and the chatter of children. Ali and Astî had been so good to him, always inviting him to their house or taking him on errands. Ali went with him to all his doctor appointments.

"*Selamünaleyküm*, may God's peace be upon you," Ali said.

"*Aleykümselam*, peace be upon you," both Buck and Nick said back.

Nick felt Astî take hold of his hands and kiss him on each cheek. She smelled of jasmine.

"Hi, Astî," he said warmly.

"Hello, Dr. Hart."

He had given up trying to break either of them of their formality.

"This is a great day," he said.

"Yes indeed, Dr. Hart," Astî said.

Expectant silence overtook the room.

After a moment, Nick spoke, "Well? Where is that handsome boy?" He reached out his hands.

He heard Ali say something in Turkish. Then he felt small hands on his knee. He reached for them and took them in his hands.

"*Selamünaleyküm,*" Nick said to the child.

"Peace be upon you, Dr. Hart," the tender young voice said.

Nick was instantly transported back to the operating room at King's. The beautiful child with the big ears laid out on the operating table with a broken leg. The same sweet voice. Tears overflowed his eyes.

"Hello, Ibrahim. Wow, you are speaking English now," he said through his tears.

"Yes, Dr. Hart, but I'm not so good, I'm afraid."

"I think you never sounded better, Ibrahim."

Nick reached for the boy and brought him up close for a hug. He felt Ibrahim wrap his arms around his neck and squeeze tightly. He let the embrace go deep.

When they both needed a breath, he set the boy on his knees and patted his head. Ibrahim's hair had grown out, but he still had oversized ears. He could feel the boy staring at him. He wondered if the white clouds in his eyes scared Ibrahim.

Nick and Buck had turned the whites of his eyes into a joke. Buck had often teased Nick that if his head were shaved and he grew a Fu Manchu mustache, he would look exactly like Master Po, the blind guru from the *Kung Fu* TV series. Nick had teased back, "Only if I can call you Grasshopper and you'll sit at my feet awaiting wisdom." They both found this immensely funny, since Buck's new prostheses were lime green. Nick had learned to believe the best way to deal with affliction was with humor and love.

"How was your trip back to Turkey?" Nick said toward Ali.

"Wonderful," Ali replied. "Better than the last time."

Ali and Astî had just returned a few days ago. They and Maggie had spent months traveling and filling out paperwork until the adoption had been finalized. Nick wouldn't have been surprised if Ali had to grease a few palms in Istanbul to get it done. Ali would do anything for the boy and was not about to leave him without a family.

Ali had shared with Nick that when they'd returned to King's from the hands of ISIS, Ibrahim was, indeed, healed. Even Ali called it a miracle.

"I have something for you, Ibrahim," Nick said, reaching beside his recliner to bring up a large package that Astî had helped him wrap a few weeks earlier. He felt Ibrahim take the present.

"Go ahead, son, you may open it," Ali encouraged.

Ibrahim tore off the wrapping and squealed with delight. Then he hugged Nick tightly around the neck. Nick had bought him a limited-edition World Cup soccer ball.

"Thank you, Dr. Hart."

Nick sensed that the boy was staring at him and figured he really was frightened by his frosted eyes. He felt Ibrahim touch his face and run his fingers over his brow.

Nick felt Ali come closer, watchful of the boy. "Son, be careful," Ali said.

"Dr. Hart," Ibrahim said. "That is not supposed to be there."

Nick didn't understand. "What is not supposed to be there?" he asked.

"Those clouds aren't supposed to be there. I saw you in… that place."

Nick could tell the boy was struggling to find the words in English.

"It was beautiful. Your eyes were as clear as the water," Ibrahim said.

Nick jerked his head back in searing pain. He thought Ibrahim had accidentally poked his eyeballs, because each globe burned as though it had been marked by a hot branding iron. The agonizing pain made his head spin. He covered his eyes with his hands and held his head. He thought he was going to pass out.

SEVEN DAYS LATER

It was a beautiful day as Nick sat in his chair, enjoying the blue sky and observing a bird at rest on a branch. He felt a light breeze gently blow the curtain aside, letting sunlight filter through the window.

The local eye surgeon had not been able to explain Nick's pain, nor could he explain the fact that the scarring over Nick's eyes was cracking and dissolving like ice on a frozen river after a long winter. None of the doctors could explain it. But Nick knew, and all his true friends knew. Ibrahim had once again ushered in a miracle. It was impossible to explain and impossible to deny.

Nick looked down at the Bible in his lap and read to himself from the Book of Revelation: "Then the angel showed me the river of the water of life, as clear as crystal, flowing from the throne of God and of the Lamb, down the middle of the great street of the city. On each side of the river stood the tree of life, bearing twelve crops of fruit, yielding its fruit every month. And the leaves of the tree are for the healing of the nations. No longer will there be any curse. The throne of God and of the Lamb will be in the city, and his servants will serve him. They will see his face, and his name will be on their foreheads. There will be no more night. They will not need the light of a lamp or the light of the sun, for the Lord God will give them light. And they will reign forever and ever."

Nick wiped tears from his newly restored eyes. Not only had his physical eyes been opened, but the eyes of his heart were now able to see with new clarity. For the first time in his life, Nick saw and accepted who he really was—and whose he really was.

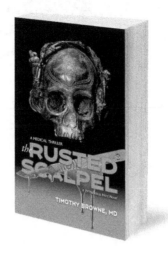

THE RUSTED SCALPEL

A DR. NICKLAUS HART NOVEL, BOOK 3

Dr. Nicklaus Hart returns from responding to a massive earthquake that rocked the Middle East, allowing an ISIS terror cell to enter the ancient area of Mesopotamia. Captured, tortured and blinded by the hands of the radical terrorists, Nick arrives home a broken man. He has lost everything he holds dear—his sight, independence, profession and most of all, hope. But at the bottom of the pit, God sends him a lifeline and restores his physical and spiritual vision.

Faced with reinventing himself, a pharmaceutical company in Singapore offers Nick a position on the dark side of medicine. The drug company's slogan, *Better Living Through Science*, is actuated as it develops medications that manipulate the brain chemicals, but at a significant cost to the patient. Nick exposes the dangers of the drug in the jungles of Borneo amongst orangutans and the original headhunters—the ancient Iban tribe.

But Nick continues to dream, hope against hope—even when the outlook doesn't warrant it—not looking for it in the lesser comforts of life or a medicine bottle, but by abiding in the truth, where he finds the greatest hope of all...love.

AUTHOR'S NOTE

My Dear Reader,

Thank you for taking this journey with me into ancient Mesopotamia. Our collective history grounds us in this region—full of mystery, intrigue and yes—conflict. If we could hear the cries of the people that have fought and died over this land, it would be deafening. To this very day, the battle continues as ISIS tries to establish their caliphate, believing that this would usher in the end-times. It is important that we all understand and gain wisdom to know how to pray. This radical ideology cannot be won on the battlefield with more guns and bombs.

Lord, give us wisdom.

The images, the suffering, the horror of the earthquake that you read in *The Tree of Life* are based in reality and my experience in the massive earthquake that hit Haiti in 2010. Responding with Hope Force International, I arrived at ground zero three days after the devastating quake. Even to this day, my words escape me to capture the absolute horror and devastation we entered. As I wrote *The Tree of Life*, I struggled with how real and descriptive to make the scenes. I know they are awful, but they barely scratch the surface. Also, understand in the midst of that horrendous affair, there were great acts of kindness, heroics, sacrifice, and love. Two weeks after caring for lines and lines of broken and battered people, our group was taking medical supplies to another hospital. We were stopped in downtown Port-au-Prince by a massive traffic snarl. With destruction all around us, the city was at a standstill. Then something I will never forget happened. Thousands of Haitians, broken and battered, people who had suffered unimaginable tragedy, who had lost everything including many of their family members, began to worship the Heavenly Father. A song started somewhere in the heart of one and spread and continued to spread until every person, as far as I could see was on their knees or standing with their hands raised, worshiping God. Lord, have mercy.

Finally, my friend, this story is for you. We are often confused when our faith and beliefs do not match up with what we experience in life. It seems that no life is carefree. I don't know what you are going through, but if you are living life, I suspect it is something. Possibly financial strains, problems at work or home, personal struggles, issues with your children or parents, addictions, anger, bitterness, maybe even feeling that the world would be better off without you. We all seek relief from the pains and strife that life throws at us unexpectedly, like an earthquake that shakes our world. I don't understand suffering. I truly don't. And worst of all, the world will do its best to beat us down. "You are not good enough, you don't have what it takes, what's wrong with you"—all an attack on our identity. But what if we truly knew who we are and whose we are? What would our lives be like then? In that search, we may find ourselves longing to return to union and intimacy with God. To do that, we must first understand who we are in His eyes. We long to once again walk with God in the garden in the cool of the day–and intimately know Him and be known by Him. The good news is, we are already complete in Him, already eating from the tree of life as we abide in Jesus–He in us and we in Him.
Lord, give us understanding.

May your eyes be open to the truth… *Timothy*

Please visit www.TimothyBrowneAuthor.com
*and sign up to receive updates
and information on upcoming books by Tim.*

 Agape
Orthopaedics

MINISTRIES

There are many wonderful organizations throughout the world helping the poor, the broken and the destitute. They can use your help in reaching the world. Here are some of my favorites that I have personal experience with:

Mercy Ships
    https://www.mercyships.org

Hope Force International
    http://hopeforce.org

YWAM Ships
    https://ywamships.net

SIGN Fracture Care International
    https://signfracturecare.org

Samaritan's Purse
    https://www.samaritanspurse.org

Wounded Warrior Project
    https://www.woundedwarriorproject.org

(top) Devastation of Port-au-Prince, Haiti 2010 Earthquake.

(left) Patients waiting in the courtyard of the hospital for further care.

(above right) Young girls who lost their entire families, waiting in courtyard for further treatment.

(bottom) Orphans surround Dr. Tim and his computer.

CPSIA information can be obtained
at www.ICGtesting.com
Printed in the USA
LVHW022242210720
661210LV00001B/4

9 781947 545168